THE LORDS OF
VAUMARTIN

THE
LORDS OF
VAUMARTIN

Cecelia Holland

Houghton Mifflin Company
BOSTON   1988

For information about permission to reproduce selections from this book, write to Permissions, Houghton Mifflin Company, 2 Park Street, Boston, Massachusetts 02108.

Library of Congress Cataloging-in-Publication Data

Holland, Cecelia, date.
   The lords of Vaumartin / Cecelia Holland.
     p. cm.
   ISBN 0-395-48828-1
   1. France — History — 14th century — Fiction. I. Title.
PS3558.0348L67   1988
813'.54 — dc19   88-12836
                                  CIP

PRINTED IN THE UNITED STATES OF AMERICA

Q 10 9 8 7 6 5 4 3 2 1

Endpaper map of Paris in the early fourteenth century adapted by W. F. Shellman, Jr., from A. Lenoir's map in P. Géraud, *Paris sous Philippe-le-Bel,* Paris, 1837 (courtesy of Bruce Redford, literary executor of W. F. Shellman's estate).

FOR FRANK THOMPSON,
who gave me a copy of Froissart once

THE LORDS OF
VAUMARTIN

one

"A TRUE KNIGHT," said Isobel de Vaumar-
tin, "is as innocent as an angel, as fierce as a lion. He is God's
warrior, and by his deeds he defines virtue — what is true and noble is
what a knight does, because he is the pinnacle of manhood. God has
made it so, and so it has ever been, and will be, forever." She stared
keenly into the face of her companion. "Such men are the guardians of
our faith, our land, our justice. Do you deny that?"

Yvain de Vaumartin said, "I do not see what this has to do with my
nephew."

"He is unfit. He will never make a knight. Therefore I believe he
should never become the Sire de Vaumartin."

She watched him a moment longer, her eyebrows raised, her face
drawn taut. Yvain turned forward.

The road here was steep and narrow, winding up through the black
boulders of the river gorge. Ahead the track widened where it pushed
through the trees, and then, above the green veil of leaves, it broke into
the open along the top of the ridge. At the highest point of the
horizon, only the clouds and the sun higher, stood the two square gray
keeps and double ring of battlement walls of the castle Vaumartin, like
a gateway to the sky.

Yvain said, "Vaumartin is beautiful, as beautiful as any woman."

His sister-in-law laughed. "So she must be, to draw such poetical
words from you."

The knight ignored her. Isobel disturbed him. He had been away for
more than a year now, fighting in the war between the rival dukes of
Brittany; he had gotten used to the harsh unsubtle discipline of
fighting, where to yield was to die, and honor was in overcoming other
men. The women saw things differently, particularly this woman.

Now, with their knights and servants and pack mules behind them,
they were riding through the trees, on the black branches the spring

leaves still new and pale, the twisted trunks and roots wound like chains around the boulders of the riverbed. Yvain cast a look behind him, over his shoulder at the file of men-at-arms and mules that followed them, and turned again to his brother's wife.

"When does Everard come of age?"

"He is fourteen now," she said. "In two years, he will be — supposedly — a man, and Vaumartin will be lost to Josseran forever."

Yvain raised his eyes again toward his home. The castle was hidden behind curtains of greenery and the upthrust shoulders of the mountain. He turned and laid his full and open gaze on his sister-in-law, veiled in her smiles.

"Josseran has ruled over Vaumartin for ten years. When Everard comes of age, if he is so meek as that, will he not see the wisdom of letting Josseran go on with it?"

As soon as the words left him, she was wheeling toward him, her blue eyes dark with rage, and her hand fisted, the knuckles white as wax. He drew back, surprised, as he would never have drawn back from a man who threatened him.

She spat her words at him. "Vaumartin is ours! Josseran's, and mine — why should we depend on the whim of some weakling, some changeling — why should any right be heard but ours? We have proven our right to rule here — we have given our blood, our heart's blood for it! For Vaumartin's sake, we must continue here."

They rode abruptly out into the sun again, as if into a wave of light. Isobel lowered her head, her hand raised before her eyes to fend off the glare. Yvain pressed his lips together. They were mounting steadily toward the castle, each step above the one before, so that the horses labored, the sweat standing out dark on their shoulders, the sun fierce on them, testing their right to reach Vaumartin.

The tall castle there was the key to the south, dominating the river valley that connected the heart of Brittany with the Loire and its broad fields and rich villages. One of Yvain's ancient ancestors had put the first stones together on the mountaintop, back when there were kings still in Brittany; other Vaumartins had raised the keeps, the walls, torn this road through the forest. When Yvain rode forth with other knights, in the endless war, it was Vaumartin he fought for, it was Vaumartin the other knights respected in him, the strength in his arm, the fire in his belly, all branch and trunk of this root. Isobel was right; Vaumartin could not fall into the hands of a weakling.

He said, "What says Josseran of this?"

"He hates the boy," Isobel said. "As well would any worthy man — he is a feeble enough creature, always dreaming like a girl, or bent over a book." Her gaze returned to Yvain, searching his face, hunting the way through his thickets of doubts. "He should be a monk. That's what he is suited for."

"That may be," said Yvain, and he saw how that made her smile. The great double gates of the castle loomed over them. They rode into the paved courtyard, and from the stables the grooms came running to hold their horses. Others of the household swarmed out of the hall to greet them. Yvain dismounted, relieved. The welcoming uproar and the crowd protected him from Isobel's whispers, and he moved in among his men, glad of their noise, to settle them for the night.

"You ran away again," Josseran said.

Everard, his nephew, heir to Vaumartin, stood before him, his hands fisted behind his back. He said, between his teeth, "I did not run away."

Josseran sprawled out in his great carved chair. They were in the hall; behind them the servants were dragging out the tables to be laid for the evening meal, bringing the benches out from the walls, putting up the shutters over the windows against the evil night air. Josseran had been out hunting all day and still wore his leather jerkin stained with blood from the butchery of some stag. He looked tired. He stroked his fingertip over the arm of the chair.

"You were supposed to be at your lessons with the priest. He says yesterday you spoke perversely to him —"

"The priest," Everard said, contemptuous. He hated the priest, who could answer no questions, who could only prattle about the things he had learned by rote, prayers and platitudes.

Josseran cocked his eyebrows at him. "He says you twisted his words and the words of the Holy Bible until he misspoke himself before all the other boys. This is very serious, Everard."

Everard turned his head and stared away to the side, toward the blank stone wall. He could not deny that, so he denied what he could. "I didn't run away."

He had gone down through the forest to the river, to watch the water run over the stones, to think and make waterspinners of reeds and listen to the birds, to be alone. He wished he were there now. Abruptly his clenched resistance to his uncle yielded to a rising, gut-churning remorse that he could not be what they all wished he was, and he stiffened himself into a fury against it, and faced Josseran again.

"I am the Sire de Vaumartin," he said. "I can do as I want here. If I care to go —"

"Be quiet," Josseran said, without raising his voice, his finger flicking at the carved wood of the chair arm.

Everard shut his mouth.

"When I was your age, I ran away," Josseran said. "But I ran away to tournaments, to horse fairs, to fights — I ran away to be a man before they would let me be one, but you run away from your manhood. Père Hébert says you're shirking again at the practice grounds."

Everard said nothing. It was true, anyway; he hated the practice with swords and shields as much as he hated the priest and his limp circular answers. His insides quivered again, treacherous, guilty. Sometimes it seemed to him he hated everything in the world, most of all himself. His gaze locked on Josseran's fingertip, prodding relentlessly at the arm of the chair.

"You are a Vaumartin," his uncle said. "In there somewhere is the heart and soul of a knight, and I will shape you to it, Everard, if I must use hammer and anvil and fire. Now —"

Abruptly the door at the far end of the hall flew open. Someone cried, glad, "My lord! My lord, my lady has come!" Everard wheeled, and Josseran bounded up from his chair.

In through the door spilled a tide of travel-worn people, pages and servants and men-at-arms, all speaking at once; home at last, they pulled off their hats and coats, they reached out to the folk in the hall in glad greeting. Josseran strode down past Everard toward the door. The boy stood where he was. Around him this merry homecoming frothed and lapped like the sea rushing in around a rock.

At the door, just as Josseran reached it, the lady Isobel appeared. She was beautiful. Everard knew all the tales about her. At the court of the duchess of Brittany, where she had spent the winter, doing what mattered there to Vaumartin, the troubadours made songs about her beauty and sang them under her windows, pinned roses to her chamber door. It was said two knights had fought to the death over a miniature of her. Her face was smooth and well shaped as a carved jewel. When she threw back the hood of her dusty cloak her hair gleamed. Her eyes shone at her husband's approach, she held out her arms, and Josseran engulfed her in his embrace.

With a murmur of pleasure the whole of the hall turned to watch. This too they were famous for, she and Josseran; they loved each other with an open passion like a flame.

Everard looked away again. He felt guilty watching them, and envious, crooked and evil. Quietly he edged down the hall to the door at the back and went away.

"I am the Sire de Vaumartin." He said that often, using it as a sort of incantation to ward off the attacks of Josseran and Isobel, but it was not true.

He went up to the top of the great keep, where a little catwalk led along the edge of the slate roof, and sat there looking out over the forest. A pair of swallows had made their nest under the eave of the tower, and they flew back and forth past him, almost within reach. The sun had reached the western horizon; above it streaks of flame-colored cloud lay like reefs along the margin of the night.

It was Josseran, his uncle, who was truly the Sire de Vaumartin. To Josseran the serfs came, with their first fruits and their offerings, their quarrels and their failings, and Josseran judged them and helped them. Josseran it was who took up his sword and his shield and rode out to fight against the enemies of Vaumartin, while Everard sat in lonely places and watched the world as if he were outside it.

Now, even now, with his mind seething, and the guilt eating up his soul, he watched the birds and wondered how they flew; his eyes took in the deepening violet color of the sunset, and he wondered why the sky was red.

"I am the Sire de Vaumartin."

His mother had died in childbed when he was born; his father, soon after on the field of Saint-Foi in Brittany. They had left him nothing but that string of words, his title. What he really was he did not know.

The swallows were settling for the night. The red light mounted into the sky and reached around the edge of the world. When the sky at night was red like this it meant fair weather tomorrow. When the sun set ingloriously it meant storms. But why was it red, and not green?

They all told him he asked the wrong questions. He folded his arms over his upraised knees and buried his face in them.

Now Isobel was here again, Isobel, who never let him rest, but chided him for every move he made that she would not have made, had she been Sire de Vaumartin. "Changeling" she called him. Maybe she was right. Some fairy must have taken the real Everard from the cradle, and left behind a toad-baby.

He matched none of them. His black hair and eyes seemed strange in the midst of his family's fair good looks. Sometimes the old cook stared at him and said, "You are your mother's image," but the cook blathered, and half of what he said was mad.

He raised his head again, as if the red sky called him; it was dying, fading away into the blue night, the last of the streaming light draining away over the western edge of the world. Now, directly above the place where the sun had gone, a tiny light danced.

He sat up straight, his eyes sharp. Was that Mercury? The priest, besieged for more knowledge, had reluctantly taken him up onto the battlement at night, and pointed to the wandering lights — Jupiter and Saturn, Mars like a red eye, and the pure beauty, Venus. He said Mercury was hard to find. He said he himself had never seen it. He said this as if wanting to see Mercury were an unclean thought, like peeking at women in their bath.

The tiny star was setting already, disappearing into the last light of the sun. He would never know if that was Mercury. He thought of all the things he would never know, all the questions that had no answers.

Overhead the stars were coming out, thousands of stars, some flashing green and orange and white, some still and cold in the flat black sky. His spirits rose. Even if he was a changeling, despised and shiftless, yet the world was wonderful. He lay back against the slanted roof, smiling at the stars. Now his stomach panged him; he was suddenly hungry in his belly as he was always hungry in his mind.

With a wild rush the cold night blew across his back and ruffled up his hair. He got to his feet and went down again, into the ordinary light of the castle.

two

"THEN THEY ARE really going to fight, this time?" Isobel asked. "I mark, there has been much talk of it, and many loud words of heralds, for years now, without a blow struck."

"There have been blows struck," said Yvain de Vaumartin, sitting on her left.

"Not between King Edward and King Philip," said Isobel. "It is their war; they must fight it."

On her right, Josseran gave a peal of laughter. He turned, his broad leonine face bright with amusement, and looked across his wife to his brother. "So speaks the voice of one who has been there, surely."

Yvain laughed also, and Isobel flushed like a rose. Everard admitted her beauty, and in secret he had tried to write songs about her; he loved doubly to see her humbled, her pale skin suddenly fresh with color, and her haughtiness chastised. He peered around his uncle Yvain, sitting next to him, to see her, and she saw him and stared coldly at him, and her lip curled. Everard turned hastily straight again.

The servants were bringing in the dinner. While they ate, they talked about the war. A page leaned between Yvain and Everard, filling their cups. Still high-colored, Isobel said, "Well, you know, much goes on, at court — we hear much. Such as that King Philip cannot take his wife along on the march, and therefore nothing will be done, because she decides all for him." She broke off a chunk of the bread and sopped it in the gravy. "Is that true?"

Josseran shrugged one shoulder. He sat sprawled in his chair, one arm hooked over the back. "King Philip is a better knight at table than he is in the field, perhaps."

Yvain said, "It is not as a knight he fails. With a sword in his hand he is splendid. In jousts I have seen him carry off the flag many a time. But leading other men into battle he cannot make up his mind." He hacked bits off his meat with his knife.

Everard sat watching them talk. Josseran and Isobel were both fair-headed, his elder uncle massive through the chest and shoulders, slab-jawed, shaggy-browed, with rough splayed hands like paws. He had lost the ring finger on his left hand. Yvain was shorter, lighter of build, his hair darker, although not as dark as Everard's. His skin too was brown. His nose had been broken. His brow had a callus where his helmet rested.

Between them Isobel was pale as a candle, and her moment of humility was gone. She was staring at Everard, her shaven and painted brows arched.

"Everard," she said. "My little lord. How do things go with you? How went your hunt today with my lord Josseran?"

"I didn't go hunting," Everard said.

"Oh? Perhaps then you rode out with your friends among the other boys, and played at war and jousting."

"No," Everard said.

"Did you then go hawking?"

"No!"

"Well, then, Everard, what did you do?"

He glared away, across the room, keeping silent. Josseran said, "Answer the lady Isobel, boy."

Everard jerked his head up. "I lay in the grass," he said, "watching a butterfly, which was more beautiful than you, lady, and —"

"Hold your tongue," said Josseran in a harsh voice.

Isobel said, "Ah, well, I see they do not include courtesy in your lessons. Tell me what they do teach you here."

He hitched himself up on the bench. Everybody was watching him. "Arithmetic and astronomy and Latin —"

"Latin? From the Holy Bible, of course."

"The Bible, yes," he said, cautious. "Ovid, Boethius —"

"Ovid!" she said, and her eyes widened in mock horror. "That hardly seems fit matter for a would-be monk."

"I don't want to be a monk," Everard said. "It's you who keep telling me to be a monk."

"Speak properly to my lady Isobel," Josseran growled at him.

"My lady," Everard said, and gave her as false a smile as he could muster, "I pray you excuse my manner to you, which is most churlish of me, in view of your unending kindness to me."

Yvain's hand dropped heavily onto his shoulder. "What else do they teach you? You must practice at the butts by now." His voice was bland.

Everard said, "Every day."

Yvain was pushing down on him. He stiffened against it, surprised, and looked hard at his younger uncle. Yvain was watching him narrowly. Isobel had turned to Josseran, on her far side; he was holding out a tidbit of the fish to her, and she leaned on him to nibble it from his fingers; they did not mark what was happening here. Higher in his chair than Everard on the bench, Yvain was slowly leaning more and more of his weight onto the hand on Everard's shoulder, buckling him over.

The boy clenched his teeth. The weight was heavy, and he could have moved away, but he resented it; he braced himself against it, and then hardening every muscle he straightened, he took back the space Yvain had forced him from.

At that the pressure abruptly lessened. His uncle smiled at him, and lifted his hand and laid it on his knee.

"Do you like Ovid?"

Everard scrubbed at his face with his hand. He realized that Yvain had just now been testing him. Suspicious, wondering where this took them, he said, "I like Augustine better."

Yvain looked surprised. "Who teaches you Augustine?"

"No one — the priest lent me the book."

Yvain's face was wide and open as a baby's, his gaze steady on Everard. "You know, the monk's life is the highest calling a man can come to. Perhaps —"

"I won't be a monk," Everard said, "just to get out of someone else's way." He stared past his uncle at the lady Isobel.

She was eating something, her jaws moving like a cow's. She said, "Well, then, Everard, be a knight. You know your uncles are called to the king's hosting this summer, to go to fight Edward Plantagenet. The cause is just. Will you take it up?"

Josseran, beyond her, said, "My God. You don't know what you're saying."

Everard said, "You mean, go to the war?" His voice squeaked.

Josseran said, "He'd be less use than a girl."

Isobel said, "He is old enough to be a squire. If he is to be a knight, he must learn war — is that not so?" She turned back to Everard, and her face was smooth and slick, her voice oiled. "Or you could be a monk, Everard."

He tore his gaze from the smooth painted mask of her face and stared across the room. Josseran was laughing again.

"He ran away today, rather than go down to practice at the butts with the other boys. There are five other boys here I would sooner go with than him, surely." He took his winecup from one of the pages. Everybody was staring at Everard; he could hear the room growing still as more and more people stopped what they were doing to witness this. Josseran coughed, amused. "He ran away to build little watermills."

Everard said, "I'll go."

He swallowed, as if to keep these brave words from turning back and hiding in his throat.

Josseran said, "I can't allow it. I'm still master here. You don't know what wars are like, either of you, Isobel. He would be in serious danger, the whole way."

"Yet he wants to go," Isobel said, ebullient. "Let the boy prove himself!"

Yvain was rubbing his jaw, staring away across the room; the servants were shuffling in another round of meats. Everard was clutching the edge of the table, struggling with his rabbit thoughts. Josseran was wrong; Isobel knew the dangers of the war. Isobel wanted him to go because she wanted him to die.

At the thought of dying his belly caved in, his throat clogged, his breath ceased; he died a little, in the thought.

To be the Sire de Vaumartin, that meant to be a knight: to fight for God and France and Brittany and this castle, here, and the lands around it. If he could not do it, there was only the monastery, all those loveless men, praying for other people's souls, copying other people's books, serving other people's notion of the good. He sat hunched forward, his hands gripped together, seeing both these lives stretching out before him, each one a narrowing tunnel to the grave. Then, abruptly, Yvain's hand fell solidly on his shoulder.

Now he did not push him down; now he held him up.

"Let him come, if he wants. I'll watch over him. Between us we can teach him much."

Josseran said, "I cannot permit it."

Everard swung his head around and faced him. He was taut as a drawn bow. "If I don't go, what then?"

Isobel gave a light laugh, like a jester's bell. "Then you will stay here, dear little lord. With me." She showed her small white teeth; her brilliant eyes turned in triumph to Yvain. "You see, he is a coward."

"I'll go," Everard said. He looked to Josseran, behind her. "I am the Sire de Vaumartin. You must let me go, I demand it."

Josseran's brows drew together over his broad nose. He raised his hand to his mouth. Beside him his wife straightened, smiling, and turned and put her hand on his arm and leaned toward him and whispered into his ear. Everard saw that his uncle would relent; he was going to the war. On his shoulder Yvain's hand gave an encouraging squeeze. Isobel beamed at him, triumphant. She had trapped him; whichever choice he made suited her well. He shrugged off Yvain's hand and bent over the chunks of venison before him.

11

In the dark, their flesh slippery with sweat, she whispered, "I cannot bear that you must go — in the past few years we have been together so seldom —"

Lip to lip. He had never known any other woman, and never would; he loved her only, her alone, the laughter of her eyes, the wine of her mouth, the hollows over her hips, the bone between her breasts, the sweet tangle of her hair.

He said, "Alive or dead, I will come back to you, my Isobel."

They made love together, but he felt something held back in her. The ending was lonely for him. He lit a candle and set it into the sconce on the old carved headboard.

"What is it?" He lay down again on the bed beside her, the light of the candle shining on their bodies. The curtains of the bed were drawn. Outside other people talked and moved. Here he could lie naked and watch his lover, his wife, his Isobel. Between their two bodies they made a world of their own, a little Eden.

Now some black serpent had come between them, and he said, "What is it, Isobel?"

"Everard," she said. "You said yourself there are great risks. If he should fall into danger —"

She was unsmiling, her eyes bright, and her voice broke off; she put her hand to her throat. Josseran said, "I'll keep a close watch on him. Yvain and I."

She said, "Must you?"

He jerked his head back. "What are you saying?"

"If . . . something befell him, who would blame you?" she said.

The muscles in his arms jumped. "You mean — kill him?"

"No, no." She smiled. Her fingers brushed down over his chest. "But there will be dangers — I cannot bear to think you might place yourself in danger, to save one so worthless as he."

His fist was clenched. Her words wounded him. "He is my brother's son. When my brother Clair lay dying he gave this boy's life into my care."

"Ah, Josseran," she said. "For the sake of Vaumartin —"

"When he sees war, he will choose the monastery," Josseran said, roughly. His hand opened, and he laid his palm down on her belly, caressing the soft flesh. "Or he will thrive, and become a man."

"And take Vaumartin from you," said Isobel, steadily.

Josseran stroked the flesh of her belly. No one would ever take what he loved from him. There were years to go before Everard came of age, and anything could happen in that time, and God was just: God would not let him lose Vaumartin. Yet her words lingered, like an itch in his mind. He moved his hand up over her belly to the white globe of her breast.

"Forget about Everard," he said. "You are my dominion."

She reached out her arms to him. She said nothing to him, and her lips parted, her thighs rose, parting, and yet in the back of his mind he wondered if she would love him so much if he lost Vaumartin. He pressed himself down upon her, watching her face, to see if she held back from him.

Her eyes fluttered closed. He thrust hard with his hips, rudely bursting through the gates of her body, and she cried out.

"Watch me," he said. "Pay heed to me, Isobel — to me —" He lay down on her, his forearms on the bed on either side of her head, and thrust hard at her, hurting her again, making her feel his weight and his power, and yet, using her, subjecting her to his will, he wondered with a little panic what he would be, who he would be, if he had not Vaumartin.

three

"WE'VE ALWAYS FOUGHT the Plantagenets," said the knight on Josseran's far side. "It's God's cause, like stepping on snake's eggs."

Ahead, the brilliant red banner, the Oriflamme, consecrated to God and France and glory, floated like a smear of blood against an overcast sky. Everard drew in his breath and let it out again in a noiseless sigh.

He had been madly excited when they followed that banner out of Paris, more than a week ago, part of such a great army of knights and men-at-arms and servants that the ground itself trembled under their horses' hoofs. The English had then been only a day's march away. The smoke of burning villages had risen like plumes in the sky to the northwest. Every moment Everard had thought to see the leopard banners of King Edward, to hear the brass horns blare, and to charge into battle.

Since then they had ridden along, day after day, the English scurrying away from them, always just out of reach. They turned west, and the English veered north. They went north, and the English swerved away to the west again. They passed the English camps with the fires warm on the ground; they reached looted villages while the flames leapt from the thatched roofs of the houses. They rode into the town of Airaines to find the enemy so recently gone that the dung of their horses smoked, the meats for their dinner hung half-cooked on the spits.

There King Philip had loitered awhile, dining on Edward's fare, hoping to swing around and trap the Plantagenet's smaller army against the river Somme, but while Philip tarried, the English broke through at La Blanchetaque and escaped when the tide went out and left the river shallow enough to ford.

At that King Philip led his men all back into Abbeville, where they ate well, and drank, and told stories, and polished their weapons, and Everard began to think they would never fight.

"It was the curse of the Templars that brought this on us," said one of the knights.

"The Templars," Everard said. He turned to his uncle Yvain, on his left. "What have the Templars to do with this?" They were marching again, going north this time, following the Oriflamme up through the ripening corn and orchards of Ponthieu.

Yvain smiled down at him. His horse was a full hand taller than Everard's little chestnut palfrey. "The Order of the Knights Templar was a crusading order, the richest in Christendom. King Philip the Fair — the grand-uncle of this Philip — he wanted their money, and he grudged them their power, and so he condemned them on charges of witchcraft and heresy —"

"Of which they were guilty," said another man, sharply, and crossed himself. "Don't overlook that, my lord."

"— and burned them at the stake," said Yvain, as if the other man had not spoken. "And from the crackling flame the Master of the Temple cursed the king, and so it was that within a very short time —"

"Ten years," said the other knight.

"— Philip was dead, all his three strong stalwart sons were dead, and all their sons were dead. And so the end came of the House of Capet, which had been kings of France since time out of memory."

Everard shivered; he imagined the roaring flame, the voice from the flame. "God is just," he said, and crossed himself.

All the men around him laughed. Josseran swiveled in his high-pommeled saddle to join the conversation. "God is amused, perhaps. When the last Capetian died, there were two choices for the throne of France —"

"Three," said the other knight, and Josseran and Yvain together barked their laughter and gave him a friendly silencing stare.

"Two that mattered," Yvain said. "There was Philip of Valois, who is now the king, and rides ahead of us with his companions, hoping that someday in his lifetime he will join battle with the other choice, who is Edward Plantagenet, king of England."

"The grandson of Philip the Fair," said Josseran, "and who therefore has the better claim, actually."

"At the time we had to choose, he was a boy of sixteen," Yvain said. "And his mother, although she was the daughter of Philip the Fair, was a whore, who had murdered her husband, and who was living openly with her lover under the same roof as young King Edward. Nobody wanted that brought to fair France."

"So the council of the peers of France named Philip of Valois to be our king," said Josseran.

Everard leaned around Yvain to see the other knight. "Who was the third claimant?"

"One even younger than Edward," said Yvain.

"The grandson of the eldest son of Philip the Fair," said the other knight. "Charles, his name is — heir to the kingdom of Navarre, in the south."

"He doesn't matter," said Josseran. "Not now. We elected Philip of Valois to be our king, and he is our king, and that's the end of it. As we are going to prove, surely, if Edward ever lets us. Ho, there, what's this?"

A youth, gorgeously dressed in red and gold satin, was riding back through the advancing army, his gaze fixed on Josseran and Yvain. Reaching them, he flung up his arm in greeting.

"Well, hail, my lord de Vaumartin, the king sends his best regards, and hopes to find you well."

"God keep King Philip," said Josseran. "I hope he has sent you with some orders for me. I am sick to death of riding along in his dust."

"Indeed he has, my lord. He has bade me ask you to take your men and go off toward Crécy, which is north of here —"

"I know Crécy," said Josseran, impatiently.

"So he said, my lord, and therefore chose you for the matter. He wishes you to ride out as fast as you can, and see if you can make contact with the English, and give him some report of what they are doing."

Under his breath, Yvain said, "God be thanked, we'll get to fight, maybe." He lifted his reins, and his horse snorted.

Josseran flung up his hand, signaling the knights behind him. "The king honors me with this chance for glory." He spurred his horse, edging it sideways, out of the general march; turning, he looked down at Everard. "Stay by me, hear?"

"I will," said Everard. His horse was following his uncle's without any bidding of his. Yvain pressed on beside him. Down the columns behind them all the knights who followed the green banner of Vaumartin were peeling away from the army. Everard's skin tingled. His horse began to sidestep, snorting. Josseran called out, hoarsely; they all broke into a gallop.

The sky was full of rushing clouds. Now, as they left the king's army, the sun broke through, and a sudden bright wash of light gilded the field of corn before them. The knights spread out in a broad crescent, galloping after Josseran through the planted field; at its edge the ground fell away in a gentle slope.

There they formed together into a column again, to pass through the stand of trees that grew along the little stream. Under the trees the air was dank. Mushrooms grew thick on the leafy ground. On the far side of this wood, Josseran drew rein, turned to face his men, and gathered them all around him.

"Now, mark this. Ahead of us" — he waved — "lies the village of Crécy. You will know it by the spire of its church. The land beyond it is heavily wooded, and I do not believe that King Edward will lead his army into it, where he cannot keep them well together. Therefore he must either turn and march back the way he came, which is folly, since it will bring him face to face on the road with King Philip, or he will stand there, and wait for us. Or he will try to lead his men off to the east, down that way."

He pulled off his helmet and wiped the sweat from his face. Everard looked to his right and to his left, seeing how all these knights waited on him, respecting his skill at this, and he himself faced his uncle again, keener.

His heart was thumping unevenly. He hated being afraid.

"My brother Yvain will take half of you that way, toward Crécy, and see if Edward has pulled up to make his stand there. I will lead the rest of you around to the east, to see if he is trying to slip away from us again. Form a line, and follow close, because the land is broken, and the forest covers much of it." Josseran nodded to Everard. The helmet had left a red line across his forehead. "Stay by me, boy, mark."

"Yes, uncle," Everard said. His voice broke with a squeak, and all the men laughed.

Josseran put his helmet on again. The harsh planes of his face disappeared behind the smooth curved cheekpieces. Everard rode up beside him, and they split away from Yvain and started down a path that skirted the foot of the hill and wound off into the trees.

The other knights followed in a close pack. There were three of them. At first they kept still, looking keenly around them, but after a few moments they began to talk and joke.

Josseran twisted in his saddle. "Keep still! Do you want to warn everybody that we are coming?"

Beside him, Everard peered forward down the path. It wound off across a little dent of a stream bed and through an oak wood, dark as a church, but beyond that the sunlight reached the ground, and he guessed there was a meadow, or more fields. As they rode into the oak wood he shivered. The cool and the dark seemed alive and watching. Through the corner of his eye he saw some small creature whisk quickly away up a great tree trunk. Beside him, Josseran turned again and snarled at his men to still their voices. A bird fluttered away from their approach with a flash of white-barred wings. The path narrowed down to a thread. Josseran ducked under an overhanging branch, and they came out onto the edge of a meadow.

"Yonder is the road east," Josseran said, waving away ahead of them, where the trail skirted the meadow and plunged into the wood again. He drew his horse to a stop, and the knights gathered up close around him, while he looked from side to side, his hands braced on the pommel of his saddle.

Abruptly, decisive, he turned. "You, Martin, take these two and follow that road, there. See if any great number of men have passed along it this day, and then come and join me again back there" — he waved back up the track they had just taken — "where we separated from my brother. Everard, come with me."

Martin raised his hand. The other two knights rode after him, and Everard followed Josseran away to the west, toward the dark oak wood.

He hunched his shoulders, loath to leave the warmth of the sunlight. Josseran led him into the trees, and the cold still air fell over him like a cloak. The ground climbed under their horses' feet, and Josseran swerved and rode higher yet, forcing his mount through veils of green brambles, up toward the summit of this ridge.

"If I were Edward," he said, "I would make my stand by Crécy, on some ground that favors him. His army's much smaller than King Philip's; he cannot hope to win a battle in the open field."

He spoke quietly, looking keenly around him all the while. Everard, beside him, ducked down below a swaying branch. They reached the top of the ridge.

Before them the ground dropped steeply away; they looked out over the rolling green tops of the forest trees, toward the west, where at the very edge of the world the horizon was blue with mist. Much closer, at the margin of the forest, was a church spire, in the midst of red-tiled rooftops, and around it the ordered green of tilled ground.

"That's Crécy," said Josseran.

Everard stood in his stirrups, easing his aching thighs. Directly below them, under the old oak trees, was a heap of trimmed logs. "What's that?"

"Some woodcutter's work," Josseran said.

An axe lay on the ground some little way beyond the logs. Everard said, "He must have just been here."

"He's here still," Josseran said. "Hiding."

"Why does he hide from us? Isn't he French, like us?"

Josseran said, sharply, "What do you care? What kind of question is that?"

Everard was peering around into the shadows under the trees, looking for the woodcutter. It came to him suddenly that everywhere around him, hiding from him, were the common folk who worked this land, who planted the corn he had just trampled through, whose villages burned. He turned to his uncle. "Why —"

"Damn you, Everard, you ask too many questions!" Josseran turned and struck him. "Pay attention to me, or you'll get us killed. Now — come along. Keep your eyes open, damn you." He swatted at Everard again, and the boy dodged. Josseran reined his horse around hard, shoving Everard's lighter mount on ahead of him, down the steep slope.

Halfway down it, Josseran said, harshly, "Wait — hold up!"

Everard jerked his reins taut, and his palfrey stopped, shifting its hoofs restlessly on the broken ground. The slope here was studded with rocks. Leathery gray lichens grew in patches on them. Josseran crowded by him, went down a little way, to where the slope flattened out, and dismounted.

There the ground was torn, the black earth turned over the upper layer of leafy humus. Something heavy had passed this way recently. Stooping, Josseran put his hand to the ground, feeling the tracks.

The forest around them was utterly still. Everard lifted his head, wondering where the birds were. Then, suddenly, above him, he heard the clink of iron.

A yell burst between his lips. He wheeled. His horse half reared, snorting, and over the crest of the slope above him three knights galloped, headed straight toward him, drawing out their swords.

These were English. They came at him like arrows. Their bellowed war cry made him yell. Wrenching his horse around, he headed it at a dead run down into the trees below.

Josseran shouted, flinging up one arm. Everard's wild flight carried him within a few feet of his uncle. Josseran's horse bounded sideways, out of his path, and let out a shrill neigh that rang through the trees. Half galloping, half sliding, Everard's horse careened down the steep slope, while the boy clung to his saddle, the reins flapping in his hands.

The ground flattened out, and the palfrey regained its balance. Everard turned, looking back, knowing he should go back to aid his uncle, but the horse was gathering itself to flee again, and the English knights were pouring down the hill, and a wild panic mounted like a sheet of fire in his brain and he swung around again and pressed himself down to his horse's neck and drove his heels into its flanks.

His horse raced three long strides across the flat ground. Then abruptly, almost under its hoofs, the land pitched off again into a sheer rocky cliff. The horse lurched to one side, trying to save itself. Everard screamed. His feet came out of the stirrups. The horse stumbled, caught itself, staggered up again, and fell, and Everard flew off.

He landed rolling, the breath knocked out of him, and flung out his arms to keep from going over the steep cliff. Scrambling up, he looked around for his horse, but the palfrey had found a trail and was already disappearing into the trees, its red-gold tail like a banner.

Everard stopped. Panting, he looked back up the slope, where Josseran had his foot in one stirrup, his reins gathered in his hand, his horse bounding and leaping away from him. Just beyond him, the English knights, five of them now, cocked up their swords and swung out to assault him from several sides.

The trees in their way slowed them just long enough for Josseran to fling himself up across his saddle. Lying across it, both legs still on the same side of the horse, he bolted down toward Everard, the English streaming along behind him. Everard ran a few steps to meet him, his hands out. Josseran was galloping straight toward him. As he rode he swung his right leg up over his horse's rump, and coming upright in his saddle, he gathered his horse up and steadied it. Everard reached both arms up for his uncle's help, but Josseran swerved to avoid him and charged away and left him there.

Alone, abandoned, Everard whirled to face the English. Their swords raised, their horses' hoofs like scythes that tore the soft earth, they thundered down on him through the trees. He flung up his arms to cover his face and dove toward the shelter of the nearest tree, and the English hurtled past him, after Josseran, bellowing as they went. Then, down over the top of the hill, came another wave of mounted knights.

Everard wrapped himself around the foot of the oak tree, his face pressed to the raw earth, the ground shaking under him; he stiffened his muscles against the pounding hoofs, the slash of the swords. Something struck him in the back, and he whined. He clutched his arms around his head. He tasted blood in his mouth: he had bitten himself. His terror was like a whirlpool in his belly, sucking him down. The roar and thud of the hoofs faded.

"Everard," said his uncle Yvain's voice, cool, above him.

He looked up, his wits scattered, and drew a breath, amazed at being alive. The other knights had passed on by him. He turned and looked up at Yvain, on his great war-horse, beside him.

"Come on, now," Yvain said. "Get up. You're all right. We've run them off."

Everard got to his feet. His legs were wobbling, and he sat down hard on the ground again and had to pull himself up on the tree behind him. "Where is Josseran?"

"Let's go find him."

"Did he get away?" Everard held up his arm, and his uncle grasped his wrist and helped him vault up behind his saddle.

"I don't know," Yvain said. "Let's go see."

"I —" Everard, clutching the saddle's cantle with both hands to stay on, squeezed his eyes shut, and lowered his head. "I was afraid. I ran away, and he . . ."

Again he saw Josseran, half on, half off his horse, charging down toward him, past him, away from him, leaving him there. But it was his own fault. He had fled first.

Yvain said, quietly, "Keep still, boy. Say nothing."

They rode on through the wood, and the trees gave way to a broad fallow field, where some sheep were grazing. At the far side ran the road, and by it Josseran's knights were gathered.

Among them was Josseran, with Everard's horse by the reins.

"There he is," Yvain said. "Remember, say nothing."

Everard's heart was pounding. He should have stayed there, he should have stood with Josseran; again he had proven himself unworthy. At the thought of facing Josseran he cringed, and pressed his cheek to Yvain's armored back.

The knight reached out behind him and awkwardly patted Everard's thigh. He reined his horse into the midst of the knights.

"He's whole," he said, in a falsely hearty voice. "No harm done."

Josseran said, "I'll do some harm to him."

Everard straightened, gathering the words to apologize, but Yvain had bidden him keep silent, and he did. Josseran had his helmet off. He was staring at Everard, his jaw set like rock, and his eyes blazing.

"He ran like a girl."

"Here, Everard, get on your horse," said Yvain, and edged his gray stallion over side by side with the chestnut palfrey. Everard slipped into his own saddle. He could feel the stares of the other knights on him, all around him, a hedge of thorns.

"His horse took off with him," Yvain said mildly.

"He's a coward," Josseran said. He wrenched his horse's head around. "Who were those knights?"

"Foragers," Yvain said. "From Edward's army, which, as you said they would be, are drawn up on a ridge, just beyond Crécy, where there is a mill. They are going to face us there. It's well-chosen ground — we will have some difficulty routing them from it."

Josseran was glaring at Everard. "Especially with such as this to do it with." He struck at Everard with the back of his hand.

"Leave off," Yvain said, sharply. "They came on him from above, unexpectedly —"

"He left me there!"

"You left him," Yvain said, and Josseran clamped his jaw shut, his eyes glittering under the fierce bushy brows.

They swung around, riding side by side, the other knights trailing along after them; their voices rose in a babble, and Everard could hear his name spoken, and laughter, and sneers. He hunched up his shoulders, riding along between his uncles.

"The horse bolted," Yvain said to him, a question in it, or an invitation.

Everard lifted his head. "No," he said, in a low voice. "Josseran is right, I ran away." Tears stung his eyes. He was going to cry, and disgrace himself utterly.

"That's honest enough, at least." Yvain reached out and gripped his shoulder. "Take heart, boy. The first time I saw battle I ran like a corncrake." He gave Everard a rough comradely shake. "The next time, you'll do better."

Everard looked up at him, grateful, and to his surprise Yvain gave him a broad smile and a wink of his eye. Maybe it wasn't so bad, then. His uncle's arm still lay across his shoulders, their horses so close his leg was pressed against Yvain's horse. On his other side, Josseran grunted, looking away — Josseran, who had left him, who hated him.

But Yvain leaned toward him and kept hold of him. Yvain did not give up on him. Everard collected himself, straightening, his shoulders back. He felt Yvain beside him like a second self, giving him courage. Maybe he would get another chance, maybe Yvain was right, and he could prove himself more worthy. He swallowed, feeling better, and looked up at his uncle with a surge of love.

four

JOSSERAN COULD NOT LOOK at Everard. He led his men south up the road away from Crécy, back toward King Philip and his army.

Everard had fled away, he told himself. Everard was a coward.

A blast of cold wind rushed into his face. The sky was darkening, although there was still some of the day left; a storm was sweeping in on them. They would not fight this day, save as they had already fought. Yet he longed for battle, to wipe away the metallic taste of sin that lingered on his tongue.

He kept his eyes turned away from Everard, away from Yvain. One hand on his hip, he pretended to be studying the terrain off to his right.

Everard had run, but Everard was a boy, and weaponless, and the English had attacked suddenly and in greater numbers. Even against his will Josseran admitted that Everard's running away was excusable.

His own running, his refusal to help his fallen nephew, that was not.

Isobel had said, *Do not put yourself in danger, for the sake of this weakling.* She was a woman. She knew nothing of chivalry. A knight put himself at risk every day, for the sake of the weak and the helpless, and Josseran had failed in this. He had let his temper overcome his honor.

Yvain knew it. He saw that in Yvain's face, in Yvain's championing of their nephew, the arm around the boy's shoulders, the gentle words. Later, he knew, when they were alone together, Yvain would have harsh words for him.

Under a sky turning black as a bruise, they rode on up the broad track between the cornfields of Crécy, and there they met King Philip's army.

In the vanguard marched a troop of Genoese crossbowmen, all in their armor, and carrying their bows. Josseran swung his own men out to one side, trampling down the wheat, to let them pass by and to fall in with the first mounted companies of the royal army.

Here King Philip rode beneath the triple-tongued Oriflamme, curling and uncurling in the breeze, its silks as red as the noble blood of French chivalry. On his left hand were the Sire d'Aubigny and the Sire de Beaujeu, and on his right the blind king of Bohemia, who had fled his contentious throne for the ease of Paris, and who now went forth in support of King Philip, in search of excitement, a knight on either side to lead his horse.

The king lifted his hand, and Josseran saluted him and swung his horse around to ride beside him.

"Your Grace," he called, loud enough for all to hear, "God has at last given us what we all desire. The king of the English and his knights have finally come to earth; they have taken up a position on the ridges above Crécy, to do us battle there."

From the knights around him there went up a bellow of a cheer. Abruptly the horse under him leapt, as the whole column surged forward, eager, toward their enemy.

"God be thanked," said the king. He was tall and brawny, and behind the cheekpieces of his helmet his face glowed with high color and his eyes shone. "Now shall I prove the justice of my cause!"

Another roar went up from his knights. At a quicker pace they swept on down the road. Josseran twisted to look around him for his brother and his nephew and his knights, and saw them crowding in behind the king's companions, struggling for riding room in the mass of men hurrying down the road toward Crécy.

"Where do they stand?" King Philip shouted. The wind was rising again, hissing in the fields, and off in the distance a low rumble of thunder rolled.

"Their position is very strong," Josseran shouted, trying to make himself heard above the thunder and the clamor of the great army. "Tomorrow, when we join battle —"

At this suddenly there went up such a shout that his words were drowned. The army had come up to the summit of a low hill, where the road curved down into the village of Crécy. The Genoese bowmen were striding off down the road into the long shallow valley where Crécy village stood. And beyond them, along the top of the ridge, were the English, thick as standing trees along the rising ground, their silky banners fluttering and their lances pricking the sky.

"There — there —"

A sharp gust of wind swept up the road into Josseran's face. It was beginning to rain. Josseran turned in his saddle, looking behind him, back to where his own little army rode, under the green banner of the Vaumartins with its gold cross. Yvain was there, Everard beside him, the boy's dark head like a flower among the helmeted heads of the knights.

"Hold," the king shouted. "Hold, now —"

Josseran's horse snorted, skittered, and suddenly half reared. He jerked his attention forward again. The Genoese, sighting the enemy, were screaming and shouting and banging their crossbows on their shields: but they had stopped, also, and were blocking the road.

"What is it?" asked the blind king of Bohemia. "What is it? Are they before us, the villains?"

"Yes," said one of the knights. "The English are drawn up on a slope before us, not half a mile away, as I judge it — I see their archers, very well set up; we shall have a hard time breaking through them. And his knights are all on foot. They are ready for us."

The commander of the Genoese crossbowmen was forcing his way back through the last ranks of his men to the king. "Your Majesty! Your Majesty —"

The hallooing of the Genoese drowned his voice. Josseran wheeled around toward the king.

"Your Grace — we must gather all your commanders, and come at this in some order —" Like the galloping hoofs of a wild hunt, a rumble of thunder resounded along the sky, coming ominously closer.

King Philip said nothing. His hand was fisted on his thigh. He was staring across the valley at his enemy, while all around him his men shouted and pointed, and their horses leapt.

"There are the English banners!" A knight leaned toward the blind king, almost directly in front of the Sire de Vaumartin, and began to describe the sight before them. "There are the leopards of the Plantagenets. I see Northampton's emblems, and Warwick's bear — the finest jewels of English chivalry await us here!"

Josseran's horse reared up again. He and the king had stopped, the Genoese before them blocking their way, but the rest of the army was still moving up behind them. The road was so close and crowded now that his horse, coming down on all fours, hit the king's a glancing blow on the shoulder with its hoof, and the king's horse shuddered. A drop of rain struck Josseran's cheek. It would be disastrous to charge down this road in a rainstorm. He jerked hard on his reins, trying to back up his horse, and the stallion snorted and pinned down its ears, and under him he felt its muscles bunch; it was going to kick out, to make room behind it to move into. Josseran eased his grip on its mouth. There was nowhere to go. He slackened his reins.

"We cannot fight today," the captain of the Genoese was saying, standing there before the French king's horse. "Let us go make camp, and rest, and tomorrow —"

The rain was falling harder now, loud on the helmets and shields of the knights. Josseran pressed his horse closer to the king, wanting to counsel agreement with the Genoese captain; half the royal army was still well back down the road.

Suddenly, painfully loud, a roll of thunder battered the clouds overhead. The king sat in his saddle, frowning, the rain running down his face, while the Genoese captain shouted from the ground, but the words might as well never have been spoken; in the thunder and the rain the king could hear nothing.

As they hesitated, another large company of the royal army pushed in among those already facing the English. On either side the great army was spilling out over the fields, crushing the young corn, and spreading off down toward the valley, toward the English. The thunder pealed again, so loud the Sire's horse squatted down, startled, but already along the western horizon the sky was blue, and the rain was lessening, and the sun was coming out.

"We cannot fight!" the Genoese screamed, his face wine-red, his voice at last clearly audible.

From behind the French king came an answering shout: "Fight! Fight!"

As the knights behind the king forced their way closer, they saw the English, and pressed on more eagerly. Josseran felt his horse yield a little to the push, and blind Bohemia raised his head, cocking his ears, his eyes like pearls.

"Fight!"

Suddenly the whole army surged forward. Under this pressure, the crossbowmen began to shout and thump their shields again, and slowly advanced, cautious, the road running still with the rainwater, and the sun, in the west, now blazing in their eyes. Josseran swung around toward the king, amazed, waiting for Philip to give an order to hold, but the king said nothing. His mouth worked. His eyes darted from side to side, and his lips parted and his tongue licked out.

"Fight!"

The king of France sat there in his saddle, staring down the road at his enemy, doing nothing, and down Josseran's spine ran a prickle of wild fear. From long experience he knew that sensation: the battle was beginning. The king, doing nothing, had lost command over it. Whatever happened now was in God's hands. Josseran wrenched his horse around, and from behind him now came the blast of a trumpet.

"Fight! Saint-Denis — Saint-Denis —"

Before he could work his horse free, the men around him were charging.

Shoved on ahead of the knights, the Genoese trudged forward, unwilling, their bows cocked. The sky was clearing. Wraiths of mist curled up from the ditches and the fields toward the late sun. As the crossbowmen moved forward through this drifting haze, the knights behind them spurred their horses into a gallop.

There was no room. The bowmen blocked the way forward, and now, on the hillside before them where the Plantagenet waited, English archers raised their long yellow yew bows and sent their first flights of arrows into the air.

"On!" someone was screaming, close by Josseran. "On! On!" He thought it was blind John of Bohemia, but the rushing knights around him were crowding him away from the king and his companions. Josseran looked back one last time, over his shoulder, back toward his own green banner.

Yvain was there, with Everard beside him. Yvain flung up his arm, hailing him. Josseran gave him an answering wave. His horse lurched. He was caught in the charge. He could not look backward now. With his right hand he jerked out his sword; with his left he set his shield, and sinking his spurs in he bellowed his war cry and plunged forward, into the battle, toward the English enemy.

Yvain shouted, "Everard! Stay by me!"

The boy heard, somehow, in the confusion, and reined his little horse hard up against his uncle's. Before them, in the wild tumult of the charging army, there was no longer any sign of Josseran. The mass of knights behind them on the road thrust them steadily forward. Yvain swung his great war-horse up beside Everard's palfrey, and without the spur both horses broke into a gallop.

In a mob of men so dense there was no space between them to fall, they charged down the road toward the English. Arrows hissed and whined in the air overhead, and there were dead men ahead now, on the road, the Genoese, dying under the English arrows, dying so fast that abruptly the whole great troop of crossbowmen whirled and tried to flee. At that the French knights pressing after let out a howl of rage.

"Cowards! Kill — kill!"

They plowed into the surging mob on the road, trampling down the Genoese, and hacking at them with their swords.

"Get out of the way!"

"Cowards — slay them!"

The arrows slipped into the mass of bodies, and gaps appeared among them; Yvain's horse trod on something soft and nearly fell, and his rider swayed wildly. He let out a yell. Beside him Everard leaned over and thrust out one arm, as if to defend his uncle, and the horse's hoofs struck solid ground again and the great muscles gathered and Yvain de Vaumartin hurtled forward into the battle.

He wrenched his sword from the scabbard; he forgot about Everard. Ahead of him still were only Genoese, ducking and falling and dying, clogging the road, but beyond them now he saw the flash of the sunlight on helmets, the raised wall of shields.

Those were knights. Those were his enemies. After him his friends came, so fast and so thick they thrust him on before them, faster and faster. He drove his spurs into his horse's flanks, and the great brute neighed and lunged forward. The road bent upward again. A knight in red armor charged straight at him, his sword raised.

They struck blows. The clash of sword on sword shivered his arm to the shoulder. His throat was stopped with fear and he could not shout his war cry, but his arm belonged to God, and God as ever ennobled him; he struck and struck, watching as if some other man did this work. The surging of the half-mad horse under him rocked him violently out of his saddle, and he lost one stirrup. Something rang off his shield so hard there were bells in his ears. Another horse crashed into his from behind, and his mount stumbled.

There were knights all around him, English knights, on foot, screaming in their bastard French. He howled in fear, lashed out with the strength of fear, driving them back, meeting one blade on the edge of his shield so that the sword clattered from its owner's hand. His horse charged, giving him an attacking angle on the man before him, and that man disappeared before his sword; Yvain had no feeling of having struck him down, but he was gone, and the horse was struggling on, going uphill now, straight into the sun.

Yvain flinched from the brilliant sunlight. Half blinded, he found his other senses unlocked: the stink of blood made his stomach roll, the shrill screech of iron on iron stood his hair on end. His horse stumbled, nearly throwing him. He hacked behind him with his sword, hitting only the air. Swinging forward again, he faced a lance coming straight at his face and ducked. The shaft went over his shoulder, and he reined his horse hard around into the horse of the other knight, keeping the English lance cramped and useless, and thrust and stabbed and chopped until the other knight was gone.

Still there were more, always more. He could not see another Frenchman. His horse was staggering on the steep slippery hillside. It went to its knees, and then from his left a battle-axe swept down and struck the great horse just in front of the wither, and the blood shot up in a spray into the air and the brute sagged and fell.

Yvain shrieked. He flung himself on the man who had slain his horse, an English foot soldier who with both hands raised his battle-axe above his head. Yvain lunged, his sword thrusting forward and all his weight behind it, and drove the blade into the man's chest and through and out the other side, with such a force that he went to his knees as the Englishman fell.

Abruptly, to his amazement, he saw Everard just beyond, on foot, carrying the stump of a lance, parrying off blows with it, driven to his knees as his uncle watched. Yvain staggered toward him. Raising his sword, he made a shelter for his nephew against the rain of blows. Everard wheeled, his face white, the thin stem of the broken lance in his hands, placing himself to protect Yvain's back, and in all the tumult, in the noise and fury, Yvain felt a stab of pride in this green boy, who had found his courage at last.

The sky above him darkened again. The English were assaulting him from two sides, their swords like thunderclouds against the sun. He struck hard and low, to bring them down, and a body crashed down before him; he thrust out with his sword, and from his left a blade swung like a scythe in the ripe corn and struck through his right arm at the elbow.

There was no pain, only a tide of blood from the butt of his arm. He slumped down, the world growing all strangely white around him. Everard wheeled around, standing over him, protecting him. Yvain could not regain his feet; his body seemed long and limp as a willow switch; he struggled to stay conscious. His arm gushed rhythmic spurts of blood. Above him Everard was parrying off blows, holding off the English, giving him a space to die in. Abruptly the enemy turned away; there was a moment's lull.

Yvain flung up his head, too heavy now for his neck, and Everard knelt down and his arm went around Yvain and he held his uncle tight against him, and Yvain laid his head against Everard's shoulder.

"I want to go home," he said, dazed; as his blood flowed out his senses were fading away, he seemed to be a boy again, in the wood by Vaumartin, with his brothers Josseran and Clair; he was tired, and the night was coming. "I want to go home —"

"I am with you," Everard said, and held him, and thus, in his nephew's arms, Yvain de Vaumartin gave up his life on Crécy field.

Josseran never saw his nephew and brother after the first charge. His half-maddened horse carried him in the midst of a great band of knights straight down the slope. He gathered himself, pulled his sword out, got his shield snug against him; the French knights were so close around him, so tightly packed around him, that he was afraid he would never see the English, never strike a blow.

The great charge reached the foot of the slope and turned uphill, galloped west up the hill, and abruptly the clouds parted, and the sunlight, brighter for the rain, met them like a wall of fire. Josseran flinched, his arm up. Beside him someone screamed. It was raining again, in spite of the sun. He could feel the raindrops plinking off his shield, off the shields of the men around him.

But there were no raindrops; it was a rain of arrows that fell. Now, abruptly, there were no French knights around him at all.

Struggling up the steep broken slope, the sun blazing into his face, he took a blow on his shield and struck blindly forward. His sword hit something. His horse plunged, reared, lashed out with its forehoofs, shrilling. Another great blow smashed against his shield. The sun in his eyes was worse than blows, and he swung his horse around, striking before him and behind him with the sword, and now, finally, he could see.

His horse reared again. All around him were men on foot, and they charged at him from every side; he parried off their swords with his shield, struck at them awkwardly with his own blade. Not like honest knights, he thought, in a wild instant of mirth: why won't they stand still like real men? That made him laugh; he spurred his horse forward, leaning down to strike at these enemies who came at him like hornets from the ground, and something hit him hard in the back. His horse stumbled. He felt his mount going down and threw himself free.

On foot, to his surprise, it was easier. He stood a moment, looking around him. The old windmill stood directly behind him, at the top of the ridge. The leopard banner of the Plantagenets fluttered from its peak. Off to his left in a great wedge the French knights had slowed their charge; they were struggling uphill against the packed ranks of unmounted English, and beyond them, more English were running down the slope, to take the French from the side.

All around him were eddies of French and English, fighting. A riderless horse galloped past him, its reins whipping, and he ran a few steps after it, hoping to catch it. Then suddenly before him was a wild-eyed man with a long knife, who screamed and lunged at him.

Josseran flung up his sword. The knife came at him like a snake's tongue, slipping in under his own blade, and he sidestepped. The Englishman let out a yell in some language not French. Josseran pretended to trip. The Englishman reared back his arm to strike, and Josseran put up his sword and the other man ran himself onto it.

He looked surprised; even dead, he looked surprised. Josseran had to put his foot on the man's chest to draw his sword free. His mouth was dry. His belly fluttered with panic and his arm was too heavy to lift. Behind him a horn blew.

He wheeled. Down the slope behind him came another charge of the French knights. Before they could reach the English they were stumbling over the dead men and dead horses that littered the low ground; loose horses, galloping wild here and there, broke the charge.

It would do no good. Josseran wiped his hand over his mouth, his chest constricting. This was a disaster, here. King Philip had led them to a disaster. The English were pushing down the slope on either side of the French; they were surrounding King Philip's army. The French had no hope of winning this battle now.

Josseran staggered away, across the slope; the muscles of his thighs burned, his feet like weights at the ends of his legs. Suddenly he thought of Yvain, of Everard, and he whirled again toward the battle.

Above him, near the mill, several horns sounded, over and over. He wheeled. In a broad arc a crowd of English knights swept down the ridge toward him, headed for the battle beyond. As they rode they stood in their stirrups, they raised their swords over their heads and shouted their battle cries. Their surcoats were spotless, their swords gleamed, unbloodied. They were fresh as maidens to this fight, while the French waded in mud and blood, exhausted.

Josseran scrambled across the stony slope, tripped over a tangled bush, and fell headlong. Ten yards away lay a dead knight, his shield under him. Josseran ran up to the corpse and pulled the shield loose, and as the English charge reached him he flung the shield out sideways, and with the edge swept the legs of the first horse cleanly out from under it.

The rider catapulted out of his saddle and slammed to the ground. The other knights charged straight past Josseran. He turned, panting, to see them strike the mass of the French knights from the side and drive them back across the marshy lowland.

This battle was lost. Josseran threw down the shield he had picked up. There were loose horses everywhere, wild with fear and the smell of blood. If he could catch one he could get out of here. Wherever Yvain and Everard were, he could do them no good now. He pulled off his helmet and his leg armor and hurried after the nearest horse, away from the battle behind him.

five

EVERARD LAID YVAIN DOWN on the torn
and bloody earth; the roar and crash of the battle around him
sounded far away. He gripped Yvain's hand. Every kindness his uncle
had given him arose again in his mind, and tears burst from his eyes.
The blood all around him was Yvain's, puddles of it, sticky and
stinking. The hand in his was already growing cold. He sank down,
shivering.

A blow glanced off his back, and he flinched, his arm up. A man
with a club was coming at him, his stick raised to batter him again.
Everard lurched up onto his feet. He snatched up his uncle's sword, not
to save himself but to protect the dead flesh that he had loved, and with
all his strength he slashed down and broke the man before him through
the skull.

As that body fell away, a horse plunged up toward him, and its rider
struck down with his sword, and Everard met the blow with the blade
in his hand, and the sword rang and shivered so that he dropped it. He
ducked. The horse reared again, its hoofs above his head. He saw his
death before him, but the great iron-shod hoofs missed him. Cowering
over his uncle's body, he saw the knight veer away to meet an assault
from the side.

"Valois!"

"Plantagenet! Plantagenet!"

Over his head the sky darkened in a gust of arrows. Someone nearby
cried hoarsely, "Mercy — I yield!" A horse thundered down on
Everard, and he flung himself across his uncle's body, protecting it; he
could not bear that the great hoofs should tear Yvain's flesh and break
his bones, dead though he was. The horse swerved to avoid him.
Something struck him lightly on the arm and bounced away, and he
looked down and saw an arrow lying in the mud beside him.

He put his hands on his uncle. He felt himself swollen, bursting, as if his grief became another man inside him, who grew too big for a boy's frame.

"Yield," a harsh voice said, in bad French. "Yield."

Everard straightened; three or four foot soldiers were around him, closing cautiously on him, daggers and clubs in their hands.

"Yield!"

He screamed. He caught up whatever lay near his hands and flung it at them — stones, grass, the broken arrow; he leapt to his feet, and when they closed in on him he kicked and thrashed and bit at them. They knocked him down and pushed his face into the dirt.

"Yield!"

He lay there on his face as they bound him up. He tasted mud. His cheek ground against the dirt. Through the tail of his eye he could see them stripping his uncle of his armor and his clothes, rings, spurs, even the little wooden cross around his neck. The man inside Everard began to roar. The boy Everard only wept, and turned his head away.

They took him to the earl of Warwick, who said, "I knew Yvain de Vaumartin, and Josseran, his brother. Are you their kinsman?"

Everard said, "Yes."

The man before him sat relaxed on a little stool, wearing only the dirty buff-colored quilted padding that went under his armor; his big hands, loose on his knees, were bloody and bruised. He looked Everard long in the eyes.

"Are they dead, then, on this field?"

"Yvain is dead," said Everard. "I know nothing of Josseran."

Shaking his head, the earl dropped his gaze a little, his mouth kinked. "Then it is true — we have brought the best of them down, here, with a sheaf of cloth-yard arrows."

He said this to himself, without congratulation; Everard clenched his teeth and kept silent. He could not bear to give this man so much as an unnecessary word.

The earl faced him again. "Your kinsman was a great knight, and had I been favored enough to take him I should have demanded a ransom worthy of his blood and his prowess, but you are only a boy. For the respect in which I hold your house, I shall have no ransom of you. You will stay this night here, but in the morning you are free to go back to Vaumartin."

"I want my uncle's body," Everard said.

"If you can find it." The earl's eyes widened. "You are Josseran's son?"

"My father was Clair de Vaumartin," Everard said, unwillingly.

"The Sire de Vaumartin. I remember him, a valiant and cunning man." Warwick paused a moment, but Everard would not look at him, would not be drawn into talk with him; he felt weighted down, dull, and sour with hatred.

At last the English knight said, "Well, then, let it be your duty to become the knight he was. Give me your promise that you will not make war on me now, and I shall give you the freedom of my camp."

Everard said nothing.

"Give me your word, or I shall have to bind you."

"Bind me, then," Everard said, and shuddered, from head to foot; then he lifted his eyes and stared at the earl. "I will not promise you anything."

The earl's eyes widened, and his big battered hands closed into fists. "This is not the courtesy your uncle would have offered me," he said.

Everard bit his lip, furious. He saw that sword again slicing down, chipping through his uncle's arm, that English sword.

"Well, then." The earl thumped his knees. "You are only a boy, you will do no damage to any but yourself, should thoughts of vengeance lure you into dangerous adventures. I have no fear of you. Go, do as you wish. I would have tendered you the honors and respect due the son of your house, had you shown me a gentle manner. Go."

The boy turned and walked out of the tent. He walked on legs like sticks of wood; he was exhausted.

It was dusk. The muddy slope where the English had made their camp spread away before him, thronged with people, scattered with the bright leaping beacons of their cookfires. Everard walked away from Warwick's tent, down through the camps of lesser men. Around many of them sat French knights, taken captive, and he looked for Josseran but did not see him.

Josseran was probably dead, too. Everything he knew was dead.

Slowly he walked around the edge of this place, between the first of the campfires and the old mill. Two strings of horses jogged toward him, and he moved out of their way. Coming to a little tree, its leaves and green boughs half chewed away by the English horses, he sat down at its foot.

His mind was empty. He could not weep any more for Yvain.

Leaning his head back, he stared into the darkening sky, and all he knew was a kind of dull pain, an unassuageable longing that this day should not have been.

Slowly he became aware of a noisy crowd swarming toward him, coming over the hill behind him, past the old broken mill. He stood up, wary. Past him came a stream of mounted knights, whooping, waving tokens of their victory over their heads. In their midst, crowded and cheered, rode a boy not much older than Everard himself.

This boy wore full armor. In the uncertain summer twilight, Everard thought it looked black. His helmet was off, and his shoulders were wrapped around and around in a filthy piece of cloth. A banner: a conquered flag. As Everard watched, other men rushed up from the camp below to meet the English heroes.

The boy in armor stopped. The men around him fell back, giving room, and from the crowd that came to give honor to the conqueror stepped forth a man so richly dressed Everard knew him at once for the king, Edward Plantagenet himself. For a moment the king and the boy faced each other, triumphant.

"Your Grace," the boy said, in a clear tired voice. "My father, my king, I lay my victory at your feet." He knelt, uncoiling the ragged banner from his shoulders, and spread it out at the feet of the king.

All the men cheered. Everard bit his lip, suddenly more angry than he had ever been: how could they cheer over so many dead men? He tasted blood in his mouth; he had bitten his lip open.

Before him, the king reached down and raised his son up, and embraced him, and all the English army cried out in one voice. "All hail King Edward! All hail Prince Edward, our Black Prince!" Everard turned and went away, up over the hill, toward the battlefield.

He searched through the night for his uncle's body. Once or twice he fell asleep, lying on the ground, the stink of blood in his nostrils, but he dared not rest too long. Wolves and vultures prowled the field, and human scavengers as well, looting the corpses that lay so thick on the low ground, and he was determined to find his uncle before they did. At last, just before dawn, when the morning star hung in the sky like a crystal, he came on the body.

By then it was nearly morning. He sank down next to the corpse, afraid to touch it. It was not his uncle any more. Yet toward this meat he felt an obligation more important than his own life, and when the light began to creep up over the edge of the world, he gathered the stiffened stinking thing up onto his back and, crooked under its weight, trudged away across the field.

The English were everywhere. They stopped him every few steps to demand his name, to know where he went, to know who the corpse was. None offered to help him. They were robbing the bodies still, arranging ransoms, getting themselves organized to march off; they did not care about one boy and one body. The sky was laid over with slate-colored clouds that seemed to press down on the field of Crécy like the lid of a coffin. In the low ground, deep mists had formed during the night, clammy cold fogs like the congealing air. Everard shuffled away down the road, going toward the church spire in the distance.

The men who had captured him had left him his clothes, and in the village he gave his shoes and coat to the priest of the little church, to buy space for his uncle in the churchyard. As he set about digging the grave, a little crowd of villagers gathered along the edge of the yard. The priest, who helped him dig, asked, "Where is the king? Will he bring another army?"

"I don't know," said Everard, who also did not care.

"Are the English coming this way?"

"I don't know," Everard said again.

He had never seen such a tool as the shovel with which he dug this hole; the rough wood tore his palms, the iron-shod blade bit the earth with a harsh grating whine that jangled in his ears like broken bells.

In the face of the boy's indifference the priest ceased to ask questions, but from the side of the churchyard, a village woman called out, "Who will protect us, if the king is gone?"

Everard straightened up, leaning on the shovel; his arms hurt deep as the bone, from shoulder to fingertips, with the weight of the earth that would soon press down upon his uncle. To the peasant he said, "Take your children, woman, and whatever is in your pantries and your butteries, and go hide with them, in the belly of the earth, at the top of the highest hill, because nothing stands now between you and the English, and they are devils, demons, evil spirits and worse."

He looked down into the uneven pit he had dug, and saw it was big enough, if not for a man to lie comfortably in, then big enough to pack away a stiff and decomposing piece of meat. Throwing down the shovel, he put the corpse into the ground.

The priest stepped forward, mumbling prayers, but Everard thrust him off. One hard look kept him away. Everard knelt at the side of the hole. He put one hand down to touch the dirt. His uncle was dirt now, like this dirt. His chest was sore with grief. Suddenly he remembered the severed arm; he should have searched that out also, and buried it here with the rest. The sore spot in his chest grew and grew, filled him up, and welled over; hot tears splashed down his cheeks. He struggled to fit prayers to his frozen lips. He prayed to God to take the soul of Yvain de Vaumartin and give it safe lodging in Heaven. His mind yearned passionately for the missing piece of his uncle's arm. For a long while, his prayers exhausted, he knelt by the open grave and did nothing.

Far away, somebody shouted, and the villagers stirred; swiftly they went away from the churchyard, and the priest too bustled away. Still Everard knelt there, until the priest came to him and said, "The English are coming. You must take shelter."

The boy rose to his feet. In the hole his uncle lay crumpled and filthy. With the shovel and his feet and hands he spilled the raw earth over him, piled it up high above the grave, and beat it down nearly flat.

"Say Mass for him," he said, to the priest.

"I will," said the priest, and held out Everard's shoes and coat. "Here, take these. You cannot go far without shoes."

"How far must I go?" Everard asked.

The priest did not answer, but watched as the boy put on his shoes again, and his coat. They went together to the gate into the graveyard, which opened on the broad road.

"Here," said the priest. "This may keep you for part of your journey, at least."

He held out a small loaf of bread and a little leather flask of wine, which Everard took, and stuffed inside his shirt.

"Which is the way to Brittany?" Everard asked.

The priest pointed south. With the same hand, he made the sign of the cross over Everard and murmured a few words of blessing. Everard set his feet upon the road and followed it.

SIX

THE ROAD LED HIM south to Abbeville, on the river Somme, where the gates were shut and guarded by clamorous mobs of townspeople, carrying rakes and hoes and clubs of wood. Knights in full armor and crossbowmen by the dozen walked the ramparts of the town's double walls. Everard crossed the bridge over the Somme there, part of the swelling stream of people fleeing from the English.

He overheard the people talking, on the road around him, each speaking with perfect confidence, as if somehow he had stood on a cloud the past few days, and seen everything that went on.

Some said that the king of France was dead, or captured, and that the English were marching on Paris itself, and would have the whole realm in the hands of Edward Plantagenet before these very folk could walk across the Abbeville bridge.

Others said that devils had risen from the earth at Crécy and taken English armor and joined the army of the Plantagenet, and in the guise of ordinary men were now raping and burning and looting the whole north; and still others said that the sky above Crécy had been filled with angels, who bore up the souls of the French knights as they were killed, and that the humbling of the king meant that Christ was coming again and the end of the world was at hand.

As these crowds flooded over the Somme, they bought bread from the people of Abbeville, and paid for it with rumor. So the panic spread from Crécy, as if something had broken there in the foundation of the realm, and the cracks spread out from it in all directions.

Everard stood between two of the houses on the bridge at Abbeville. The river wound away from him between the slanted red rooftops and pale straight walls of the town, away to the harbor, where he could see the masts of ships tossing in the violent wind off the Narrow Sea.

The battle at Crécy and the death of his uncle had fallen behind him, were vanishing swiftly into the depths of unreal memory. Now he struggled with the future.

He knew the way back to Vaumartin; all he had to do was keep on putting one foot before the other, and the road would take him there. He knew also what awaited him there. Isobel waited for him, who hated him, who wanted him dead, or shunted away into a monastery cell. Josseran, if he still lived, would be there, who had abandoned him once already to the English, and who, without Yvain to temper his will, would soon find a way to take all that rightfully belonged to Everard.

Everard felt himself to be a boy no longer, a helpless servile boy no longer. The battle had toughened him. He felt within himself a new heart, made strong with rage. He would not walk tamely back there, to those people who despised him, to suffer whatever they wished to do to him. When he returned to Vaumartin, he wanted the power to do as he wished.

At the end of the bridge, he came to a fork in the road. An old man sat there, toothless and ragged, begging for his bread.

Everard asked, "Where does this road go?" He pointed to the right fork of the road.

"South," said the old man. "To Caen, Lisieux, and Brittany." Unquestioned, he then pointed out the other road. "That is the way to Paris."

"Paris," Everard said, and walked forward a few steps.

He had no money. He was hungry, and his shoes, not made for walking, were wearing through; soon he would be barefoot. He had no weapons. He knew no one in Paris. He would be alone there, utterly.

So be it, he thought; this is meet and just. He would begin with nothing but himself. He would make his own way. Then, when he had become his own champion, he would go back and take what belonged to him. He would have his revenge on Isobel and Josseran. His feet were already moving, his step springy, his eyes keen. Swiftly he walked away down the road to the east, the road that led to Paris.

King Philip said, "God is against me. God Himself." He raised his winecup to his lips; his throat worked in long swallows until he set the goblet down empty.

Josseran glanced at the knight on his left, saw in that man's face his own dismay, and leaned urgently forward toward the king. "Your Grace, you must collect yourself. France relies on you — on us —"

Philip was shaking his head. "God has passed His judgment on me. More wine." He coughed.

They sat in the hall of the castle La Broye; it was the deep of the night, but the servants had lit such a great fire in the hearth that the light washed the whole room. Josseran laid his hands down flat on the table. Around him sat what was left of the king's council, and his heart quaked to see it, because so many of the best and noblest men were gone.

Those that remained hardly spoke. Their faces were slack, their ears heedless of the king's words, their gazes avoiding him, their attention turned inward, each to his own thoughts. Their servants hurried around them, filling their cups, and bringing them such meats as the castle kitchens had hastily prepared, but the lords of France sat like gray and dusty stones in their seats. Josseran himself had to force his gaze toward the king.

He said, "Your Grace, we must at least discover what is left to us of the array of France. Send heralds to the camp of King Edward, and ask to know what knights and lords he has taken prisoner, who will be ransomed, to return to fight beside us."

King Philip reached an unsteady hand for his winecup. "God is against me," he said, as if he had not heard Josseran speak.

At that Josseran shrugged, and turned his head away. He thought of his brother Yvain — of his nephew.

Yvain would watch over Everard. But there was Vaumartin to think of, now.

He turned to the king again. "Your Grace, the English will not stop here. They will strike again, and my heart tells me they will strike at my own castle, Vaumartin, which stands athwart the Breton road."

"If God chooses —" The king coughed, and did not say more.

"God gave me Vaumartin," Josseran said, "and I am going there, to hold it against the English. If my brother comes, send him after me."

The king said, "Go. Run, like the rest."

Josseran gripped his temper tight; now that the thought had formed in his mind that Vaumartin was in danger, he trembled to be so far away from it. Rising from his place, he went down the length of the table, and around the end of it, and walked away down the hall to the door.

The castle was full dark. In the two great courtyards the lesser men were sleeping, exhausted, while their horses stood with drooping heads beside them. Josseran went among them, bending down here and there to rouse his own men, of whom about one half were left alive.

Of each one, he asked, "Did you see my brother, in the battle? Did you see him afterward?" They stared back at him with glazed eyes, and no one answered him, either way.

Then he said, "Get yourselves up, and get on your horses. We are going back to Brittany." That brought some life back to them. They raised themselves up, and took what was left to them of their weapons and armor, and got their horses ready.

While he was doing this, another French knight came to him and laid his hand on Josseran's arm.

"Where are you going?"

"Back to my land," said Josseran. "Back to my heartspring."

"What of France?" this knight asked. "You owe the king some duty still, do you not?"

"I owe it to *my* king," said Josseran, his temper rising in his throat like a sword drawn up in its scabbard. "This Philip is no king of mine, not after what he did today. Not after what he said tonight."

The knight made no answer to that, but took his hand away, and so Josseran led the last of his men out of the castle La Broye.

Wherever they went, on their way home, the news of the terrible defeat at Crécy had already come. In the villages and on the road, when folk heard that he and the weary band of men who followed him had fought at Crécy, they turned away.

Near Nantes, he heard that King Edward had marched north from Crécy, off to attack Calais, on the Norman coast. That eased his mind a little. Even so, Vaumartin drew him like the well of life.

In every village, of every traveler he passed he asked about Yvain, but got no word of him; he guessed Yvain was behind him still, Yvain and Everard. When he thought of Everard at all, he felt a grim satisfaction: Crécy would have laid Everard's soul bare. After Crécy the boy would beg for the peace of the monastery.

When he rode at last into castle Vaumartin, and his wife Isobel met him, she was dressed from head to foot in black.

Without words, she embraced him; her lips were soft under his, and she stroked his cheek. Her face was radiant. She said, "God be thanked you have returned to me, husband."

He stood with her hands in his, looking down at her. Around him the great walls of Vaumartin were strong and tall, and he felt safe enough at last to draw a free breath. He said, "Have you had any word of Yvain?"

Then she drew out her right hand from his grip, and reaching into the bodice of her dress she brought forth a little chain, with a wooden cross dangling from it, that he knew well.

He took hold of the cross. "Where did this come from?"

"The earl of Warwick, of the English, sent it to me," she said steadily. "No word, and nothing else, save this cross."

Josseran lifted the cross to his lips and kissed it. In his chest there was a hard knot of grief. He walked a few steps away from her, thinking of Yvain.

He said, "God have mercy on him. He was a great knight, a great knight." He turned to face her, putting out his hand to her.

She took it. She said, "Do you have any word of Everard?"

He looked into her face; he said, "No, nothing."

"Then he is dead also," she said.

His belly contracted. He remembered, at Crécy, how Yvain and Everard had charged side by side into the battle, and he knew that what she said was true, but in her voice he heard a sort of triumph, which chilled him.

"I shall send to the English," he said. "They may have taken him prisoner."

She said, "They would have given us word, if they had taken him. He is dead."

He looked her full in the face, and said, "You do not know that — not certainly."

"He is dead," she said, and her voice sang with victory. "You are the Sire de Vaumartin, my lord."

Then she smiled at him, a smile full of secrets, as if they had conspired together, and their conspiracy had come to success.

He said, "Do you think I killed him?" And he crossed himself, his brother's little wooden cross clutched in his fist.

She lifted one shoulder in a shrug. Even in black mourning clothes that drew the color from her skin, she was beautiful, her face flawless, unmarked by suffering, by guilt, by understanding. She said, "What difference does it make? The changeling is dead, and you are the Sire de Vaumartin."

He thrust her away. "I did not do it!" His voice rang out. Around him the whole courtyard seemed to boom with his voice. He looked around him, at the people turning to look at him, at the high cold walls of Vaumartin. They would all think it, even if it were not so — he had the profit of it. Like his fist clenching over the little wooden cross, his heart closed around this guilt. Long-striding, he stalked past his wife, into the hall of his castle.

Isobel went into the chapel and knelt down at the altar, to thank God for her husband's deliverance, but she could not lose herself in her prayers.

All had happened as she had wanted it; Everard was gone. No one could ever accuse her of murdering him. She was really guilty only of wanting it. He had chosen the way himself, chosen his own death, a stupid, silly boy, unworthy. Now Josseran was Sire de Vaumartin — she was Dame de Vaumartin.

Yet there was no peace in it, in her mind, in her soul. Something in it twitched and thrashed, as if buried away alive.

Before the old wooden altar, its paint worn away along the top, she knelt in the sweep of her black mourning gown, and lifted her face to the suffering face of the Crucified One, and suddenly, vehemently, too late, she wished she were innocent.

seven

L EVERARD SPENT his first night in Paris in the great cathedral of Our Lady, on the island in the Seine that sailed through the middle of the city. The church was so vast it was like being inside a mountain, and with its soaring peaks and stone worked smooth as glass, it seemed much like the magic mountains of the old stories, beyond the grasp of men. He fell asleep staring up into its dizzying vastness.

He woke with the first gray stony light, as a procession of monks and priests with tall candles in their hands paced chanting down the nave toward the altar. Their candles, with their holy yellow glow, made the church seem darker and more cavernous. High above them, brightening in the dawn, the blue-and-ruby windows of the clerestory shone forth like visions floating in the air.

While the priests sang a memorial Mass, Everard went around the great building, looking at everything; his eyes seemed always drawn upward, his head always cocked back. At first he saw only the great statues that filled the niches around the many altars, but as the daylight grew stronger, painted figures appeared everywhere, as if coming out of hiding — stiff and solemn saints in blue and gold, white angels and red-and-black devils, and wild beasts, crowding the choirs, climbing the spines of the vaults, tangles of faces and hands and monstrous wings, creatures foul as Hell itself, and fine and wonderful as Heaven: a cosmos made of stone, and peopled, in the grace of God's sunlight, with marvels.

At last, hungry, he went out of the cathedral. An old graveyard took up one side of the church, and in front of the porch was a large irregular pavement, where now some people with carts and packs were beginning to set up a market. He drifted around this place for a while, hoping to find something to eat; the great numbers of the people made him shy.

The streets that left the paved square were narrow and filthy, lined with shops and houses that stood one wall against the next, their fronts flush with the edge of the street, and their penthouses built out over the street, so that even in the bright day the place seemed gloomy. Through these streets like tunnels, stinking and dark, the people of Paris hurried, each with his gaze narrow like the street, focused only on his own mighty business.

Ragged filthy beggars whined at him from the porch of a little church. He followed a milkmaid awhile, as she went from door to door, selling pails of milk, but when he asked her for some of it she snarled and threw a stone at him. A horseman galloped up and by him, the hoofs clattering and slipping on the slick pavement, as Everard and those around him flung themselves against the nearest wall to escape trampling. He passed two men on a street corner fighting over which would sell his pots there; a little crowd gathered to cheer the battle on.

A pieman hawking meat pies came by him, shouting his wares in a singsong voice; the steaming aroma made Everard's stomach cramp.

At the opposite end of the island from the cathedral was a castle, with crenellated towers beyond its massive wall, and in the open courtyard people were gathered. He went in among them, really hungry now, desperate, and when he saw a purse tucked invitingly into the belt of a fat man, he grabbed it and ran.

The fat man shrieked. Everard fled, and the whole mob chased him out through the courtyard gate and down through the streets that suddenly seemed as wide and open as the church nave, with no place to hide. He dropped the purse; he ran until his breath gave out, and finally dodged into an alley and hid behind a rain barrel. Slowly his pounding heart slowed, his burning lungs eased, and he saw that no one was going to catch him, but still his skin crept.

He decided then not to try to steal anything more; he was no good as a thief.

Following the constant crowd, he crossed the river to the south, where along the river's edge the housewives of the city were washing their white linens. On the grassy bank above them, under the plane trees, fishwives and winesellers and cheesemakers were haggling over wares brought down the Seine in flatbottomed boats. There seemed to be food everywhere, none of it for him.

This bank of the Seine was more open than the island, or even the north bank, where great stone towers and houses lined the broad street along the river, and lines of rooftops showed beyond like the fading peaks of mountain ranges. On the Left Bank, where he now found himself, the steeples of the churches rose up among the leafy crowns of trees, and there was space between even the meanest houses. The people walked slower, and stopped to talk in the street, or by the wells. Pigs rooted in the ditch along the edge of the street. A cock crowed at him from a low-hanging eave. Walking along a winding street, the screams of playing children in his ears, he came on a man unloading firewood from a wagon.

Everard paused, watching, and this man at once called him to help him and gave him a halfpenny for stacking the wood in his houseyard. With the money in his hand, Everard said, "I am hungry — where might I eat?"

"Try the White Rose — she'll give you a pork pie and a tank for half a penny." The man winked at him. "A bit more, if she likes your looks."

Everard went the way he pointed, crossing the broad dusty street that led back to the bridge onto the island, and walking down a narrow rutted lane.

This took him into a place that he thought at first must be a monastery. In among the broad grassy fields, there were no houses, only great slab-sided ill-kept halls like barns. On the street he passed several men in long black gowns like priests, who greeted him in Latin. At last, on a street that wound down toward the river bank, he found a tavern with one white rose painted on its sign and another sketched across the front of the building, the green stem twined around the corner.

In the sparse grass between the tavern and the street, two men in black gowns lay with their heads in their arms. Everard peered curiously at them as he passed, and nearly stepped on a boy who sat in the doorway, eating a piece of bread.

"They're just drunk," this boy said jovially to him. "The Picard nation celebrated here last night — a little too hard, I guess. Drinking up the surplus, they call it."

"The Picard nation!" Everard said, amazed. He stopped beside the boy; delicious aromas of garlic and onion and meat reached him from inside the tavern, but his curiosity overruled his belly. "What is this place, anyway?"

The boy looked sharply at him. His black hair hung down long and greasy to his shoulders. Stuffing his bread in his mouth, he thrust out his chest and, mimicking Everard's Breton accent and Everard's way of standing, he peered around him and said, "What is this place, anyway?

Maybe it's Heaven! Maybe it's Hell! Ask them." He laughed, jabbing his thumb at the two drunken men. The lump of bread was still wedged in his cheek; he got up, dusting his hand off. "Come inside, country boy, you look hungry."

Everard went after him into the tavern. A long, low-ceilinged room, it was almost empty now, save for the wooden benches scattered all around, and an old man slumped listlessly on a stool in a corner with a tankard in his hand.

"Mother!" the black-haired boy shouted. "La Belle Rose — come give a tank and a loaf to my fool here, who doesn't know what the universitas is!"

The universitas. Everard straightened, putting it all together now: this was the great Studium of Paris, where scholars came from all over the world to teach and to study: the universitas was the guild of their masters, although many, like this boy, used the word to refer to the place in general. The priest at Vaumartin had told Everard of it. He had spoken of it as a sink of Hell, eaten with the worms of doubt and disbelief. Everard, who had always tried to think the opposite of the priest, had imagined it like a great white castle, tower rising upon tower, full of noble, learned men and wonderful books. Now, stepping over the drunken men to reach the tavern door, he wondered if for once the priest had been right.

Out of the back of the tavern came a tall woman with flaming red hair.

"Mother Rose!" the black-haired boy called, and flung open his arms. "I've brought you another hungry belly to feed."

"Bah," she said. "Get your lazy unwiped behind out of here, Flippo. As for your friend, he can eat if he has the money, or he can go home with you and let Italo feed him."

Flippo shook his head. "How sad, and after all I've done for you, Mother." He backed up, edging toward the door.

Everard went by him toward the redheaded woman, holding out his hand. "I have money. Please — I'm hungry."

"God's balls," she said. "Another Breton goat-boy." She peered into his palm, took the halfpenny, and nodded to him. "Sit down."

Everard sat down on a bench, and a moment later she brought him a piece of a savory pudding and a tankard of beer. Flippo sat beside him.

"So, country boy, what brings you to Paris?"

Everard mumbled something around a mouthful of food. Flippo

reached casually for the tank of beer, and Everard moved it out of his reach.

"Oho," said Flippo. "That's not very friendly." He wiped his hand on his shirt. "Here. How's your luck today? Want to try my game?"

Out of the wallet on his belt he took three walnut shells and a coin, so old and bent and cut it rocked on the flat tabletop. He lined the walnut shells up on the bench in front of him, hid the coin under the middle shell, and began to shuffle all three back and forth around the top of the bench.

"Now. Which one's got the money under it?"

Everard had been watching, his mouth stuffed with pease pudding, and he put his finger on the middle shell. Flippo groaned.

"Well, you caught me. You're pretty sharp, for a bumpkin. Let's try it again."

He set his game up again on the bench. Mother Rose was staring at them from the far side of the room.

Again Everard found the coin with no trouble, which seemed to annoy Flippo, who flung his hands up, tossed his black hair, and scowled.

"You're a sharper, aren't you?"

Everard laughed. The pudding was gone; he drank the last of the beer and wiped his mouth on his sleeve. With his belly full he felt much better.

"All right," said Flippo, "I'll tell you what. Put up your own penny, and if you win this time, you take mine. If I win, I'll take yours. How's that? Fair enough?"

"It would be, if I had the penny," Everard said.

"Oh, come on, you've got a penny, surely. Everybody has a penny." Flippo shook his wallet, which clinked convincingly. "Come on. Just a penny. You're so sharp, you'll win right away."

Everard's gaze went to the walnut shells. It seemed a quick easy way to get his next meal, but he did not have the penny, and as he thought it over, he saw no reason why a stranger like this boy would want to give his money away; it was a trick, somehow.

He said, "I have no penny, Flippo."

"That belt, then. If I win, you give me the belt, but if you win, you take my penny."

"That's no penny you've got, either," Everard said, nodding at the poor broken little coin on the bench.

Flippo grunted. Getting up, he scooped the walnut shells and the

49

chip of money into his hand and dropped them into his wallet. "You can't trust people's looks any more at all," he said, glared at Everard as if Everard had cheated him, and walked out of the tavern.

The red-haired woman gave a grunt of low laughter. She said, "Cute enough, goat-boy," and came across the room to take the tankard from him. "Stay away from Flippo, if you're smart."

"I need work," Everard said.

She walked away across the tavern. "Go to the Place de Grève, over on the high bank, that's where they hire day labor."

He went after her a few steps. "Don't you have any work I could do? I —"

She wheeled around, her eyes flashing, and spat. "No! I have no work for lazybones goat-boys. Now get out, before I get my man there to pitch you out on your Breton backside!"

Everard glanced at the old man in the corner, who was dozing over his ale. The woman seemed more capable. As he hesitated, indeed, she raised her fist, and hastily he backed out the door.

Thereafter, whenever he could, he went to the White Rose, especially in the afternoon, after the Studium's ordinary lectures let out, when the place was crowded and uproarious. The scholars wore monkish black, and many had their heads tonsured, but they loved dice games and drinking and songs, they loved to pull the serving girls into their laps and stick their hands under their skirts. Every morning Everard went down to the Place de Grève, on the north side of the river, and made his day's penny unloading barges, and in the afternoon he went up to the tavern and diced and drank and practiced his Latin on the scholars.

After all his quarrels and struggles with the priest of Vaumartin, he had considered himself well provided with learning, but these scholars could recite at great length from books he had never heard of. They loved to argue, and the winner of any argument was he who could summon the most authorities to support his cause. Usually the question was witless, such as whether angels had gender, or if Adam had a navel, but sometimes they argued matters that seemed to Everard to strike his own soul — what was real, what was right, what was worth doing in the world — and they did it with a passion and a certainty that he envied.

They came from all over Christendom, these scholars, many of them no older than he was; some were rich, but most were poor, as poor as he was. They were homeless, hearthless, kinless men, as he was.

Even so, they had their place, the Studium, and their quest. If they had no things, yet they had ideas about things. He had nothing at all.

That tormented him. At the crossroads back in Abbeville, he had sworn to make of himself such a champion that even Josseran would quail before him, so that he could return to Vaumartin and seize his birthright back again. But here he gained no ground toward that end. Every day was a struggle merely to ease the pinch in his belly. His home was a flour sack under the eave of the White Rose, which he paid for by hauling and chopping and digging like a serf. Vaumartin and his heritage seemed lost to him utterly.

He swore to himself, over and over, that he would never forget who he really was. When the moment came when he could stand forth as a champion, and demand what was truly his, then he would shout out his name for all to hear. In the meantime, better that Everard de Vaumartin not exist. If Josseran learned he was alive, and found him like this, Everard would be helpless. So when the scholars asked him for his name — when Mother Rose, sharp-eyed, pressed him about his home — he put them off, he looked away, and mumbled something false.

Nonetheless, they came to know him. One night he got into an argument with a German scholar, and being in need of a telling remark, he made up a bit of an idea that supported his position. He attributed this homemade wisdom to Aristotle, whom the scholars called simply the Philosopher, holding him in greater reverence than any other authority, even the Bible.

The scholar whom he was contending with looked impressed, and hesitated to say more. Everard said, "You recognize the words of the Master, of course? *De sententia?*"

"Oh, yes, yes," said the German. "I remember it exactly. *De sententia.* You have it right."

He was one of the rich ones, wore a gown trimmed with squirrel fur, took a servant with him everywhere to carry his books and winecup and money. Probably he had the servant study for him as well. Everard smiled at him.

"You have a wonderful memory, then, because I just now invented the whole thing; Aristotle never wrote anything called *De sententia* that I know of."

Some of the scholars at the same bench had been listening, and when he said this they roared, delighted. The German student flushed red and backed away from Everard, muttering about not hearing him properly. One of the men laughing on the bench reached out and thumped Everard on the back.

"Well played, by God's eyes! I'll take you to my lecture on the Decretals — you'll confound my master, who knows nothing either."

Another of the scholars said quietly, "False knowledge confounds everybody." He frowned at Everard. "You should enroll in the Studium, boy, and find out the uses of truth as well as the uses of ignorance."

Everard burned at this reproach, and blurted out, "I see no value at all in your arguments, save to win drinks from one another."

The scholar nodded at him. "Then let me put it to you in your own terms. If you do not practice with your sword, when you must fight with it, you will fail. So it is with the nobler instrument, which is the mind."

Everard had not considered that he might belong in the Studium. Slowly he said, "How does one enroll?"

"Find a master. Pay your fees. Find a room somewhere, an inkwell, a supply of quills —"

"Who is your master?" Everard asked.

"Mine? Angulanus. Humbert van Ecke. But he will not take you."

"Why not?" Everard sat up straight, his hands on his chest.

The scholar nodded at him. He had wide-set gray eyes, and he did nothing quickly. He said, "Because you are wellborn, but here you are living in the street. You are a runaway monk — although in truth you have not got such a look about you — or you are someone's bastard — something anyway on the wrong side of the blanket. Who would have anything to do with you?"

Everard brooded on that. It shocked him that the gray-eyed scholar had known so readily that he was noble-born. It comforted him also, in a way, that his true identity still clung to him.

A few days later, Flippo came back.

Everard was in the yard behind the tavern, turning over Mother Rose's garden with a spade. The black-haired boy ambled in quietly and leaned against the fence behind him.

"Still here, are you? She must have a kindness for you."

"Hello, Flippo," Everard said.

Although it was cold, he had his shirt off, not wishing to get it any dirtier that it already was, and he worked steadily to keep warm.

Flippo watched him a moment and said, "There's somebody who wants to meet you. Why don't you come home with me? You'd like my house, anyway — we'll get something to eat from my mother."

Without pausing in his work, Everard said, "You have a mother? And she admits it?" From the tavern came a low laugh; Rose was watching out the pantry door.

Flippo said, "Come on, drop the shovel, this is boring. My mother will give you a cup of beer, too."

"I'm not done yet," Everard said, and now Mother Rose came out of the tavern.

"You! Get your little lying tongue out of here. He's busy."

Flippo slid away down the fence like a drop of oil down a hot pan, and was gone. Mother Rose turned toward Everard, her hands on her hips.

"Get back to work. I'm not paying you a limp carrot or a watery egg white unless you're done by sundown."

Everard had not stopped working all through this, but he saw no reason to tell her so; he cast over a shovel of dirt and plunged the blade back into the earth again. She watched him awhile, her gaze remote, and went back into the tavern.

eight

AFTER THE BATTLE at Crécy, the English
marched north, to the coast of Normandy, and laid siege to the
city of Calais. This city, strongly walled and fortified, lay opposite the
English coast, across the Narrow Sea, and if he possessed it the
Plantagenet would be the more able to jump back and forth between
his own kingdom and luckless France.

Calais resisted, but King Edward was patient.

In the next summer, after his terrible defeat at Crécy, when again he
could call his vassals to their annual duty of sixty days' armed service,
King Philip summoned all his tenants and their armies and led them
away to Calais, to raise the English siege. Then Josseran de Vaumartin,
with his men-at-arms and knights, went up from his own lands, and
rejoined the king.

Beaujeu said, "They have lain under siege in that city, for upwards of
a year — they must be eating the spiders and mice by now. Watch out,
the ground here is all muck."

Josseran lifted his reins, steering his horse after the Sire de Beaujeu's.
The air smelled of rot and damp. They were riding along the margin
of the swamp that lay between Calais and King Philip's new camp,
sprawled over the meadows and scrublands behind them. Even at
night, Josseran could well make out where Calais stood, beyond the
intervening trees and marsh.

On the top of the highest tower in the city flapped a banner sewn
with the fleur-de-lys, King Philip's emblem, lit up by a leaping
bonfire, erupting torrents of sparks. The clamorous blaring of trumpets
around it had not ceased since King Philip's army arrived, earlier in the

day, and the cheering of the people of Calais was as loud as the horns, exuberant at their coming deliverance.

Beaujeu said, "This won't be easy."

Josseran peered through the darkness around them. He had been to Calais once or twice, and each time, being a fighting man, he had marked how the city lay, neither on water nor on land, because the sea came up to its very walls on the one side, and this great marsh guarded the approaches to it on the other. Between the far side of the marsh and the city's walls ran a strip of drier ground, and on that King Edward had laid down his army and arranged his siege engines, out of reach of the new-arrived French.

"There's the bridge," Beaujeu said, and inclined his head.

Ahead of them a bridge arched over a canal. The road over it, he remembered, was the only sound way into Calais. Torches fluttered and roared on its railings, and Josseran could make out the shadowy figures of men moving around in the wavering reddish light.

"Those are English," said Beaujeu. "Lancaster commands them."

Josseran pursed his lips. Everybody knew Henry of Lancaster, who had fought in France most of his adult life: French mothers used his name to terrify their children. In his mind Josseran formed an image of the land around the city.

"Along the shore," he said, "is there no way by the sea? I thought I remembered —"

"Sand and dunes," said Beaujeu. "Treacherous footing."

"Yet at low tide it might be possible," Josseran said. He swung around, looking back toward their own camp. He had seen local people there, when he rode in, selling fish to the other knights. They would know the tides, the paths through the coastal dunes.

Beaujeu said, "We must have some way to compel the king."

He reined his horse around, a big man, gray-bearded, who sat slumped comfortably on his horse with an older man's lack of interest in appearances, and stuck his fist on his hip.

"To tell the truth, my lord de Vaumartin, I see our task here nearly impossible, but not for reasons of the lay of the land. Have you seen the king yet?"

Josseran had his back to the French camp. He was scanning the land around the bridge again. "No, I paid my respects when I joined the army, but it was the prince who received me — Normandy, Prince John."

Beaujeu grunted. "Would that he led us — he at least will come to some decision, although most of the time it's the wrong one."

"What do you mean?"

"Since Crécy, the king has been like a man haunted," Beaujeu said. "You yourself — would you trust any command he gave you?"

"If I agreed, surely," Josseran said.

"If you agreed. But wars are not won by men who stop to think if they agree with their commander's decisions," Beaujeu said. "Philip sees the worst in everything. For fear of evil consequence he cannot make up his mind. He sees Crécy again in everything; his will is paralyzed."

From the blazing tower in Calais went up a great thunder of a cheer, and Beaujeu twisted to look that way; his saddle creaked. Josseran scratched his chin.

"How would you do this, then, my lord?"

"The object must be to put great numbers of our knights into Calais itself," said Beaujeu. "Then they could issue forth in a charge, and we could catch King Edward between them and us, here by the marsh."

"If we sent the best knights we had to steal toward the city along the coast, then with all the rest attacked the bridge, we could distract the English here enough for the men on the beach to get into the city. We must get some local guides — go when the tide is down, tonight, or tomorrow morning —"

"That's desperate," said Beaujeu. "Yet it's a plan, at least. We must show the king we mean to do more than just camp here and wait all summer."

"Will the king agree?"

"No," Beaujeu said. "But if he sees we are determined, he will agree to something."

"Then that is what we will do," said Josseran.

He turned his horse; Beaujeu rode up beside him, so that their stirrups rubbed together. In the silence and darkness around them, the uproar from the tower of Calais seemed a puny vainglory. They rode back toward the camp. The marshes smelled heavily of rot and slime. Here and there among the dark clumps of trees, as they rode by, Josseran saw a sudden red-gold gleam: the torches of Calais shone on some pool of standing water.

His scalp prickled up. Over there, beyond those thin stands of trees, were the men who had humiliated him at Crécy, who had cut down Yvain. He longed to force them to their knees. Until he saw them humbled, he himself was humble, cramped and low, less than a man.

The French camp was stretched out across a strip of an old field, still rumpled from the plow, and on this ground the knights and their followers had built campfires, were raising tents and putting up pennants; strings of horses stood snorting in the dark, neighing and stamping their feet, calling for water and feed.

With Beaujeu, Josseran rode up into the next camp, where over the fire piled up with brush two hares were roasting tandem on a spit. A dozen knights and men-at-arms leaned on their saddles around it. They were staring away toward Calais, their eyes drawn by the blaze beyond the marsh, the banner fluttering over Calais.

Josseran said, "I cannot bear to think what tales they tell of us, over there in English Edward's camp." The men by the fire growled.

Beaujeu, lounging in his saddle, explained their plan to send a band of men in along the seacoast, while the rest of the army made a foray at the bridge, but Josseran dismounted, and squatting on his hams, eye to eye with these knights, he talked about the king, and Crécy, and the need to strike now.

"The king will not do this willingly," he said. "We must call for a council meeting, with one mind, and there we must force the king to our will."

One of the knights held back. "We just got here. My horses are tired."

Josseran said, "Well and quickly done, this plan can put us on top of things here. If we can force Edward off that land just below the wall of Calais, he will have nowhere to go — we will have him running."

The other knights' eyes were sharp and intent. They nodded at Josseran, and murmured to one another, and getting up they put on their swords and followed Josseran and Beaujeu on to the next camp.

There Beaujeu and Josseran spoke as they had before, Beaujeu from his horse, and Josseran on foot, nose to nose with the listening men, and again most of the knights came along with them. In a growing band they made their way through the camp, going from fire to fire and talking to the others, until everybody there could see that something was going on, and even those men who had not heard them trailed after them, and so they came to the king's tent.

King Philip had brought his eldest son with him, the duke of Normandy, Prince John. When the crowd of knights swarmed up to the King's pavilion, they found this young man sprawled out on a carpet before it in the light of several torches, playing at draughts with another man.

Neither of them stood, although before them now came many of the most noble lords in France; Prince John stared at the checkerboard awhile, frowning, as if his game mattered more than his army, while the other player lifted his head and surveyed the crowd with a lofty look.

"Who is this fellow?" Josseran asked.

Beaujeu murmured, "Charles d'Espagne, he's called — a prince of Cerda, adventuring around France, as so many of them do these days, living on our king's bounty." He raised his voice. "My lord prince, we seek the hearing of your noble father, should the king stir himself to come forth and give us his attention."

Prince John lifted his hand and waved at him. "It's the middle of the night, Beaujeu. The king has gone to sleep."

"Then wake him," Josseran called out, harshly.

The Spanish adventurer leaned forward, his hand shielding his mouth, and whispered to Prince John. The prince laughed, and looked around, lounging on his elbows.

"Tell me what you wish. I shall be king, one day, and I will hear you."

From behind Josseran, a low growl went up, and several of the knights began to shout, "The king! The king!" and stamp their feet.

John lost his smile. Beside him Charles d'Espagne began to finger his long Spanish mustache. The prince got to his feet, raising his hand, and called, "Now, calm yourselves — the king is indisposed. Let me hear what the matter is, and in the morning —"

"We will be heard now," Josseran said, standing forward. "Call forth the king —"

At that moment the door of the tent was swept back, and King Philip himself stepped forward.

The crowd hushed. Josseran shut his lips, his bold edge blunted; this was his king, in spite of everything, God's annointed. Beside him, Beaujeu lowered himself carefully down to one knee, and Josseran did so also, and behind him the whole crowd grunted and clicked and shuffled and sank down in obeisance before Philip of Valois.

"Who comes?" the king said, and trudged out another step into the night. The torchlight spread over him, tall and stooped, a cloak pulled around him. "Who wakes me from my sleep, hah?"

At that from the tower of Calais there went up a sudden boom of noise, and cheers and roars from the people of the city. The king squinted in that direction.

"Your Grace," Josseran cried, seizing this chance. "You hear the people of Calais, calling you to their rescue. For their sake we've come all this way. Now we must strike boldly, to prove to them our will and our power, and get our revenge on King Edward!"

A yell from the others punctuated his speech. The king only blinked at him. His face looked older than Josseran remembered it, gaunt and seamed and sagging, the flesh dry under papery skin. He said, "We have just this day arrived before Calais. Soon I shall send heralds to His Grace the king of England —"

Josseran took a step forward toward him. "Your Grace, Calais is desperate. A day, or another day, may mean nothing to us, but to them it will be days of hunger and death." He gestured toward the English. "The longer we are here the more ready the English will be for us."

The king drew his cloak tighter around him. His shoulders were hunched. His body seemed only a frame for the cloak hanging limp around him. He raised his gaze again toward the tower booming and blaring in the distance, to the fleur-de-lys banner glowing in the bonfire light.

Plaintively, he said, "I cannot see, in the dark — I must see how the land lies — I must make plans —"

"We have a plan, Your Grace," said Josseran.

Prince John had gotten to his feet, Charles d'Espagne with him, whispering again in his ear, and now the prince turned to Philip and tugged on his arm.

"Let me lead these men — I shall lead them —"

The king's face tightened; lifting his arm, he thrust off his son. "You shall, shall you? What a fool is this, here!"

Josseran said, "Your Grace, tonight — this very night — a bold move will wipe out the shame of Crécy —"

"Crécy."

At that word the king's hands on the cloak drew together again, bundling him deeper into the folds of fur and cloth. His head sank down.

"Tonight," Josseran said, "we shall force a way into Calais, and raise the siege, and send King Edward —"

"You fool," the king shouted, and his eyes blazed. "Tonight? You'll do it tonight? Isn't that what went wrong at Crécy — we got there, saw them, and charged, without thinking, without planning —"

"This is different," Josseran said. "Here we must have a bold move, something quick and decisive." From the crowd behind him came calls and whistles, supporting him, but some others began to shout in favor of the king.

"Heed King Philip! He's right —"

"There is no need for hasty decisions. Hear the king out —"

"My lord de Vaumartin," the king said. "You say you want to send men along the coast. Have you found a guide? Do you know the tides here?"

Josseran's jaw muscles worked. A silence fell over the crowd, and he wondered where Beaujeu was — wisely holding his tongue, he realized, letting Josseran take the full blast of the king's foul humor. He said, "No, not yet, but —"

"Then," said the king, "I command you to do so, with such as will follow you, and when you have seen the whole of the problem, come and speak to us about it, and we shall move on from there. Hah? Is that agreeable to you?"

Josseran raised his head, surprised. "Your Grace, I am delighted at this honor! I —"

"My lord!" Prince John sprang on his father from the side. "Send me to command them, my lord."

"Yes," said the king, and his hand fell to the prince's shoulder. "You go with him. You and my lord Charles." He was turning, going back into his tent. Josseran's hands drooped. He saw that the king was only getting rid of him — the king expected this to come to nothing.

Prince John wheeled, his face taut with purpose. "Then I shall do it! Charles, you are my second in command, and who else —"

"The scheme is mine," Josseran said.

"Then you shall come also," said the prince, looking beyond him, for his friends in the crowd, and some few of these began to step forward, calling to him. Josseran stepped back. At least they would be doing something. He started back to his own campfire, to give such orders as were necessary to his men, to collect his weapons, and get a fresh horse.

It was nearly dawn before Prince John had gotten his company together. They set off to the south, to skirt the marshes around Calais, twenty-two knights in no particular order, with the prince in their midst drinking from a flask and talking of his great deeds among women. The Spanish prince, Charles, clung beside him so close their stirrups might have been tied together.

The marsh gave way to scrubland, where pigs rooted, and the serf children who herded them scampered up the trees at the approach of knights. The sun was rising up through heavy mists. Josseran rode along ahead of the king's son, whose tales of lechery grew louder and less convincing as the sun came up.

"My lord de Vaumartin," the prince said, suddenly, "I am told you have a beautiful wife."

Josseran's back stiffened; around him the men who knew him cast sharp glances from him to Prince John. They were riding down a cart trail between a stand of nut trees and a hilly pasture.

Reining his horse back, Josseran said, "My wife would not suit you, my lord, being faithful as well as beautiful."

"But she is beautiful," said John, and leered.

"She is more beautiful than a spring flower," said Josseran. "She is the only star in Heaven, when she shines, but she shines for me alone." They were rounding a curve, and the harsh salty air blew straight into his face; ahead of them lay the sea, grumbling and thrashing.

John still had the leer stuck on his face. Beyond him Charles d'Espagne tugged on his sleeve and whispered to him. Josseran waved on down the road.

"Here is the coast, my lord — we should be seeking out a local man to guide us."

John grunted. His shoulders moved, putting off such dreary occupations. "You," he said, gesturing to one of his friends. "And you. Go fetch us some peasant." His head swung toward Josseran again.

"So far, you mean, she shines for you. But she's never known a prince, I am sure — has she?"

Josseran said, "My lady is beyond your reach, my prince."

"Bah. When I've beaten the English — You ran away, at Crécy, didn't you?"

Behind Josseran, someone gasped a soft oath. Josseran got a grip on his temper; he swung around to face John squarely, his hand on his hip. "I did not run away. I fought through to the end of that Hell into which your father, a man of power, led us."

"But you lost," John said, grinning at him.

Josseran clenched his fists on his reins. He studied the young man a moment, seeing his splendid size and broad shoulders, the might of his arm, and the bland baby-wide innocence of his face.

"No," he said. "I did not lose there. Your royal father lost there, and you might look at him, now, and see what it was he lost. My brother rode into that maw of Hell, and died, and my nephew rode into it, and he did not come back again, but I came back, and I still have my honor. Your father the king lost his, and with his, yours also, my prince. You may gain it back, but not by sniggering words about other men's wives — not by conquests in the sheets." Josseran flung his arm out, pointing toward Calais, behind the hills and trees. "Lead us to a victory, my prince, and you will have your Valois honor."

"Amen," a knight beside him cried, and several others joined him. "Lead us to a victory!"

John was glaring at Josseran. He said, "You have no right to speak so to me. I am your future king!"

"Remember," said Josseran, "that being high you may fall much farther than lesser men." He reined his horse around; up the cart path John's two knights were riding, and before them they herded along a peasant in a brown smock and bare feet.

They rode a few strides more, coming out between two old grassy dunes onto the long flat beach. The sand was pale as the mist, and where the mist still hung low over the rolling waves and the surf, the beach disappeared into a haze that rumbled and shook under the sea's assaults. To the south the broad sweep of sand and dunes ran in a long slow curve that vanished into the misty distance; to the north, toward Calais, the dunes rose in heaps, like frozen waves, capped with short spiny grass.

Now the sea rushed in around the dunes' feet, slopped and sucked and burbled in and out of the low ground between them. The rising sun was fighting through the gray haze; the wind against Josseran's face was damp and salt. He rode off a little way, toward Calais, and picked a way in through the dunes.

Tangles of driftwood like old bones lay in the hollows under the sand hills. Pink and yellow flowers clung to the slopes with runner vines like nets. Something bolted away from his approach, but he never saw it; the dunes rose around him, featureless and confusing, and swiftly he saw that without a knowledgeable guide they would soon be lost here. He rode back the way he had come, to find Prince John arguing, red-faced, with another knight, the peasant standing between them.

"I say we take him back to the king," said the knight, an older man, balding. "That's what the king said we should do — come down here and see what the land's like, he said, or something like it, and then go back and talk things over."

John sneered at him. "That's small glory for a night's riding, isn't it? Here, you." He put out his foot and kicked the peasant in the shoulder. "Can you lead us to Calais?"

"To Calais, master?" The peasant's eyes rolled; he shot a look down the coast. "You mean — by the waves?"

John drew his foot back and kicked him again. "Do you know who I am? Who's your lord?"

"Master —" The peasant bobbed up and down in a bow, smiling, his eyes sleek with fear. "Please, master —"

"Who taxes you? Hah? You pay service, don't you? To whom?"

The peasant's face cleared a little; this he understood, and he straightened. "The Abbot of Vere, master." He turned and lifted his arm to point. "I'll take you —"

John kicked him again. The peasant dodged most of the blow. Josseran, watching from one side, lifted one leg up and crooked it around his saddlebow; he was beginning to see they would be here awhile.

John leaned over the peasant to bellow at him. "Do you know who I am?"

"Master —" The peasant bobbed up and down again; his forehead pleated with bewilderment. "No, master —"

"I am the son of the king of France," John shouted. "I am the prince royal of France!"

The peasant's mouth worked; he looked desperately around him at the knights on their horses, looming around him, and bent down to his knees, mumbling something. John smiled, pleased.

"You will take us to Calais," he shouted down at the peasant. "If you do, there will be gold for you. If you don't, I'll have you beaten to a blood pudding, do you understand me?"

The peasant said, "Master, I cannot —"

John lifted his hand, and the knight to his left stepped down from his saddle. The serf cringed down on all fours. Josseran grunted, contemptuous of this quivering thing that could not even stand up straight. Even before the knight reached him the serf was screaming.

"I'll do it — I'll take you —"

"Good," John said, and raised his face and smiled all around him, triumphant.

"Not now." The serf, panting, raised his head, and seeing that the knight stepped back, he got slowly up onto his knees.

He cast a look around him at the waves, at the men watching. "Later. When the tide ebbs."

"Excellent," said the prince. "We'll wait here, then."

Josseran bit his lips shut against his objections. He watched the serf narrowly, expecting him to try to escape, but the serf only sat down on the sand, his arms around his knees, his hair in his face like a veil.

Prince John bellowed to one of his men to bring the draughts board, and with Charles d'Espagne at his side and his other slick-tongued friends he fell to playing draughts and arguing and talking about women. In this wise they waited all through the day, until in midafternoon the peasant went down to watch the sea, and announced that the tide was ebbing.

Then John ordered his men into their saddles, and they set off along the margin of the sea.

With the tide out the beach was broad and sloping. The peasant led them at a trot along the foot of the dunes, where the high tide had left heaps of driftwood and seaweed like green hair on the sand. The flat beach below it was pocked with the holes of clams and crabs. The barefoot serf ran along at a steady jog, the horses streaming out behind him.

John said, loudly, "This seems not so treacherous a way as many would have me think." He gave a shrewd look at Josseran.

The beach curved on away from them, and the peasant slowed. Pointing, he warned them to follow close to his track, and not to veer off from it. The sun was hot and bright on the dunes, but where the waves lapped a mist was already forming, gathering from the spume of the breakers, lifting up from the wash of the sea, and ahead, the sun gleamed on the top of a ridge of fog lying like a dune of misty air over the beach.

In a file the knights rode after the peasant into the fog, and abruptly the air was cold, the sun was gone, and they could see only a little way ahead. Some of the knights broke out of the file and galloped down toward the sea, flirting with the waves. Josseran kept his gaze on the serf, whom he did not trust.

The peasant's back in its ragged smock bobbed along just ahead of Prince John. There was dried blood on his shoulder. He jogged along at a steady pace, his footprints clear in the wet sand.

The boom and crash of the breakers sounded to Josseran's left, seeming far away, although once or twice, to his surprise, little wavelets crept up almost to his horse's feet. Behind him, a knight shouted, and he turned.

The knights behind him had scattered widely over the beach. Now, abruptly, too late, they were rushing to fall back into line, but one had gone too far, almost to the sea's edge, and there the sand caught him.

Barely visible in the fog, his horse was struggling to drag its feet out of the muck, and as it struggled it sank in up to its knees. It reared and bounded forward and this time went in up to its belly.

"Hold," Josseran roared, and the whole column halted. Out there beyond a blank and treacherous expanse of sand the horse floundered and heaved itself up a little, but its haunches sank deeper, and a wave rushed in and broke around it. Trapped in his saddle, the knight waved his arms and yelled, and the horse gave a neigh of terror.

Josseran looked behind him, at Prince John, who sat in his saddle and stared and did nothing. Josseran sprang down from his saddle.

"Come — we have to save him!"

Under his feet the sand was reassuringly firm. He pulled off his cloak and surcoat, and several of the other men, seeing him do this, did it also. Another wave flooded in around the trapped horse and its rider. The horse flung its head up, its gaping nostrils ringed with red, above the muddy slop of the breaking wave.

Josseran called out, "Here — make a line." He pushed a laggard man into place before him. The others, wiser, were wrapping their cloaks around one another's middles, clutching one another's belts, making a human pier out to their endangered fellow. "Hold one another —" He glanced up, seeing Prince John come back to watch this from the safety and height of his own saddle.

The prince said, loftily, "Proceed, my lord," and waved his hand at him.

Swiftly Josseran made a knot in the end of his cloak.

"Hold my belt — hold on to one another." He went from one to the next up to the head of his line, and with the knotted cloak dangling in his fist, and the man behind him clutching his belt, he led them out toward the surging sea-wave that swirled around the floundering, desperate horse. Under each tentative step the sand was hard, until suddenly he put down his foot and his shoe disappeared into an inch of fine muck.

They were still far from the knight on his trapped horse. Josseran lay down on his belly and squirmed out across the sand; the man behind him seized his ankles. The yielding surface of the beach quaked beneath him, but it held his weight, spread out as it was, and so he drew near to the trapped knight.

"Here!" He tossed the knotted end of his cloak to the knight, who seized it and held tight.

"My horse —"

"We'll get the horse next," Josseran cried. "Come — quick!"

The knight dove toward him. The wave shrank and slipped back away from him, leaving him and the horse above the breakers, but when the knight's feet touched the sand he sank in as if into water. He sprawled across the surface, as Josseran did, and with both hands clutched Josseran's cloak. Josseran braced himself against the weight of man and armor.

"Pull!"

The whole line hauled steadily back, and Josseran skidded backward, dragging the knight after him. Then abruptly the sand beneath Josseran was hard enough to stand on, and he rose, breathing out a sigh.

The horse blasted another desperate neigh. The sea rose again around it, breaking over its empty saddle. The knight was struggling on his knees in the surging foam. Josseran leaned out and gripped him by the front of his surcoat and with main strength and the strength of all the men behind him hauled him onto dry ground.

"My horse —"

One of the other knights said, crisply, "Make a rope of belts and cloaks." Josseran, the man behind him still clutching his belt, crawled forward to the yielding sand again, lay down on it, and inched his way out over the treacherous sucking sea bottom.

The waves rushed in again. He had to hoist himself far up off the ground to breathe. His hands sank down to the elbows into the soft water-laden sand. In a corner of his mind, he realized that the peasant had lied; the tide was coming in again. While the wave retreated he scurried forward, swimming through a stream of water and sand. The sea swept in around him again, and on the foam-dappled surface of the wave, the reins of the thrashing horse floated toward him.

He lunged, sinking to his knees in the sand, and caught one rein. The man behind him had let go of him, but at once reaching hands gripped the seat of his breeches, dragged him back, and got a better hold on his thighs. When he dragged his feet from the clinging muck there was a loud smacking sound, like an obscene kiss.

"Pull!"

Josseran wrapped the rein around his wrist and slowly eased his weight against it. The horse was snorting. Sea foam splattered its face. Straining forward, its head extended in a line with its neck, it struggled up and lunged forward through the clinging sand; its efforts drove it deeper, but it gained a few inches toward the beach.

Now the other knights had made a great long rope of their clothes and belts. As Josseran with the bridle urged the horse on to another lunge toward safety, the other men rushed in and flung the makeshift rope around its rump.

"Heave!" Again, with all their strength combined, they dragged on the horse, and the horse clawed with its forelegs, heaving its hoofs up through the sand and down again, and swimming thus in the loose sand, with the men hauling it, the beast struggled up to the shore.

Josseran's arms hurt. The knight went to his horse, which was covered with sand, and began to feel its legs, murmuring to it. Josseran strode down along the top of the waves to Prince John, perched dry and idle in his saddle, and said, "This serf has lied to us. The tide is coming in."

The serf still stood just behind the prince's horse. Charles d'Espagne, beside him, swung his horsewhip around and struck the man lightly on the shoulder.

"No, no," the peasant cried. "It's only here — I warned you." He looked up at the prince on his great horse above him. "I warned you! Remember?"

John said, "He said the way was treacherous. Come along, it's getting cold here."

Josseran growled at him. Turning to his horse, he stabbed one foot into the stirrup and swung himself up into the saddle, and with the others he followed Prince John away up the beach.

nine

THE FOG THICKENED. They rode along past
clumps of mud like half-buried heads in the sand, past old dunes
that the sea had eaten hollow at their feet, so that the stringy roots of
their coat of grasses hung down beneath in webs and veils. Seabirds
screamed nearby, but in the fog Josseran could not see them.
Sometimes the sea foamed and broke under their horses' hoofs;
sometimes they could hear the waves crashing, off to their left, but saw
nothing but a long flat stretch of damp sand.

They came to a place where the sea splashed and surged along the
foot of a dune, and the guide led them around inland, down a trail
where they went single-file, nose to tail to avoid getting lost in the fog,
up through low wind-curried tangles of seabrush, and down again
twisting and turning, to a beach of cobbles.

Heads down, the horses picked their way slowly through this field of
wet rocks, their hoofs slipping on the smooth stones. The sea
murmured and chuckled in the darkening fog to their left. Josseran was
cold, his hands frozen, his clothes soaked from his submergence in the
waves. He wondered how far they were from Calais.

He thought of Isobel, as he often did, in such instances as this; he
thought of touching her, of listening to her laugh, and his memory
built around him that space that they alone shared, that private world.

"Hold," John called, ahead of him, and put up his hand.

Torn from his comforting thoughts, Josseran reined in. John was
talking to the guide, and the serf was pointing ahead, and saying,
"Wait here, just wait." He scampered away into the dunes.

John eased himself in his saddle. "Does anyone have any more
wine?" His friends hurried to take him a flask.

Josseran dismounted, stretching his legs, and working his arms and
shoulders to get some warmth back into them. The young knight who
had been trapped in the sand came up to him.

"Thank you," he murmured. "I was foolish — stupid — to get myself in such trouble."

"Learn from it," Josseran said, curtly.

"I will," said the young knight. He held out his hand. "Michel de Ravennois, my lord, at your service."

"Josseran de Vaumartin," said Josseran, and did not add the conventional amenity, but they shook hands.

The night was falling around them, as if the fog thickened and grew darker. The young knight, Michel, said, "I brought a loaf — I am glad of that, now — I hope you will share it with me."

Josseran was looking toward Prince John, wondering where the serf had gone. He said, "I have my own dinner." He had known there would be nothing to eat in Calais. He faced the knight again, putting off his growing vague alarm. "How is your horse?"

"He's sound."

"Good. Such a thing as that could bow a horse's tendons. I have seen —"

He stopped. Under the low talk of the other knights, and the grumble of the sea, he could hear something else, a clicking, a low irregular rattle, as if shod horses were walking on rocks.

Michel was saying something; Josseran raised his hand, and stepped back, looking back through the gathering gloom toward the cobble beach. The rattle was too uneven to be hoofbeats. He went several strides away down the beach, toward the field of cobbles, and in the deep twilight watched a wave rush in across the stones, shifting them, rolling them together; when it drew back the ticking and banging of the jostled stones was louder yet.

Josseran wheeled. "Where is that serf?" He strode three long steps toward John and broke into a trot.

The prince still lounged in his saddle drinking and talking. Josseran went up to him and pulled on his leg.

"Where is your peasant now, my lord? Hah? The tide is coming in behind us."

John stuck his cork back into his flask with a thump of his palm. "He went to scout the way ahead."

Josseran wheeled around, seized his horse's reins, and swung into his saddle. "He's abandoned us here." Twisting, he flung his gaze up and down the beach in both directions. The fog and the darkness surrounded them; he could see nothing. "And a good place to do it, too," he said, and faced the prince.

John's face had tightened into a petulant scowl. "Well, that's a dungpit." He looked around him, as Josseran had, and said, in a false voice, "Oh, he'll be back. Let's wait for him."

As he spoke a wave rushed up and curled its foamy edge around his horse's fetlocks. Josseran gritted his teeth.

"I told you he was lying!"

He shouted this at the prince, who glared at him, and turned and bellowed, "Make a light! Let's have a torch, here!" Josseran reined his horse around and rode back a little way.

He could shout at the prince, but it was his fault as much as John's; this had been his idea.

He remembered how they had swung up through the dunes to get here; he wondered if they would be able to find their way back. Now, banging and rattling, the whole cobble beach was under the slop of a great breaking wave, and he wondered if they could even reach the dunes.

Michel had ridden up to him. "What's going on?" Down the beach, around the prince, a light glowed suddenly, filmy in the mist.

Josseran said, "I think the guide's gotten us lost."

Two of the other knights were moving up beside him. One murmured, "I knew that jack had a shifty look about him."

From the pack of men around Prince John, now, came a loud halloo; they were trying to call the serf back. Josseran's horse sidestepped, lifting up its feet. Gurgling and giggling, the sea was grabbing at its hoofs.

Josseran said, "We have to get off this beach. Come on."

All the other men began to talk at once. "There's that trail back there —" "Let the horses take it, they'll guide us back —" "But the tide —" "Let's go, let's get out of here!"

Josseran said, "I'm going that way." He pointed to the north, up the beach.

John gaped at him. Beside him, Charles d'Espagne gave a disbelieving laugh.

"I said I would go to Calais," Josseran said stubbornly. More than anything else, he wanted to be quit of John. "I am going to Calais. Any who will join me, come."

He backed his horse out of the close pack of other knights and started away at a trot down the beach. Behind him someone laughed. He did not look back to see if any followed, but he heard hoofbeats coming after him.

His horse jerked to a stop, its forelegs stiff, its breath blasting in snorts. The beach had ended in another half-gnawed sand dune. The three men who had followed closed around him. One was Michel de Ravennois, the young knight Josseran had saved.

"Oh, God," one of the others breathed.

Behind them, on the beach, the yellow glow of John's torch was bobbing. The prince and his friends were going back the way they had come. The fog was enveloping them, dimming the little light, and abruptly one of the three men with Josseran reined his horse around and galloped away after the torch disappearing into the mist.

Josseran said, "Go, then, quickly — if you choose."

The other two said nothing. They sat there in their damp saddles, the fog thick around them, and watched the torch fade away to nothing. Josseran nudged his horse forward, into the lapping sea along the foot of the sand dune.

The horse strode out freely for a few yards and then slowed, snorting, its head down. The sea sloshed around its fetlocks and slapped up against the soles of Josseran's shoes. The other knights had not followed him, but waited behind him, beyond the foot of the dune that leaned over Josseran, pushing him down over his saddle.

With a snort his horse wheeled around and galloped back to the other horses, and he let it run, the reins flapping, back to the shelving beach above the breakers, where the other knights waited.

Brought so quickly in between them, Josseran said only, "Let's try inland."

They said nothing. He could not make out their faces, for which he was grateful. Dismounting, he led his horse along the landward side of the dune, searching for a trail up to the top.

The trail led through knee-high brambles and sawgrass, the fog swirling thick and cold around him, but as the ground under his feet leveled out and he climbed to the top of the dune, suddenly he rose out of the fog, into the clear blue evening, with the moon shining.

One of the other knights sighed. "Thanks be to God," he said, and they all crossed themselves.

They stood at the top of a cliff. The half moon shone above them, and the stars glittered in the sky, but before them, covering the sea, the beach, all the low ground, lay a thick fog, on which the moon shone blue and silver. A few yards down the cliff was the ruin of an old tower, two or three round courses of stones still standing together, and the rest scattered around.

Josseran rubbed his chin. "We could wait until morning," he said, and glanced at the others.

Neither of them spoke. Michel de Ravennois got his loaf from his wallet and chewed off a piece of it.

Josseran said, "Or we can go on. Calais must not be so far away, now — we have been riding nearly a day, surely."

He turned, scanning the fog to the north, but the night enveloped everything. The ruin of the tower made him think that the city was close by — that this was an outpost of it — and he tried to see if another such tower stood inland of this, but beyond the dunes only the tousled heads of trees showed against the clear dark sky. Neither of the other knights spoke. Josseran girded up his courage. He had brought them here; he was their leader.

"We'll go on until the moon sets." He turned, looking for the trail through the wiry wind-driven brush; his feet found it more readily than his eyes. Leading his horse after him by the reins over his shoulder, he went through the jumbled stones of the tower, along the top of the cliff, and silently the other knights followed.

They slept when the moon went down. Josseran dreamt of Isobel, and with the sunrise woke, shivering, longing for her. A strong breeze was blowing off the shore, sweeping the fog away, and the whole sea glittered, the waves rising from it like snow-capped mountains. A flight of little birds raced by, in perfect formation, inches above the foam-laced green water. Josseran led his knights off down the beach to the north.

As the sun mounted in the sky, it dragged a haze after it, and the breeze slackened. By noon the air was still again, and the fog lay in rumpled layers over the dunes and the sand. Twice they had to leave the beach to climb the dunes and pick a way through the bewildering featureless landscape of hummocky sand and low brush.

They had nothing left to eat, now, and nothing to drink; nobody spoke. At last, in the late afternoon, they rode along a wedge of pebbly shore to the bank of an inlet or stream, and beyond, half a mile away across the beach, the walls of Calais appeared before them in the sunlit mist.

The city was built on rising ground, its towers and houses of gray stone, and the wall around it was of gray stone, ranging down into the sea in successive banks. Between these walls and the riders lay a broad and seemingly empty beach. To the right, on either side of the brackish water of the inlet, were the low trees and spiky grasses of the marsh.

To the left, on the ocean, Josseran saw the wooden towers of English ships, rocking and bowing with the waves. They seemed far off. He wondered if they could sail close to the shore here, and threaten any army that came by this way. The waves were breaking far out from the shore, in line after line of white crests; he doubted if the ships could get very near, but if they had catapults on board, or crews of archers, they could protect this beach.

In any case, they certainly could spy on any movement of knights along it. Even now, he thought he saw a flash of light from a masthead, and wondered if it was a signal to the land.

Michel dismounted and knelt by the stream to cup up a handful of the water and taste it. He spat it out. "Brine."

Josseran grunted a laugh. "What did you expect?" His mouth was gummy with thirst; his horse breathed in regular soft blasts of wind, its ears switching from side to side.

The other knight said, "So — there is Calais. Now, even if we do reach it, there's no food in there for us, and what good will we be to them — three more hungry men?"

Josseran wheeled toward him, unreasonably angry. "Why did you come, then?"

The knight shrugged, his mouth bending into a smile. "I trusted you more than John to get us through. Now, I say — let's go back. Tell the others we've found a way here —"

There was a sudden loud hiss in the air, and a thunk. The knight's voice cut off. His eyes opened wide in surprise, and he pitched forward, an arrow between his shoulder blades. Josseran yelled.

"Go!" He gripped his reins, bending forward, and drove his spurs into his horse's flanks.

The horse bolted forward. Its ears pinned back, its shoulders driving, it thundered into the little inlet and across, sending up curtains of spray. Josseran glanced back once to see Michel de Ravennois charging after him.

His horse stumbled on something in the riverbed, and he almost went off; under him the animal caught its balance and heaved itself up again and he clung to his reins and the horse's mane. There before him lay the walls of Calais. He charged toward the city.

From the shrubs and marsh to his right, a line of horsemen galloped, swinging out to intercept him. Englishmen.

He gathered himself. A wild energy surged through him. After all the frets and doubts of the march along the beach, here at last was that which he understood, that which he lived for. He reached across his body to his sword and drew it free and steadied his horse and charged.

Behind him, Michel de Ravennois was shouting a hoarse war cry. The Englishmen veered around, to come at Josseran from both sides, and Josseran chose the three men on his left and reined his horse toward them.

He went straight at them, cutting down their angle; they clashed together with a wild whine of metal on metal. Josseran swung his sword at waist level, felt the shock of contact, and with knees and heels kept his horse driving hard past the English knights, who had to slow and wheel to follow him. One of them fell. Another sent his battle-axe straight at Josseran's head, and he ducked, and as he ducked stabbed backward with his sword.

His horse staggered. He lost a stirrup. The battle-axe sang by his face again. Its edge glittered. He chopped awkwardly up at the Englishman's arm and his sword bit into armor and his belly clenched and he smelled blood.

"God help me!" That was the English knight. "God save me!"

Josseran's horse was bleeding from a gash down its neck. It galloped on, straight down the beach toward the city. On either side, an English knight ranged up, and Josseran veered the horse over and crashed into the enemy on his left.

The impact jangled him. He could see nothing but a confusion of sky and armor and horses, but he swung his sword, again and again, more to ward off blows than to deal death, and his horse spun around and reared and gave a loud neigh, and coming down to all fours it was running again, its head and neck level, the reins loose. Josseran flung his gaze around him.

Three English knights were galloping after him. Behind them, several more surrounded Michel de Ravennois, unhorsed and fighting on foot in their midst. Josseran heard his wavering voice raise his war cry again. After that he heard no more from Michel de Ravennois.

His horse was limping, tiring. He bent over it, calling to it, steadying it with hands and legs. Ahead the gray wall of Calais ran down into the sea, but there was a little gate in it, and Josseran sent the horse on the last of its strength into this shelter.

He leapt from his saddle, his sword in his hand, and put his back to the wooden gate. The English knights were hurtling down on him. He could see their eyes behind the cheekpieces of their helmets. With his left fist he hammered on the gate.

"Let me in — I am French — I am friendly — let me in!"

From behind the gate someone shouted, "Stay out there, fool — there's nothing in here for you!"

The English were reining their horses in; they had him trapped here now, and he beat on the gate again, desperately, and called, "Let me in, for God's love!"

"Stay out there," the same voice answered him. "You'll do as much good dying out there as starving in here."

Josseran snarled an oath. The sweat was running into his eyes and he scraped his hand across his forehead. He took his sword with both hands and rushed out to attack the nearest of the English, before they could settle on some plan to take him.

The Englishman wheeled away from him. He was smaller than Josseran and his footwork was awkward, and with three blows Josseran had him down on his knees. The other knights lunged at him, but they came both from the same side, and he sprang lightly around to keep the fallen knight between him and them, and with a great two-handed blow he knocked the fallen knight sprawling across the sand.

"Ah! Who's next?" He waggled his sword over his head. "Shall I choose? You!" He charged toward one of the other two, and that man shied off, skipping back out of the way. Josseran would not leave the shelter the gate gave him, and dropped back.

"What — cowards, are you? English cowards? Come to me, and let me prove to you what manhood is —"

The third knight shouted something and rushed at him, his sword too high; Josseran undercut him, got him going one way, and met him with the edge of his sword at waist level. The knight sagged, gasping, and went to hands and knees.

"That's two," Josseran roared. "I'll take on your whole army, English cowards!"

The one remaining hung back, but behind him came several more knights, leisurely approaching, Michel de Ravennois's horse among them, his body thrown over its saddle. These men arranged themselves before Josseran, trapping him against the gate that would not open, and stared at him.

"Who will fight me?" Josseran shouted. "Who is brave enough to match a knight of Brittany, hah? Anybody?" He whirled his sword over his head, afraid that they would send for a bowman.

One of the knights pulled off his helmet. He had an air of confident command, although he was very young. On his upper lip a faint chestnut fuzz of a mustache showed, pearled with sweat.

"Who are you, noble knight? Give us a name to attach to the deeds we'll tell today, in our camp, when we have dispatched you."

"I am Josseran de Vaumartin! And speak it with respect, whether I die here or no!"

"Vaumartin," said one of the other knights, in a voice ringing with recognition.

"Well, Josseran de Vaumartin," said the young Englishman, "I will greet you with respect, as the only man of Philip's whole army to reach Calais. But I see no need for such a noble knight to die. You see that you have no chance here, save by the mercy of God. Yield to me now, and save that mighty arm for another battle."

"Give me your name, then," Josseran said. "I will not yield to a lesser man, not though it means my death."

"Judge for yourself, then," said the Englishman. "I am Edward, duke of Aquitaine, and prince of Wales."

Josseran lowered his sword. Surprise and relief softened his muscles. Across the space between them his gaze met the Black Prince's, and he said, "I yield, then, to another warrior," and held out his sword.

L ten

THEY TOOK HIM straight to King Edward Plantagenet, who also recognized his name.

"Vaumartin." The king was standing at the foot of a towering wooden scaffold built before the Calais wall; his archers were scurrying up and down it like monkeys. Like all this camp, it was well made and well done. Edward had a broad red face, with piercing pale eyes, and the chestnut hair of his kindred. "What is it they say about Vaumartin — who holds it holds the throat of Brittany?"

"I have never heard that," Josseran said. "But it is true enough."

He suspected now that they favored him for his castle's sake; Vaumartin had saved him.

"Well," said the king, "my son tells me you have the mightiest arm he has seen yet among French chivalry, and I love to honor such men as you, even if you fight against me. Give me your word, and you shall be free in my camp."

"You have it, Your Grace," Josseran said.

"And I will ask you to do me the favor of dining with me, later in the day, at my tent."

"Your Grace, I am much honored."

"You honor yourself," said King Edward, and gave a loving look to his son. "He does not praise men often for their valor. Particularly not Frenchmen."

The prince said, "I love a true knight." He smiled at Josseran. "Besides, he is a Breton."

He led Josseran off to the horselines, where Josseran tied his injured war-horse to a rope stretched between two stumps. There the prince left him. He worked around the horse, tending its wound, and soaking its legs in cold water.

Being in this camp made him feel better, even though it was his enemy's camp. The small details and ordinary things of this life had always reassured him, his competence at them, their obvious value; he shook off some of the feeling of failure that still overhung his mood. He told himself he had done well enough, to reach Calais, and certainly had lost no honor.

Yet men had died, because he led them there, to that beach. He had rescued Michel de Ravennois from the sea only to lose him to a sea of Englishmen.

Around him lay the English camp, orderly and clean, all the men in good spirits, although they had lain here at this siege for upwards of a year. This was good soldiering, Josseran thought, looking around him, and compared it with the slipshod lazy ways of the Valois. That made him feel better, somehow, about Michel de Ravennois, who if he had been better led might still be alive.

Later, with Prince Edward, he went to the king's tent, where to Josseran's amazement there were women. King Edward had brought his queen, Philippa of Hainault, who was immensely pregnant, and several of her women, all very pretty.

"My lord the king loves to look on beautiful women," said the Black Prince.

"Beautiful women are one of this world's chiefest ornaments." Josseran was sitting beside him at the table, which was makeshift enough: planks of wood thrown across trestles, and covered with sheets of cloth. Across the tent, vast as a church in the midst of her women, the queen sat placidly as if she were in her garden; her plump motherly face was overcast with the brown mask of pregnancy.

"As for myself," the young man said, "if I had a wife, I would cleave to her."

Josseran said, "I also," and a look passed between them; at once they knew each other better.

The king entered the tent, and all there rose to honor him. There was plenty to eat, meat and fish, and wine in plenty, although the plates were slabs of bread, and the lesser men shared their cups. Here and there, as they ate, men got up and raised a cup and spoke in honor of the king, calling for the fall of Calais, the humiliation of King Philip, the ruin of the Valois, the desolation of France.

"Do not take this ill," the Black Prince said quietly. "It is only our custom here, to make warlike speeches."

"The same custom holds in France," Josseran said. "It is an easy way to gain the king's eye." The prince laughed, reaching for his wine.

He rose in his place, his cup in his hand, and all around the tent a hush fell. The prince raised his drink in a salute.

"Let us remember that a great warrior needs a mighty enemy. As knights we test our mettle against other knights — we keep one another strong, we drive one another to such feats of courage and strength that uplift the world. Therefore, to the chivalry of France!" He raised his cup to Josseran, beside him. "God keep you all, brothers in arms!"

Josseran sat where he was, his face hot with embarrassed pleasure; all around the tent the other Englishmen boomed out their salutes, adding such great names of the French knights as each man knew best. When they were done, and drinking, he rose up himself, in silence, and in silence offered his cup, and drank, one of them, although they fought against one another, one of the greater community of chivalry.

At this moment, while they were all still warmly wrapped in fellow-feeling, a messenger came in.

"Your Grace — my king — there are men here, noble and valiant men, from King Philip of France, requesting a hearing of you."

King Edward drained his cup and held it out to be filled up again. The young page who ran to take it looked much like him: another of his many sons.

"Then send them in. The rest of you, pay heed, and do nothing for which I must reproach you before everybody."

Josseran leaned back, his hand on his belt, looking to the door of the tent; he was eager to see who was here from King Philip. It did not surprise him when the Sire de Beaujeu came in, with a train of lesser men behind him.

Beaujeu advanced through the tent toward King Edward, bowed, and began to speak in a loud voice.

"Your Grace, I am very glad you have consented to hear me. I come from King Philip with his greetings and his hopes that you and your whole family are in good health."

He stopped and bowed with ponderous ceremony toward the queen, in the midst of her ladies. She smiled, her hands in her lap, plain as a cow among the beauties who attended on her.

"Now," said Beaujeu, his voice ringing like a clarion, "I have come to tell you as well that King Philip cannot find a way through the morasses around you, in order to bring you to battle. Therefore he asks you to come forth, to meet on ground of some mutual choosing, where your army and his can engage each other, so that great deeds can be done to glorify our chivalry, and so that God can make known His justice and His purpose here in France."

Josseran wiped his mouth. A swift glance up and down the room showed him the other knights leaning forward, their faces taut with excitement. Now at last all this would come to something.

King Edward's expression was calm as a shopkeeper's. He laid his forearms on the table.

"My purpose in France is already very clear, I think, my lord. It is to take Calais, first, and the whole of his kingdom, later, and toward that end I am progressing."

Josseran straightened, startled. The room was absolutely still. Behind Beaujeu the other French knights stood with chests thrown out, lofty frowns on their faces, and their hands on their sword hilts.

Beaujeu lifted his gray head. "No human purpose comes to anything, save it reflects God's will. A battle between us will reveal God's will in this."

The page had come back with King Edward's cup. The Plantagenet glanced at his son and with a touch on the boy's shoulder sent him on around the table to Beaujeu, to give into the French lord's hands the king's own cup.

Then Edward said, "I have made myself clear. Calais will be mine very soon. I see no reason to divert my power here into a pitched battle. If Philip can raise this siege, let him try it; if he cannot, let him take that for a pronouncement of God's will, and leave off."

Shocked, Josseran reminded himself he was a prisoner here, and held his tongue, and did not move, lest his gesture betray his thoughts. Beside him, the Black Prince shifted in his seat, and the lord of Vaumartin glanced at him; he saw the young man's jaw clench, and lowered his gaze.

"Is that then your word?" Beaujeu said. "You will not come out to do battle with King Philip?"

"It is my word," said Edward calmly.

Beaujeu gave the cup to the page. "Then I shall take my leave of you, Your Grace, my purpose here concluded."

He bowed to the king, turned and bowed again to Queen Philippa, and with no further words he walked out of the tent, and the rest of the French lords followed him. Outside their voices rose in a roar of comments, which the falling flap of the tent quickly shut off.

King Edward swung his level look around the knights sitting all around his tent. He said quietly, "Many of you will argue with me — or would argue, if I gave you the chance — but I will hear nothing of it. I mean to build a kingdom in this place, stone by stone, and I will not waste my strength debating the set of each piece. Go back to your dinner. Let's hear some music, too."

Josseran raised his head, and found the Black Prince watching him. In the prince's face Josseran saw reflected his own tortured thoughts. They were knights; to reject a pitched battle was to deny them something more dear to them than bread and wine.

The prince said, in a harsh, unnatural voice, "Sire — my king — I support your choice." He lifted his cup in a salute and drank deep from it.

Josseran drew a ragged breath. The Prince's speech was honorable, but Josseran did not drink, although all around the tent men hurried to add their voices to the clamor of agreement.

He remembered admiring the order and purpose of King Edward's camp, and now he saw something else in Edward's purpose, some larger frame that made little of knight's deeds.

They said they honored him here for his valor, but King Edward put no worth on valor. It was Vaumartin they had saved him for, his castle, his power; they wanted Vaumartin. He had been a fool to feel one of them, to be proud of their respect for him. He raised his head, alone, surrounded by enemies.

Twice more King Philip sent envoys to King Edward, demanding that the Englishman lead his army out from the sheltering marshes to an open ground and engage there in chivalrous combat, but King Edward each time refused. On the tower of Calais the bonfires had gone out, the trumpets had stilled, the cheering of the townspeople had died away; the fleur-de-lys banner drooped like a rag from its staff.

One morning when Josseran woke he saw that the banner had been cut down entirely, and looking toward the marshes, he saw, beyond, a rising column of black smoke. King Philip was burning his camp; he was marching away.

Later that day Calais surrendered. The Black Prince and Josseran went to witness it. The French commander, his arm bandaged and bound to his chest, walked out of the city with his sword reversed, and after him followed six of the chief men of Calais with ropes around their necks. They all went to their knees before Edward Plantagenet, and delivered themselves and their city into his hands.

King Edward would have hanged these men for holding Calais

against him, but the queen suddenly appeared, escorted by her ladies, and she threw herself at her husband's feet, pleading for an end to bloodshed. Edward's grim face softened. He lifted her up, her little white hands in his, and kissed her, and gazing fondly into her uplifted eyes he told her that for her sake he would spare the burghers and their city from punishment. Then the burghers too joined in his praises, and acclaimed him as their noble and compassionate master.

The Black Prince murmured, "You see the lady behind her, in the rose-colored gown?"

Josseran picked out a fair-haired girl, swan-necked, among the women attending the queen.

"That is his paramour," the prince said. "She is the reason my mother the queen is here at all, so that he can have his leman."

Josseran shut his lips tight together; he stared at King Edward's shrewd, high-colored face. This was a show, then, a little pageant. The Plantagenet played everthing around him as if it were a chess game. Under his graces and elegance Josseran saw the truth in him cold and hard as a heart of stone. He thought, Which is the better king, between him and Philip, then — the one who cannot live what he believes in, or this one, who believes in nothing? There was a foul taste in his mouth. He turned away.

Later, Prince Edward came to him, while he was packing his horse, and made him the gift of a ring.

"You have been most generous, my lord," said Josseran, stiffly. He stood sliding the ring on and off his finger, uncertain how to take the young man's kindnesses, if not as calculated as his father's.

Young Edward put his hand on the war-horse's thick mane. "I hope we meet again, Josseran. You and I have much in common, I think."

Josseran wanted to see him as a friend, and put out his hand. "God keep you, my lord."

"And you." The young prince clasped his hand in a vigorous shake. "I will not offend you — as I think my lord father offended you — by saying I wish you fought with me rather than against me."

Josseran was surprised. "I do not remember he said so."

"Yet he offended you," said the prince. "I saw it." He backed up, going, and waved to him. "Travel well, Josseran." Turning, he walked back through his father's camp. Josseran mounted and rode away.

eleven

LATE IN THE SUMMER King Philip slunk back into Paris, one day after the news arrived of the fall of Calais. Having no work, Everard went up to the north bank of the river, to watch the king ride by.

He never got a clear look at the king; Philip's friends surrounded him, a fence of bodies in blue and green silk. They could not shelter his ears from the boos and hisses and whistles of the crowd. Hoots of laughter and derisive jeers marked the king's passage all the way up the Draperie to the Great Bridge. The tall stone fronts of the buildings resounded with insults. The overcast sky itself seemed to rain down shame on King Philip's head.

The fury and boldness of the people startled Everard. As the king rode by, men bounded out of the packed ranks of the onlookers and ran along beside the horses, screaming insults at the king, asking him, Where was Calais? What had he done with Calais? Everard expected the king's knights to charge into the mob, to scatter them, at least, if not punish their insolence, but the Valois's escort rode along in a tight mass behind him, their lances bolt upright, staring straight ahead as if they noticed nothing. They too, clearly, were ashamed of the king.

Everard walked along behind the thick of the bystanders, his gaze on the cordon of noblemen who surrounded the king: if he could reach the king, somehow, he could lay his case before him, and get Vaumartin back.

There was no way for a ragged nameless streetboy to reach King Philip. On the far side of the Great Bridge, where the king went into his palace, Everard walked on, over the Little Bridge, down into the Studium.

All afternoon he hauled wine tuns for Mother Rose, in return for his supper and a place to sleep. Slowly the great front room filled up with scholars. Everard sat in the corner, by two men playing a game of tables on the bench. One of the serving wenches brought him a cup of beer and stood talking to him, her head to one side, smiling.

"Did you see the king today, Everard?"

"The king," said Everard. "The Flemings have it right, he is a foundling certainly." He drained the tankard and put the cup back on her tray.

She said, with a sideways look and a twist of her hips, "I'll bring you another — just be sure Mother Rose doesn't see us."

"She has already," Everard said. Mother Rose was crossing the room toward them like a great ship breasting the waves.

The girl went swiftly off in another direction. Everard sat back on the bench. He had already had one argument with Mother Rose over the girls.

She reached him circuitously, stopping here and there to talk to one or another of her custom. When she finally came up beside him, she said only, "Did you go up to watch the king?"

"I told you I did."

Solid as a post, she faced him, her arms wide, her hair like sun-burnt wheat. "You couldn't find any work, then, at the Place de Grève?"

"It was a slow day."

"You should be looking for better work, Everard, you know. You can't live all your life like this."

He stiffened. She had been on this subject now for days, every time she talked to him. "I've paid you, one way or another, for every crumb I've gotten here, Mother."

"It's for your sake, not mine," she said, indignant. "I'm only thinking of you." She snapped her fingers under his nose. "And keep your hands out of Annette's bodice."

"Can she still put her hands down my breeches?" he asked, and she slapped him.

"What a dirty tongue!"

He grunted at her. "Why not? You insist on meddling with my life — how is that so different from her grabbing me by the balls?" His voice trailed off, his attention caught on two people coming into the tavern. Mother turned to look where he was looking.

The first was Flippo, whose real name, Everard knew now, was Filippo del Borgo; Everard had not seen him in some while, since

Mother Rose had thrown him out of the White Rose for stealing drinks. Thin and pale, he slithered through the noisy crowd like a night creature, looking all around him. He saw Everard and Mother Rose and stopped.

Behind him came an older man, taller, in a long black cloak, with an air of assurance that seemed to take over the room.

"Italo del Borgo," said Mother Rose, under her breath, and wheeled toward Everard. "Stay away from him."

Flippo was leading his father toward them. Everard drew his feet up, angry with Rose, and watched the big man coming through the room.

There was something arresting about Italo del Borgo; every move was polished, adroit, exact. His face was smooth and round as an egg. His large, dark, expressive eyes bulged. On his lips a constant smile played. He was looking at Everard with an open intense interest, and Flippo came on ahead of him and said, "Here he is, Everard. I thought if you wouldn't come, I'd bring him to you, see? This is Italo del Borgo, the very famous alchemist and magician."

Mother Rose said, "I told you not to come here."

"Yes," said Italo, in a silky voice. "An understandable prohibition, considering, but I exempted him from it so that he could lead me here to meet our young friend." He turned, and blessed Everard with the effulgence of his smile.

"I meant you!" Mother Rose said. She glanced around, to make sure no one was watching, but more and more people were. She faced Italo again. "Get out. There's nothing here for you."

"Isn't there?" said Italo, unruffled. He looked straight into her face, and raising his hand he made a sign with his fingers.

Everard's gaze sharpened. He tried to follow the quick twitchings of Italo's fingertips. Mother Rose, closer, saw better than he. She took a step backward, looking confused.

"Get out," she said, but she was not looking at him any more; her gaze moved fitfully around her, as if she had forgotten what she was doing. "Go on," she said, softly, fretful, but she herself was going, wandering off across the room. Everard sat up straight, impressed, and turned his unblinking attention on Italo del Borgo.

"Well," said the magician. "Now we can talk."

"You are an alchemist?" Everard said. "I don't see what use I would be to someone like you. Why don't you raise a demon?"

The magician's smile broadened. "Now, now, my dear, give me at least a hearing. There is a certain enterprise I am advancing, and I think you are one I might use in it, that's all."

"I will do no devil's work," said Everard, and crossed himself.

"Oh, nothing wicked, nothing of the kind," Italo said. "Just some gold money, which I am sure you could put to use, couldn't you?"

Everard looked him over again. The magician's clothes were ordinary enough, except for the great black cloak that he flared and swung around him like wings. He had a sleek air of secret amusement, as if he knew more than other people. Everard glanced away, across the room, toward the wine tuns.

Mother Rose stood there. She had recovered her forceful frown and was staring straight at Everard, her arms folded over her chest. He smiled at her, who let this wizard frighten her in her own tavern.

"Why don't we go back to my house?" said Italo. "It's not far, and more comfortable — we can have a cup of decent wine there, and talk at length." He cast a disdainful look around him at the tavern. "Leave these fools to their Sic et Non."

"While we cleave to our hocus-pocus?" Everard said. He glanced at Mother Rose again, wanting to be sure she saw him leaving with Italo. "Very well, I'll come." She glared at him; he smiled at her again and followed Flippo and the magician out of the tavern.

Italo's house was in the countryside across the Great Street from the universitas, near the church of Saint-Andri, where there was a little well called Saint-Andri's Water. The alchemist's house had gardens around and behind it, although the front of it was square up to the street, and it stood two stories high under its pitched roof. Besides its main hall, it had a separate kitchen and a pantry, and when Everard first went into it, he thought it was enormous.

Within a day it had shrunk down around him like a trap. Flippo and Italo were pleasant enough, even fawning over him, but the house also contained Elisabetta, Flippo's mother, who spoke no French, and who hated Everard at once. Every time she saw him she gave him such a black look that he went cold. Once he heard her arguing savagely in a corner with Italo, and by her gestures he knew she was savage about him.

When he asked Flippo why she did not like him, the boy shrugged.

"Papa's always bringing someone else into the house — she's just tired of having to feed strangers."

"I did not ask to come here."

Flippo shrugged. "Never mind. It won't last long." Everard did not ask him whether it was Elisabetta's fury or Everard's presence here that would not last.

They were in the room they shared, in behind the pantry, at the back end of the hall. Besides the bed, the room was full of lumber, boards, and wooden crates, piled up across the wall at the foot of the bed, which left barely enough space in the room to get in and out the door. In this narrow area Flippo was pretending to be tired, making a great business of stretching and yawning and climbing into bed. Everard, who lay next to the wall, had seen him do this the night before also.

He said, "How long must I stay here?"

"Oh, not long — you did very well today, I was amazed, you learned it all so fast. You have a good voice for it, too, although your accent's really . . . Now we must only wait for the clothes."

Everard said nothing. All day Italo had taught him speeches and phrases in Italian, made him walk around and stand in poses, and bow and gesture and even take off a hat he did not have. The masques he had seen once at the court of Brittany had consisted of such things as these; and soon he was to have special clothes, too. He wondered what masque Italo was putting on, and why.

Now he feigned sleep. Flippo was snoring like a dog before the fire. For a long while the two boys lay side by side on the bed, both utterly awake, until at last Flippo eased himself quietly off the edge and crept away across the room.

Everard opened his eyes slightly, enough to see the other boy move a crate at the end of the wall, step in behind it, flat to the wall, and quietly disappear downward into the floor. A moment later the crate rasped back against the wall again.

Everard got out of the bed. When he leaned over the crate to see what lay behind it, he found only the wall. He shifted the crate a little and waited. When nothing happened he moved it a little more, away from the wall, and uncovered the edge of a hole in the floor.

A breath of cold dank air reached him. He pushed the crate aside and bent over the pit, wondering where Flippo was. It was black down there, lightless as the womb itself, and he went back for the candle.

That light showed him a short drop down through the floor into a room or cave below, with walls of gritty white stone. Flippo was nowhere. Everard dropped feet first down into the cave, the candle shielded in his hand.

All around this room were more crates, strings of onion, sausage, garlic, a heap of turnips, a row of cabbages on a shelf. At the far end five wooden steps led up to a door at the top of the wall, and Everard climbed them on his toes, two steps at a time, and put his ear to the door panel.

He could hear nothing. Cautiously he reached for the latchstring, expecting to find Flippo in the pantry, munching on his mother's tarts.

The door opened into the pantry, but the room was dark. Flippo could of course have already left by the door into the hall, except that it was strange he would go down into a cave in the ground to get to a room he could reach so easily from his own bedroom.

Everard went back down the steps into the cave. There seemed no way out but to go up again, and yet Flippo was not here. He turned, raising the candle over his head, looking at all the walls and the floor too.

All the walls seemed solid, square, their edges meeting, but at one corner the shadow was strange, and when he went there, he saw that the two walls here did not quite meet, but left enough of a space between them for a man to slide through sideways.

This little opening led to another room, bigger than the other, with two or three more openings leading away from that. Still there was no sign of Flippo. Everard chose one exit at random and went into a narrow, twisting tunnel.

The walls dripped; under his feet sometimes the floor streamed with water. Once the tunnel closed down so tight that he had to crouch and go along crabwise. Then it came to an end.

He straightened, slowly, one hand over his head. The candle was guttering. He was wondering why this tunnel went nowhere when he thought to look straight up.

There over his head was a shaft cut through the stone. He put the candle down, and pressing his hands and feet against the sides of the shaft he climbed up into it. Almost at once he could taste fresh air and hear the wind blowing. He climbed up through a fringe of grass into the night darkness and looked around him.

He was in a graveyard somewhere. Around him stood old stone crosses and the overgrown mounds of graves. His hackles stood up on end. Quickly he looked around to see if anyone witnessed this. Pulling himself free of the tunnel, he went through the graveyard to the high bank of earth that surrounded it.

On the far side was a meadow, and beyond that, to his surprise, he saw the squat undecorated spire of Saint-Andri's church. He was across the rue Saint-Germain, a good quarter of a mile from Italo's house.

The candle in its holder was still in the tunnel below. Thoughtfully he went back down the shaft, picked up the candle just as the flame flickered out, and in the darkness felt his way back to the room where he and Flippo supposedly were now sleeping.

Some while later he woke to hear something move in the corner. He lay still, his eyes closed, as Flippo crept back up through the room; for a while Flippo haunted the corner there, bending and stooping in the dark, until at last Everard's curiosity overcame him and he sat up in the bed.

"What are you doing?"

Flippo wheeled, his jaw falling open, and hid something away in his shirt. "Nothing — nothing — I was using the chamber pot."

Everard laughed at him. "That's the chamber pot, under your shirt?" He reached for the candle.

"Don't strike a light!"

The single high window of the room let in enough of the moonlight to show Everard the shape of the jug Flippo was hiding, and he laughed again.

"That's what you do at night, is it? Go out and steal things, Flippo? Like a rat, running around the city at night?"

Flippo's face hardened. He turned, stuffed the silver jug into the crate beside him, and lunged toward Everard.

"You're no better than me. You and your high-flown ways — you're no better than me!"

"I don't rob," Everard said. He lay down in the bed again, rolled the blanket around him, and turned his back to the room.

"You're no better than me," Flippo said again, stubbornly.

Everard said nothing. In a moment Flippo crawled into the bed beside him, put his back to Everard's, and went to sleep.

In the morning, to Everard's disgust, Italo took him out in the garden and washed him. The alchemist was in a bubbling good humor. Bits of knowledge spilled from him like water boiling over the edge of a kettle. "I've heard it said the Cathayan people wash themselves every day with water, and that has yellowed their skins like a tanned parchment. Hold still, you are too filthy even for a page of the duke of Naples. That's why the Cathayan people all have the plague, because they submerge themselves in water, which is why I am throwing the water over you rather than you into the water. Hold still, damn you."

Naked and shivering, Everard turned around and around, as Italo poured bucket after bucket of water over him; afterward they scrubbed at the stubborn places. Now and then Italo would suddenly speak one of the Italian speeches Everard had learned, and Everard had to reply properly. Italo took a pair of shears and trimmed his hair, and they oiled it and combed it.

Clean and dry, Everard went into the hall again and stood before the fire. Italo brought out a suit of clothes, complete from smallclothes to shoes. Everard was disappointed. He had hoped to become something exotic and exciting, but he had caught enough hints already not to be surprised: they were getting him up as a page.

The clothes were very fine. It felt good to put on fresh silk smallclothes and new stockings. There was also a pair of red velvet breeches and a short coat, with undersleeves of gold satin, and a big flat soft hat of red and gold. He thought the clothes were gaudy, and said so.

"Well," said Flippo, "what's to say to that? I wish I had some clothes like those, I'd give anything to do this, and there you are, saying they're *gaudy*."

Italo said, "Leave him alone. He's a little prince, for now. You may think it's gaudy, but it looks proper. Here, put the shoes on. This is the way the best folk dress, you know, there's a rule of sumptuary, put dark people in bright colors."

Everard sat down to pull the shoes on. Italo went to the stairs and shouted for his wife.

"They'll need a little fitting here and there," he said, coming with a smile up the hall. "But in truth you look very well in them."

Everard plucked at the long toes of the shoes. "How am I to walk in these?" He had gone barefoot for so long that even this soft leather chafed his toes.

Elisabetta came down to the hall, grumbling, a basket over her arm. Her daughter came with her, Flippo's little sister, whom they worked like a slave; there was another baby someplace, and Elisabetta herself was enormously pregnant again. Kneeling down before him, she gripped the jacket and jerked it, moving him around like a piece of wood.

"When are you going to tell me what's going on here?" Everard asked Italo, over Elisabetta's graying head.

Italo was chattering at his wife in Italian, his hand waving, as she plucked and prodded at Everard's coat. Everard ignored the handling.

"You have to tell me sometime, don't you? Why not tell me now?"

Italo said, "You'll learn what you need to know."

Elisabetta was pinning up the hem of the coat. Italo stood back, watching with a smile of broad satisfaction. "This will be magnificent," he said. "This is going to work out very well — very well indeed, I say." He smirked at Everard. He had a large head, with big, expressive dark eyes, and his skin was pale and soft. There was something soft and sinuous about his whole manner, like a cat; it was easy to imagine him performing magic tricks.

"I want to know what's going on," Everard said, "or I'm leaving, now." The jacket pinched a little, and with a shrug of his shoulders, he eased the tight undersleeves.

Italo at once was nodding, pleased, pointing to Flippo.

"There, see? That you could never learn, that comfort in the clothes, that convinces me more than anything he could say. Now, listen, Everard, what I tell you you must reveal to no one else — no one, you understand? Because I will know that you have betrayed me." The magician's eyes opened wide, gleaming. "And I have — you know — such knowledge of you now, and scraps of your hair now, hidden away, your nails, such things as I would need to lay a spell on you that would rot your insides out."

"I won't tell anybody," Everard said swiftly. "But I want to know what's going on."

"Elisabetta —" Italo spoke a long rattle of his own speech, and his wife, on her knees, lifted her head, surveyed Everard, and began to put her pins and scissors away in her basket. She nodded at Everard and tugged at the jacket, and carefully he eased it off.

Italo sat down on the bench before the fire. He said, "Now, listen, Everard. You know that every feast day Prince John and his friends hold court at his house of Saint-Ouen, south of the city."

"No," said Everard, "I didn't know that."

"Well, he does. Now, soon, it will be Martinmas, and on that day the prince and his friends are having a tournament at Saint-Ouen, and the king himself will be there."

"A tournament," Everard said, with a little start of excitement. He thought at once of Josseran, who often went to tournaments.

"Yes," Italo said, his wide soft face brimming with smiles, "you'd like that, wouldn't you — to go to see the tournament — to see all the noble lords and ladies — maybe even rub shoulders with the king?"

Everard's mind was leaping on, inventing a meeting between him and Josseran, in front of a great gathering, in front of the whole world, in front of the king himself, Josseran withering before Everard's accusation, Josseran yielding, Everard at last restored in glory to Vaumartin.

"And if they ask you who you are," Italo said, "you must tell them that you are the page of the duke of Naples."

He was leaning his arm on the table, watching Everard closely. Everard, in his smallclothes, went a little nearer the fire.

"The Lord of Naples is the king of Sicily," he said. "No one will believe me."

"Oh, they will, who understand," Italo said calmly. "In the great world — that is, among alchemists and magicians and such — we all have our titles. Not like ordinary titles. When they ask about your master, you must tell them he is a very great magician. But no more." He lifted his hand, palm toward Everard. "Let them get curious."

"They'll throw me out," Everard said.

"You must conduct yourself confidently, and choose whom you speak to well — no poor men, no monks — the younger men, the flash dressers with bells on their shoes, the ones playing dice, not the ones on the jousting field. Women of all kinds, all sorts." Italo lifted his forefinger toward his nose. "But you must say nothing, if they press you. The first time, we want only that they come to know you. The less they actually know, the better."

Everard grunted, distrustful; he glanced at Flippo, leaning his chin on his hands on the far side of the table.

"So," said Italo. "Will you do it? Steal into the king's tournament, and go about, and sow my seeds for me? If you do it, I promise you, you will be well rewarded."

Flippo said, "I'll do it — I told you —"

"Shut up," Italo said, without even glancing at him. His gaze was fixed on Everard. "Well?"

"I'll do it," Everard said.

"Excellent," said Italo. "Filippo, fetch a jug. We'll drink on this — on our enterprise together." His face widened with a buoyant smile. Everard slid down onto the bench, his hand on the table, hoping Italo could not read his thoughts.

PRINCE JOHN'S GREAT MANSION of Saint-Ouen lay on the road south of Paris, in a forest of oak trees and meadows. Everard went in sitting on the back of a wagonload of wine tuns, which carried him through the back gate and around behind the sprawling house. In a copse of shrubbery he put on his new coat and his hat, and thus easily he walked off into the crowd that swarmed over the grounds.

No one challenged him. Hundreds of people strolled through the gardens behind the house, or sat on the greensward drinking wine and talking. There were servants everywhere carrying trays and baskets of food, bearing cups and messages, some in the livery of Prince John, some few in the livery of the king himself; he saw others in colors he recognized, with a little shock of surprise, from festivals and tournaments he had gone to in Brittany — the Sire d'Albret, the prince of Foix, Beaujeu, de Nesle.

It seemed like years since he had fled. Actually he had been nameless only some fourteen or sixteen months. He felt very comfortable moving around in the gardens of the prince. He smiled at people, nodded and bowed, murmuring greetings, and no one questioned him at all. He belonged there.

He ambled down past a pond at the foot of the garden, where a flock of ducks was fighting over bits of bread some little noble children threw them, and stopped to watch two men playing tables on a stone bench; in the pruned and trellised rose garden beyond, three musicians were fumbling through an Italian song, and Everard agreed with the old man standing next to him that the lutenist was fair, but the voices terrible.

"They should not undertake that which they cannot perform," the old man said. "And you, my young lord, you are —"

"Everard de Vaumartin." He saw no reason to carry through Italo's program in this; he intended never to see Italo again. He bowed to his companion. "One with no gift, and very little undertaking at all."

The old man found that amusing, and they laughed together, talked about the first melee of the tournament, which had taken place that morning, before Everard's arrival. A page came and murmured to the old man, who with a few words of excuse went hastily off.

Everard sauntered away toward the tournament ground. On a stretch of flat low ground a furlong from the house a fence had been thrown up, all fluttering with the pennants and scarves of the knights. Now the oval space was an empty stretch of pounded grass and gouged earth; it was nearly noon and no one was fighting, because of the heat and the audience's preoccupation with their dinner. He hung over the fence a moment, as he had done as a little boy, his arms hooked over the top, his nose full of the smell of dust and horse sweat and man sweat and blood.

His spirits soared. He felt home again. He belonged here, with these elegant people, in this life of ease and honor and grace. They recognized him as one of them; here at last, the truth in him would come to light.

The king's pavilion stood just opposite him, draped with black. Everard strained his eyes, reading the pennants flying from every peak and staff.

The green and gold of Vaumartin was not among them. He made his way in through the little village of tents, looking for Josseran.

On every tent pole a banner fluttered. He walked the whole length of the campground, reading the banners, but he did not see the green-and-gold cross among them. Disappointed, he told himself that even if he could not confront Josseran here, he could still find the king — lay his wrongs before the king — and get justice.

As he rounded the end of the tournament field, a loose horse came galloping toward him.

He dodged to one side, toward the rickety fence. At the sight of him, the horse shied violently back. It was a tall slab-sided chestnut, with a white streak down its face, and the reins of its bridle flying over its wither and between its legs. With a snort it bolted forward again, swerving to get past him.

"Stop him!" a groom screamed. "Stop that horse!"

Everard leapt into the horse's path, and the brute veered, its head flung up, and tried to dash through between him and the fence. He ran yelling at it, waving his arms, and the horse lunged back on its haunches. Dust sprayed up from its sliding hoofs. At once the grooms chasing it leapt on it and seized the reins, and one bounded onto its back.

"Thank you," said the man gripping the runaway's reins. His accent was Breton. "If he'd gotten past you, we'd never have caught him."

Everard was dusting the grit and sand off the front of his coat. He said, "It was nothing. I'm glad you've got him now."

"He's messed up your clothes."

"It's nothing," Everard said again.

The man staring at him was clearly not a mere groom, although he wore plain hose and a jerkin. Suddenly he thrust his hand out. "I am Jean de Quercque-au-Lesaine. By your voice you're another son of Brittany. Come with me, have a cup, and I'll get my boy to brush your coat."

"I am Everard de Vaumartin."

They shook hands. "I understand you were the champion this morning," Everard said, having heard this from the old man in the garden.

The knight laughed. Leading the horse by the bridle, he started back around the fence toward the scattered tents. "I did fair enough, as they say. Today you win, tomorrow you lose."

He was above middle height, his brown hair a little shorter than the current fashion; his eyes were deep-set, hollow, the skin sunken and dark around them, giving him a dissipated look, and his front teeth crossed. They went around the tournament ground to his tent, where a little crowd of knights was sitting around drinking from a breached wine tun.

"Got him, ah, Quercque?"

"Shouldn't you manage your horse a little better?"

"Maybe you should take out whatever it is you poke up under its tail there, Quercque."

The Breton knight handed his horse to the groom and led Everard into the middle of the company, said his name around, and nodded to a squire to bring him a cup of wine. Everard sat down on a camp stool. This tent, like most, was not of silk but of common canvas, pegged up with sticks and rope, and decorated only with a ragged pennant. Pieces of armor, saddlecloths, clothes, and boots littered the ground around it.

The five or six knights lolling around the wine tun were all of the same cut as their host. They wore plain shirts and hose, one his linen gambeson, stained dark with sweat, his big feet bare as a baby's. Chunks and crumbs of bread lay on the ground all around them, and bits of cheese, the remnants of their dinner. A mastiff slept at the door of the tent.

"Did you see that two-handed backhand swing of Normandy's? What a champion he is."

"Would he be such a champion were he not the king's son?" said another, a brown-haired man with a lean face like a hatchet and a quick, snag-toothed smile. He had a heavy, mealy accent Everard did not know. "That's what I say. I'll call him a champion who begins with nothing and makes his way to glory by God's grace and his own strength of arm."

"Wagner," said a short, sleepy-eyed knight, "you speak so because he is not your king."

"Nor yours, yet, Saint-Born," said Wagner.

"We'll see how good his two-handed backhand is," said Jean de Quercque, filling his cup at the broken wine tun. He raised it up in a salute. "To my sweet lady, loveliest and most virtuous of all women!"

They all drank deep to that. Everard, looking from one to the other, saw their easy comradeship, their pleasure in one another's company, and remembering his cold and lonely life in Paris consoled himself that soon he would have back the life where he belonged.

"Can you beat him?" the short man asked Jean de Quercque.

"Who — Prince John?" Quercque laughed. "I can beat any man alive, when my arm's right and my horse is willing."

"Are you to meet him in single combat, then?" Everard asked.

"In the challenge round," said the hollow-eyed knight.

"If you can take Prince John down to a mercy," said Wagner, "you'll win the whole tournament, Quercque, and remember that you swore you'd stand us all a banquet if you did."

"When did I say that? You'll beggar me, holding me to promises I made in my cups!"

"Ease off, Quercque, ease off," cried another. "If you win you'll think no price too high."

The knight stretched a little, lounging on his stool. "I don't enjoy the winning any more. It's the service of honor I do it for, and there's times —" He wagged a finger, giving them all a lesson, the prerogative of the victor. "There's times when honor is served in other ways than winning. When some poor bumpkin's up against you with his balls in one hand and his sword in the other, sometimes it's best to let him think he has a chance." He reached for his cup. "That way, you know, there's honor even in losing."

Quercque, so saying, his head to one side, assumed a noble loftiness of looks that set him over all their envious jeers. Someone else said, "Well, Jean, we'll see — when you fight Normandy."

"Normandy's no problem," said Quercque.

"He cheats," said the German knight, Wagner.

"You would not be bold enough to say that to his face," said the short knight, Saint-Born.

"He'll be king someday," one of the Frenchman said. "Some things are more important than chivalry."

At that Jean de Quercque stiffened, his face cold. "Without chivalry the world would be a den of brigands and harlots."

"Amen," said Wagner, and several of the other growled in agreement, bad-tempered suddenly, glaring at the Frenchman who had spoken against their honor.

Wagner turned to Everard. "Your name is Vaumartin, you said. You must be a kinsman then of the Sire de Vaumartin."

Everard almost said, "I am the Sire de Vaumartin." Instead, he said, "Josseran is my uncle." His belly tightened. "Is he here?"

The other knights laughed. "Josseran de Vaumartin is not fast friends with Prince John," Quercque said.

"Nor would the king like to be reminded that Josseran de Vaumartin was the only knight of France to reach the walls of Calais." Saint-Born took Everard's cup and dipped it into the tun.

"He is a mighty knight," said Quercque. "I would give much to test my arm against his." He turned toward Everard, sharp-eyed. "You are his nephew? I thought his brothers were dead. Yvain, I know, died at Crécy."

"Yes," Everard said, and crossed himself. "God have mercy on him."

Yvain's name had drawn the tears up into his eyes, like salt drawing blood from an open wound. The knights were staring at him, their looks intent; suddenly he did not want their probing, their prying. To them, clearly, Josseran was a great champion. Without him here to defend himself, anything Everard said against him would seem underhanded backbiting. He thought again of the king, who, they said, hated Josseran; he would take his grievances to the king. He stood up.

"I must go, I —"

"I'll walk with you," said the knight, and got up. The squire gave a few swipes at Everard's coat with his brush. Everard sought some excuse to avoid Quercque's company, but the knight insisted on going with him.

When they were a few steps from the tent, the knight said quietly, "That is a great name — Vaumartin, you know."

"I know," Everard said.

"In that case," said the knight, "perhaps you ought to think twice about appropriating it." He gave Everard a pat on the shoulder, turned, and went back to his tent.

Everard stood frozen in his place, his face blazing with embarrassment. It had never occurred to him that anyone would think he was lying. He had thought they would accept it utterly.

Slowly he grew aware again of the hurry and noise around him. He trudged away down the length of the fence.

The king's pavilion rose up before him, a great deck of striped silk, rising and falling with the wind as if it breathed. Everard gathered himself. His heart was racing. Around him, the crowd was thickening; soon the afternoon's single combats would begin. He had to reach the king soon, before other matters distracted him.

In the back of the pavilion was a little wooden stair, where the servants were going in and out, with trays and cushions and cups, pieces of paper, flowers, and ornaments. Everard went to it and looked up into the pavilion, where a woman laughed and a lute was playing, and quietly he climbed up the stair.

No one stopped him. He edged in beside a page in a blue coat and turned his gaze around him.

Diffused through the silken curtains, the sunlight swept out bands of color, green and purple and dark green and violet. The discreet music of the lutes blotted out the sounds of the crowd outside. The woman on the far side laughed again, her silver lace headdress bobbing. She was not pretty enough to wear the paint she did. On a cushion beside her, a small boy dozed, and on her other side, padded and supported by cushions, an old man snored away inside a great fur-lined robe.

Everard looked around him for the king; he remembered Philip from the march to Crécy, a big man, in the prime of life, but no such knight lounged here, in this hot, crowded place.

"My lord Charles," called the woman in the silver cap, "my little prince, now come away from the wind, you'll fall ill again."

At the front of the pavilion, three boys were fighting for space; the tallest and thinnest of them twisted toward her. He had a homely, pale, old man's face, with the long Valois nose. "It's about to start again, madame — there, I see the gatemen coming!"

Startled, Everard realized that this boy was Prince Charles, the king's eldest grandson — that this overpainted woman was his mother, the duchess of Normandy. She leaned forward, her voice sharp. "Your Grace! Your Grace!" She seized the old man beside her by the arm and shook him. "God's bones, he sleeps like a corpse. You! Musicians — shut up!"

The lutenist stopped abruptly. Everard gaped at the old man stirring now in the fur robe.

This was the king, then. Everard's jaw fell open. He stared rudely at this husk, this relic of a knight. Roughly the duchess of Normandy gripped the old man's arm and shook him. "Wake up, Your Grace!"

With a snort and a snuffle, King Philip lifted his head. "Eh! What? What?"

"The joust's beginning again, Your Grace," said the duchess. "You told me to wake you. You —" Her gaze came straight to Everard, still staring amazed at the old man. "A cup of the red wine for his Grace the king."

The king's jeweled cup lay in the fur beside him. Everard picked it up, his throat tight, his knees loose, and as he had done before, at Vaumartin, serving his elders, he took the cup across the pavilion to the table where the ewers of wine were waiting. No one looked at him or questioned him; they took him for granted. He carried the cup back and held it out to the king.

The old hands came out toward it, veined and knobbed, trembling, and Everard had to put the cup into the king's grip. Then behind him the crowd around the jousting field let out a clamorous roar.

He backed away quickly to his place among the pages. After the jousting he would ask for audience with King Philip. Now, out there, on the jousting ground, the dust rose in a cloud, and the hoofs of the horses pounded.

"Who fights? Who's on?" the king shouted, in a breathy voice.

"It's Father!" one of the boys cried. "Father — Father!"

The king drank half his wine and flung the cup down, drenching his own clothes and part of the duchess's skirt. "I want to see. Help me there."

Everard hesitated only a moment. With two others of the servants he went up and helped the king out of his throne and toward the front of the pavilion. The king leaned heavily on him, one arm sprawled across his shoulders.

"Let me see my son fight!"

Other servants flung back the front curtains of the pavilion. The king lurched forward toward the very edge. Everard braced himself against the sagging unbalanced weight.

The jousting field spread out before them. Two knights were riding up toward the pavilion, one from either end, their lances at salute.

One was splendidly equipped in black armor, with red and blue plumes in his helmet, and riding a magnificent bay horse. The other knight rode the slab-sided chestnut with the white streak down its face that had led Everard to Jean de Quercque.

The king raised his hand, and the two knights bent their lances down to him.

"Fight on," the king shouted. "Fight your best, for Jesus Christ, for France, for your sacred honor!"

At that the crowd beat their hands together and shouted and cheered. The knights bowed again to their king and rode away, the duke of Normandy to the left, Jean de Quercque to the right.

At opposite ends of the field, they turned and faced each other. The crowd hushed, waiting, so quiet now that for a moment Everard could hear the banners and pennants on top of the pavilion snapping in the wind.

With a shrill brass blare the horns blew. The two knights galloped together down the center of the field; as their horses hit their stride, they swung their lances down and crouched behind their shields.

They came together with a crash, and both lances shivered cleanly. The voice of the crowd rose in a whoop, and the two horses galloped apart again, down to the far end of the field, where their squires ran out with fresh lances.

The king said, "A fair run. He sits so well on a horse, my Johnny."

Beside him, on the far side from Everard, one of the boys gave a muffled cough. The king struck hard at him.

The horns shouted again. Again the knights rushed together, their horses hurtling down the center of the field, and this time Jean de Quercque's lance splintered, but the duke of Normandy's struck the Breton's shield square and held.

A yell went up from the crowd. Jean de Quercque swayed, half out of his saddle, his horse scrambling to keep its feet under its toppling rider. Normandy wheeled his bay horse. Swinging his lance around, he made straight for the struggling man.

"Give him a chance," said the duchess, under her breath. "That's not fair."

"Winning is what matters," the king shouted. "Get him, Johnny!"

The crowd had stopped cheering. Clearly most of them agreed with the duchess. Normandy set his lance at Jean de Quercque's body and put spurs to his horse. The Breton hauled himself back into his saddle, but he had lost one stirrup; as the duke hurtled down on him he pulled his horse around into a rear and the lance slipped by through the empty air, inches from his elbow.

The crowd yelled, appreciating the desperate horsemanship; they all favored Jean de Quercque now. Everard, still tense under the king's weight, watched the Breton knight wheel and collect his horse in the middle of the field and draw his sword.

Normandy still had his unbroken lance. He let his horse carry him away down the field, to get a good running start, and swung around again, couched the lance, and drove straight at the Breton and his sword.

Everard gritted his teeth. This then was their honor, their chivalry. He watched Jean de Quercque dodge and duck, fending off the lance with his sword, while his horse worked him back and forth across the field. The crowd began to yell, derisive, calling for a fair fight.

"They're fools," the king said harshly. "He'll win, that's what matters."

Abruptly Normandy raised his lance, as if he meant to throw it down. The duchess murmured. Jean de Quercque lowered his shield arm, relaxing, and before he could move, Normandy swung the lance around hard and knocked him from his saddle.

The king shouted and beat his fists on the shoulders of the servants holding him up. Everard turned his face away from the field. He did not want to see the Breton knight harried up and down on foot, and now his ears told him that Jean de Quercque saw the uselessness in that — he was giving up.

Cheated. Everard turned his head, looking behind him into the pavilion. His belly hurt, his shoulder hurt where the king had pummeled him. He met the eye of one of the other pages, and the boy came forward and slid between him and the king, taking over his place. Everard went back toward the stair.

He would get no justice here. He had been a fool to think the king would have any ear for him. He had thought that Italo was preparing him for a masque, and so he had: this whole court was a masque, a falsehood, a hoax. He went down the stairs at the back of the pavilion, longing for open air.

As he went down the little flight of steps, his gaze fell on the king's cup, lying at the back of the pavilion. If he left now Italo would think he had failed — would never believe that he had been here. He could not endure that Italo, even Italo, should think him a liar. He reached out his hand for the cup, put under his coat, and went out of the pavilion.

The whole great crowd now was massed around the fence, cheering and singing; the next combat was on, and the sound of hoofbeats rose like drums into the dusty air. Everard went away across the lovely grounds of the house, through the garden, where now at the side of the pond a cook's boy was luring in the ducks with bread, to catch one for someone's supper. Before Everard reached the gate, he took off his fancy coat and rolled it up with the king's cup in the middle, and in his shirt he went out onto the road to Paris.

There, on the sides of the road, just beyond the gate, were crowds of beggars, old women in rags, naked children, cripples and dodderers, so thick along both sides of the road that no grass showed between them. As he came out they raised their voices in a chorus, their hands out, palms cupped. "Alms, alms . . ." He walked through their midst with a stony heart, his eyes straight ahead.

In the deep of the night, he reached Paris again, coming in through the fields below Saint-Andri, and made his way into the graveyard there. In the overgrown corner he found the hole down into the tunnel, and through the subterranean way he crept along to the rooms under Italo's house, and went up through the pantry into the hall.

There on the table he left the fancy coat and the hat, folded neatly, with the cup on top. In only enough clothing to be decent he went down again through the tunnels and out across the graveyard to the little church of Saint-Andri and knelt down there before the altar and prayed to God for guidance.

He knew nothing any more. His heart was an empty vessel. What he had believed was false; he dared believe nothing else, for fear it too prove false. He had walked out of the world, when he left the house at Saint-Ouen; before him now lay a featureless landscape, a gray blur that was his future life. Desperately he filled his mind with prayers, to cast out fear.

The church was old and humble, with its ancient wooden Christ, its stone floor worn in ripples by the knees of worshipers. Save for two guttering candles, it was still and dark; no one disturbed him. He prayed all night for God to give him help, to send him some sign. In the dawn light, as the carved features of the crucifix before him became distinct, he was too tired to pray, too tired to think or even to be afraid, and he trudged away, out of the church, across the wakening city to the White Rose.

thirteen

IN THE NEXT FEW WEEKS, Flippo came several times to the White Rose, but Everard kept out of his way. He told Mother Rose to tell Flippo that he had disappeared. With the fall harvests going on, barges came down the Seine every day, full of produce, and he got all the work he could do at the wharfs along the riverbank.

Up the rivers with the high-piled grain and tuns of wine came tales of a great earthquake in Italy that had cracked the seams of the earth and let some foul contagion out of Hell; when he was not hauling and lifting Everard sat on the wharfs with other men and told such tales, and made up wilder stories yet. Paris lived on gossip.

The White Rose was on the rue de Guellande; the next street turning left was the rue du Fouarre, and it was on this narrow curving street, overhung with old plane trees, that the Studium had its lecture halls. Huge as haybarns, carpeted in straw that, the scholars loved to say, had gone unchanged since Peter Abelard first spat the errors out of his mouth, the buildings loomed up on either side of the street like churches of reason. There one winter's day Everard took himself to hear a lecture of Humbertus Angulanus, Humbert van Ecke, the last nominalist in Paris.

Angulanus was an old man, bald above the ears, with such a drapery of hair below that his head seemed to be rising up like the sun through gray mists. The crowd to hear him was so great that Everard could just squeeze in the door.

Before him stretched the cavernous lecture hall, strewn with benches like jackstraws. Rows of scholars packed them end to end, their books open on their knees. Before them all, perched on a stool, Angulanus swiveled his head to sweep the crowded room with his gaze, and lifted his voice.

"My question today is this: whether the World is in the Mind, or the Mind is in the World."

Poked into a corner, Everard heard these words, and a shudder passed through him; his heart leapt like a war-horse that hears the trumpet call to battle.

In the White Rose he had heard scholars debating this question, which was really only another version of the controversy over universals. It had been dry words, before, but Angulanus in his high, strong voice transformed it into the stuff of Everard's own life.

"There have been those," Angulanus was saying now, "who have taught that only words are real, words and ideas, and that all the phenomena of earthly life are but manifestations of the Word Eternal." He swept the room with his gaze again, his look a scythe to cut down the weeds of falsehood.

"This cannot be so! For what comparison can there be between the evil and wretchedness of the manifest world and the Eternal and the Divine?"

To Everard, who all his life had heard that the Word was God, it was as if the shutters had fallen off the windows of his soul, and the great wind of truth was roaring through, scouring his mind clean.

If the things of the world were merely a reflection of God's Mind, then they were as God meant them to be, and it was sin to question it. But if that premise was false . . . like a man struggling through an impenetrable jungle, he seized Angulanus's idea as if it were a broad highway to freedom.

Angulanus thundered, "The names of things are mere conveniences, constructions of the minds of men. It is the things themselves that are real — life itself that is real — the world itself that is real."

Then in losing the name of the Sire de Vaumartin, he had lost only words, not his essence. What he had been born to be, he remained.

At that the door behind Everard opened, and the beadles came in, slapping their broad-bladed paddles against their palms, and Everard slid away around the side of the room and dashed out before they could catch him. The paddles of the beadles were undeniably real.

He waited outside all the rest of the morning. With the nominalist doctrine burning in his brain, he found fascination in the random fall of a leaf from one of the great plane trees.

The world of the realists was cold and still as a crystal. All that mattered of a man was that he mirrored — imperfectly — the perfection of eternity. Everard by this doctrine had already failed.

The nominalists gave him value in himself, although he struggled with the thought, and could not really think of any proof. His ideas did not have the soaring logic of Angulanus's; his mind limped and staggered after unreachable flashes of insight, while the old man's thoughts seemed to stride the cosmos like the giants in the stars.

He watched the leaves fall, in the winter wind, each leaf unique and necessary, each one different, like each life.

When the nones bell rang, and the door of the hall opened before the outcoming tide of scholars, Everard went around to the back of the hall and waited for the master.

Angulanus emerged almost at once, but surrounded by scholars. Babbling at him, their black gowns swirling out behind them as they bustled around him, they bundled him away down the rue du Fouarre toward the river, where the masters of arts had a house. Everard trailed along a hundred feet behind them.

At the masters' house the crowd of scholars kept at Angulanus so long that Everard began to lose heart. He had missed a day's work to come here, and unless he could persuade Mother Rose to give him some bread he would go hungry, and he was cold. Still he waited, and when he saw the last of the scholars leave the house, he went in.

Angulanus lived in a room at the top of the stairs. Everard went up quietly to the door and knocked.

"Open it."

He opened the door, and went into a room under the eave, much longer than it was wide. Below the open window there was a writing table with a row of inkhorns along the top. A big stack of books stood on the floor beside it, between Everard and the old man, who sat on a stool with a book on his knee.

When Everard came in, Angulanus looked surprised, straightened and stared at him. "Who are you?"

In his best Latin, Everard said, "My name is Everard. I want to study with you."

Angulanus shut the book and set it on the table beside him. "No more of a name than that? Where do you live?"

"Here. In Paris. I — the woman at the White Rose lets me sleep in the attic."

"In the attic." The old man's eyes were sharp. "Have you no family?"

"No, I have no family, master."

"Bend over, if you please." And when Everard hesitated, wondering what he meant, the master reached out and firmly pushed him down, so that he could see his hair. He was looking, Everard realized, for signs of a tonsure. His hand rested briefly on Everard's crown, an impersonal pressure.

"Well, Everardus Atticanus, your Latin is excellent."

"Thank you, master."

"But I will not have you as a student."

"But — why not?"

"Primarily, it is the wrong time of the year to begin studies —"

"I'll come back."

"Secondarily, you have no money to pay me."

"I'll get the money somehow — I work, usually, during the day —"

"Which you could not do and study also." The old man reached for the book on the desk. His voice was almost gentle. "Which is my third reason, the fourth being that you are not telling me the truth about your identity, and therefore I cannot trust you."

He opened the book again, and bent his gaze toward it. Like a door closing, he shut Everard away from him. Everard stood there a moment, struggling for the courage to tell him the truth, but he could not prove who he really was, and he could not bear that Angulanus also think him a liar. At last he turned, his legs stiff, and walked woodenly away.

Mother Rose knew it was no use to be kind, since it only led people to expect more kindness, whereby they lost their courage. When halfway through the afternoon Everard dragged himself into the tavern and dropped into his corner like an old cloth doll, she made him scrub the pots and haul water and wood into the kitchen before she sat him down and put a bowl of stew in front of him.

As he ate he livened up. She was watching her new cook struggle with a pie crust, and every time she glanced at the boy he looked brighter. When he was done, and took the wooden bowl out to wash, she went after him.

"What's wrong with you? You're droopy as the rat hound's orphan pup."

"I can't get into the Studium," he said, baldly.

He scrubbed his bowl clean in the tub of water on the back step. She gazed at him, amazed.

"You want to study? Why? Do you think you'll make a nice priest?"

That made her laugh, and she thumped him on the head, pleased with him, who always surprised her. "Can't you learn enough from my boys here? Get them to tell you what you want to know."

"They don't know anything," he said. "All they know is what they've been told."

She caught him by the chin — his beard was growing out, thin and fine as baby hair — and turned his face to look at her. "Do you really want this? To be a scholar?"

"Yes," he said. He got hold of her wrist, pulling her hand away from him.

"Then have faith — you'll get it. God answers every prayer." She chuckled. With a pinch she let him go. "That's how He punishes us for our sins. Go in there, start that tun of Rhenish for me, before the Picard nation arrives."

He went back into the tavern. She threw out the new cook, who could not make piecrust, and did it herself.

fourteen

THE CROWD at Orléans was still cheering. Josseran was last to ride from the lists; as he went out the little gate at the end of the fence, a dozen men rushed to hold his horse, to take his lance and shield, to offer him a cup of wine, a napkin to wipe his face.

"Magnificent," one man said, hoarsely. "You were magnificent."

Josseran crossed himself. "God favored me today." He stepped down out of his saddle, feeling every ache, every bruise; suddenly he was exhausted.

"Favored you!" They roared around him, jubilant. "He gave you the arm of Hercules! The strength of Atlas!"

He drank off the cup pushed into his hand and reached for another of the dozen held out to him; his groom led off the red roan stallion. As the horse went off, its head low, Josseran reached out and patted its rump, thankful for its skill and strength.

"That blow you used to unhorse Prince John —" A lanky knight laughed into his face. "Come along — come now — you must sit down, let us honor you, champion of Orléans!"

Josseran said, "In a ten-man melee the victor does not win, so much as he survives, by luck more than skill. Luck and God's favor."

"Luck is the residue of grace," said one of the men he had just beaten. "I have waited a long while to match myself against you, Vaumartin — and you exceeded my expectations for it, let me tell you!"

Boisterous, they led him off to a pavilion behind the lists. He looked around him, hoping to see Isobel; it was unlikely she would come down into the dust and muck of the camp, and so she had not. When he looked across the broad, trampled fighting ground, he saw her still in the prince's pavilion, sitting between the duchess of Normandy and the countess of Aumale.

He lifted his hand to her, and far across the field, across all that lay between them, she flung up her arm in answer. The lavender scarf at her wrist fluttered. He reached up to his chest, where above his heart a similar lavender scarf was fixed to the breastplate, and tore it loose and kissed it, and then with the other knights he went off to a tent, and let them get him out of his armor, and bring him more wine, and pile him up with their praises and admiration.

While he was sitting there, relaxing in idle talk, one of the knights he had just beaten sank down on his heels beside him.

"My lord," this man said, "I should tell you that at a tournament at Saint-Ouen last summer there was a boy who took your name in vain."

"What?" Josseran said, blankly. The wine was muzzing up his thoughts.

The knight rubbed his hand over his face. He was a tall lean Breton, with hollow eyes; Josseran remembered him as a tireless and canny fighter, whom he had been lucky to unhorse. Now this knight said, "I met a boy at Saint-Ouen who pretended to be a kinsman of yours. He even called himself de Vaumartin."

"Did he," Josseran said. His voice rang in his own ears, unnaturally loud.

"When we pressed him, he backed off," said the Breton knight, whose name, Josseran remembered now, was Jean de Quercque. "He looked of gentle breeding, but he was rough, you know — his clothes were wrong, too flashy, and he had work-worn hands." Quercque nodded to him. "I thought you should know of it — it is a compliment, I suppose, when impostors choose your name to shelter in." He slapped Josseran's knee. "You were splendid today. I hope we meet again sometime, and I may make a better opponent for you."

"You were good enough," Josseran said, and shook his hand. "Thank you."

In the prince's pavilion the air was stuffy and ripe with the overbearing scent of lilac, which the duchess used to excess. Isobel said, "I think I shall walk, a little, until the next joust begins — will you join me, my lady?"

The duchess leaned on her cushions. She had been drinking unmixed wine in great quantities all day and her face was red. "No, no, you can go, my lady de Vaumartin — leave me to my own joustings." She smiled into the face of the Sire de Nesle, sitting on her left. "Sir knight, you will couch a lance with me, won't you?" She giggled, her fingers to her lips.

The knight muttered something. Clearly her boldness embarrassed him, as she intended it to. Isobel rose, shook out her skirts, and with her page and her waiting woman made her way out of the pavilion.

Outside the air was sharp with autumn; the wind swept up the soft slopes from the river, bending the trees and calling in their branches. Isobel strolled out away from the crowds and bustle by the tournament grounds. The page ran on ahead of her, jumping and chasing the last few birds of the autumn.

The tournament field was on high level ground, overlooking the river. On the broad rounded slopes the grass was brown and crisp with last night's frost; with every gust of wind the trees that filled the deep creases between the hills cast away their cloaks of leaves. Down to the southwest she could see the gray spires of Orléans, city of princes.

"I wonder that my lady duchess does not guard her tongue," said the waiting woman. She had served Isobel since her babyhood and had the privilege of free speech with her. "Does she not know, my lady, what rumor says of her?"

"I don't think she cares," said Isobel.

She lifted her face into the cool breeze. "Was he not wonderful? My Josseran. I thought I would burst with pride in him."

"He was a true and perfect knight," said her woman. "Who is this, now, coming after us, my lady?"

Isobel looked back the way they had come. The airy silken heads of the pavilions lined the far side of the field; across the intervening green walked a man in a red doublet and a tall red-and-gold hat.

"Charles d'Espagne," Isobel said, displeased. She put out her hand to grip her woman by the arm. "Stay, whatever he says."

The woman said nothing, but drew closer and held Isobel's hand like a little girl. The courtier came toward them, smiling, with many bows. His smile showed his eyeteeth.

"Sweet lady, many congratulations to you, whose champion so honored you with his gallant chivalry in the lists."

"My lord," Isobel said, coolly. The page had come back, his coat disheveled, and stood before her.

"I wonder if I might walk with you," said Charles of Spain. "Such a beauty as you lifts my heart."

"My lord, you are too kind."

"My words do you no justice, lady." He glanced at the woman, at the page. "Send off your servants, that we may talk freely."

She tightened her grip on her woman's hand. "Speak as you will, my lord — these people are as close to me as my own husband."

At the mention of Josseran, his face clouded, as she had hoped. Quickly she walked forward, going back to the pavilion.

The courtier fell into step beside her. He had long thin white hands. Rumor had it that Prince John had promised to make him constable of France, when John was King. Josseran said that was a joke, surely — Charles d'Espagne never drew a sword, never even put on armor; to give him command over all the knights of France would make a mockery of chivalry.

Now, leaning toward her, he murmured, "I come as the sparrow of a greater man than I, lady, to offer you his bounteous praises, and the honor of his love."

She did not even bother to look at him. "You may tell Prince John I am the wife of Josseran de Vaumartin, which is the greatest honor and delight any woman could wish for."

"A true heart is a glory in a woman," said the courtier.

They walked on a few more strides; they were nearly in among the pavilions now, close to mobs of people, and she quickened her stride. Charles d'Espagne put out his hand and stopped her.

"Dame de Vaumartin!" he said, rolling the words on his tongue. "Yet — you know — something your dear husband said to me, once, at Calais, got me thinking, and I asked some questions, here and there, and found — you are not really Dame de Vaumartin, are you?"

Isobel stiffened, cold. "What do you mean?"

The brim of his hat shaded his eyes like a mask. His smile was full of teeth. "I mean that the previous Sire de Vaumartin was a boy yet, at Crécy, and he vanished there — no one knows if he died, or was taken prisoner, or had some calamity occur that left him alive but unknown. So he may yet be in this world, and if so, lady, you are not the Dame de Vaumartin. And your fine brave husband is not the Sire de Vaumartin, but only a common knight."

She glared at him, furious, hating him so much her look should have withered him like a desert wind. She said, "Leave me, my lord."

He did not leave. Bold, in front of her servants, he reached out and took her hand and said, "Prince John would confirm you in the titles, I am sure of it, if you showed him a little kindness."

She wrenched her hand from his grasp. Between her teeth, she said, "Leave me, my lord."

His smile slipped. He took a step backward, with a flourish and a bow, shot a glance at the woman and the page, and said, "Good day, lady." Turning, he walked off toward the prince's pavilion. The back of his coat was creased. Isobel tore her gaze away from him.

Her attendants were still a moment, awkward, the woman avoiding her look. The page said, "My lady, you dropped this." He held up her lavender scarf. Isobel took it from him with numb fingers and crumpled it in her fist.

Josseran said, "I have to talk to you."

Isobel raised her eyes to his face. They were in the great hall of the castle of Orléans. Around them crowded the greatest men and women in France, splendid in velvet, damask, silk and satin, gold leaf and silver embroidery, humming with gossip and rumor. When the duke of Normandy appeared they would all sit down to eat supper. Isobel was hot, and her feet hurt; she longed for the peace of Vaumartin.

She said, "Can we go outside? The prince will be here in a few moments."

They had not been alone together for days, it seemed, even sleeping in the same room with other people, their servants in the bed with them. Isobel swallowed the tension in her throat.

"It's stifling in here," she said. "It's hard to believe it's almost Christmas." She laid her hand on his arm; she had resolved not to tell him about Charles d'Espagne's words to her, since she knew how he already loathed Prince John.

Under her fingers Josseran's arm flexed. "Let's go out to the courtyard."

They made their way through the crowded hall. At every step someone called out Josseran's name. Isobel leaned on him, letting him pick their course. At the cool air that met them at the doorway she gasped with relief.

They went out into a small courtyard between the hall and the chapel. Here also there were little groups of people, talking and laughing and drinking; although the night was falling, the light of the torches burning on the wall cast a wavering twilight across the middle of the pavement. Josseran led her around to an angle where the chapel's wall met the battlement, and where the torchlight did not reach.

He turned to her, and she lifted her face; they kissed. For a moment, locked in his arms, her eyes closed, she forgot the world and the court, she gave herself up to the little world of their love. She stroked her hands down his arms, remembering his tireless strength in the lists.

He said, "Isobel, today — someone told me Everard is alive."

"Everard," she said. She backed up a step, her hands leaving him; she felt as if he had driven a knife into her belly. "Who told you that? It's a lie!"

"No one told me — outright — but a knight who was in the melee had seen him. He didn't know who he was, he thought the boy was lying, using the name —"

"He was," Isobel cried, desperate.

"Keep your voice down," Josseran murmured, and flung a look to either side, into the dark. "The way he said it — I know it is the truth, Isobel. Everard is alive —"

"No," Isobel said, and she turned to him, and clutched his arms, and gave him a shake. "No. Look at me. You must not believe this. Today —" She collected herself, to tell him this, knowing the unpredictable force of his temper. "Today Charles d'Espagne came to me — with loathsome propositions —"

Josseran's head reared back. "I'll kill him!"

"Hold! Wait, heed me, do you think I gave him hearing? Trust me! I sent him off, I heaped scorn on him, but he said — Josseran! Heed me!" She pulled on his sleeve. "He said that they know that Everard's death was never confirmed — he said you are not really Sire de Vaumartin."

He flung off her hands; his face was rigid. She reached out to take hold of him again, and he thrust her off again. She could not see his expression, only the shape of his profile against the uncertain torch-light.

She said, "You must never admit that Everard may be alive. If he is, then he has not come forward."

"He was at Saint-Ouen," Josseran said. His voice was harsh, metallic, ugly. "He must be in Paris, or near there."

"Josseran!" She got his arm and pulled him toward her. "Forget him! You must not —"

He said, "He is my nephew, my blood and bone. My brother Clair gave him to me. I —" His voice sank suddenly to a murmur. "I failed in my duty — I abandoned him — I robbed him of his birthright."

She wheeled around toward him, her temper snapping. "You did what was necessary! Vaumartin is ours."

His hands rose to his face. To her astonishment he sagged, his shoulders round, his face buried in his hands. "Oh, God, forgive me —"

Her knees shook. A wild terror filled her, that his strength would fail her, that he would yield and fall and leave her alone, and she cocked her arm and slapped him hard across the ear.

"You coward!"

He wheeled toward her. Before she could see what he did, before she could avoid it, his blow struck her face. Her eyes bleared. She wobbled back and came up against the chapel wall behind her; her elbow rasped on the stone.

They stared at each other. Neither of them spoke. All around her left eye the flesh throbbed and ached, and her arm hurt where it had struck the stone wall behind her. After a moment he turned and walked away across the courtyard, but he did not go back to the hall; he went around the building, staying outside, in the darkness.

Isobel touched her face. For a moment she stood there, indecisive, wanting to call him back, but afraid of his anger. Under her fingertips the flesh around her eye was already puffy. She could not take this bruise into the hall. In the crowded castle of Orléans there were fewer places for her to go than for Josseran, but one was behind her, and she went into the chapel, found a corner, and prayed to God that Everard was dead.

In the morning, at Mass, Isobel would not look at Josseran. She wore a veil over her face, hiding the marks where he had hit her.

He had not seen her since their quarrel. He had spent the night in the hall, drinking with other men, saying nothing to anyone, struggling with his shame.

Now, in the chapel, made gorgeous by gold lamps and hangings, and stuffed with the flower of the French court in their rose satins and jewels, he stood side by side with his wife and did not touch her, and in his belly his shame simmered and brewed, a caustic stew, to burn them both.

She had brought this on them. She had given him the idea of abandoning Everard. She had driven Everard off.

His head pounded. He had drunk himself into a stupor, thinking about his nephew, about Prince John lusting after his wife and threatening his dominion, and he could not think very well even this morning. He raised his face toward the altar, his chest tight.

The chapel was magnificently appointed. Tall painted screens set off stalls along either side for the royal family, whose city this was. Prince John sat in the frontmost stall, facing the altar. Josseran's hand tightened into a fist.

The king was not in Orléans. The king, some said, now spent his days in prayer, on his knees, or writing long letters to the pope arguing for the proposition that immediately on their dying the blessed saints came at once before the Face of God, rather than having to wait for the Last Judgment; or else how could prayer to the saints achieve anything at all? He left his kingdom in this world to Prince John.

In the afternoon, there would be another joust. Josseran would have his chance then to deal with Prince John.

That stiffened him. That he understood, it was clean and easy, to fight, to overcome his enemies. He glared at Prince John again, safe inside his fancy screen.

The prince seemed to feel the weight of his hatred. He turned, showing his face. Someone came up to him from the crowd, and John stooped to hear, his hand cupped to his ear.

Isobel murmured something to Josseran. He glanced sharply at her, but her head was bowed, her fist at her breast; the heavy veil blurred her features, so that he could see only the curve of her jaw, the hollow of her cheek.

He glanced at Prince John again, but the royal stall was empty. The prince had gone out through the side entrance. Josseran made a small sound in his throat, gratified, as if somehow the fury of his look had driven out the prince.

They knelt for the Adoration of the Host. All around them, folk shuffled forward, heads bent, hands pressed together, toward the altar. Josseran did not receive the Eucharist; in such a bloody frame of mind as his, it would have been a sacrilege. Nor did Isobel, but stayed beside him, her head bowed. He glanced down at her again, struggling with his feelings.

She had hit him first. As soon as he thought that, regret filled him; he longed with his whole heart to be back there again, in that moment before he struck her, the thing undone.

"Oremus." Tiny in the golden candleglow of the altar, the priest blessed them, and with all the rest he went down on one knee and prayed to God to forgive him, unworthy, unworthy, unworthiest man in France.

Still, when he rose up, his heart was still rotten with sin. He took his wife's arm to lead her from the church, and her touch set his teeth on edge: it was all her fault, she had begun this. He longed to see Prince John out ahead of him, beyond the tip of his lance. Someone was calling to him, smiling and bowing, and he called and smiled, waved and bowed, his face smooth as a mirror, while his belly boiled with rage.

In the courtyard, folk milled around, meeting one another. On the step somebody pushed by him, so hasty in going that he stepped on Josseran's shoe and did not turn to apologize. Isobel moved a little away from him. There seemed fewer people in the courtyard than there had been in the church; he wondered idly where they were all going to. The Sire de Beaujeu came up to him, and they stood discussing the war in Brittany. Needing quiet, they moved out of the crowd toward the wall. Isobel lingered nearby, looking around. She had not spoken to Josseran since he hit her. Yet it was her fault. Numbly he faced Beaujeu and talked about supply lines and siege engines. When Isobel abruptly went off, he hardly noticed; neither did he heed the steady rumble of wagon wheels going by in the street just beyond the wall.

Beaujeu said, "You'll fight today, won't you? You were very impressive yesterday."

"God favored me." He crossed himself; glancing over his shoulder, he looked for Isobel.

She was coming toward him, her skirts in one hand, her face still shrouded in the heavy veil. Beaujeu gave him a sharp look. Belatedly Josseran realized that the veil betrayed him; everybody must know that Isobel, vain as she was, had to have pressing reasons for hiding her face. His thoughts tumbled; he watched her come up to him and pull the veil up and over her head, careless of Beaujeu standing there, exposing her face to open view.

Her eye was ringed in dark purple. Josseran said, "No, cover it," and put up his hand to the veil, but she caught his wrist.

"Josseran," she said. "Don't you have ears? Listen to the wagons. Look around — people are leaving. Can't you see?" She flung her arm around at the courtyard. He raised his head, puzzled, wondering what she meant, and it was true that people were hurrying up the steps into the castle, down the lanes between the buildings, rushing away, instead of lingering in the courtyard to talk. He looked down at his wife again.

"There was a dead rat in the kitchen this morning," she said. "That's why John left the Mass —"

"A rat," he said, slow-witted, and a moment later the word jumped into his mind.

"Plague," he said.

Isobel clutched his arm. He turned to Beaujeu, who shook his head. "I know nothing. If it's true . . ." The older man was backing away, his mouth caught in a smile, but his eyes suddenly shiny with fear. "Good day, my lord."

Josseran wheeled back to his wife. "Get your servants ready. I will see to the horses. Come to the gate when you are ready. Be quick."

She nodded; her face was pale, the great bruise livid at the edges. Her eyes were huge with fear and pain. Abruptly he leaned down and kissed the bruise and kissed her mouth. She caught him around the neck and held him tight, her lips on his. They straightened; she pulled the veil down over her face and went away toward the hall.

Vaumartin. Abruptly he longed for its safety, its walls, its weight of name. All the things that had mattered so much to him, a few moments before, were meaningless now: Prince John and their feud, Everard, his wife's treachery — it all shrank down to nothing. He had to get back to Vaumartin. He turned on his heel and strode toward the stable.

THE WINTER ENVELOPED PARIS in a bone-cracking cold. At Candlemas there was ice on the Seine. No more barges came up the river, and Everard walked the streets, calling out his willingness to do any job; he swept out chimneys and dug latrines. When there was no work at all, he went up to the little bridge, where the booksellers had their stalls, one jammed against the next on the downstream railing of the bridge.

Books were expensive. Everard could not buy the cheapest volume, and because he had no master, the booksellers would not, as they did with the scholars, let him rent the books and take them home. Instead, he hoarded up his pennies until he got the book's hire and leaned against the side of the stall, reading that way and coming back day after day until he was done.

When they got used to seeing him there, the booksellers showed him what was under their shelves, the outlaw books, thin stacks of paper slapped together between boards, William of Ockham, Marsilius of Padua, whom the pope had condemned.

In these books he found the nominalist arguments that underlay the lectures of Angulanus: God was irreducibly distant from the world and from men, inaccessible to reason; the order of the world could not bind Him; not even the priestly order of Mother Church was a reflection of Him. All that was real — all that reason could detect — was local, temporary, changing, and changeable, the fragments of order.

Leaning on the rail of the Little Bridge, his fingers numb with cold, Everard thought these words ought to thunder off the page, and that kings and princes must tremble with terror just to know they were written down somewhere — it amazed him that the emperor supported these men, although of course their doctrine leveled the power of the pope, the emperor's ancient enemy.

But it threatened everything established, this doctrine. By exercise of simple logic, it undercut the meaning of every order, every law, every authority in the world.

Everard himself had nothing, and no law allowed him anything, no authority enforced his desires. He spent all his spare money to read, and so had no real home still, but lived in the garret at the White Rose. When Mother Rose caught him with one of the serving wenches, her skirt around her waist, his breeches around his ankles, the redheaded tavern keeper threatened to throw him out, and he left.

It was too cold to stop moving, and he wandered around the streets, feeling his life draining away from him in day after day of mindless labor, other men's ideas, quick ruts on the stair of a tavern, getting drunk, dreaming of Vaumartin. Humbertus would not accept him. But there was another master he knew of, whose doctrine he could learn.

His mind made up, he went across the Great Street to the quartier Saint-Andri, to the house of Italo del Borgo, the very famous alchemist and magician.

Flippo answered the door. His eyes widened with surprise to see Everard standing there; he quickly came out onto the flat open stoop, shutting the door behind him.

"Keep quiet," he said. "My mother's sick in childbed, upstairs." He jerked his head up toward the second-story window above them. "What do you want?"

"I want to see Italo," Everard said.

Flippo's lip curled. "What makes you think he wants to see you?"

"Doesn't he still want someone to help him get patrons at court?"

"Yes, well," Flippo said, "you didn't do so well at that, did you? Now, get off! Get out of here. He's got me, I handle things for him, get off!"

He backed up and shut the door in Everard's face. Everard lifted his fist, to hammer on the door.

His gaze climbed to the window overhead; he was loath to disturb Elisabetta, and he had no real assurance that Italo was even there. He went down the three steps to the street and walked away, down to the rue Saint-Germain, to the Saint-Andri graveyard.

Italo said, "Is there nothing more in the pot? God's bones, I'll be glad when she's up — you cook as if we are all birds."

The older daughter whined at him. Italo, Flippo, and Giulia were gathered by the hearth, the only light in the hall coming from the fire on the hearth. It was almost full dark outside and the windows were shuttered. Everard pushed the pantry door silently open and slipped into the hall behind them.

"It's hard, doing Mama's work," the daughter shrilled, casting up her hands. "If you would help me —" she turned, saw Everard, and shrieked.

The two men sprang to their feet, wheeling toward him. Everard raised his hands, to show himself harmless, and made Italo a short bow.

"Good evening, Master Magician."

Flippo gawked at him. The daughter was standing as if turned to stone, her hands to her face. Italo grunted.

"I told you to block up that tunnel!" He swatted Flippo across the arm. His face turned toward Everard. Across his balding egg-shaped head his frown spread in furrows like a plowed field. "What are you doing here, Everard?" he said, coolly.

Everard had hoped for more enthusiasm from him. Collecting himself, he said, "I came to offer you my services again. I realize that the last time was — unproductive, but —"

Flippo sprang forward. "He ran out! Didn't he, Papa? He ducked out on it and ruined the whole thing!"

Italo put out his hand and stopped him. "Keep quiet." He jacked up his eyebrows at Everard. "Yes, I'd be very interested in hearing what actually did happen at the king's tournament. Come, sit down. I don't think there's much left to eat, but you can have a cup with us. Giulia —"

Flippo bit his lips. His look at Everard was murderous. Everard looked away from him, his muscles tight, wishing he had thought this through better, and went up to the hearth and sat down beside Italo.

"I did not do what you told me to do," Everard said. "I had — other things I — personal matters." He stared into the fire. "But I could have done what you asked. No one questioned me. I could have made your name known to many people, even to the king himself, perhaps."

"You're lying," Flippo burst out. "You didn't see the king."

Italo snorted at him. He was watching Everard with keen interest, his lips unsmiling, his eyes avid. "You saw that cup, Filippo. You know what I sold that cup for. He saw the king, indeed. So, Everard, now your — personal matters are taken care of, and you're willing to serve me? Why should I believe you?"

Everard said, "Because you want patrons at court, and I can move freely at court."

"Sometimes." Italo stroked his face. "Under certain circumstances. Rumor is, the king's failing. Soon we'll have Prince John for our king."

"John will be no better," said Everard, remembering the joust against Jean de Quercque.

"He is vigorous, young, strong," said Italo. "The kingdom will thrive on his youth."

Everard gave him a sharp look. "I did not know you for a realist, Italo."

The magician made a laugh deep in his chest. "Do not pin your names from the universitas on me, boy. I am conversant in such arts and secret knowlege that the magpies know nothing of — nothing!" He flourished his right hand over his head, and his eyes flashed. He stared at Everard a moment, to see if his rhetoric had its effect, and then suddenly jerked his gaze toward Flippo.

"He can sleep in your bed again. I suppose there's no use — or sense, now — in plugging up the tunnel." He nodded at Everard. "We'll have to talk things over, and see what can be made of you. Perhaps you will make me an apprentice." He smiled. "Welcome, Everard."

In the morning when he woke up Flippo snored on asleep in the bed, and he had to crawl over him to reach the floor. The bed was full of fleas. He shook out his shirt carefully and held it in the beam of sunlight coming through the window, but as soon as he had it on, he felt a track of bites across his stomach. Scratching, he went up to the hall.

Elisabetta was there. Thin and pale, she looked at him indifferently and brought him a slab of bread and some cheese, and even spoke to him a little in Italian.

He said, "Where is your baby?" and made rocking motions with his arms.

Her face dropped, she looked suddenly exhausted, and she said nothing, only made the sign of the cross, so he knew the baby had died. A little later, he saw her by the fire with the older baby, a pretty, fair-headed little thing called Sylviane. She cooed to it and cuddled it, and pressed her face to the little girl's, but she never smiled. She seemed half gone, as if her soul yearned after the dead child's.

The girl Giulia came groaning from the kitchen, complaining in Italian; by the fire, her mother turned and chattered at her, their dueling voices rising higher and higher. Everard drifted toward the stairs, looking up, wondering where Italo was. Then suddenly Giulia was tugging on his sleeve.

"My mother says, if you're going to eat, you can work." She thrust an empty pail at him. "Please, go fetch me some water from the well. The yoke is by the door, there."

Everard took the pail; Elisabetta was glowering at him, as if she thought he would refuse. He went to the door for the yoke and the other pail. When he set the yoke on his shoulders, the little girl Sylviane let out a squeal of pleasure, and came tottering across the hall to join him.

Elisabetta gave off a sudden burst of Italian. Giulia said, "Take Sylvie — she likes to go to the well." She turned back to the kitchen. Everard went out the door, the yoke on his shoulders, and Italo's child, crowing and buoyant, scuttling down the steps ahead of him.

It was some weeks short of spring; the row of trees behind the well was still a rank of bare spikes. A flock of white hens pecked and scratched in the gutter in the middle of the street. The little girl made a short charge into their midst; they scattered, squawking, and Sylviane sat down hard on her bottom. Everard stopped and set her on her feet again.

Her hair was a mass of gold curls. She looked like Italo. Wriggling out of his grip, she set off down the street again, teetering and tottering like a drunkard.

Everard followed her. The street here was more an irregular court than a straight-going way, its sides defined by the fences and front steps of the houses along it. The deep ruts in it were full of scummy water. Halfway to the well he passed the largest house in the quartier, the house of Bonboisson the vintner, whose shop took up the whole front of the building. On his sign was a bunch of purple grapes made of wood. Behind the shop was his family's living quarters; they had two stories, a separate kitchen, and glass windows.

At the well several of the local women were gathered to gossip; they left off their talk as he approached, and watched him with an undivided scrutiny the while he drew the water and filled the buckets. He paid no heed to them. In their black gowns and white coifs they reminded him of the village women of Brittany, although Breton women wore their coifs in great starched loops and wings, and these women merely wrapped their heads up in linen.

Everard had already heard the old story that Saint Andrew, passing by, had preached here, converting several heathen, and, requiring water for their baptism, had thrust his staff into the ground and brought forth the spring; the neighboring churches still sent to this well for water for their fonts. It had a bitter taste. He drank some of it while he was there, needing a little sanctity.

Sylviane scrambled around on the well. Several times he lifted her down from the stone coping around it, until she broke away and ran into another street, directly away from her home.

This path ran off north toward the river. Two huge wooden shoes hung down over the first two doorways, proclaiming them cobblers' shops. Beyond was a fallow field, a distant orchard, and a cluster of rooftops. Sylviane slowed, and he caught her, awkward with the yoke on his shoulders, and got her running back in the right direction.

People were going in and out of the bakery just off to the right of the well. Everard wondered if Elisabetta had bought there the bread she had given him for breakfast; it had been very good bread. A white goat was browsing on the thatched roof of the house beyond, and beyond that, another wall of naked trees rose up to fringe the sky. This much, then, was Saint-Andri's quarter.

Home to him, now. He had a sort of family, now. It surprised him to like that. With the yoke on his shoulders, he strode away down the street toward the alchemist's house.

sixteen

"FRIAR BACON'S SALT, that is, Solomon's salt, which is sulphur, and Peter's salt," said Italo lovingly, "and ground charcoal." Before him on the table stood a collection of strangely shaped pots and glass jars, which he lifted, fondled, put down as he talked.

He scooped up a little handful of the grit he had just poured onto the table and twisted on the bench and flung the powder into the fire. There was a flash of brilliant light and a crackle that seemed to come from inside Everard's ears. He gasped, and Flippo crowed.

"Look at him. Not so high-bellied now, is he! You see, you bumpkin, what power is. Show him again, Papa."

Everard reached across the table for the powder, heaped on a piece of paper, but Italo caught his wrist and held his hand away. "Ah, no. Such things are not for apprentices. Sit back."

"Tell me again," Everard said. "Sulphur —"

"Peter's salt, ground charcoal." Italo dusted his hand against his shirt. His eyes were half shut; he looked sleek and soft, like a cat. "It cannot be damp at all, or it will not work."

Everard said, "Do it again," and Italo laughed. He reached out carefully for the paper and slowly, carefully tipped the powder back into its flask.

"Not for you, yet, boy. Not yet."

He mixed a powder from a vial, a liquid from a bottle, and suddenly had before them a sizzling froth, bubbling up and over the cup that had easily held everything before, spilling onto the table, dripping down onto the floor. Flippo hooted at him again.

"Look at him!"

Everard sniffed, smelling vinegar. "Tell me what those things are," he said.

"No, no," said Italo, with a soft catlike chuckle. "Not for mere apprentices. You'll have to learn a little first. Now, this —" He lifted up a squat little jar, stopped with a plug of glass. "I wish I had more of this. I've heard this matter just lies around on the rocks of the desert, in the eastern countries, burning by itself. Now, we could make something of that to impress my lord our gull."

Everard leaned back, his eyes on the collapsing froth. His nose still noticed a vinegar smell in the air.

"When are we going to try the court again?"

"When the king returns to Paris," said Italo.

"The king's in hiding," Everard said. "The king may never come back to Paris. Why don't we approach the prince? He is here often, and he loves to spend money, they say."

"Well, he's not here now," said Italo, and shot a dark look at him. "I will decide these matters. You will do as I say, without question. Without question! Do you fathom me?"

Everard joined his hands together in front of him on the table. A hot flush climbed into his face. He was thinking of the priest of Vaumartin, who had hated questions. Italo glared at him still.

"I will choose who is to play my lord the gull, boy. I will devise the game, and the stakes. You are merely one of the pieces! Keep that well in mind. I can replace broken pieces."

Everard grunted at him. "No questions at all? Not why do these things happen — why does the powder explode — why does the vinegar mixture bubble?"

"Why?" Italo said, blankly, and jerked a smile over his face. "What sort of question is that?" He leaned forward over the table, his eyes blazing. "God makes tricks. The whole world is one trick after another, boy, don't you realize that yet? These are just tricks, God's jokes. That's why."

"Tricks," Everard said heavily. "That's all it is to you?"

"Do you think God is too good for tricks?" Italo leaned toward him, his voice falling to a whisper. "God is the first trickster, the ultimate prankster. You know what His first and best and favorite trick is, boy? Death. That's God's joke on us. He bestows on us this life, heart and soul and brain, these hands, these arms, this mouth, this cock — the whole world to use them in — but just as you're beginning to understand how to live, you realize that life is slipping away from you — He's taking it all back — and by the way He expects you to adore Him for His generosity!"

He shouted the last of it, in a sudden roar of temper, thundered with his hands on the tabletop, and abruptly calm again leaned down for the ewer of wine. "That's the trick, boy."

"There must be something else," Everard said.

"Well," said Italo, pouring wine into their cups, "maybe there should be something else, but there isn't, Everard." He nodded toward the ewer. "Pour me another cup, and then get down to bed. I'm tired of dealing with ignorance."

Everard gave the mattress of the bed a violent shake and settled it again on the rope springs. Flippo came down the three steps into the little room.

"Listen, Everard," he said, "you know I go out at night, sometimes."

"Yes," said Everard.

He did not want to talk to Flippo; he was brooding over what Italo had said. He laid the blankets out straight on the bed and sat down on the frame to take off his shoes. Flippo went to shutter the window. The room dimmed.

"Anyway," Flippo said softly, "I know places now where we can gather in a wagonload. But I need help carrying it off."

"Help," Everard said, his attention snagged. "Where are you finding so much to steal that you need help in carrying it away?"

Flippo snickered at him. "You haven't been listening to the gossip. There's plague in Paris. All the rabbit-hearts are leaving, all the wellborn and well-off."

Everard said, "So you go and loot their houses? God, what a paragon you are, Flippo."

"Don't call me that," Flippo said. "It's Filippo."

Everard didn't bother to answer him. He lay down on the bed, his arms crossed behind his head. In the dim light the alchemist's son hovered around the room like a dirty angel.

"I see what you're doing — taking my father from me — worming your way in here, trying to take my place with him. You think you're better than me, but you want what's mine, so you can't be."

Everard said, "Go on, Flippo, go steal. Just don't wake me up when you get back."

Flippo called him a gutter-name. Everard shut his eyes. The crates and lumber in the corner scraped and banged, and there were the sounds of Flippo lowering himself through the hole in the corner, and then stillness.

Everard resisted believing what Flippo had said, about stealing his father, but he knew that it was true. He lay still awhile, waiting for sleep, his thoughts downcast. What was worse than Flippo's charge was the feeling that he had chosen wrong. He had come to Italo for power and wisdom, but all Italo could give him was tricks, deceits, pranks and games. He lay there a long while, wondering if Italo was right, and tricks and games were all there was, or if it was only that tricks and games were all that Everard deserved. Finally he rolled over, his face to the wall, and blanked his mind, and lost himself in sleep.

seventeen

IN THE MORNING Flippo was sick. Waking
next to him, Everard was aware even before he opened his eyes of
the heat of the other boy's body. He recoiled away out of the bed and
called Italo, but it was Elisabetta who came.

Flippo moaned. The fever blazed in his skin, in his breath, in his
lusterless hair. With Everard's help Elisabetta got his clothes off, and
while they were moving him he vomited.

The stench made Everard's guts roll. The vomit was a tarry black,
like crushed soot, like old ink. Everard backed away, into the doorway
of the room.

Crooning reassurances, Elisabetta struggled to lift her son up into
the bed again. Her thin bony back was to Everard. The brown hair was
slipping down from its tight bun on the top of her head. He glanced
over his shoulder, into the hall, thinking of running away.

Elisabetta turned toward him, her face desperate, and said something
pleading in Italian. With her eyes on him he could not refuse her. He
went down into the room again and lifted Flippo and turned him while
she cleaned him and straightened his bed.

Everard sat by the fire and ate a bit of bread and drank watered wine
for his breakfast, and Elisabetta came to him and made the sign of the
cross over him and sprinkled him with something, holy water,
perhaps. Her eyes were dull, her attention inward, or elsewhere. Her
mouth was set like a line chiseled into rock. Italo came down the
stairs.

"Filippo's not sick," he said, very loudly, before anybody else had a
chance to say anything. "He's just drunk or something. Don't tell
anybody." He sat down at the table. His broad, pale face was as

unruffled as ever. As always he had some bit of knowledge to put forth, some fact to protect him from the truth.

"I have heard when the plague struck Milan, the duke ordered his men to board up the houses where it first appeared, with all the people in them. They'll do that to us, if they think —"

He broke off. Still his face was clear of care, a maniacal guise of confidence. Everard got up from the table and went to the door.

From here he looked up and down the street. It seemed the same as ever, coming narrow up from the rue Saint-Germain, broader where the cherry tree stood in front of the priest's house, broad still and dirty where it passed by this house, curving around toward the well.

In front of Bonboisson's house was a wagon. Between it and the house, the vintner's family ran in a steady stream, back and forth, carrying armloads of goods, and casting them into the wagon. Everard went out onto the back step to watch them. They climbed into the wagon, the vintner in his black coat taking the reins, his wife beside him, their several children in the back, and with a whistle and a shout they drove off. As they rolled away, something fell out of the back of the wagon and lay there in the street, and they did not come back for it, they did not even slow or turn to look.

They rounded the corner past the bakery and were gone, and then again the street seemed the same as ever. Elisabetta's white chickens fluttered in the dust. Two little boys from the cobblers' shops ran along kicking a ball back and forth between them. A woman came out of one of the other houses and went to see what the Bonboissons had dropped.

Everard turned away, back into Italo's house. His belly hurt; his head began to pound. A dull terror filled him. He thrust it away. Nothing would happen to him. He had just come here, nothing would happen to him, he did not belong here. He felt suddenly far, far from himself, looking down from some great distance, safe and far. He crossed himself, and went to see how Flippo did.

Italo went out; Giulia sat in the hall praying. No one but Everard helped Elisabetta. Still thin and frail from childbed, she fought for her son's life with a one-minded passion, and Everard brought her the water and wine she asked for, sat with her while she prayed, helped her bathe Flippo and turn him over, although the stink of everything that came from him was overpowering: his sweat, his urine, his vomit, everything black and stinking. Under his arms, in his groin, in his neck, the flesh began to swell, turn shiny and black.

Elisabetta muttered in Italian. She made signs in the air; she got some of Italo's sulphur and sprinkled it around Flippo's bed. The swellings grew, like tiny heads straining to pop through the distended skin. She took a knife and blessed it and cut into them. Everard could not bear to watch her and had to turn his head away. What oozed out of the lumps was neither blood nor bile, nor any other healthy humor, but a black gritty stuff, like char, like Friar Bacon's salt, as if Flippo burned alive inside. In the evening, in spite of everything she did, he died.

Elisabetta and Everard wrapped the body up in a clean sheet. He expected her to weep, to mourn, but she did only what was necessary, she moved with a spare economy, as if she saved herself for an ordeal to come. Italo returned, and he was trying to convince them not to take the body away where anyone could see it when they heard the ringing of a bell in the street.

Elisabetta opened the door. Standing on the step, they all watched a cart roll up the street.

A skeletal white horse drew it. Holding the bridle there walked a man in a gray robe, the hood pulled over his head so that his face was invisible, a pitchfork over his shoulder. As he walked, he cried, "Bring out your dead, bring out your dead!"

Everard could not move. His terror held him fast, there on the step. Elisabetta started down to the street; Italo gripped her arm and said sharply, "No! Don't," but she shook him off and went down into the street and raised her arm to the cart as if she were hailing a peddler with something she wanted to buy.

The leader stopped the bony horse. The two men who followed him reached into the cart and took out their pitchforks. Elisabetta led them up into the house. Everard shrank back from them. As they passed him he smelled the ineffable sweetness of roses. From the flaps and seams of their robes there peeked out the pink and white blossoms of roses. They came out carrying Flippo, one at his head, one at his feet.

Italo said, "No, it's not plague. He was drunk. It wasn't plague." He reached out to grip his wife by the shoulders and said into her face, "It's not plague." Tears streamed down his face. She looked at him almost with indifference and freed herself from him and went out after her son; when they threw Flippo onto the back of the wagon, on top of other cold white arms and legs and chests, she reached in and tucked the sheet around him.

Everard's head throbbed. He started back into the house, and under him the floor gave way, the world fell away; soundlessly he collapsed into Italo's arms.

Elisabetta washed Everard and wrapped him in a blanket and laid him down in Flippo's bed. She stroked the boy's forehead, blazing hot, and gave him water to drink, although he vomited it up again at once. Then she ran up the stairs, to her own bed, where Italo lay thrashing and screaming, and bathed him, and gave him water that he threw back at her, black and stinking.

When she needed more water she looked for Giulia, to send her to the well, but Giulia wasn't there. She called, but Giulia did not answer, and she never came back again.

With the buckets in each hand Elisabetta went to the well. The street was empty, save for chickens and dogs and pigs. No women loitered at the well to share gossip. When she turned the squeaking winch handle to raise the water, the sound brought someone to the window of Rogier's cobbler shop; she saw a face peer around the shutter, and she herself turned away.

There was no time to grieve, or even to be afraid. In her house, now, everything she knew and loved lay in the path of a vengeful God. She knew what she had to do, and she did it, although God Himself fought against her, and she knew she could not win.

Everard lay in a close world of fire and soot and pain, and from it he called out, and she came. From some cool space beyond this one she reached in to him, touched him, brought him water. The pain spread through his body, and she soothed him in her foreign tongue, in words that did not matter; the voice alone mattered, her voice and her faithful attention.

She took her knife, and stabbed the great boils swelling out of him. The pain made him scream.

He clung to her hand. "Don't leave me — don't leave me —" He felt himself poised at the top of a long irreversible fall. She told him to pray, and she prayed over him. She wrapped him in a dry blanket, and when it was soaked through she brought another. When he began to shiver she tucked hot bricks against his sides to keep him warm. She never gave up. He was there on the edge of the abyss but she held him fast. He saw the other people dropping into the black pit below him, heard their screams and smelled them burn, but Elisabetta held him up; by threads of her fierce will she bound him to the living world, and bit by bit Everard grew stronger again.

Sometime after midnight Italo died also. Elisabetta, dozing in a corner, woke to find him cold.

She could have screamed, or cried, or torn her hair, but all of these things seemed pitiable before the enormous terror that had come over them all. She went to the cradle, where Sylviane still slept, lifted out the child, and took her down the stairs into the hall.

There was only a little bread left, some beans, and a piece of cheese. She nursed the child, daubed some honey on her fingers, and gave her a white chicken feather to play with. Then slowly she went toward the little room in the back, where Filippo had died, where Everard now was dying.

When she opened the door she thought he too was dead, he lay so still. She almost shut the door again, unwilling to face another corpse, until he whimpered.

She went down the little steps to his side. The stink was unbearable here, closed in as this room was; her shoes slipped in the vomit caked on the floor. Bending over him, she laid her fingers to his forehead.

His skin was cool. As she touched him he moaned again.

Now she dropped to her knees. Her heart was thundering. He was alive, he had lived through the fever; at least for now, he was alive. She knelt there in the filth and prayed to God in gratitude. Tears rolled down her face; she shook with sobs. Now, when she had some hope at last, she gave herself over to the luxury of grief.

Everard was still too weak to rise, too weak even to eat. She steeped herbs in wine and fed this infusion to him drop by drop. At noon the death-cart came by again, and she let the men into the house to get Italo.

As they went by her she held up her skirts, to keep even the hem of her garment from touching them. Murderers, they were, these men in robes gray as fungus, condemned men brought up from the bowels of the city prison to gather in the dead. To them this was a respite, what they did. They loved the plague; it was their master, their familiar. Heaving Italo up out of the bed, they tweaked his flesh and poked him.

"Here's a good dinner for the devil, hah!"

"He'll need a gravy — this meat's a little tough."

They laughed, going down the stairs. Elisabetta held the door for them, but she turned her face away, afraid they might guess that here one had escaped them.

She stood on the step to watch where they went. Their tinkling bell led them off down the street, past Bonboisson's, and she herself went out to the street to follow their course around the well. The cart rumbled up before Rogier's, and the gray men went in with their jokes and their pitchforks, and came out again with bodies. They went on to Blisane's shop and took out bodies.

Elisabetta's chest was tightening, as if her flesh were failing. She was dizzy; she nearly lost her balance and fell as she stood there in the street. The cart rolled away toward the bakery, and stopped again, and again the door opened, and again they brought forth dead. She swayed back and forth, she clutched her arms against herself. Running back into her house, she found Sylviane playing on the floor by the hearth, and scooping her up Elisabetta pressed her face to the child, and the hot tears spilled down her face.

Everard woke, too weak to lift his head, too weak to call. He wondered if he was dead, if this was what being dead was like, this utter exhaustion.

He lay for a long while, feeling the warmth in his limbs, the slow beating of his heart, and knew he was alive. He slept; he woke again.

She did not come. His belly growled with hunger. There was a pitcher by the bed, which he struggled to reach; he drank the last few drops of wine in it, wondering why she did not come.

Finally he dragged himself up out of the cot. His limbs shook with weakness. Leaning on the wall, on the bedframe, he crept up the steps.

The house was silent. It felt empty, a great hollow shell around him. He sat down on the floor, his head nodding under its own weight, and somewhere upstairs a child cried.

Sylviane.

Slowly he drew himself toward that sound. Crawling across the floor, he reached the foot of the stair, and there slept for a while, his head on the step. The child's crying woke him again, deep in the night, and he began the slow climb up the stairs on hands and knees and belly.

When he reached the bedroom at the top, the dawn light was breaking in pale shafts through the cracks in the shuttered windows.

He had never been in this room before. Heavy wooden furnishings crowded it; the great bed was beautiful, with a fringed canopy, carved posts, a rich man's bed. In it Elisabetta lay, and she was ablaze with the fever, and her neck was swelling black.

Everard leaned against the bed and gripped her hand, the hand of her who had brought him back from death. She paid no heed to him. He looked desperately around him for water, for a knife to pierce the black bubo big as a melon below her ear. Sylviane screamed in the cradle, and Elisabetta opened her eyes.

"My baby," she said, and feebly her limbs moved, as if she were trying to rise.

Everard said, "Be still. I'll help you. Rest, Elisabetta."

She spoke again, in Italian, but every word was clear to him.

"Take care of my baby."

"I will," he said. "I swear it. I will."

She shut her eyes. He held fast to her hand, but he had no power to save her, and within a little while she was dead too.

He could not give her to the death-cart, but he was too weak to bear her to the churchyard, to dig a grave. Instead he dragged her, slowly, resting often, down into the warren of tunnels beneath the house, down to the deepest of the niches carved out of the white rock.

It was not consecrated ground. He had heard that those buried in unsanctified ground could not find Heaven. Kneeling down beside her, in the damp, sour-smelling space, he crossed himself and prayed for her, and to her, who had saved him, whose presence here would surely consecrate this ground. In the back of his mind, the thought lingered that she should stay here, in this house, where she belonged — that her spirit would protect it.

The crying of the baby roused him from his numb and weary prayers, and he climbed back up to the warmth of the hall.

There was nothing in the house to eat but a few handfuls of beans. He soaked them soft and cooked them to a tasteless mush. The little girl would not stop crying; even as she ate she cried for her mother. Everard held her on his lap before the fire and let her suck on his fingers.

There was no one else in the house but him and the baby. He could find no trace of Giulia or Italo; he wondered if they had died while he was sick, or if they had run off. Every time he heard a sound outside the house he turned toward the door, hoping to see Italo come in. In his arms, Sylviane slept at last.

He scrubbed his filthy room — Flippo's room — and washed the blankets and hung them along the fence to dry in the sun. Leaving the baby to sleep, he went out to find more food. The street was deserted. In Bonboisson's house, the four glazed windows were broken. Even the chickens and pigs were gone, although it was the height of the day. By the well, a dead rat lay stiff in the dust.

The two cobbler shops were shuttered tight, but to his surprise, there was smoke rising from the back of the bakery, where the ovens were, and he went to the door of the shop and knocked.

The door opened a little, but no one looked out, no one spoke. To the dark behind the door, he said, "I need bread."

No one answered, but the door stayed open, and he heard feet shuffling away; a moment later a hand held a round loaf around the edge of the door to him. He took it, fumbling in his purse; in Italo's bedroom chest he had found some money.

He said, "How much is it?" Willing to pay anything he had.

Behind the door there was a laugh, closer to weeping than to mirth. The door shut again.

When he returned to Italo's house the baby was feverish.

His heart contracted to a cold lump in his chest. If she died he would be all alone — all alone. She screamed in pain, kicked and thrashed. He remembered what Elisabetta had done, and bathed her, kept her in the cool water as her skin burned.

She sobbed for her mother. She began to tremble, and he took her from the water and wrapped her in a blanket and rocked her, all through that night, before the fire, rocking her back and forth, fighting his own exhaustion. Elisabetta had saved him; he dared not fail to save her baby. She sucked frantically on her fists, on his fingers, on the corner of the blanket, but when he tried to feed her she vomited tides of black. Her body seemed to wither in his grasp.

In the pit of the night, when only his will was awake, his will failed also, and he dozed off, the baby delirious in his arms.

He woke sprawled on the floor by the fire. The child was gone. He sat up, hungry, stronger than before. In the fireplace the last hot coals hissed and sizzled; it was raining; drops of rain fell down the chimney and burst on the hot embers. He got up to his feet and went down the hall, looking for Sylviane.

He called her name. She was not in the hall, nor in the kitchen. Then he saw the front door was open, and he went out onto the steps of the house.

The rain was falling in a fine gray mist, veiling the street, hushing the whole world with its whisper. Like a benediction it fell; cleansing the world. There, in the muddy street, was Elisabetta's child.

She was naked. The marks of her mortality showed on her body like seams, black streaks below her arms and over her belly. She stood with her head back, trying to drink the falling rain, and she slipped and fell in the mud.

Everard went back to the hall for a blanket and hurried out to her. When he lifted her up, covered with mud, she smiled at him. Her skin was cool, her senses whole; the terrible assault had passed lightly over her innocence. He wrapped her into the blanket and went down to the church of Saint-Andri, and there in front of the homely old Christ he knelt down, meaning to give thanks to God for sparing him and Sylviane.

He could not summon the words. The child dozed in his arms, her head heavy on his shoulder, smelling of urine and stale milk. He wondered if God had let him live for some reason, or if it was mere chance.

He could not believe it was chance. He would not live his life as if it mattered no more than a whim. Kneeling there, he began to think that God had called to him, saving him, saving Sylviane. He swore to God that henceforth he would seek always to do that for which God had deemed him worthy to be saved.

He felt holy as he thought this, and high-minded as he put it in his prayers, but he knew himself: he had failed before. It was easy to make a promise for eternity, but he lived day to day. The child was heavy. Soon she would be hungry. He gathered her up in the blanket and trudged away down the street again, back to Italo's house.

eighteen

THROUGH THE HEAT of the summer the city lay helpless under the Death. There was nothing to eat, no wine, no cider, no beer; the riverbanks were deserted, the marketplaces empty. In the streets even the wild dogs shunned one another.

Two days after Everard got a loaf of bread at Ferrière's bakery, he went there again, but there was no answer to his knock. He found another baker, three streets away, who for a halfpenny would pass a loaf through a hole in the door. The death-carts came to the street and took more bodies from Rogier's cobbler shop and from Blisane's; when no one answered at the baker's, they broke the door in and brought out all that were there. They had been dead for days; they were stiff as flagpoles.

Every time he saw a death-cart, he looked into it, searching for Italo among the gray strewn corpses.

Walking past Bonboisson's deserted house, he heard chickens cackling, and got in through a shattered window. Elisabetta's flock had made a roost of the hall. In the back he found a cask of wine, and thereafter he and Sylviane ate eggs and drank wine with their bread.

She cried still for her mother. Every night, he held her by the hearth and rocked her until she cried herself to sleep, and he held her not only for her comfort, but for his. Yet there were times when he despaired of keeping her. It was hard enough to feed himself, and she was a constant trial, clinging to him, crying, demanding what he could not give her, waking him out of his sleep, sleeping when he wanted her awake.

Sometimes he thought of leaving her at the Hôtel-Dieu, on the Island, where the nuns fed the poor and took in orphans, but when he thought of Elisabetta he was ashamed. He reminded himself that she had given this child to him, not to the nuns. God had given this child to him. And the corpses were everywhere, the dead were everywhere, in the carts, in the silent houses around him, where he imagined the

Death sat down to table and dined on the bodies of his neighbors, but the child was alive, warm and wild and alive. He needed her. As the days went by, as he cared for her day after day, he loved her.

The death-carts rolled along the streets, gathering in their harvest. North of the river, they took the bodies back to the great cemetery of Saints-Innocents, but south of the river they bore them off outside the line of the ancient wall, into the fields, and threw them into a pit there and scattered earth and quicklime over them. Once or twice a day, a priest came out and blessed the whole place at once.

The stench of this mass grave was unspeakable. Yet Everard had gone there; he had seen the new bodies piled on the old, the old piled on the bones. Around the edge the wildflowers grew, nodding marguerites, yellow and white, and little blue angel's-eyes.

He stood there, before this community of the dead, and wondered how many were left alive in Paris. There seemed to be acres of dead bodies here. Yet in the city more died every day; he saw the carts roll by piled so deep with corpses that they had to rope them on.

He did not know why he had come here, but he felt guilty at leaving them, as if he deserted them, going back into life. That night, for the first time, he wept when Sylviane wept; the awful smell of the mass grave made him sick for days afterward.

He took Sylviane with him when he walked across the Great Street to the rue du Fouarre.

What he expected to find, he did not know. Surely there would be no scholars in the Studium, and there were none; the White Rose was shut up, with no sign of Mother or her drunkard husband or the serving girls, and the doors of the lecture halls were boarded. He went up to the house where Master Humbert van Ecke had denied him, and that house too was dark and deserted.

He knocked on the door anyway, a little wistfully, as if some spirit of learning might come out and make him welcome. No one answered. With Sylviane dozing on his shoulder, he turned away.

"Ho."

He wheeled. There above him, in the second story, a window opened.

"Who is there?"

It was Angulanus himself. His bald head poked out the window into the sunlight. Everard backed up to show him his face.

"It is I, Master — you may not remember me, I came to you last year."

The old man rested his arms on the windowsill and frowned down at him. "Yes, I remember you — Atticanus." The old man's eyebrows wriggled up and down. "Come in."

Everard went through the door. The child was heavy on his shoulder. Inside the dark house, he stood a moment, his nose itching from the dank moldy air; the dim ramshackle hall around him was full of trash. He could hear the rats scurrying and nibbling in the shadows. Remembering his way up the stairs, he climbed to the next story and found the room where the old man sat, surrounded by his books.

"So," said the old man, speaking Latin. "What brings you here? Is this your child?"

"Yes," said Everard, to avoid long explanations. He sat down on a stool, looking around him longingly at the books piled on every shelf and table. Sylviane slept in his arms. "Is this again the wrong season to come asking you to teach me?"

The old man smiled at him. "There are no fruitful seasons left to any of us, boy. No reason to teach anyone anything."

"Why are you still here, then?"

"I am working," said Humbertus, and laid his hand down flat on the paper on his desk, half-covered with writing.

"If there's no reason to teach there's no reason to write," Everard said. "I need to learn, Master — I have to make some sense of this. There must be questions that have answers. I need to know what they are."

The old man said, "What questions matter in such an hour as this?"

"I need — I want —" He cast his hands upward. "Why has God done this to us? Or is that a question without answer too?"

Humbertus stared at him from beneath his thick gray eyebrows, and suddenly he began to laugh. He shook his head.

"Boy, He has struck at us because we deserve it — you and I deserve it, because we want to answer questions."

He slumped forward, his shoulders drooping. His long black scholar's gown was rusty with wear, frayed at the edges of the broad floppy sleeves. Lifting his hands, he pressed them to his face.

"All my life I have struggled for reason, for knowledge of the world, and so I drove God, the Unknowable, out of the world. I put Him up in the sky somewhere, up safe out of my way, that I could loose the power of my reason.

"But without faith to guide me, my reason leads me in circles."

The old man covered his face with his hands. Everard licked his lips, unnerved at the old man's despair. Humbertus raised his head from his hands, his face gaunt with anguish.

"It is useless to multiply the entities, so the Inceptor said, yet the entities do nonetheless multiply. There must be a reason for everything, he said. Faith is not enough. Therefore God sends me a Hell of reason. I can stuff my head with knowledge, but without the eyes of faith I see nothing, I am blind, and the entities are everywhere, they feed on my doubt, the more I question the thicker they swarm around me, taunting me, they poke and prod and gibber in my ears, my eyes start, my skin crawls, every single hair erects itself, while my reason, useless in the dark, cries, 'What? What? Nothing is there!' "

He turned his head away. Everard sat still a moment, and then his hand gathered into a fist on his knee.

"You, too — even you tell me not to ask questions."

Humbertus lifted his head and stared at him, and his face was smoother, his body loose, eased for a moment of the suffering of his thinking. "No. I will never tell you that. I do not believe that. We must seek knowledge. We must struggle to understand. Faith by itself is unacceptable. God did not make us men that we might refuse to think. There must be system in the cosmos. It is our purpose to discover it."

He lifted one hand and let it fall.

"Yet the system mocks me. Behind each order lies a greater disorder. Each answer only leads to more questions. And with God expelled from the world, the world itself is withering up, dying like a plant uprooted from its nurturing soil."

"Is the plague then God's punishment on us?"

"The plague is the absence of God. It is not real — it is the absence of reality, it is nothingness, the seed of nothing in each of us which grows and grows in the space that we should keep filled with faith in God — grows and grows until there is nothing left but despair, and doubt, and meaninglessness."

Sylviane woke; she lifted her head, damp blonde curls sticking to her cheek, saw the old man, and scrambled to sit up. Master Humbertus looked her over.

"You should take her out of Paris. Here she will surely sicken and die. Find someplace, somewhere, beyond the reason of men, where God still dwells in His creation, where the world is still whole, and there, perhaps, you might live on. But not here."

"The plague has already assaulted her," Everard said. "She lived. So did I."

The old man's face sagged. His eyes blinked, as if at a sudden invasion of light. He leaned toward Everard. "You lived!"

"The child's mother died. If any of us deserved life, it was she, who championed us against the Death itself. Therefore God is not sparing us for the sake of our goodness, or slaying us for asking questions, since He took her who was good, and spared me, who questions all."

Humbertus said, "You lived!" He reached out with both hands and gripped Everard by the sleeves, and a broad smile broke across his face like the sun rising. "You lived!"

Everard said, "God saved me for some reason. I believe that — I refuse to believe it was an accident."

The old man drew his hands back, into his lap, and stared at him. "Tell me then who you are."

Everard told him, as sparely as he could, beginning with the night at Vaumartin when Isobel had goaded him into riding out to war; the old man listened keenly, although Sylviane scrambled noisily in and out of Everard's lap, and finally ran out to boom and shout on the stairs.

At the end, Everard said, "God favors me, then — isn't that what it means? That someday I shall return to Vaumartin?"

The old man's eyebrows jerked up and down. He said, "Perhaps." He turned, reaching into the stack of books on his paper-littered desk. "Or — perhaps — He has sent you here, to heal an old man's double-hearted soul." He held a book in his hands, and he stared deeply into Everard's face again. "Do you still wish my teachings?"

"Oh, yes."

"Then —" He set the book down on Everard's knee. "Take this book, which is Donatus's *Grammar*."

Everard reached for the book. "Are you giving it to me?"

Angulanus laughed. "Perhaps. You can copy it, if you wish. If you memorize it, you will have it with you in a more convenient way. Come back to me when you are finished and I shall lecture on it to you." He pushed at Sylviane, who had run in again and was trying to get down from Everard's lap. "Get her out of here." He spoke French now, as if the smaller creature required the lower language. "She'll dirty my books. Go on, go read that." He turned away, reaching for his pen. Everard, delighted, seized the book and caught the child up with his free arm.

"I have no money."

"Money is worthless." The old man leaned his arm on his desk. "Who knows how many may live through this terror? One at least shall carry learning and reason with him." He nodded at Everard. "You have already paid for this, I think. Come back when you have Donatus mastered."

Everard said. "I will. I'll work hard, I promise you."

Humbertus waved impatiently at him, and turned to his writing. Everard went away down the stairs.

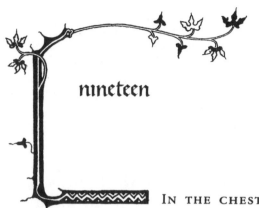

nineteen

IN THE CHEST in Elisabetta's bedroom, he found paper and ink and quills. Sitting at the table in the hall, he copied out Donatus's *Grammar,* while Sylviane whooped and scrambled around him.

She drove him nearly mad sometimes, interrupting him as he struggled with a particular construction, dragging his attention away from the flow of sense. Once, while he was deep in his book, she ran away out the door, and he gave up nearly a whole afternoon searching for her, desperate with worrying about her, hunting up and down through the whole quarter until he found her under the steps of the abandoned bakery. He whipped her then so hard that her screams brought a woman out of Rogier's cobbler shop down the street.

She said, "Ah, leave her be, the poor creature — leave her be — is there too little pain in the world for you, that you'd make more?"

So saying, she sat down on the step of the shop, under the sign of the shoe with the paint peeling off the toe and heel, and stared away into the empty street. Everard went toward her, Sylviane in his arms.

She said, "Has it passed by?"

"How many are left in your house?"

"Me. My old mother, the crone —" She laughed unsteadily, and raked her hand through her hair. "My daughter. At Pentecost there were eight of us. Has it passed by now? Is it over?"

He said, "No — no, I don't think so." The day before, on his way to buy the bread, he had seen three of the death-carts, high-piled with their harvest, in the rue Saint-Germain.

What he said seemed not to reach her. With her left hand she was smoothing her hair back from her face, stroking the hair back, over and over. Her gaze was fixed on the empty air. "Have you anything to eat?"

"There is bread at the baker's in the rue Probe. I have some eggs. Some wine."

She leaned forward over her knees and began to weep. He clutched the child tighter. The woman's grief frightened him; he had steeled himself against such giving way, guarding himself against pain, numbing himself, but her sobs cut through this armor. He could not go off and leave her, as if she did not matter. Timidly he moved closer to her and put out his hand to console her.

She wheeled toward him. What he had dreaded now occurred: she flung herself on him and clung to him, shaking with weeping, engulfing him in her sorrow. He sagged under her weight. Her tears dampened his shirt. The last of his reserve gave way. He began to weep. He thought of the dying, of the dead everywhere, and a huge hard mass in his chest rose and dissolved and rained from him in showers of tears. He clung to her as she clung to him, Sylviane between them crying also, until at last they were empty.

A little while later, as he labored over his book, Rogier's widow came to the back door, and he gave her some eggs, and she gave him half a cheese. After that they shared whatever food they had; they went to church together and to buy bread, and sometimes she watched Sylviane for him.

He read grammar, and Master Humbertus lectured to him and questioned him and seemed surprised at his understanding. It was simple enough to Everard. Next he studied rhetoric, copying out long passages from Cicero and Seneca; these exercises bored him, although they improved his Latin, and sometimes, as he walked home from the rue du Fouarre or as he searched through the deserted markets and the barricaded shops of Paris for a handful of beans or a flask of oil or a few turnips, pieces of what he had memorized floated unbidden into his mind, and he raged at Cicero, balancing words and phrases like a mountebank juggler while the whole world died. He raged often at Humbertus for making him study such irrelevance.

Yet he lived for those moments in the old man's room. Each book Humbertus gave to him he devoured, reading each passage over and over, because when each was mastered, he could go back across the Great Street to the rue du Fouarre. Face to face with Humbertus over a book, he forgot the plague, the famine, the loneliness, he even forgot Vaumartin: between them, they made a new world, with no misgrown corrupting past.

The old world still infected Humbertus. Once, lecturing on a speech of Cicero's, he flung the book down.

"Why has God set us down here and given us no power save to wonder at it? By the sweet wounds of Jesus Christ, the soulless cow in the field has a barn to come home to at night, and the gift to know the way, whether the cowherd come or no!"

Everard said, "God tests us, maybe." He looked out the window, down to the street, where Sylviane was chasing the birds.

"Ah, you think so," Angulanus said, and his head bowed again. "If He tests me, then, I am found wanting, boy. I have failed, because I have no strength left, I sit here, day after day, waiting for the Death to come for me, and there are times I wish it would hurry."

Everard said, "You should go out. You are too alone here. Come to my house — "

The old man grunted with laughter. His broad forehead furrowed up. "Yes? Come live with you, I suppose? You will be the father, and I the son? You'll tutor me in life, as I tutor you in books?" He laughed again, harsh, and turned away. "No. I'll stay here, boy. I am too old to go out now, too old and too afraid."

Everard could say nothing to him. Angulanus's despair touched off an answering fear in him. He turned his head again, seeking an antidote, and watched Sylviane trying to climb one of the great plane trees along the rue du Fouarre.

"Only a child can be happy now," the old man said. His voice was listless. He picked at his robe where it covered his knee. "Maybe to be happy ever you must be a child. So it was with the blessed Francis."

He lifted his head, seeing something not there any more. "I joined the Franciscans because of Francis," he said. "I heard stories of him, how he preached to the birds, how he talked to flowers. How he rejoiced in the sunlight, and lay down to sleep under no blanket but the moonlight. I was a boy on the verge of manhood. My beard was sprouting, my voice cracked, there was hair around my penis, my thoughts were violent and filthy. I thought the blessed Francis would cleanse me."

Everard said, "Why did you come here, then?"

"My order sent me here." Angulanus gave another hoarse laugh. "The priests and the monks, you know — they abhor Francis. As soon as he was dead and sainted, safely tucked away in Heaven, they made his teachings anathema. You cannot simply wander through the world, talking to flowers and birds, finding God everywhere, and letting Him care for you like a loving father. Oh, no. Such a life makes priests unnecessary. The Franciscans now must all obey the rules, live in monasteries, devote themselves to study of the proper kind and to prayer for souls, especially those souls rich enough to endow monasteries with gold and land and power."

He stretched, sighing, his shoulders moving under his black robe. "So I came here, and they seduced me with my own powers of reason, and I got drunk on reason, and I lost my faith, if I had it ever."

Everard was wondering how the old man sustained himself; he decided at once that when he came again he would bring Angulanus food and wine. He leaned forward, intense, wanting Angulanus to see how important he was to Everard.

"Were it not for you, Master, I would go mad. Your books, your lectures — even such talk as this — "

Angulanus turned toward him, bending toward him, his face so soft and full of yearning that he seemed abruptly to be that child he had spoken of. He gripped Everard's hand, and he said, "Help me."

"Master, I — "

Then Sylviane burst into the room, smelly, dirty, noisy, hopping on one foot. "Papa, Papa!" She hopped toward Everard, holding up the other foot, the sole blackened; she had a splinter. He drew her into his lap, gave Angulanus an apologetic glance, and with his belt knife worried out the ragged bit of wood.

"Papa." She flung her arms around his neck, half choking him, and climbed down, and in an avalanche of noise she rushed away again.

The old man was frowning at her. His hands were drawn back into his sleeves. The moment had passed. Everard wondered what he had meant, what help he needed.

He did not ask; Humbertus had withdrawn into his dignity again, was poking through his books again, muttering to himself. Brisk, distant, he wheeled around and dumped another heap of books in Everard's lap.

"Here, Everard. The old logic. *Categoriae, De interpretatione, Isagoge.* Go. Come back when you have read them."

On Assumption Day there was a procession from Notre Dame to the monastery of Sainte-Geneviève, to ask God to deliver Paris from the Death. The bishop himself led it, although he was an old man and feeble in his limbs. Some of his canons supported him. After him came the monks of Saint-Denis, carrying before them a golden reliquary with their most precious possession, the Blessed Virgin's own tears in a vial of crystal. The monks of other houses joined the procession, each with a prized relic or statue. The ordinary men and women followed.

They made a pitiful little straggle of a parade, winding through an empty city. A few chanted. Most had no heart for that, but trudged along in silence, with bowed heads. Many of the penitents went down on their knees, and crept along over the stony ground, leaving streaks of blood to mark their way. Others struck themselves again and again with their fists until their faces were as black with bruises as any plague victim's.

What good this did was hard to tell. On the way back from the procession, many of them fell down and died, and the death-carts came along and lugged them off to the mass grave.

Everard wondered sometimes if the plague had reached to Vaumartin. He thought of Vaumartin as an island in a flood, raised like Ararat above the sickly humors of the world. In Vaumartin there was no death.

Often, after their supper when he held her on his lap to help her go to sleep, he told Sylviane about Vaumartin, as if it were an old tale. Someday he would take her to a great castle, and there they would be happy, with plenty to eat, and people around them to wait on them. He told her about the wonderful clothes she would have, remembering Isobel's clothes, the long silk gowns, the headdresses.

What she understood of that he did not know. She was learning how to talk. He spoke to her sometimes in Latin, and she learned a little of the high tongue also.

He thought all this no harm, but then one day as he was getting her dressed to go to Mass, she looked into his face and said, "Go Vartin?"

He laughed, startled. "No, not today." She sighed, her face drooping, so downcast he decided not to tell her any more.

To Humbertus he told everything. They had plunged together into the study of Aristotle's Logic. Nearly every day, in Angulanus's office, they sat nose to nose and went at each other from the opposite sides of an argument.

They began with the usual exercises of the schools, the nature of angels, whether the saints saw God, whether Adam and Eve had sex in Eden before the Fall. Everard enjoyed even these practices. The joust of words was like a wonderful game, like wrestling with an angel; the satisfaction of composing a perfect argument elated him.

What he loved best was when Angulanus shut the book and they talked of what was going on around them.

This the old man did more and more often, as the summer waned. One day in the early fall, around the feast day of Saint Francis's Stigmata, he show Everard a letter from the canon of Notre Dame, asking him for his opinion on the question whether the Jews had brought the Death on Christendom by poisoning the wells.

Everard said, "If the Jews were poisoning the wells, then the plague would strike only where there were Jews. Yet I have heard of the plague in Cathay, and whole monasteries are full of dead men."

"Jews have feet," said Angulanus, "and can climb even monastery walls. Indeed, they are merchants, and peddlers, and so are often in monasteries, especially rich ones."

Everard touched his chin, where his beard was growing long at last. "Do they poison themselves, then? Because I have been to the Juiverie, and they are dying there also. There is no profit for them to destroy the whole world if they themselves perish."

"For the sake of the hatred they bear us, which, if you have been in Juiverie, you will have noticed: they despise us."

Everard straightened. "Yet they have lived among us for generations, and have not done it before." He paused, seeing the weakness in these negative arguments. Angulanus smiled at him.

"You begin convinced they are innocent."

"Yes." Everard nodded at him. "The Bible is the work of Jews. In it is no poisoning of wells. Rather, the Bible is itself a well of knowledge, and from it we have drawn forth the waters of truth that nourish us. If there were poison in the Jews, it would have rotted us long ago." He shook his head, pointing to the letter. "No, in this, Master, there is a simple violation of Ockham's Razor. To charge the Jews is to admit an unnecessary entity. The plague comes from God. It is punishment on us for our sins. There is no need to argue deeper than that."

Angulanus was fingering his beard. "Does every act of reason begin with an act of faith?"

"Shall I argue this, Master?"

The old man smiled at him. "You just have." He took the letter and carefully folded it. He twisted suddenly to look out of his window. "See, now, the daylight is fading. The fall of the year is on us. Let us share the bread you've brought, before you have to go." He reached for the basket of bread that Everard had brought with him, took out the loaf, and cut it in half.

Everard said, "How did you get this letter? Did you have any other news?"

"They say William of Ockham is dead, in Germany, and also the men who condemned him to the pope. Like a blast of God's breath the plague scours the world of good and evil both."

Humbertus broke the loaf in half and set one half before Everard. "Your child is properly fed?"

"I left her with my neighbor."

Humbertus said, "The king is not well." Chewing, he leaned his elbow on the desk and stared at Everard. "Not with the plague, he is not to die so fast as that. But he is dying."

"How did you learn this?" Everard said.

"I went this morning up to Notre Dame, and there met with the bishop and other men." He waved his piece of bread at Everard. "That surprises you, that I left the house."

"Yes," Everard said. "It does. You were afraid, before."

"Many things would surprise you," said the old man. "Eat."

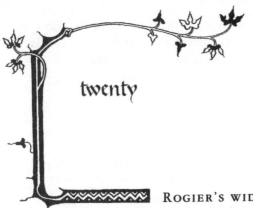

twenty

ROGIER'S WIDOW SAID, "You've heard that
the queen is dead of the plague? And the duchess of Normandy?"

Everard wrapped another egg in straw and fit it into the basket.
"Where did you hear that?"

She laughed. "Do you think Paris has stopped gossiping, just
because the Death is killing everybody? When a Parisian dies, his
tongue is the last thing to stop moving." Leaning her folded arms on
the table, she watched him cut the loaf of bread in half. "Where are you
taking all this food? To that old man? What a waste."

"He is my master," Everard said. "Will you keep Sylviane by you
today, while I go over there?"

"She is a hellion," said Rogier's widow. "As soon as I turn my back
she runs off. I'll lock her in the cellar one of these days."

"I'll take her with me," Everard said.

"The duchess of Normandy!" The cobbler's widow shook her head.
With one hand she propped up her chin. "The daughter of an
emperor, Everard, dug into the earth like an old bone." The abruptly
she sagged, she slumped, she buried her head in her arms and began
to cry.

"Now, come —" He went around the table to her, embarrassed; she
did this often, she came to him to cry with him. He put his arm around
her shoulder and gave her a little squeeze, as if pushing her into a
smaller space would stiffen her. "Come, now," he said, and held her,
and she turned her face against him and leaned on him and wept as if
she enjoyed it.

She left, after a while, consoled. He struggled against the shameful
sense of power that it gave him to console her. With the basket and
Sylviane, he went across the Great Street to the Studium, but when he
came to the house in the rue du Fouarre, Angulanus was not there.

That alarmed him. Angulanus had always been there whenever

Everard came. Lately he had been going out, exposing himself to trouble, to the Death.

The room was the same, full of books, smelling of ink. Everard left the basket on the floor inside the door and went down again to the street.

Sylviane whooped. Her face was smudged with dirt. Her bare legs churned. She ran ahead of him down toward the river, where the broad grassy bank met the water. Having nothing else to do, he let her lead him away through the meadows where the scholars used to play their games of ball; he watched her climb a tree, and stood with her on the pebble shore across the narrow water from the island, showing her how to skip flat stones on the water.

The great plane trees were blowing and bending in the wind. Daisies like little suns spangled the meadow. As he walked through the knee-high grass the swallows swooped around him, skimming the earth, veering in sudden twisting turns to soar up toward the broad blue sky. The plague touched these creatures not at all. Humankind died and rotted away while the whole wild world went on around them, untainted. For an instant, his mind low, he saw the race of men as a wound in the world, which the Death was healing over.

Sylviane, her arms wide, ran after the swallows, pretending to soar as they did. Her voice rose in a shrill wordless cry.

They crossed over the Great Street again, near the foot of the Little Bridge. Just beyond the second tower of the bridge's gatehouse, Everard paused, startled.

When he had first come to Paris the wide south bank, sloping down from the foot of a row of tall windblown trees to the river's edge, had been a string of fishmarkets and horsemarkets. Through the plague summer the deserted beach had grown up in weeds and grass and brambles. He had come here often with Sylvie, and had seldom seen another human being there. Now, as far as he could see, there were people.

On the river a boat drifted, the sailor trailing a fishing line over the stern. Where the water lapped along the stony fringe of the bank, there were baskets of laundry, and two women, their skirts tucked up, were stooped to float white bubbles of linen on the surface of the water. Three or four people were picking berries in the brambles; here and there someone led a horse down to the high grass.

He laughed, shaken, amazed. Long-striding, he went after Sylviane down to the margin of the river, and a new sound struck his ears.

Across the way, on an old stone bridge pier, there was a mill. Silent for months, today the great wooden wheel was lowered down into the bulge of the current, and its roaring voice carried bull-throated across the water.

He laughed. "Sylvie —" He ran to find her, where she waded after water striders and frogs. "Sylvie — Paris is alive again. Look!"

She cast a single indifferent glance at the mill, turned to look into his face, and hugged him. Whatever made him happy contented her. She planted a wet kiss on his cheek. Buoyant, he carried her away, up the river, to find Angulanus.

When he reached the rue du Fouarre again, the old man was sitting in the grass in front of the house, under a tree. Instead of his black scholar's gown he wore the brown robes of a Franciscan. Everard's steps slowed. He let Sylviane slide down from his arms to the ground.

"Master," he said, uncertainly.

The old man turned toward him. "Well, Everard," he said. "You are here to say goodbye to me."

Everard went down on one knee beside him. "Goodbye? What do you mean?" Sylviane stood a little way off, watching them, one finger in her mouth.

Angulanus turned toward him. "You recall I said one day that you would be the father and I the child, Everard. I said it then as a bitter ignorant jest. But it has come true. You have brought me forth into the world."

"Master —"

Angulanus reached out and grasped his hand. "I am going out to find God, Everard. To put myself in God's hands, as the blessed Francis did."

Everard let out a gasp. With both hands he held on to Humbertus, as if he could keep him there. "But — the city is coming alive again. I heard the mill turning. And there are people going about — " He saw Humbertus smile, and, desperate, he leaned toward him, pleading. "I'll go with you."

"No," Humbertus said. "Here you must stay. I have given you my teaching, and you must take it forward, into whatever it is that God means next for the world. I have never had such a student as you, Everard. Your mind has taken the system of logic as a sword takes its edge."

"You've only begun to teach me! I need you!" He thought of days without Angulanus, without the fierce discussions in the little room, and his spirit sank. "I have so many questions — will you leave me with no answers at all?"

"I have given you better than answers," said Humbertus. "I have shown you the power of logic to discover the answers for yourself. Come with me."

Everard followed him into the house and up to the little room, talking with every step.

"You must not go! How will you live?"

"God will care for me."

"Master — I need you still. You must tell me — help me — show me how I can recover Vaumartin — "

At the top of the stairs, Humbertus wheeled toward him, his face taut. "Hear me, Everard. I have given you the means to distinguish between the true and the false. Now, use it! This question of your old home of Vaumartin is false. What is true in your life is there before you — do not neglect it to chase after an illusion."

Everard jerked his head back, startled; he felt the old man had betrayed him somehow, and he turned his head away, struck to the heart. Humbertus went on into his room.

"Come here!"

Swallowing, Everard followed him.

"These are yours," Humbertus said.

He stood beside his desk, and on the desk were two piles of books.

A low half-worded cry escaped from Everard. He went toward the books, his hands out. Humbertus smiled at him, and took him by the wrist and laid his palm on the first pile.

"These books are sound and healthy — Donatus, Aristotle, Euclid. Keep these on your shelf. But these —"

He shifted Everard's hand to the other pile, smaller.

"These books are full of wasps and biting flies, Everard. Keep these books somewhere out of sight." In spite of what he said, he stroked the worn cover of the top book with his fingers in a kind of caress. "Here is Bacon, and Grosseteste, and that sweet devil Eriugena, who began it all. These books will lead you to the stake, if you let them."

"Master, you must not go," Everard said. "If you will not stay for my sake, there are other students — the Studium will open again —"

"The Studium," said the old man, with contempt. He went by Everard to shut the door, and turned, his eyes fierce. "The Studium is a grave of the mind. Take what you need from it, but do not expect to make a home of it. I have a note — " From the desk he took a piece of paper. "Show this to the rector, and they will admit you. There will be many a young master eager for a new student, especially one such as you. Find one who looks you in the eyes."

"Where are you going?" Everard said.

"To find God," said Humbertus.

He sat down on his stool, his hands tucked between his knees, and stared at Everard.

"I could not go, before. My own reason weighted me down and kept me here. Now I have passed my need for reason on to you, and I am free to seek faith. Now, do not argue with me, but heed me."

Everard licked his lips. He longed to reach out and seize the old man, to hold him there, but he saw by Humbertus's face it was no use, and his arms fell to his sides.

He said, "I owe you so much, Master."

"You will repay me," said Humbertus, "if you go forth into your life, and keep your eyes turned forward, and do not look too much behind you to the past, which is gone and dead. Speak the truth to every man, as straightforwardly as you know. That takes more courage, sometimes, than to draw a sword and strike him, Everard.

"Yes," said Everard.

The old man's eye's were blazing. He stared into Everard's face a moment in silence, and then said, "Do not let the Studium seduce you as it did me, Everard. Keep faith."

"Yes," said Everard. His cheeks were stiff and oddly cold. Abruptly he realized he was crying.

"Everard, every man dies. What matters is not to try to escape death, but to live more of life."

"Yes," said Everard, and bowed his head, and wept.

"Goodbye."

"Wait — Master, I will walk with you — "

"No," Angulanus said. He went to the door and opened it.

"Just to the edge of the city — "

"No," Angulanus said, and went out.

"Master —"

On the stairs there was a last footstep. Everard stood up, staring at the door. A wave of terror swept over him: he was alone, alone.

He collected himself. Somewhere nearby Sylviane was singing. He took a step forward, after the old man, but Angulanus had told him not to follow. He sank down again on the stool.

After a moment, he turned to look at the piles of books beside him.

He had never owned a book before. He put out his hand and touched them. Now he owned an armload of books. A wealth of books, a dominion of books. As his hand stroked the plain wooden board that covered the top of one volume, his heart leapt. His. Angulanus had left him his books. He swelled with a sudden rising energy and will and happiness. Humbertus was gone but he had not gone: his center was here, his essence, his books. Swiftly he gathered them up into his arms.

There were too many to hold. He looked around him for something to carry them in.

The basket still stood on the desk. He snatched it up, but it was still full of food, and he had to take that home again: eggs and bread were too precious to cast away. He went into the back of the room, looking around him.

There in the back, hanging on a peg, was Angulanus's black scholar's gown.

He reached out and took it down, but he did not wrap the books in it. Instead, carefully, he slipped his arms into the sleeves, shrugged his shoulders into it, and drew it together in front of him. It fit him very well. He smoothed it down, his hands trembling.

In a corner he found a leather sack, probably made to carry books. Angulanus had not gone, he told himself. Angulanus was in Everard now. And in fact he felt a new energy, a new vigor in him. Calling to Sylviane, he slung the bag over his shoulder, took the note and the basket of food, and in his black scholar's gown, a scholar now, he strode out to the rue du Fouarre and went home.

twenty-one

JOSSERAN SAID, his back to her, "You should stay abed again today, all day."

"I cannot rise," she said, her voice flat.

"I am going out." He sat down on the edge of the bed, to let his servant put his shoes on. "We need meat. I shall take Richard and Simon and run the deer."

Since they had come back to Vaumartin, one jump ahead of the plague, he had shut everybody up in the castle and let no one in or out, save himself and the two others, to go hunting when the larders were empty. Thus far the plague had taken no one in castle Vaumartin.

The siege was wearying, nonetheless. Little by little Isobel had lost her color and her quickness; now she stayed in her bed nearly the whole day, every day, with her women to entertain her, reading and sewing and talking.

He stood up, still with his back to her. They had argued, the night before; she still had strength for that. He could not bring himself to look at her.

She said, with an edge in her voice, "Stay away from the village."

His head bobbed in a short nod. His servant brought him his leather jack, although the late summer's heat was already blazing in the sky beyond the window, and held out his dagger to him, which Josseran took and sheathed in his belt.

Isobel said, "What we talked of, last night —"

"Do not speak of it," he said. His voice grated, harsher than he meant it to be.

"You know I am right," she said. "Put it out of your mind."

He tramped away across the room to the door. "I am going," he said, and went out.

He took with him the boldest of his men-at-arms, as he always did, and with their bows and dogs they left the castle, riding wide around the village at the foot of the ridge. As they rode up the next hillside, he turned and looked back at the village, wondering what went on there.

It looked no different than it ever had, all the years he had lived here, a ring of huts around a common green, with the great wall of the ridge overshadowing it, the castle above it as if in another sphere. Thin spines of smoke rose up from three or four of the huts; the rest looked cold. Were those folk dead, then? He would not go there to find out, nor would he suffer anyone else to go there, and he turned in his saddle now and led his men on up through the scrubby hillside.

In the broken forest over the top of the hill, the dogs startled their first buck, a three-year-old whose horns were just budding, which led them in a wild chase down through the gorge of the river, bounding through fields of black boulders, the dogs yelling after it. Josseran, his bow ready in his hands, saw the white scut of its tail flash, and once when the buck paused on the high ground just ahead of him, he had an instant's broadside look at it, but he never loosed an arrow. The buck vanished into the dense trees where the river's ravine widened.

There, in a patch of meadow, they killed some hares. They worked their way north, through stands of oak and open grasslands, and started another deer, which they killed when the dogs trapped it against the rock-tumbled foot of a cliff.

While his men dressed the deer, Josseran went on foot down along the cliff's base, to where a spring bubbled up, and drank of the cold bitter water. He took off his shoes and put his feet into the pool.

His mind seethed against Isobel. Face to face with her while she screamed at him, he could think of nothing to say to her, but now a thousand evil words flooded into his mind; he imagined himself cutting her down with his tongue, as she sliced and bruised him with hers.

He knew he would never say these things to her. When they quarreled, he could either turn and walk away or he could strike her with his fist, but he could not wither her with the blast of his words, as she did to him.

In the clear cold pool, his feet looked ashy white, his ankles seemed broken where his legs entered the water. The wind came sighing through the tall trees around him, and then down the cliff wall beside him a little spray of pebbles bounced and rolled, splashing finally into the water.

He looked up, the hair standing on the back of his neck. The rock soared up away from him toward a little patch of blue sky. Whatever had sent the pebbles rolling had disappeared. In the world's youth, he knew, such places as this had harbored fairies, goblins, the daughters of the sunlight. One of those women, tall and slim and golden, might just now have run along the cliff face, and with her light foot dashed a cascade of stones down on his head. With a sudden passion of regret he longed to see her, to capture her, to embrace her; he yearned for the lost Eden of love.

His men called to him, and he put on his shoes and went back.

They rode around in a broad curve through meadow and forest, where the wild birds raised storms of song, and the small creatures fled to cover at their approach. In the early afternoon they spooked up another stag, this a huge old forest monarch, with a rack on him like two tree branches. All through the daylight they pursued him, seeing him ever on the next hillside, going up as they went down. Twice they lost him utterly, and Josseran sidetracked and backtracked with the dogs until he found the scent again. At last, in the twilight, the dogs dragged the stag down, and Josseran with a single arrow freed its spirit from its ripped and bleeding flesh.

The stag fought against dying, its wide eye bulging; even dead, its eye stared at him. His heart quaked with sudden pity for his magnificent victim, even as he gloated in his triumph over it.

With their prey they rode home again, exhausted, through the deepening gloom. They carried the two dressed carcasses slung between their horses on poles, and the hares hung from their saddlebows: everyone in castle Vaumartin would eat well this night. Swinging wide to avoid the village, they came into the plowed and planted ground where the serfs grew their crops.

Shoulder-high to the horses, the wheat stood heavy-headed, bearded like the mountain kings, the dry stalks singing in the night wind. With every gust the ripened seed scattered across the field, veils of blown wheat, showers of seed, a golden treasure thrown to no one. The time to harvest had gone past, and no one had come to cut down the stalks, to bind them, to thresh them; they who had planted in the spring were dead in the fall, and the results of their labor rode the rising evening wind and fell ungathered to the earth.

He wondered if any man would ever harvest wheat again, if ever again the world would be as it had been, before the Death came.

When he came into the courtyard of his castle, he knew at once that something was wrong, from the way the people turned to look at him. His first thought was of Isobel. Two steps at a time he went up the staircase to the room at the top of the tower.

She lay where he had left her, in the great bed, the curtains drawn back to let in some air, and her women around her. She was not dead; her head turned when he came in, and her hand moved on the coverlet, but she was still and pale.

He sank down on the bed beside her. "What is it?" Her hand was cold as the water of the fairy pool.

Her waiting woman said, "She miscarried. Right after you left, she lost a baby."

"A baby," he said, stupidly. His hand tightened on hers; he lifted her fingers to his lips. He had not even guessed she might be with child.

On the pillows her white face turned toward him. "You killed it," she said, her voice a murmur.

He let her hand go. "I did nothing."

"You killed it. With all this talk of Everard, of finding Everard again."

Her face rolled away from him. The woman bent over her, crooning to her. Josseran turned away.

Through the years of their marriage they had been often apart, and he had not wondered much why she did not bear children; he had thought it would happen, in God's time. Now it had happened, and God had blighted the fruit of her womb. He got up, his legs stiff and awkward as stilts, and crossed to the window.

The stars were coming out in the black cauldron of the sky. He leaned on the sill of the window. She was right, the child had died for Everard's sake. Their sin would be barren. No son of Josseran's would inherit Vaumartin.

For months now they had argued about Everard, until his very name lay like a naked sword between them. Looking out on the jagged ridges of the mountains, Josseran promised God that he would find his nephew, if he still lived, and make amends to him.

How he would do this was unclear to him, since around him now was Vaumartin, his castle and his name, and he could no more give that up than he could strip off his own flesh. He crossed himself. To

God he vowed again that he would seek out Everard, and he begged God not to let Everard die in the plague, not to let Everard die of any other evil, but to preserve his nephew, until Josseran reconciled himself with him.

Behind him in the great bed there was a low soft sound, like the wind through the seeding wheat, which was Isobel weeping. Josseran lowered his head down between his arms, down to the cold stone of Vaumartin.

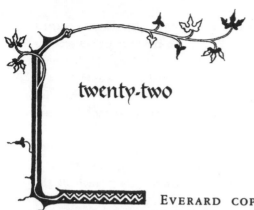

twenty-two

EVERARD COPIED PARTS of Humbertus's great volume of Aristotle and took the copy to his usual bookseller on the Little Bridge, who paid him a penny a page. The bookseller was pleased to see him. "Too mean to die, eh? Too tough for the Death to gobble." The bookseller himself had spent the past year in the country, sweating and praying. Now the plague was gone, and there were people in the city to buy books. Scholars at the Studium to rent them. He said, "What else can you get me, master? I have Aristotle already."

Everard thought of the other books, hidden away under the bed in Italo's house. "What else?"

"Odd books. You know, rare books. Hard-to-come-by books."

"You mean heresy," Everard said.

"Well — I didn't — "

Everard leaned on the bookseller's counter and stared into his eyes. "For such books as that — if I had them — I would expect a better price. Two pennies a page at least."

The bookseller harrumphed and grumped and pulled on his mustache. "Exactly which books are we talking about, now?"

"What are you interested in?"

Beneath the merchant's bushy eyebrows his eyes shifted, looking up and down the street; his thick lips pushed out as if he were kissing money. "Well — say — Ockham? Jandun?"

"What about Roger Bacon, or the Bishop of Lincoln?"

The bookseller's whole face sharpened, going lean and tight. "Bacon. I would pay twopence a page for the *Compendium*. Do you — " His voice dropped to a murmur. "Do you have Olivi?"

"Olivi. I don't think so." He had barely heard of the Joachimite John Peter Olivi.

"Well, copy me the Bacon, then. I have a certain buyer for the

Compendium." The bookseller slapped his counter. His face smoothed out again into its bland public mask. "Don't let the wrong eyes see you doing it, master."

With his smooth inkstained hands he arranged his volumes on the shelf. His stall was no more than three walls and a roof, propped up with stakes and rope; every night when he went home he took his shop away with him in a two-wheeled cart.

Down the way, at the foot of the bridge, a juggler with a monkey had drawn a little crowd. There was room on the bridge now for such antics. Before the Death, the shops had crowded every inch of the railings, so greedy for space they left scarcely enough room for traffic to squeeze through. Now two wagons abreast could cross the Little Bridge from the City Island to the Left Bank, and meet very little traffic coming the other way.

The bookseller leaned over the counter of his stall and shouted to his neighbor. Everard went back through the gate to the quartier Saint-Andri.

With the money he made copying books, he enrolled in the Studium, in the Picard nation, under a younger master who had studied with Humbertus, and who looked him in the eyes. Through the summer he struggled to amass money so that when the lecture halls opened in September he could give all his time over to study. The copying was more work than he had ever done, cramping his fingers, kinking his back as he bent over the desk, bedeviling his eyes.

Nonetheless, it was good work; he memorized things as he copied them, Bacon, Eriugena, Grosseteste, on whose ideas his mind soared as if on wings of grace.

Sylviane was a constant fret. Sometimes he tied her to the table by a long length of cord, so that she could move around without escaping him. Sometimes Rogier's widow would watch her for him, although she had more than enough to do now, running her dead husband's shop by herself, and when she lost her temper, she beat the child, which dismayed him.

"You should marry," the widow said to him one day.

He had come to trade her one of the chickens for the repair of his only shoes. She turned them over in her hands and shook her head.

"More holes than leather, Everard. You ought to get married. Find a wife to take care of you and Sylvie."

"How can I get married?" he said, and laughed.

"I am getting married," she said, calmly. "Blisane and I are getting married. We shall put our shops together." She put his shoes down and went back into the dark of the shop. The place smelled strongly of alum and leather. When she came back, she had another pair of shoes. "Here. These will fit you well enough, but I'll need two chickens."

"This hen and some eggs," he said. "I cannot give up more."

She shrugged. "You are lucky I care about you, Everard," she said, in an aggrieved voice.

"I know," he said. "I am very glad for it, mistress."

She laid the shoes down on the counter and accepted the hen with both hands. "You should marry Jeanne Bonboisson."

She gestured across the street, toward the house of the vintner, who had come back recently with his family, now that the Death was gone. Already they had replaced the broken glass in the windows and repainted the wineshop's sign with its wooden grapes. On feast days he saw them all together in the church, the vintner massive and slow-moving, his wife beside him, his children ranged around him, and his widowed sister.

This widowed sister was Jeanne Bonboisson. She was older than Everard, a plain woman, small and slightly made, with the spare dry look of a woman who had borne no children.

He reminded himself that he was Everard de Vaumartin. Through his veins coursed the finest blood in Brittany, the blood of counts and dukes, of ancient kings. It was an insult to his nobility to consider marrying a vintner's sister.

The Bonboissons knew none of that. The Bonboissons knew him only for a poor and nameless scholar, probably not good enough for them.

One Sunday at Mass he stood behind the Bonboissons, and all through the prayers he found his gaze straying again and again to the little widow. She was diligent in her prayers; even when the two giddy girls beside her laughed and waved to nearby friends so that the mother leaned around Jeanne to slap them, the vintner's sister ignored it, still as a stone in a rough current.

The back of her neck was white and tender. A tendril of dark hair had slipped from her coif in a wild curl. He brought his eyes forward again, ashamed of himself for spying on her.

"Dancing on a grave," said Mère Bonboisson. "That's what they're doing."

"Better to marry than to burn," Jeanne said. She was churning the butter, and her wrists hurt.

"God did not deliver us from the Death that we should make merry," her brother's wife said sharply. "I expected a more uplifted mind in you, Jeanne. You girls, mark what I tell you."

Her daughters murmured in agreement. Out of their mother's earshot, they giggled and gossiped around the cobblers' wedding, made jokes about old feet in new shoes, but they knew the face that Mère Bonboisson wanted hung on everything, and around her they were always very glum. Jeanne hauled the butter crank up and down, up and down. She had hoped, at first, that they would go to the wedding, that they would have a little gaiety at last, but now she saw her hopes dashed.

Her brother came in the door from the hall. "Jeanne, will you come, please?"

Jeanne straightened, her hand on her back. Mère Bonboisson said, "She has not done with the butter. What do you require? I shall do it, or one of the girls."

Bonboisson's mouth quirked in a humorless smile. "This you cannot do, mistress. Jeanne, come with me."

"The butter cannot wait," said Mère Bonboisson, but Jeanne was already leaving the churn, wiping her grimy hands on her apron. She went through the door ahead of her brother.

"Get one of the girls to do it," he said, behind her, and closed the door on his wife's objections.

Jeanne went into the hall. At the far end, by the hearth, a man was standing, and she paused, just inside the door, waiting for her brother to come. He swung the door shut behind him, and she followed him toward the hearth.

"Master Everard," he said, "this is my sister, Jeanne, who is, by God's will, a widow now. Jeanne, this man is Everard le Breton, who lives across the street from us, in the alchemist's house."

Puzzled, she said, "I am pleased to meet you, Master Everard."

He was no stranger to her; since she had come to live here, after the Death, she had seen him often in the street with his child. He was young, scarcely twenty, and his looks had much affected the Bonboisson daughters, who thought him very handsome. Jeanne was inclined to agree with them. She could not imagine what he had to do with her.

Bonboisson sat down heavily on the bench. "Master Everard has come to ask me for your hand in marriage, Jeanne."

"He has?" Suddenly her legs quivered. She sat down also on the bench.

"I am not a man of means —" Everard began, in what was obviously a prepared speech, but Bonboisson quieted him with a look.

To his sister, he said, "Since you are a widow, I am inclined to allow you your own will in this, Jeanne. I may tell you that Master Everard has informed me his property amounts almost to nothing, since the alchemist's house actually belongs to the child, and his prospects are very uncertain."

Jeanne clenched her hands together in her lap; her heart was pounding. She tore her gaze from the intense dark gaze of her suitor to look her brother in the face. "May I then speak to him myself?"

Bonboisson lifted his head up, frowning. "That seems forward and unwomanly to me."

"I cannot see how I am to have my will in this if I cannot speak with him myself." Jeanne twisted her hands together, the palms slippery with sweat.

"Very well," said Bonboisson. "Speak."

She turned to the young man, who was now staring into the fire, as if to separate himself from them. She said, "You should know, Master Everard, that I cannot bear children."

He turned toward her, the firelight on the side of his face. "God has already given me a child."

"The alchemist's child," Bonboisson said.

"She has no one but me, sir." He faced Jeanne again, his eyes direct; he had a very fierce look to him, like a fire burning in him, and a way of standing as if the world were his. "I am in my first year at the Studium, mistress. All I have to offer you is myself, my house, and my child."

"You are not a priest," she said.

"No, nor will make one, I promise you."

That made her smile, and he smiled also; yet he still seemed very serious. She had seen him with the child, laughing, carrying her about. That was why he wanted a wife: to care for him and the little girl while he plunged his nose into his books. She wondered, only for an instant, what he looked like without his clothes.

She stood up and held out her hand to him. "Thank you, Master Everard. I shall consider it."

"Thank you, mistress."

His hand closed on hers in a tight grip, as if he shook a man's hand. She murmured something and went back toward the kitchen, her hand tingling.

When she opened the door, the two daughters leapt back away from it; they had been listening at the latch. She came through the door and they sprang on her.

"What did he say? Wasn't that Everard?" The elder clutched at her sleeve; the younger clapped her hands together.

"Jeanne, why did he want to talk to you?"

"Girls, come sit," their mother called, from the sunny part of the kitchen, and they hovered a moment longer, their eyes wide and bright, before they hurried off under her wing again. Jeanne followed them into the sunlit area before the open door.

"Well," said Mère Bonboisson. "What was that about?"

Jeanne sat down on a stool. "The man from the alchemist's house has asked me to marry him."

The two girls screamed. Mère Bonboisson's mouth dropped open. Through the back of the kitchen came the vintner himself, solid, slow-moving, to fix Jeanne with a bitter look.

"That was more forward than I like to see my sister."

"I thought I was mannerly enough," she said.

The two girls fluttered and murmured together like little birds; now the elder, Marie, suddenly cried out, "Oh, Jeanne, how wonderful!"

Triumphant, the younger cried, "We'll have to go to this wedding!" and covered her mouth with her hand, her eyes popping.

Her mother wheeled around to fix them with a glare. To her husband, she said, "Is this the truth, Bonboisson?"

"All true," said Bonboisson. He frowned at Jeanne. "To speak to him like that — you cannot mean to consider this proposal seriously."

The girls were giggling and muttering together again. Mère Bonboisson leaned over and slapped the nearer of them.

"I have a widow's rights," Jeanne said. "You said so yourself. My property is mine —"

"God's word is very stern, that widows ought not to remarry." Bonboisson went striding off across the kitchen, his arms milling. "You should have refused him at once. Now he'll think he has a chance."

"Why then did you even call me out there?"

"To tell him no!"

Mère Bonboisson said, "Certainly she will tell him no." She did not bother to look at Jeanne; she reached for her tatting board. The two girls were struggling to keep their faces properly glum and pious, but their eyes shone.

Bonboisson stalked back across the kitchen. "What will you tell him?"

"I think," Jeanne said, "I should like to know more about him."

Mère Bonboisson said, "She will tell him no. A widow's duty is to her family. I need her here." Above the board her fingers looped and wound the white thread into lace. "After all we have done for her, she will remain here."

Jeanne crossed herself. Saint Paul had said that for a widow to remarry was a sort of adultery, but the Apostle had perhaps known nothing about sisters-in-law. "I should like my own home again."

Bonboisson loomed over her, his heavy-jowled face set in its perpetual frown, and looked from her to his wife. He must have seen how things went between them, or guessed. His hand fell on Jeanne's shoulder.

"I shall make inquiries of him."

"No good will come of this," Mère Bonboisson said crisply, shuttling the thread between her fingers. "No good." She nodded toward the churn. "Finish the butter, if you will."

Jeanne got up and went to the churn. Her back still hurt, but as she lifted the handle her gaze caught on the looks of her two nieces, vivid with secret delight, and she lowered her head to hide her excitement.

twenty-three

IN THE LATE SUMMER King Philip died, and Prince John became the king of France.

Everard took Sylviane to the City Island, to the great cathedral of Our Lady, to watch the new king crowned. The cathedral was magnificent, so set about with tall wax candles that the air itself seemed to shimmer. Sylviane and her father were crowded into the back, with the other ordinary people, but she perched up on his shoulder, her hands on his hair, and looked out over the heads of the vast mob toward the altar, as if she were looking into a golden box, and there, far far away, a tiny man knelt, while another tiny man, like a doll all dressed in gold, raised a hand over him to bless him.

Her father had told her that one of these men was the new king, and so she supposed the other must be God, the King of kings.

Afterward people sang in thunderous voices that rang through the cathedral; there were sermons, which she slept through. When she woke up, her father was carrying her through the crooked crowded streets of the Island to the courtyard of the royal palace. There, as the people crammed into the space before the gate, the king appeared before them at a window, and everyone cheered.

Then the king began to throw money into the crowd, and other people, wonderfully dressed, appeared on the wall and flung little sweetmeats down to the children. Sylviane escaped at once from her father and ran through the mob, whooping, chasing the little pasties and candies that sailed through the air and skittered over the pavement; she fought fist and foot and tooth for a piece of honeycomb, and thought King John the wonderfulest king in all the world.

She said so to her father, as they went back home. "I hope he is king forever."

Her father only grunted at her. He held her firmly by the hand, having spent most of the afternoon trying to catch her. His hands were smudged with ink. As she walked beside him, she looked up at him, hoping everyone else saw that they were together. When she grew up she meant to marry him. He was very handsome, her father, more handsome even than the king.

She told him that, too, and for a moment thought she had said the wrong thing, because he made a face, but then he scooped her up in his arms and held her tight to him, and she yielded herself to the complete grace of his love.

When they were in their own street, though, another man came up to her father and said, "Good afternoon, Master Everard. Our king is safely oiled, is he now?"

Her father stopped, and even took his cap off. "Good day to you, Master Bonboisson."

Sylviane clung to her father's hand and pressed against his leg, looking suspiciously around at this stranger. He was no real stranger, since he lived across the street from them, behind the wineshop, but he was old, and he never smiled. She pulled on Everard's arm.

"Come, Father."

Bonboisson frowned down at her. "This is the child?"

Her father picked her up; her father held her, safe in his arms, at eye level with the other man, and she put her arm around Everard's neck, to show how much she loved him. "Sylviane, say hello respectfully to this good man."

She did as he told her. Bonboisson made no answer; he said only, "I shall be sitting in my hall this day, Master Everard, and I would be pleased to see you there within the hour, if it is possible for you."

Everard stiffened. Sylviane felt the shock of his surprise all through her own body. He stammered something to the other man and, carrying her, strode swiftly toward their house, almost running. When they were alone in the hall she said, "What is it, Father?"

"Nothing. You go and play now. Here." He helped her take off her dress and her good stockings. "Stay close by, Sylvie. I am in no mood to go running after you again."

"Father — " Naked, she jumped up and down in the middle of the floor. "What's the matter?"

"Nothing, baby. Here." He had gotten her everyday stockings and smock from the cupboard, and helped her put them on. There were holes in the knees of the stockings, holes in the toes. He had promised her new ones at the beginning of the summer, but every time she asked for them, he reminded her of the loaf of bread she had thieved from the cupboard, as if a loaf of bread could have been spun out into a new pair of stockings, had she only not eaten it up.

She watched his curly dark head before her, as he knelt before her, pulling the stockings up. She bent down and kissed the top of his head.

"Now," he said, "go and play."

He straightened, his face wild. His hands flew over his clothes, pulling at his coat, at his belt, at his hair. He had shaved his face earlier, for the king's sake; she thought he looked wonderful, like a knight in a tale, except he had no armor. What was he going to do? He seemed on fire with purpose. His coat had a hole at one elbow. She pointed this out to him, and he flung his hands up.

"I can't sew," he said to her, like an admission of sin. "Now, go out and play. I will call you in later for supper."

"But where are you going?"

"Just over to Bonboisson's house, you heard him. Now go!"

He chased her out, which alarmed her, and she hid behind the corner of the house and watched him stride forth, stiff and straight, toward the house across the street. She wanted to follow, to spy on him, but she didn't dare; instead, she crept under the step, curled up in the dusty warm darkness there, and waited until he should come home again.

As she waited in the dark, she told herself again the story he had told her long ago, about the great castle where they would go one day, and have servants to wait on them, and wonderful things to eat, and beautiful clothes: the castle Vartin, half the way to Heaven.

Bonboisson poured a young red wine into two of the three cups on the tray. He said, "This came up the river a few weeks ago from Burgundy. It is a little unfinished yet, but will serve." He held out one of the cups to Everard, who feared spilling it and took the cup in both uncertain hands.

Solemnly each man lifted his cup. Everard, who could seldom afford to drink wine, took a deep swallow, felt the warmth and well-being of the wine course through him, and began to relax a little.

After his first meeting with Bonboisson, he had expected no more. The vintner had made it clear that he thought Everard no fit match for his sister, and the sister herself had seemed cool to it. Yet now Everard was sitting in Bonboisson's hall, sharing wine with him, waiting for the sister to appear.

Bonboisson said, "I should lay up a wine like this for a month at least, perhaps more, depending on how much I can acquire of it. The flavors are all at odds now — it needs to blend." He set down the cup, empty. "I have made inquiries of you, Master Everard."

Everard cleared his throat, although he had nothing to say.

"All say you are constant, because you are still here, which the women seem to make a deal of. Your manner is pleasing, another advantage with the women. Tell me what you plan to do, when you have done with the Studium."

Everard gripped his winecup like a shield before him. "I — Master Bonboisson, in faith I must tell you I have worked hard and long merely to be able to study. What happens afterward — "

Bonboisson reached for the jug of wine. "What faculty do you intend to study under?"

"The faculty of arts, sir."

"Grammar and arithmetic? Logic? Then when you have your license will you teach other scholars?"

"I —"

"In my trade I need men around me who can read and figure. More, I need men — men I can trust — who know the laws."

Everard said nothing. Everything about Bonboisson was heavy, solid, and certain, allowing no questions. Then the door at the far end of the hall opened, and Jeanne came in. He stood.

Small in her plain gray gown, her hair hidden under a white coif, she came up to the hearth, and she put out her hand to him, as she had the first time. She said, "Welcome, Master Everard."

Bonboisson had risen when Everard did. He motioned his sister to the stool beside him, and said, in a sour voice, "Now I suppose you will speak for yourself again, Jeanne."

She bowed her head a little, and said, "It is your part to speak for me, brother."

Bonboisson grunted. Everard guessed that much had gone on between them over this, and he eyed the woman again, covertly, wondering if she was contentious — suddenly he imagined how a contentious woman might roil up his life, and his nerves fluttered, panicked.

The vintner was saying, "We shall agree to this match between you and my sister, Master Everard, if we can come to some suitable arrangement of her property and your prospects."

Everard sank his head down between his shoulders. In his cup half the wine waited, undrunk, and he reached out his shaking hand carefully and set the cup down on the table. He said, "I am not a tradesman, sir."

"No, clearly, you are no tradesman. What you are is a great mystery to all of us. The purpose of marriage, you know, is to bring together two of like birth and circumstances, but no one knows anything of either your birth or your past circumstances, and that ignorance is itself a sign that something's amiss."

Everard stared at him a moment, hostile, and finally said, "I shall go now, sir, if you please."

"No, no, no. I am not going to let you go, young man. You offered for my sister. I am merely placing your offer on practical grounds. Sit down."

Everard sat down.

"Times have changed. No man knows really what the balance is any more. Therefore, we shall take you as you are. You have skills of word and number that will be most useful to me. I propose this: that you marry my sister, who has property of her own, money, household goods, suchlike things. Sufficient dowry in any case that you will be able to finish your studies in comfort. When you are finished, you will take up work such as you and I agree will benefit us all. And you will study the Roman law."

Everard said, "The best faculty for Roman law is at the Studium of Orléans. I do not mean to leave Paris."

"You could study in Orléans for a few years. I have kindred there, who would take you in — "

Everard swallowed; his gaze slipped toward the woman sitting demurely on the bench, her eyes discreetly lowered, and he said, again, "I will not leave Paris. My home is here."

"My sister's portion," said the vintner, "amounts to the sum of one hundred sixty livres."

Everard stopped, stunned. The woman sat with her hands still in her lap; she had small hands, but he had marked before, when he shook her hand, that they were strong and rough from work. One hundred sixty livres was an enormous sum of money to him.

He stiffened himself against the pull of all this money; he faced the vintner again, and again he said, "I will not leave Paris."

The merchant stared at him, his face unreadable. The silence stretched out long and taut between them. Everard waited, his gaze steady on the vintner's, and at last the older man moved, shifted his eyes, and said, "Well, then, perhaps we can let that part of it go."

Everard's muscles eased. He glanced again at the woman perched like a little bird on the bench. Bonboisson was talking again. "I have looked into the matter of your house, the title to which, incidentally, although not entirely without confusion, does seem to devolve on Italo del Borgo's child; since she is a minor and a female as well there will be no problem in transferring her rights to you."

"It's her house," Everard said stubbornly, but he was beginning to realize that they meant to make this match. He thought abruptly, idiotically, of Sylviane's stockings, of the holes he could not mend. There would be no more endless copying of books just to buy a loaf of bread. There would be someone to sew up the holes in his coat, someone to cook and clean, someone to watch the child when he went to school. There would be bacon and butter and wine.

"Well, then," said Bonboisson, "I suppose we are agreed."

Everard's belly fluttered with panic. He turned toward the table and reached for the cup of wine.

"Lady," he said, unsteadily, "will you drink with me?"

She lifted her face, calm, unknowable, alien to him. "If it please you, Master Everard."

They waited only long enough to publish the banns, and then they were married, in Saint-Andri's church, by the new priest, Father Pascal. The young priest, shy and inexpert, stumbled over the vows, and the serving boy had to prompt him. The whole of the quarter came to watch. When Everard led his new wife from the church, they sang, wound flower garlands around them, and danced them back home in their midst.

Just before they reached the house, a half-dozen knights on horseback galloped down the street, scattering everybody out of the way. Everard caught his new wife around the waist to lift her out of harm.

Thus, for an instant, she was in his arms; the weight and warmth of her body startled him. Looking down into her face, he saw the blush rising in her cheeks, and her eyes were bright. Her body was pliant in his grasp. She made no effort to pull away, and he bent his head and kissed her.

The folk around him hooted. Ashamed, he drew back, and she slipped away from him, but his lips still burned. When he kissed her, she had kissed him back, eagerly, passionately. His blood leapt.

Bonboisson had given three casks of wine to the wedding party, and by the custom, the new bride and groom had to sit in the hall and drink with their neighbors until the first cask was gone. Sylviane sat beside Everard, her face dark with anger; she gave only hard looks at the new wife, but Everard, his blood warming with the wine, with the closeness of this woman who was now his, hardly marked his little daughter. Then at last they went up to the bedroom.

On the threshold, Jeanne said, too brightly, "This is a very fine house — it seems not so roomy from the street." Her cheeks were pale. She was a little dry stick of a woman, but his mouth still remembered the warm exciting touch of hers. Still in a falsely cheery voice, she said, "Where did the alchemist make his gold?"

Everard laughed. He knew what sort of stories the quarter's rumor mills ground out about Italo, even now, with Italo long dead. "Italo made no gold. Italo made nothing real, only fraud and dreams. Except Sylvie."

His new wife sat down on the stool beside the bed. "Sylviane is very pretty. She does not like me, though, I fear."

"Is that so?" He looked at her sharply, surprised at that. "She and I have been alone here for years — she's only grown used to it that way." He saw her casting around for something else to say, and thought she wanted to put off what they had come here for. He said, "Lady, if you would prefer, I could sleep downstairs."

She lifted her face to him, her eyes wide; he remembered how she had insisted on speaking for herself when he first asked for her, and now she spoke for herself again; she said, "I did not marry you to sleep alone."

"Well," he said, livelier, eager, "well, then, I shall shut the window."

They lay together in the dark, and he said nothing to her, but afterward, in the dark, he said, "What would your other husband think of this?"

"Ah," she said, and stretched her arms over her head. "He would have wished it. He took all the joy he could of life, did my Antoine."

She told him a little more of Antoine, of their house in Orléans, of the wasting disease that took him from her, inch by inch, in the year before the plague came.

"Was he rich?" he asked.

"No, not rich. We had a quiet, hard-working life, very orderly. A well-made life."

"Ah," he said, and laughed, a ragged edge to his laughter. "A well-made life. That is just what I have not."

She wondered what he meant. She thought she should say something, to comfort him, perhaps, but she knew him too little. Suddenly he caught her to him again and kissed her hard.

"Good night, wife."

"Good night," she said, wondering.

twenty-four

"THE DEATH HAS DESTROYED the Studium," a tall scholar was bawling, as he sat perched on a bench in the White Rose, a winecup in his hand. "Where are the great masters — Ockham and Jandun, Angulanus and Riolus? Dead or scattered. Where are the scholars who made the universitas of Paris renowned throughout the world?" He shook his head sadly. "Gone, gone — all gone."

It was still only midafternoon, and the tavern's long low public room was only half full. Among the black-robed men and boys who sat around it one raised his voice in a jeer. "What's the matter, Tomas, won't they give you a hall for your lectures? Talk to your winecup, it'll hear you."

General laughter followed this jibe. Everard stood in the doorway a moment, getting his eyes used to the dim light.

He had not been in this room in three years. Every day for months now he had come by here, but always before the door had been boarded up. Now the door was busy, opening and shutting, like the mouths of the patrons. On the bench by the wall was a board of tables, and two scholars hunched over it; the sound of the dice rattled out. Two great tuns of wine, new broached, stood at the back, with stacks of cups.

There was no sign of Mother Rose. On long legs he strode across the room to the door in the back that led to the kitchen, and brushed by a wench coming out with a tray of savory puddings. Just as he stepped into the doorway a small red-faced man in a white apron blocked his way.

"And who are you?"

"I'm looking for Mother Rose," Everard said. In the kitchen he heard women's voices, but they sounded unfamiliar.

"Mother who?" The little man's voice was shrill with impatience. "I'm in a hurry here."

"The tavern keeper," Everard said. "Mother Rose."

"This is my tavern!" The red face flared with rage. "There's no Mother Rose here! Get out — go!"

Everard turned and went out. When at last he went back, the front of the tavern was painted yellow and red; the sign was a brimming golden cup hung out on chains above the street.

Yet it had not changed so much. The Picard nation still used it for a meeting place, and the same arguments still raged around it. In fact they still called it the White Rose, in spite of the new sign and the new paint. That pleased him inordinately, although he grieved for Mother Rose.

That night he said to his wife, "When I first came to Paris, she sustained me. We had an argument, I walked out, I never saw her again."

Jeanne lay beside him, thinking of saying, "Where did you come here from, Everard?" Instead she said, "God bless her for caring for you. No one knew anything of what happened to her?"

"No one there now has even heard of her." In the dark, his voice was dull. The mattress crunched. He said, "She promised me that one day I would be a scholar. When I was living in the street, she said this." He gave a low laugh. "She even said it might prove not to be what I wanted, either."

She said, a little alarmed, "Is it not then what you want, Everard?"

He said, in a rush, "I want more than this," and then was still awhile. She put out her hand and touched him, and he turned toward her, urgent, his hands on her arms, and his breath rasping in her ear.

"God promised me a cause when He saved me from the Death." He laughed, shakily, as if the words surprised him. "He did not let me live to mete out my days in old men's arguments." He rolled away from her again. "But I cannot find my Grail."

She said, "Everard, will you ever be content with anything?"

"I am content with you," he said, and turned to her again, softer now, his hands slipping down over her body and his lips brushing her ear. "My sweet Jeanne."

She turned her face toward him and kissed him. "Sometimes you have a gift of words, Everard." Yet his talk alarmed her: she could see that he was already chafing at the Studium.

For the first half of the year Everard studied astronomy and arithmetic, which he knew little of, but in the second half of the year he went to hear lectures in logic, where he had some grounding. Quickly he became impatient with the master, whose name was Claude de Brises.

He went to two lectures, and he saw how the other scholars tamely accepted de Brises's mixed terms and negative arguments. At the third lecture, when the moment came for the students to question the master, he stood up and said, "I cannot let your errors go by without challenge. Yet all your flaws stem from one simple failing: you do not understand the system of logic."

Then Everard taught the principles of logic for nearly an hour, facing de Brises as if he were his only listener, reciting long passages of Aristotle from memory. When he was done, the scholars leapt to their feet and broke into loud applause, and Claude de Brises fled out of the lecture hall so fast his black gown flew out behind him like a rook's tailfeathers.

Everard's own master heard of it and called him to his study. He was German; his name was Lorenz von Zweibrücken. Everard expected to be dealt with sharply, but Lorenz laughed when he saw him.

"Well, well," he said, "the white knight of the inkwell. How does it, Master Everard, or should it be Master Parsifal, hah? Come sit down, fellow student, you are obviously dangerous on your feet."

Everard came into the little room, which was so like Humbertus's office that it even smelled the same; he sat down on a stool.

"I am only doing my duty, Master Lorenz. Bad masters will destroy us all. De Brises knows no more of the *Organon* than I know of Hermes Trismegistus."

"Very true," said Lorenz. A broad red scar ran down his left cheek; by contrast his eyes were soft and kind, as if his real self peered around the edge of some mask. "However, he is the nephew of the bishop of Paris, and may someday be a cardinal, you know, and it's unwise to annoy such people."

"Maybe," Everard said. "I think he found it unwise to annoy such as me."

"Apparently," said Lorenz. "The universitas has summoned him to appear before them and be questioned concerning his fitness for his license, and my suspicion is they will take it away from him. Nonetheless I feel sure he will blame that not on his poor scholarship but on you, so beware."

Everard took that warning lightly, or rather, he took it as an honor.

His reputation had spread throughout the Studium, and now even men he had never met hailed him in the street. If he stopped by the White Rose, the other scholars lined up three deep to hear him argue. With Jeanne to mind his home and his child, he could study all he wished, do whatever he wanted.

Jeanne and Sylviane got along not at all. One day the wife bade him take the little girl away, so that she could have some peace, and he led the child to the playing fields along the bank of the Seine, where the scholars played ball.

Sylviane was still caught in her quarrel with Jeanne. "She hit me," she said, as they sat in the spring sun and watched the boys kicking the ball across the grass. "She hit me here and here."

"What did you do to deserve it?" Everard asked.

The little girl's face grew solemn; she pressed her lips together, staring away, thinking out what she had said. She had wound dandelions into her pale curly hair. Nearby, someone began to play a lute. The sun was lowering, the sky to the west streamed with color, and the breeze was chilly now; it was going to rain.

Sylviane said, "What happened to my real mother?"

Everard got up, feeling the sting of raindrops in the wind. "She died in the plague, with your real father and your brother and sister." He stooped to pick her up, and suddenly saw her face go white and stiff as a paper saint's.

She said, "Aren't you my real father?"

He lifted her; he cursed himself for being stupid. "No. I am not." The rain was falling now, hard, a sudden fury, and he gathered her up and ran up the slope, into the shelter of the trees.

She clung to him as he ran, but she turned her face away. When he set her down again, under the trees, among several other people who had fled the rain, she turned that same look on him again, that pale and shaken grief, and said, "You aren't my real father?"

"Sylvie —" He knelt before her, brushing the mud from her clothes. "Sylvie, I am your father now."

She did not believe it. Her face was stiff as the face of a little corpse. Her lips were bloodless. The other people around them were watching them curiously. Everard turned his shoulder to them; desperate, he took the child's cold limp hands.

"Do you want me for your father, Sylvie?"

She nodded, her lips trembling. Tears mounted in her eyes.

"And I want you for my daughter," he said. "We shall swear a vow to each other, and that will bind us to it. Here." He laid the two small cold hands palm against palm, and covered them with his own. "Say this after me. 'I, Sylviane, do swear to be your faithful daughter, in God's eyes and the eyes of men, to love whom you love, and hate whom

you hate, world without end, Amen.' "

She repeated it after him, and her face began to ease, her mouth softened, a little of the joy crept back into her look.

He said, "I, Everard, do swear to be your faithful father, in God's eyes and the eyes of men, to defend you and sustain you, world without end, Amen."

He bent and kissed her, and she put one arm around his neck. The rain had stopped. The sun was coming out, washed bright as new money. Around them the strangers were smiling and murmuring, amused at what they had witnessed. Everard picked his child up and carried her out into the day's last sunshine.

Still she was stiff in his arms. She kept a little space between them, and her eyes were full of worry. She turned to him again and said, "Does a vow last forever, really?"

"Oh, yes," said Everard. "If God records it." He looked around him for something to use as proof that God had heard.

"Did God record our vow, Father?"

"Yes," he said, and laughed, relieved, and pointed. "For see, there, in the sky, He gives us a token." In the east, above the windy trees, was a little bend of a rainbow.

Like the sky clearing after the storm her face cleared. She looked on the rainbow with shining eyes. She flung both arms around Everard's neck and hugged him. They went on toward the Great Street; as they crossed, winding through the hurrying throng, the child leaned out from his shoulder and called to the nearest folk, "See there? That's my rainbow!" and pointed into the sky. Everard boosted her up higher on his aching shoulder and bore her proudly home.

At night he lay with his wife, and after, sometimes, he talked to her as he never talked to her in the daylight.

"I see now why Humbertus left the Studium. They are cravens — God has given them the wonderful tool of logic, and yet they are afraid to use it! They go endlessly over and over the same ground, they are afraid to go out beyond what they already know, and what they know is safe."

He had told her about denouncing the lecturer de Brises in front of everyone, and now she began to worry. She said, "Is it not dangerous to know some things, Everard?"

"Yes, but more dangerous not to know. More dangerous to condemn books than to read them."

He went on like this, angry, fiery, and she lay listening to him, although she understood little of it, enjoying the sound of his voice. At night, naked together, they seemed to know each other much better than in the day.

In the day, he treated her with a grave courtesy. He gave her no orders, but let her do whatever she wished, with the house, with the garden, with the child Sylviane.

The little girl was wild as a witch, did nothing she was told, ran off whenever she cared to and came back filthy, told lies, swore, and kicked. Mère Bonboisson said to Jeanne, "You should beat the brat soundly, every time she does the least ill. Make her frightened of you! Otherwise she'll rule over you as she does over him."

The cobbler's wife said, "Some children are like soft wax that you can mold and shape in your hands. Some are like iron."

Jeanne saw no value in any of this advice, since she had no heart either to terrify the child or to shape her like wax. So the days passed, one battle after another.

"I hate you!" the little girl cried. "You don't belong here. You aren't one of us —"

"I am your father's wife," Jeanne said. "You must obey me, because I am your stepmother."

Sylviane's face twisted into a mask of perfect hatred. "Maybe you are now," she said, her teeth clenched, "but when we go to Vartin, then you will stay behind!"

Jeanne asked him later, in the dark, "What is Vartin?"

"Vartin," he said, his voice startled. "What does that mean?"

"Sylviane told me," she said, keeping her voice steady, "that when you go to Vartin, I will be left behind."

"Oh," he said, and was for a long time quiet.

She lay there, rigid beside him, waiting. They had just made love together, and between her thighs his jism was warm and sticky. At last he said, "During the plague, I told her — to comfort her — I said someday we would go away, to a better place. I did not think she would remember."

"Then there is no Vartin."

"No," he said.

His voice quivered. She knew he was lying. In the pit of her belly there was a sudden boil of distrust.

He said, "I will talk to her. She treats you ill — I see that — I am sorry for it, Jeanne. I'll tell her she must honor you."

"What good will your speaking to her do?" she said, roughly, panicked. "She obeys you no more than she does me."

"For love of me she will love you," he said.

"For love of you she hates me," cried the wife, and she rolled away from him, her face to the dark emptiness.

After a moment he said, "Jeanne," and his hand brushed her side.

"I am weary," she said. "Leave me alone."

His hand remained on her side a moment longer. She was rigid, resisting him, and after a little he drew back, rolled over, and went to sleep.

twenty-five

IN THE SPRING, the gossips told of a great
feast at King John's house of Saint-Ouen, outside Paris, where
the king announced a new order of chivalry, the Order of the Star. At
this feast, they said, the servants brought in great roasted swans, castles
made of cake, mounds of sweetmeats. In Paris, there was such a
shortage of bread that a single loaf cost threepence. There was no salt,
no meat, no fish. Bonboisson, going to buy wine at the riverbank,
came home night after night with his wallet still full; few boats were
coming down the Seine, and word was that a band of English outlaws
had barred the river somewhere to the east and let no one through
without a toll. What wine did reach Paris was so expensive there was
no profit to be made in it: the king's agents bought it all.

When the king feasted with his friends, his stewards had to send to
Burgundy for the grain, the gossips said, because there was no grain in
Paris. At the bakery in the rue Probe the ovens were cold. Jeanne went
over the bridges to the Halles, the market near the Place de Grève; she
walked all the way from the old empty fortress called the Louvre up to
the Temple quarter, looking for bread she could afford to buy, and
when she came home, her bag was empty.

The king bought the country called the Dauphiné, in Vienne to the
southeast, and gave it to his son Charles, his heir. In a glittering
ceremony in the holy chapel of the royal palace, the sickling boy
became the dauphin. Outside, the poor of Paris crowded the courtyard
and the streets, their hands out, crying for alms.

At supper Everard cut the loaf, and Jeanne spread butter thinly on
each slice. Sylviane bolted down her piece, and said, "I want more.
May I have more?"

Jeanne said, "There is no more. Not if we are to eat tomorrow."

Everard tore his piece of bread in two and gave half to the child, who took it greedily, without even thanking him. Jeanne said, "Husband, you must eat."

He said, "This is enough."

She saw how he nibbled at the bread, chewing long at little bites, to make it last; how he smiled at Sylviane as she licked crumbs from her fingers. The wife lowered her eyes, jealous of the child, ashamed of her jealousy.

With the price of food doubling and tripling every few months, the hundred sixty livres Jeanne had brought to the marriage was vanishing from its chest as if fairies came in the night and stole it. Everard began to copy his books again to sell. His master, Lorenz, gave him a student to tutor, the pimply third son of the count of Armagnac, who knew just enough Latin to cross himself, and whose first wish was that Everard take his examinations for him.

Jeanne went outside the city's ancient wall, where hardly one stone stood on top of another. In abandoned fields there she dug old turnips. From the butchers whose shambles stood on either side of the west-leading road, she bought bones and oxtails and hoofs, which she cooked into soup.

Everard showed her the tunnels under the house. She kept her hoardings there, in the cool, wrapped up well against the rats and the wet. One day, curious, she took a candle and went back a little, through the tunnel.

The gray limestone was cold and wet; the closeness oppressed her. Then in a little niche off to one side, she came on some bones.

She started from head to foot at the sight of them, and almost dropped the candle. The bones were plainly human, laid out as in a body, only slightly disturbed by the rats; some colorless strands of hair still clung to the skull. The arms were crossed over the arched cage of the ribs. She drew closer, her heart pounding, drawn by a gleam of reflected light, and saw there, hanging down between the bones, a little cross on a chain.

She signed herself. An overwhelming wave of pity rose in her, dizzying; she felt in her living flesh these same bones, in her life this same death. Quickly she went up again into the light and warmth of the house.

Later, in bed with her husband, after their joining had opened their hearts and minds to one another, she told him what she had found.

"Elisabetta," he said. "Sylviane's mother. She saved me — nursed me, in the plague, and died —" His voice thickened and stopped, clogged with his feelings.

"You took her down there?" A panic flutter worked along her nerves. "She should be properly buried —"

He turned toward her, his hands on her, his voice fierce in the dark. "In this house she was a champion. Here she belongs — not in the pits, with every other nameless, faceless body."

She kept silent. After a moment he kissed her, and lay back to sleep, but she lay unsleeping, thinking of the bones, of the spirit that had quickened them, whose house this was. A deep uneasiness filled her; she felt like a guest here, a temporary resident. All the long night through, she lay awake, a trespasser in her own bed.

In the morning, she went down into the tunnels under the house, to the niche where the bones lay.

She took a basket with her, one she used to carry her linens to the river. Kneeling down beside the bones, she said a prayer and crossed herself. Her candle burned a little round patch of light into the surrounding darkness. The only sound was a faint dripping of water, somewhere else in the tunnel.

That which lay beside her was the remnant of another woman; she should be buried safely in hallowed ground. Yet to touch her bones seemed beyond Jeanne's power; she could not bring herself to it. The thought of what she might disturb when she moved the bones turned her to a stone.

She must be buried. She could not go to Heaven unless she lay in Christian earth — would not rise again from the grave when King Jesus marched across the sky and called the righteous to eternal life. She crossed herself again, and with her heart hammering, she began to put the bones into the basket.

She took the feet first. The many little bones were light and cold; they clattered when she set them together in the basket, and her heart clenched, her throat stopped up, and she had to draw back and cross herself and shut her eyes and fill her mind up with prayers against her terror.

She could not stop now. If she had awakened some witness to this, let her good intentions shield her from it. She opened her eyes again, and put the leg bones and the pelvis and the arms into the basket. The arched ribs, the strange small bones of the spine. Twice she reached out for the skull and twice drew back her hands again, before she was brave enough to take that too. The little cross she put into her apron.

The priest of Saint-Andri lived in the house by the cherry tree, at the bend in the street. When, standing on his threshold, he saw the bones he drew back. "What am I to do with these?"

"Bury them," Jeanne said.

He frowned at her. "Where did you find them?"

She was afraid suddenly to tell him that Elisabetta had died in the Death; it might frighten him into turning her away. Desperate, she said, "Here. This was around her neck." She held out the little cross. "She was Christian. She must lie in holy earth. Please. I thought surely you would know what to do."

He took the cross and looked at it and kissed it, and gave her a piercing look. She waited, her breath stopped in her throat, and then he nodded at her.

"Well, come with me, woman."

All her muscles slackened with relief. She stooped and lifted the basket again, and followed him away around behind his house, where behind a little orchard a gate in the wall led to the back of the churchyard. They walked up through the graves there, the young priest walking ahead, Jeanne coming after with the basket of bones. The priest took her in through the side of the church.

A few old women knelt at the altar, their black shawls over their heads, and at the back a man swept the floor, stirring a veil of dust into the slanted sunlight that came through the windows. The priest took Jeanne around into the back of the church, opened a wooden door in the stone wall, and led her down a flight of steps.

He took no candle; only a little light followed them down the steps. The air was cold and still and smelled bitter. At the foot of the stair the priest stopped, and Jeanne stopped, unwilling to go farther.

She was in a little room, lined with shelves, and every shelf was piled high with bones. In the gloom she saw skulls and leg bones and ribs, jumbled together in no order, and she put down her basket and crossed herself.

"God have mercy on them." Her voice shook.

The priest smiled at her. "God already has. These are ancient martyrs, woman — they were here before the church was built."

She wanted to go, to get back to the sunlight, but she said, "Is this consecrated ground?"

"None more holy in Christendom. We are right under the altar." He pointed up. "Do you want your basket back?"

"No." She backed away, thankful, her duty done. "Will — should there be a Mass for her?"

"Was nothing done when she died?" the priest said.

"I don't think so," Jeanne said.

The priest was staring at her again. Did he think she had done evil? But he nodded.

"I will say a memorial Mass this evening. I will include her name, if you know it."

"Elisabetta."

"Elisabetta," he said, and waved her on ahead of him, up the stairs; she went eagerly up again, suddenly light as an angel, and walked home.

In the fall, heavy rains destroyed much of the harvest; brigands burned the rest. Around Martinmas, when the light was failing, and the winter and the dark closed down over Paris like the lid of Hell, there was no bread at all, not for any price.

Then Jeanne went down to the cave under the house and brought up turnips, and they ate bitter boiled turnips, day after day, and drank water.

Everard came home through a driving snowstorm and found Bonboisson sitting in his kitchen. The smell of mulled cider filled the air; Everard gulped down the sudden spring of water in his mouth.

His brother-in-law said, "Sit down, scholar, put this in your belly." He pushed a cup across the table toward Everard.

It was full of hot cider. Everard put it to his lips and drank and drank, the taste so rich and full it brought tears to his eyes. Bonboisson watched him narrowly.

"Some of us are going to the king tomorrow, to ask him to force down the prices," said the vintner. "I want you to go with us. The more there are of us, the more weight the petition may carry, and anyway you should begin to learn the business."

Everard sipped from his cup. He had been so long on poor food that the cider was overwhelming his bowels. He got up with a mumbled excuse and went out behind the house, to the ditch there, and in the driving snow squatted and emptied himself, and as he relieved his bowels he swore and spat into the snow. Clearly Bonboisson had not given up hope of using Everard in his business. Everard had no intention of learning Bonboisson's business.

In the early morning, with Bonboisson and his two sons, who

worked in his trade, Everard went down the street to the old quarter church, Saint-Andri, and said his prayers. He was supposed to be hearing a lecture on the *Interpretations* but instead he was going tamely after the vintner to beg for bread. His resentment underlay his every word and move; at the least annoyance his mood flared to a scorching rage.

Their prayers said, they went on to the Great Street and up to the Little Bridge onto the Island. There, in the street before the king's court, they came on a little group of men.

"God's greeting to you." Bonboisson shook all their hands, and introduced his sons and Everard. There were fewer of them than Everard had expected, and he saw now why Bonboisson had wanted him to come. One of them, a fat, balding man in a fine coat, was Etienne Marcel, whom even Everard had heard of, the richest man in Paris, draper to the king.

Marcel said, "Excellent to see you here, all of you, we shall need all we can muster for this." Still wringing Bonboisson's hand, he looked around him at the little group, the men standing very close together, like sheep in a storm. To Bonboisson, he said, "Few have answered the plea. I shall remember this of you, sir."

Now Everard saw hidden reasons for Bonboisson's enthusiasm, and he turned his back on them.

"What will you say to the king?" one of the others murmured.

"I have a letter," said Etienne Marcel. "I mean to ask him to enforce the just price of food and goods. There is nothing new in it, nothing strange; this has all been done before, he need only do what has been done before."

"Will it do any good, do you think?"

"I don't know. You can see how many folk think it will by the number who have come to swell our pleas. But people are starving! Starving!"

By the look of his fat jowls he had never missed his dinner. Everard drifted a few steps away. These people around him were strangers to him, foreigners as much as if they lived in another country. He hated the jingling of their purses, their corpulence, the somber color and full cut of their coats. Since the sumptuary laws forbade them the use of bright colors, they showed their wealth by the overuse of cloth, draped in great folds and loops and pads and skirts around their unnoble bodies. He felt himself bundled up in their way of life, choked with it, bound hand and foot by it.

He began to pace up and down, each time moving a little farther from these men. He was not one of them. What he was eluded him entirely. Behold the new man, resurrected from the Death. In the next year he would incept in the Studium, begin teaching, study for his master's license, and yet that too seemed like a narrowing tunnel before him. The great faculty of the Paris Studium was theology, but theology was only words to him, arguments without ground. He began to see why Ockham himself had never taken his master's, and what Humbertus had told him came again into his mind — that the Studium would never be a home to him.

Where was his home, then — that castle on the mountaintop, its towers piercing the sky, so lofty, so unattainable that the child's corrupted name for it seemed more fit than its own — castle Vartin?

He had walked away now, all down the high gray wall to the wooden gate that opened into the yard by the palace chapel. The day was somber, the sky low with gray clouds. The snow lay over everything, crusted and pitted and filthy. Behind him the little knot of merchants waited like servants to be admitted. Vendors of offal and swill. He could go on, slip around the corner of the wall, disappear into the city again.

"Everard!" Faintly his name sounded; down there in the mass of little brown men, one raised his arm. Everard's temper heated. Reluctantly he dragged his feet back to Bonboisson.

A disdainful porter finally led them through the court and into a long narrow room behind the royal chapel. The hearth was cold. On the sills of the narrow unglazed windows the snow lay in mounds scarred with bird tracks. A tapestry covered one end wall of the room; on it, in sets of three, the Nine Worthies stood inside strange vertical lines that widened at the top to form pointed arches. Moths had eaten one of the faces away.

Behind him a voice bawled, "All hail and honor His Grace the king of France, hail, hail, our most noble lord John!" Everard wheeled around.

The merchants dropped to their knees, and Everard went down on one knee. Nothing happened. They stared at the empty, open door.

Three pages rushed in, carrying cushions and a jug, and after them several men in green coats slashed with gold satin, medals and chains around their necks, bells on their shoes, who formed a double cordon leading from the door. The pages knelt down behind them. All eyes turned expectantly on the doorway; there was a perfect hush, so that

Everard could hear someone somewhere outside calling. A distant bell began to ring, and one by one others rang, all over Paris.

"Hail, the king!"

The courtiers all bent double in bows, their hands describing scrolls in the air. The pages clapped. Through the door the king strode.

He wore a close-fitting blue coat sewn with little silver lilies, and a soft flat velvet hat on his head. Around his neck on a chain of massive links dangled a huge star of gold. He smelled like rose water and mint. The gold sheath of the dagger on his belt glittered with red crystal. He stepped forward toward the merchants, looking down on them with such a haughty contempt that Everard knew at once their cause was hopeless, and said, "What brings you here, Marcel?"

The draper, on his knees, said, "Most puissant and excellent of kings, we have come here to beg you to help us in our extremity. All Paris suffers from the shortages of bread and wine, oil and salt, meat and fish." He held out a folded paper. "On our knees we implore you to force the prices down and to order those who are hoarding grain to put it up for sale, and to do what is possible to bring in supplies from the countryside."

The king gestured with his finger, and a page leapt forward to take the letter. John sniffed.

"You who live by profit, you who feed on the sweat of others, when you cannot get by with your wretched usuries, dare you come to me? You brought this on yourselves. Had you done honest toil you would have bread. Instead you chose to fatten up without work. Now suffer! The lion wins no glory heeding the whimpering of dogs. You sully me with your mere presence, I am demeaned even in listening to you. Get you gone!"

He turned; he was leaving. Everard's mouth fell open in astonishment. The merchants still crouched on their knees, accepting this, but he would not accept it, and he leapt up onto his feet, and his voice rang out.

"Sire, if Jesus Christ could wash the feet of sinners and glorify His godhead, surely you can hear the pleas of your humble subjects and add to your majesty thereby."

All heads swiveled toward him, faces white with shock. John wheeled around, glittering, well fed, royal.

"I am king here, you are nothing! The realm is mine, to do with as I wish, and you are less even than the dirt, since you will not work the land. Now, go!"

Everard stood fast; he said, "King you are, surely, and yet subject as we all are to the King of kings, who said, 'Whatsoever you do unto the least of these, ye do unto me.' "

He heard someone gasp an oath; a hand clutched at the hem of his coat. The king's face flushed purple. He turned and snatched Marcel's letter from the hand of the page.

"Words! See what I care about your words!" He ripped the letter into bits and flung them into the air, turned on his heel, and walked out. The pieces of the letter fluttered to the ground.

The merchants climbed up off their knees, their faces turned in horror on Everard. Bonboisson lunged at him.

"How dare you speak such insults to the king of France!"

Everard gathered his breath to reply, but there was nothing to be said, really. His brother-in-law snarled, "You wretch. Whatever chance we had to be heard, you have ruined it." He turned, his hand out toward Marcel.

"The man's a fool, sir, not of my family, really, a poor scholar we suffered to marry my widowed sister on hopes he would do some good in life —"

Everard brushed by him. His cheeks burned. The pages and courtiers had all left, and he went out after them, into the courtyard.

The sun had come out, and the sky was clear, a brilliant blue above the sharp angles of the castle roofline. Three horses in splendid harness stood near the wall, the steam rising from their flanks. A man in royal livery escorted the merchants to the gate.

Outside, in the street, the little band of men broke up. Bonboisson and his sons and Everard started down through the Island toward the Little Bridge. Bonboisson's cheeks were red, and his face seemed to bulge as if containing a growing fit of temper. He glared at Everard.

"The king! The king himself, anointed with sacred oil, descended from kings — the soul of France! You spoke to him as if — Don't they teach you how to behave in Brittany?"

Everard clamped his lips shut. He stared ahead of him, down the street, grooved with wagon ruts through the snow. Behind them, now, a voice called, "Ah, Bonboisson! Wait a moment — Master Bonboisson!"

Bonboisson and his sons stopped; Everard kept on, glad of a chance to separate himself from them. But the man who was chasing them went past Bonboisson, his shoes crunching in the snow, and came puffing with his effort up to Everard.

It was Marcel, the draper. He put out his hand.

"Well spoken, sir. Well spoken indeed."

He shook Everard's hand. Surprised, the scholar glanced from the draper's jowly face toward his brother-in-law, who had come up behind

him.

"Allow me to present my brother-in-law, Everard le Breton — a scholar at the Studium."

Marcel was smiling. He was some four or six inches shorter than Everard, square as a church tower. He said, "We did not get what we came for, but to see the king scolded warmed my heart, Master Everard, indeed." He wrung Everard's hand again, nodded to Bonboisson, and went away, back toward the bridge to the north bank.

Everard and the vintners went on in silence. Bonboisson still glared at him now and then, but Marcel had trussed his tongue. At the foot of the Little Bridge, Everard went off to the universitas, and the others took their own way. Away from them, he drew a deep breath, suddenly light enough to fly, and broke into a run to get to his lecture before it ended.

That night, he lay beside his wife, and said, "I looked down on those merchants because they were not noble — yet who was noble there, in that room? Not the king, with his arrogance and his weakness and failure. Marcel, it seemed to me, was nobler than the king — first that he championed us all, and then that his heart rejoiced to see a sort of battle done against our common enemy!"

His wife said, drowsily, "What is true nobility, then? Such a rare thing, you ought not to rage against its absence but merely rejoice when you do come on it."

For a while he was still, thinking over her words, and at last he said, "Wife, I knew a woman once, who if you stood in the same room with her, no one would even mark you there, so beautiful is she, and so exquisite in her bearing, and yet of the two, you are the noble, you who give yourself for the sake of others, while she — she — "

He bit his lip, his blood burning with a long-pent rage, lest he actually speak Isobel's name. Beside him, Jeanne stirred.

"Is she in Vartin, this woman?"

He said nothing, struggling with an onrush of memory that overwhelmed the dark room, the quiet bed, with a hatred that scalded his mind. In the end, he said, tight-throated, "There is no Vartin, Jeanne."

She said nothing at all to that. He thought she was asleep, and as the fury in his mind waned, he drowsed, but then, just before he fell asleep, the bed crunched, and she moved, and he knew that she had heard every word, and that she did not believe him.

He lay there a long while, tormented. If — when — he went back to Vaumartin, and claimed what was rightfully his, what would become of Jeanne? Neither servant nor noble, she had no place in Vaumartin, no work, no power, no value at all.

Yet how could he leave her? Gentle, undemanding, she had pledged herself to him; how could he abandon her? He rolled over, trying to put his back to her, but he could not shut her out, even to sleep; all the rest of the night, he lay awake, miserable.

Jeanne had longed for children, in her first marriage. She had watched every pregnant woman she saw with envy sour in her heart; her arms had hungered for the babies other women let cry without a care. Now she had a child, and it was a demon.

When she tried to hold Sylviane, the child wrenched angrily out of her arms. When she tried to brush her hair, Sylvie seized the brush from her and threw it into her face.

"My father will brush my hair!"

Everard did brush her hair, the child sitting dreamily on his knee, lulled by his touch. He helped her dress, sometimes. He read to her from his books; he got a piece of slate for her, and a bit of chalk, and taught her to form letters and numbers on the slate.

Jeanne said, "Why do you do that? What good will come of it?"

He said only, "It gives me pleasure. And her."

Then the wife bit her lip and clenched her fists and went furiously to her menial chores, to her household drudgery, while he sat with his arm around Sylviane and showed her worthless frivolous things.

When he was gone, she took the broom and put it into the child's hands and said, "Now, sweep."

Sylviane flung the broom down. "I will not."

Jeanne picked it up and again the child cast it down. Up and down went the broom, several more times, until the wife seized it and the child both and beat the child across the backside with the broomstaff.

Sylviane screamed. "I want my father!" Tears slobbered her face, red as a cooked crab. "Only my father can beat me!"

"He is not your father," Jeanne shouted; she too was weeping, from sheer rage. "He's just someone who was living here when your real father died — your real mother —"

"He is my father," Sylviane bellowed. "We swore a vow to one another, and God sent us the rainbow!" She crossed her arms over her chest and frowned triumphantly at Jeanne.

The wife sank down on the bench, her head to one side. Her temper faded; she saw that shouting and blows would bring them nowhere. This news of the vow intrigued her.

"Well, then," she said, "he swore a vow to me, too, and I to him, you know."

"I know," Sylviane said, reluctantly, and her arms slipped apart and went down straight at her sides. "But I didn't swear anything to you!"

Jeanne said, mildly, "Well, perhaps one day you will." She reached for the slate and the chalk, lying on the table beside her.

"Here," she said. "We'll play a game. What's this?" With lines and circles she made an image. Sylviane stared at her like an enemy, but when Jeanne drew little lines for a mane down the long stick neck of the figure, the child suddenly laughed.

"That's a horse!"

She laughed full into the wife's face, and Jeanne sat back and smiled at her, pleased; it was the first time they had done anything together but fight. At once Sylviane remembered, and frowned at her.

"It's my chalk. You can't play with my chalk."

Jeanne stiffened, closing her fist on the chalk, and hot words rose again to her tongue, but she mastered herself. She said, "Well, then, here it is." She put the chalk down; Sylviane snatched it at once, glaring at her. The wife bent for the broom. The child took her slate and chalk and went into her own room and shut the door.

twenty-six

"PROBABLY THIS IS NOT your Everard at all," said the Sire de Beaujeu; he was not the man whom Josseran had fought beside at Crécy and Calais, who had died in the plague, but his son. He was sitting in an upper-story room of his Paris house, while Josseran paced back and forth between the two windows.

"Nonetheless, the coincidence is very strong," Beaujeu went on, "since this Everard calls himself le Breton, is of the proper age, and is, as you described your kinsman to me, tall and dark as a raven. He's a scholar at the Studium, of a wide and slightly tangy repute, and he's giving his inception lecture in a few days, so you may view him without revealing yourself."

"Thank you," Josseran said. "I am in your debt for the trouble you have gone to, and the care you have shown for me."

"Little trouble at all — I overheard a bookseller say the name, and asked him a question or two — nothing more." Beaujeu stroked his beard. His father had been massive, gray, slow-moving, and great-hearted; the son was taller, going to fat, given to courtier's clothes, his chivalry unknown. "I am pleased to be able to place myself at your service. What do you think of Paris?"

Josseran swung toward the window again. He had not been to Paris since before the Death, and the city shocked him. Riding in along the rue Saint-Germain, he had passed whole neighborhoods of deserted houses, roofless ruins, burnt-out shells, overgrown gardens, the whole city like a rotting corpse, around which a few survivors crawled like ants.

"It's like a dried-up pod," he said. "They must have died here by the thousands."

"It was terrible indeed," said Beaujeu, and crossed himself. "I've heard tales that would wither your soul. And it's — " He scrubbed his hand over his face. "It's not over. Everything is different. The world may not be the same again."

"Not over ?" Josseran swung around. "Has the evil broken out here again? I thought — "

"No, no. It's only that so much has changed because of it. Is still changing. The plague's like a pebble dropped into a pond — long after the stone has sunk to the bottom, the ripples spread out wider and wider."

Josseran grunted. Beaujeu sounded like a priest on a street corner, thundering words of doom to draw himself a crowd. "When is this lecture, when I may see if this Everard is indeed my kinsman?" He stared out of the window, watching the steady trickle of passers-by; even after the ordeal of the plague, Paris was busy with people, alive with sights and sounds, and it drew him. He had been too long cooped up in his castle, afraid. He wanted to plunge in among other people, to spend himself in enjoyment.

"On Saint Monica's Day. Three days hence. You have not got your wife with you?"

"No," Josseran said. He refused to think of Isobel. Turning his back to the window, he faced the Sire de Beaujeu again. "Would you care to go out into the city with me? I'm of a mind for some entertainment."

"Excellent." Beaujeu reached for a bell, to call his servant. "We can get some supper — there's much to talk about."

"You heard of John's new order of chivalry," said Beaujeu. They sat in a private room over a tavern, eating roasted quail stuffed with berries, washed down with young Beaujolais. Below them, the common room resounded with boisterous drinkers and gamblers.

Josseran leaned his elbows on the table. "Yes. The Order of the Star. I mark I was not called to it."

"Did you expect it?" Beaujeu's smile was merry. "Would you have accepted? Charles d'Espagne is the marshal of it."

"That turd."

"Indeed." Beaujeu nodded, and his servant leapt forward to pour more wine into their cups. "Some say he rules the king as well. Not a savory aspect."

Josseran was thinking again of the scholar whose lecture he would attend, wondering if this Everard was really his nephew. An uneasy tremor ran down his spine. He reached for the winecup. The door opened and the serving wench hurried in with a platter, held up with both hands, on which nestled fruit and cakes. Beneath the soft white stuff of her bodice her breasts stood up like ripe apples. When she bent to lay the platter down, Josseran cupped his hand over one of them.

She squealed; Beaujeu laughed. "If such game as that is your quarry, Vaumartin, there are better places than this. But I thought you had a loving wife."

Josseran drank deep. "God's blood," he said. "After all the troubles that have come over us, can't we lose ourselves now and then in a moment's joy?" He was getting drunk already. It felt good to be drunk, to be loose, to be free. He leaned his forearm on the table and reached for another of the roasted birds before him, surrounded by onions and garlic and green sauce.

"What's the news of the English?"

"Nothing of urgency. The Black Prince is in Aquitaine with an army, raiding here and there."

"The Prince," Josseran said, remembering the man he had met at Calais. He chewed through a mouthful of quail. "By God," he said, "of all the knights I have known, he is the one I would follow most gladly."

Beaujeu looked shocked. "He is English."

"He is an angel of chivalry. While John, you know — "

"John is the king," said Beaujeu. "He wants another war, but he has no money."

"Nobody has any money," Josseran said.

"John's need may be a little more pressing than yours or mine. He's got lots of enemies. You know Navarre is in the city — "

"Navarre! I thought he was a snotty-nosed boy."

"No longer. You have not met him?"

Josseran shook his head. "What is he doing in Paris?"

"Making trouble," Beaujeu said. "Which the king is minded apparently to give him."

Josseran pulled the quail's carcass to pieces with his fingers and ate away the shreds of flesh. "Did they ever settle the issue of Champagne?"

Charles of Bourbon, the young king of Navarre, was descended through both parents from kings of France; when, twenty years before, his claim was set aside in favor of the Valois, they had promised to compensate him with wide rich territory, but neither King Philip nor King John had ever made good on the promises.

"No. They have never given over any of it."

"God's bones, John is greedy."

"He is king of France," Beaujeu said. "The terms are synonymous."

"Then what is he doing, this baby king?" Josseran put down his knife. "What can he do?" The kingdom of Navarre was tiny and poor. A prince of France would have estates elsewhere, of course — Josseran remembered, vaguely, that Navarre held lands and fortresses and towns in Normandy and Poitou that were more important than the kingdom of his title.

"Do you want to see what he's doing?" Beaujeu said. "Finish eating, and I'll show you."

Josseran reached for his cup and drained it, held it to the servant, who filled it again, and once more drank it dry. "Let's go," he said.

"We are in a Time of Trouble! I see fire raining down from Heaven, pools of fire in the streets of Paris — "

Josseran, behind Beaujeu, cast a quick look around him. From the outside, this shop had seemed ordinary enough, a narrow building in a crowded little street.

This room here was an entryway to Hell. From the ring of candles in the middle of the room, the light flashed to a fearsome red glow suddenly to fade for an instant to a saffron gloom, blooming again like raging hellfire. Giant shadows leapt across the walls and the ceiling, and the air stank bitterly of some vile incense.

"The whole world is overturned! That which ought to be beneath is now on top. What ought to be on high is borne low, low as the dust—"

In the dark he could not tell how many people jammed this room, facing the soothsayer in his circle of candles, but there were too many to move, they clogged the space, soured the air. A flutter of panic stirred in his guts. He felt suddenly out of breath. The walls were muffled with black cloth, there were no seats, the men were crushed together here around him. Only the soothsayer, in the center, had light and space.

The prophet's arms, his wide loose sleeves like wings or blades, swung in wild loops as he spoke.

"God has forsaken His creation! We are in the hands of the Devil himself! No use for prayer, no use for piety and good works any more — "

Beside Josseran, Beaujeu grunted, and his elbow nudged Josseran's ribs. The soothsayer lifted his arms, his wide sleeves fluttering.

"Doom! Hellfire comes — it rises from the ground!"

Suddenly tongues of flame whooshed up from the floor, writhing up beside the candles like a fence of fire; the tight-packed onlookers let out a single yell of terror and shrank back. The man in front of Josseran trod heavily on his foot, and on his left someone banged into him. Beaujeu gripped his arm.

"Come on — haven't you had enough?"

Josseran let the other man guide him back through the mob, toward the door again. Behind, the soothsayer's thready voice cracked and whined.

"Treason and disaster are our daily bread! Let no man trust another. Let husband avoid wife, let son suspect father — give no ear to king, to pope, to priest — "

A door opened before him, and he went gladly through it, Beaujeu's hand on his back. In the dark street beyond he stood breathing deep, deep of cool clean air. His face was slimed with sweat.

"What was that?"

Beaujeu chuckled. "Navarre prides himself on his knowledge of wizardry."

"He is mad," Josseran said, but he wheeled, peering into the shop they had just left. "Mad, but bold enough, anyway. What does King John say of this?"

"Presumably John does not know." Beaujeu gestured. "Will not know, until the damage is done." His servant led their horses up. "If you wish, now, we shall have a good carouse — I know a pleasant tavern, with very willing wenches."

Josseran mounted his horse. "If I were John, I would hang that seer." He laughed, pleased at the thought of John's rage, when at last he learned of this: too late, judging by the crowd he had just seen around the soothsayer. Beaujeu was riding away, down the narrow cobbled street; it was a dark night, overcast, and the city gloom was like a filthy smoke in the air. Josseran turned to look back. "John's a fool. Was Navarre in there, now?"

"I doubt it very much. He disdains crowds. He's a strange fellow, not my sort, if I may say so — not my sort at all, and not just because of that." Beaujeu nodded backward toward the shop. "If I were you — "

Behind them there was a crack and a clatter of hoofs. Josseran looked back. The street ran back behind them in a pinched curve, past the shop, to a turn that led to the rue des Marmousets; around this corner now a troop of horsemen was coming, torches in their hands. The leader had a whip which he was cracking, to drive folk out of the way. Josseran drew rein.

"Come on, now," Beaujeu said hastily, and reached out to pull him after.

"Hold," Josseran said. He recognized one of the horsemen behind the leader.

Surrounded by their torches' light, the pack of men rode straight to the soothsayer's shop. The man with the whip leaned down to bang on the door and bellow something. Josseran's horse edged sideways toward them.

Beaujeu said, "Come along now, Vaumartin — that's the king."

"I know," said Josseran, and reined his horse around and started back down the street toward the soothsayer's.

The man with the whip was still pounding on the door. Behind him, the other horsemen milled around in a tight mass. In their midst King John was notable for his gaudy coat. A velvet mask hid his face, but he could as well have had his coat of arms painted on it for all it disguised him. Josseran rode up into the pack, driving his horse between John's and the next man's.

"What, King? Annoyed by the stinging of a few gnats?"

John swung toward him. The torchlight flung a wavering light over him, over the matte texture of the mask, and the moist gleam of his eyes behind it. "Vaumartin!"

"Maybe you should keep your promises," Josseran shouted at him. "Or is that too unkingly?" The man on his right reached out and caught his arm, and Josseran threw him off without even a look. Into John's face, he cried, "A little harder, is it, than chasing women and giving feasts?"

Suddenly the door yielded with a crash. The knight with the whip had broken it down. The knights around Josseran surged forward, swinging down from their horses. Then from the sprung door a crowd erupted, bolting out into the street.

"Fire! Fire!"

A wave of heat scorched Josseran's back. He twisted in his saddle. The door of the shop stood open like a maw, from which there shot a blast of heat and garish light. The inside was on fire. John swore.

"Vaumartin — " He wheeled toward Josseran. His hand went to the mask and yanked it away, revealing a face stiff with frustrated rage. "You're in this too, are you? By God, Vaumartin, you'll lose that name, if I have anything to do with it — you are done!"

Josseran roared at him, "It will take more than you to worry me, King! Lay on, if you wish — "

A wash of heat sent his dancing horse around and back several steps, to the far side of the street. He ducked to avoid an overhanging sign.

With a whoosh and a crash the flames burst through the roof of the soothsayer's shop, fountaining torrents of sparks high into the air, popping and crackling in blinding explosions in the dark sky above the king's head. The roofs on either side of the blazing shop were now smoking. The street filled with townspeople gathering to watch the fire. John's knights staggered away, their arms raised, before the glowing cauldron of the soothsayer's shop.

Josseran shouted, "Get some hooks — pull this shop down, before it sets all the rest on fire!" He backed his horse away. John was gaping around him, open-mouthed, as a brisk shouting skein of people formed, with buckets, hooks, and chains, to bring the fire down. Josseran rode away.

He caught up with Beaujeu some streets away; the other man gaped at him. "God, you are reckless!"

Josseran laughed. He was still drunk enough to feel off-center, if not enough to be glad of it, and he said, "Let's find that tavern. Navarre's young, maybe, but he's shrewd — that was cannily done."

Beaujeu made a deep unpleasant sound in his throat. They rode side by side along the street between the bridges, which ran by the palace. "John played into his hands, though, stupid fool — burning the place down. He could have set all Paris afire."

His hands braced on his saddlebow, Josseran gave him a piercing look.

"Didn't you see? The fire started inside the shop. Surely the king didn't start it. But he will be blamed for it, won't he?" He laughed, exultant on the sweet liquor of revenge. They were crossing the high point of the bridge; ahead the dark north bank loomed, picked out here and there with lights.

Beaujeu rubbed his chin. His brows pulled together over his nose. "I'm telling you, Navarre is not my sort."

Josseran gave another laugh, contemptuous. King John deserved no better. Ahead he saw the bright uproar of a tavern, its patrons overflowing into the street, and he urged on his horse. "Forget it for now — come along."

In the morning, with a headache and a rotten gut, and a mind dead sober, he thought over what he had seen and heard the night before.

John was his enemy. Time and chance and God Himself had made them so, from the first moment they met. A deadly clash between them was inevitable, but the plague had almost beggared the domain of Vaumartin; without money, without men, Josseran had no power to stand against the might of the king of France.

Yet he would not yield, and God, Champion of the Poor, had shown him the way. He asked Beaujeu to take him to the king of Navarre.

Charles of Bourbon, king of Navarre, was younger than Josseran by some years. He stood nearly as tall, but he was slender, which his dress emphasized: he wore black from head to toe, a close-fitting doublet with narrow sleeves, a plain belt of leather, no ornament, no decoration, as if to declare himself was to diminish himself. His hair was so close-cropped Josseran could not tell the color. He stood before the table of his hall and said, "My greeting to you, my lord de Vaumartin. Your name is a very famous one, and I am pleased to meet you here."

Josseran bowed and made a similar speech, phrased properly to address a man of higher rank than his. Behind the table were some other men, who watched attentively. The room around them was sumptuously dressed, with a carpet of eastern work on the floor, and Italian chairs around the polished table. Clearly they were ready here for some feast.

Navarre said, "Your feats of arms are legendary, my dear Vaumartin. I hope you are about to sit down with us at table and make a willing audience of us."

He indicated the table with his hand, as if Josseran might take a place among his guests, but Josseran stayed on his feet. He folded his arms before him.

"I am here, Your Grace, for two reasons, neither of them the telling of stories. The first is to congratulate you on your enemies, because a man's enemies are one of the truest measures of him, and to be the enemy of King John is the highest measure of all, in my mind."

Navarre straightened, stiffening, his head higher. "I despise King John," he said, in a rasping voice. "He and the other Valois have stolen everything they could from me and mine."

He turned his head suddenly, and glanced behind him, toward the men standing behind the table. Among them one young man stirred a little, his hand rising toward his face; he gave a low cough. Navarre faced Josseran again.

"Your enmity to John is well known. We share an honorable war."

Josseran said, "One in which, I think, we can serve each other, Your Grace. You can do battle with the king in soothsayers' houses, and by such clever ploys as last night's, but the day is coming when you must have a captain, an army, and a champion."

The little group behind the table began to murmur and whisper among themselves. Navarre glanced toward them again. His face sharpened; when he turned toward Josseran his eyes gleamed.

Yet he said only, "I have my own army. And will welcome you into it, Vaumartin, with much rejoicing. But before you say more, let me present to you the dauphin Charles, who is among my company today."

He stretched out his arm toward the men behind the table. Josseran's mouth fell open. All the men save one stepped back, and in their midst, the tall, pale boy stood. He coughed nervously into his hand, and made an awkward bow.

"I am very honored to meet the great champion of Vaumartin."

Josseran swung toward Navarre again. "You entertain a Valois — you talk openly of your business with a Valois prince beside you?"

Navarre said, "He is young and honorable — he repents of his family's evils to me."

The pale youth said, "I am not a party to my royal father's greed and deceit — I will go now, lest I bring contention between you two." He took a wide-brimmed hat from the chair beside him and started out of the room, and several of the others trailed after him. Josseran watched them go, his eyes narrow. He wondered who was the fool here, Navarre or this prince.

The door shut, Navarre said crisply, "The boy's useful to me. He bring me news of his father, and is malleable."

Josseran scanned the men who lingered behind the table. "How many spies remain?" he said, and shook his head. "Beaujeu is right, Your Grace. You are too subtle a sort for me." He bowed with a flourish of his hands. "I shall withdraw, if you please."

Across Navarre's face a smile flickered. "No longer eager to be my champion, Vaumartin?"

Josseran bowed again. "I think the champions you need have

different skills from mine, Your Grace." He was backing up toward the door, and now he had reached it; with a final flourish, he bowed himself out, and left.

He had come alone, his men-at-arms being still at Beaujeu's, nursing tremendous headaches. As he rode back along the rue Saint-Honoré, he noticed someone following after him.

There were other people in the street, a ragman with his bundle on his back, and a girl hawking strawberries, and half a dozen little children worrying a wretched dog trapped under a step; he went on a little, slower, letting the man following him come up closer behind him. This pace brought him to the long high featureless wall surrounding a monastery, and he rode along it, not looking back, to the corner, and there turned into a lane and stepped down from his horse without reining it in.

He pressed his back to the wall. The horse walked on several paces down the lane, where some heavy-trunked oak trees grew thick on either side, and stopped to nuzzle the ground. Furtive, the spy slid around the corner, and as he came, he was drawing out his dagger.

Josseran had him by the arm before the man knew he was there. With a yell the spy swung his long-bladed dagger at him, and Josseran twisted his arm up between his shoulder blades and tore the knife out of his grip.

"You think I'm so easily done in, do you?" He jerked on the man's arm, and the spy gave a yell like a dying rabbit. Josseran laid the edge of the spy's own knife to the man's throat. "Who sent you?"

"No one! I am innocent — I did nothing!"

"Who sent you?" Josseran roared into his ear, and pressed the knife against the man's throat until the blood slipped over the edge and ran in a red tide down his skin.

The spy twitched from head to toe. "The king!" he shouted. "The king!"

Josseran's temper boiled. "He does nothing honorably! Take it to the grave with you!" Drawing back the dagger, he plunged it into the man's chest.

The spy sagged, gone. Josseran dropped the dagger beside him, bent and pushed his eyelids closed. Long-striding, he went to his horse, waiting in the deep shade of the tree. The horse snorted softly at the smell of blood. Josseran swung into the saddle and rode away through the graveyard.

He hid himself in Beaujeu's house for another day and a half, and on Saint Monica's Day he went to the Studium, to hear the inception lecture of Everard le Breton.

The lecture had been announced for a hall in the Studium itself, but so great a crowd gathered that they moved it down to the church of Saint-Severin. Josseran took only his two men-at-arms with him, and them he left outside, on the porch, while he went in.

He had to force his way through the packed crowd, mostly scholars in their black robes, and before he got close enough to see the speaker clearly, Everard had begun his lecture.

The inceptor spoke in a strong, flexible voice that reached easily through the whole church, in a fluent Latin that Josseran could not follow, although around him, every few moments, men would laugh at a joke, or burst into excited comment at a turn of logic. Uncomprehending, Josseran stood there like a rock in the tide of words and stared up at the lectern.

His heart thundered, double speed. This was his nephew; he had no doubt of it. Age had lengthened him, his face was stronger, his bearing had a confidence and certainty Josseran did not remember in the boy — as he spoke, he paced up and down behind the lectern, now and then striking down with his hand, as if to drive his words on. It was Everard. Josseran drew back after only a few moments, worked his way to the side of the church, and went out through the vestibule.

In the little churchyard, shaded by tall elm trees, he walked up and down between rows of graves. His mind seethed. He wished he had not come here.

He had found Everard, which he had promised God Himself that he would do. His heart still galloped at the shock of recognizing his nephew. That was his blood, there, his blood and bone and flesh, his kinsman.

Now he had the duty of giving back to Everard what was rightfully his, and yet Josseran could not force himself to that. He could not even greet his nephew openly, could not shake his hand, embrace him.

A greater duty faced him now. Vaumartin lay in peril of King John's greed. Only Josseran could defend it. If he surrendered the title now, folk would think he was afraid, that he was shirking. A disputed title would give John all the more excuse to meddle, to seize everything.

Everard could talk and sway a crowd with his voice, but he was no knight; he would not fight to save his heritage. To give him Vaumartin was to lose it.

Behind him, in the church, there was a storm of applause. Everard was bringing his lecture to its close. Now there would be some prayers, and Beaujeu had told him they would go and drink, afterward, in a tavern in the Studium, and he could meet Everard there if he cared to — if it was the right Everard.

He wheeled. His cloven heart steadied and found purpose. There was one thing that mattered to him, which was Vaumartin. He went on around the church, quickly, before the crowd left it.

Richard and Simon were sitting on the porch, sharing a flask of wine. When he came around the church, they looked up, surprised; they had seen him last going in the front door. He went up toward the horses, going by them without stopping.

"Come along," he called, and gestured them after him. "It is the wrong man."

twenty-seven

IN HIS DISPUTATIONS Everard had always managed to avoid referring to the dangerous writers whose books were hidden under the bed in Sylviane's room, but after his inception, he gave his first afternoon lecture, on Aristotle's *Physics*. For an unrequired lecture it drew a good crowd, some twenty or twenty-five scholars. Everard concluded with remarks on the nature of light, beginning with Grosseteste's idea that light was the primary substance, extending as it did from its source instantly into a perfect sphere, filling all emptiness with itself; and going on to some notions of Everard's own, innocent enough it seemed to him, but interesting and elegant.

After he had done, some of the scholars came up to fawn on him and ask stupid questions. Behind them stood one who said nothing, but smiled unpleasantly, and as the others went away, Everard recognized this last fellow: it was Claude de Brises, the incompetent master of theology whom Everard had chased out of his own lecture hall a year before.

"Well," he said, fighting a sudden uneasiness, "Master de Brises, have you come back to study honestly this time?"

De Brises's nasty snake-lipped smile remained on his face. He said, "I have recovered my license, Master Everard. I am here to teach again."

Everard shut his books and stacked them one on the other. "Then I am very disappointed in the universitas. Why are you attending my lecture?"

De Brises raised his eyebrows. "Professional interest. You are well read in English authors."

"To you, it must seem so." Everard came down from the raised lectern, his books under his arm, and started toward the door; several scholars remained in the hall, where another lecture would soon be given, and they watched this confrontation with curious faces. Over his shoulder, Everard said to de Brises, "If you knew more, I would be more interested in your opinions."

The other man pursued him toward the door. "Some books it's better not to have read. Master Everard."

Everard wheeled around. "You Franciscans! Chastity, poverty, and ignorance! I suppose in your case that's making a virtue of necessity."

De Brises's smile slipped. His teeth showed in a snarl. "I shall report what I have heard here today to the rector of the universitas."

"Do so. It will amaze him to hear the ass Brunellus talk. Only speak distinctly, lest he take it for gas from the other end, which you much resemble."

The scholars around them laughed, and de Brises turned white. He lunged toward Everard, his fist raised, and struck him hard across the face. Several of the men around them dragged him backward by the arms. Everard put his hand to his mouth, which hurt; he looked down at the blood on his fingers.

"What a gift for argument you have, de Brises — the Gospel of Force."

"Heretic!"

Everard walked out of the lecture hall. He knew de Brises was not done with him.

A few days later Lorenz von Zweibrücken — Bipontianus, the scholars called him — summoned him up to his study, and they sat there awhile, talking over practical matters of teaching.

"You must collect your fees," Lorenz said. "There's a talk all around the Studium that you have not charged anyone a fee."

Everard hated money, and he said so. He was staring at the papers on Lorenz's desk.

"Nonetheless, you make it difficult on us all, when the scholars come to think they can hear lectures without paying a fee."

"Maybe I am not a teacher, Lorenz."

"That may be so. You are alarming people, also, with some of the things you are teaching. What are you looking at?"

Everard stretched his hand into the dusty air between them. Through a tear in the curtain over the window a ray of light was streaming in over the desk, turning the papers from shadowy dimness to a blazing white. "If what I see is not the thing itself, but the light only, gathered in through the eye, then within me is the cosmos, and without me only shadows of the cosmos." He raised his gaze to meet Lorenz's eyes. "Why should I turn from examination of the truth to heed the malice of the darkness?"

Lorenz shook his head, looking exasperated, his hands pressed palm to palm before him. "Everard, you must not give that lecture again."

"Ah, so de Brises has talked, has he? I wonder how much of what I actually said he managed to remember."

"Everard!" Lorenz slammed his hands down on the desk. "Heed me. Leave off that line of thinking. It's obviously heretical. You fool — Eriugena placed reason above faith, and he disappeared. Ockham escaped only by connivance of the emperor. Other people I care not even to mention by name were burned for saying what you are saying, and less forcefully and clearly than you are saying it."

"I have said nothing not logical and demonstrable by proof, Lorenz."

The German grunted at him. The skin of the long scar on his face was shiny, like parchment. Flayed. His eyes were fierce.

"You need discipline, Everard. You are brilliant but undisciplined. You know what the scholars call you, don't you — Audax Inceptor! That's not a compliment. It's time you were ordained. Get your tonsure, commit yourself to God, and give up this frivolous whoring around with banned books."

Their eyes met, and they stared at each other awhile. Everard had always thought that beneath his necessary orthodoxy Lorenz was a free thinker, and he faced his master with a sense of betrayal. He said, belligerently, "Or?"

Lorenz pressed his lips together, his brows bending down over his nose, and gave a shake of his head. "Now I am your enemy, hah? Anyone who will not join you in your reckless headlong charge must be running in the opposite direction. Listen to me. I love you. I fear for you. Heed me."

Everard sat back, his hands in his lap. "I'm sorry. I meant no — I know you are my friend, as I am yours."

"Then guard your lips." Lorenz smiled, but without mirth, his eyes still sober. He said, "Good day, Everard."

He stood, and Everard stood; they shook hands, and Everard felt as he did so that Lorenz was bidding him farewell. Bound to the Studium, the German master dared not link himself to anything heterodox. Everard went out. In the street below Lorenz's window, he looked up, and saw the German pulling fretfully at the curtain — blocking out the little hole that let in the light.

Everard had thought he could keep his mind divided into what he thought and what other people might know he thought. Now he saw that reading Eriugena and Ockham and the others had put them in his mind not like the furniture in rooms but like the dye in the threads of a fabric: everything he said was stained with their selfish freedom. Everything he said revealed him to the whole world. He walked away, shaken.

Sylviane said, "There, see?"

Jeanne shook her head. "I see nothing but scratches and lines. What does it say?"

The child turned her slate around toward her stepmother. "That says, *Sylviane. God made me. God loves me.* See?"

"Show me how to make my name."

Sylviane frowned. She had a raven's feather stuck into her sleeve, like a stray wing.

"Ah, then you cannot," Jeanne said. "I see no value in this, if you cannot write other things — "

"Here." Sylviane pulled the slate across the table toward her, scrubbed it clean with her towel, and drew on it again. "That says *Jeanne.*"

Again Jeanne shook her head. It still looked like chicken tracks. The door opened, and Everard came into the hall.

"Here, Father," Sylviane cried. "Read this to my mother, make her believe me."

Everard was taking off his black gown. He was sunk down deep in himself, his actions mechanical. Leaning over the table, he looked at the slate and said, "Ah. John. No — Jeanne." He stroked the child's face and went to hang up his gown.

Sylviane beamed at Jeanne. "You see?"

"I think he was guessing," Jeanne said. Her gaze remained on her husband.

Sylviane said, "Father, look what I found." She plucked the black feather from her sleeve and held it out.

Everard took it, gave it a swift look, and laid it down on the table. His face was drawn; he seemed to be heeding nothing outside himself. But when he went to sit down the child sprang on him.

"No! You didn't see — come look — "

"Sylviane," Jeanne said, sharply, "leave him to himself."

Everard lifted his head. "What didn't I see?"

Sylviane picked up the feather. "Come look." Gripping him by the sleeve, she pulled him away toward the door. Jeanne got up and followed.

On the sunlit step, Sylviane was saying, "Look at the feather! See? It makes a rainbow! There are rainbows in everything, Father!"

Everard sat down on the step, twisting and turning the feather in his hands. Jeanne sank down beside him.

She said, "You seem very low today, husband. Are you feeling well?"

"No," he said, and laughed, unhappy. He said, "I make a world for myself and it crumbles, over and over. I am no god. My creation dies at the first breath."

Jeanne tucked her hands inside her knees. The sun was warm, but his words chilled her, unnerved her, as if a cold wind blew. He sat with his head turned away, twisting and turning the black feather in his fingers; Sylviane sprinted away down the street, calling to someone by the well.

Jeanne reached out her hand toward Everard. "What interests you so in the feather?"

"One of God's gambols." He held the feather out to her, twisting and turning it. A flicker of colored light shone across it. "See how it makes a rainbow, sometimes." She took it, beguiled.

He said, "Aristotle teaches that the rainbow comes when sunlight shines on clouds, which is patent nonsense. Aristotle did not use his own logic sometimes."

She turned the feather between her fingers, watching the color come and go. "They are not the same, though, are they — the rainbow and the changing light on this feather?"

"I don't know." He shrugged. "Grosseteste has a theory, but it's gibberish, refraction and reflection at the same time of the same light, it makes no sense." He sounded grouchy.

She said, as she often said now, "I don't understand."

"I'll get the slate," he said, and rose to go into the house.

Later, when Sylviane had gone to bed, and Jeanne was banking the fire in the hearth, Everard came and sat down on the bench, and said, "I . . . am going to leave the Studium, Jeanne."

Her arms stiffened. Vigorously she poked at the ashes before her, trying to keep from showing her alarm. "And then what will you do?" She thought: Will you go back to Vartin, and leave me behind? "Why are you leaving? The inception lecture was a great triumph — everybody said so — "

"Too great, maybe," he said. "There are people . . . watching me now — and they mean to shackle me to their ideas, to their old ways."

She turned toward him, the fire banked, giving off only a faint red gleam that painted the high lines of his face and left the rest in shadow. "And you will not yield to them."

"I cannot," he said. "When there is so much to know, to learn, to study — how can I turn back to doing what thousands of other men have already done?"

Her heart was pounding. She thrust her hands down into her lap, thinking, unwillingly, of what the other women already said about her, as she worked and worked to keep him in seeming idleness. She said, "How will we live, Everard?"

His head swung toward her. "I thought of going to Marcel."

"Marcel!"

"You remember — the king's draper. When we went to give the king our petition — "

"Yes," she said. "I remember. Do you think he will have a place for you?"

"I hope he will." He rubbed his hands together, his face sucked gaunt. "The king has named him provost of the merchants of Paris. He will need clerks and scribes around him."

"A scribe," she said. "Is that what you want to be?"

His eyes were steady on her, the last light of the fire gathered in his look. "No one cares what a scribe thinks," he said, "and so he may think as he pleases. About rainbows, if he pleases — about the world as it is."

She saw that he expected her to speak. "Do what you must, Everard," she said.

"I knew you would say that," he said. "You have a true knight's heart, Jeanne."

There was a little silence, as with her true knight's heart she struggled not to be afraid of what lay before her. When his voice began again, it was soft and slow.

"There is no justice in the world, Jeanne. Those who are noble and honorable struggle just to live, while the base and selfish wallow in

idleness and luxuries. The Studium condemns questions and rewards
the repetition of old fallacies."

She said, "God tests us."

He laughed. He raised his head, his eyes gleaming. "So I said, once,
and do still believe it. The challenge is there before me. I must take it
up, somehow." He put out his hand to her, and she took it, and neither
of them spoke for a while; she thought he had said everything in his
mind, and she was still fighting against her fears and doubts, and
determined not to let them show.

Then suddenly he stood up, drawing her after him. "Come, wife.
Let's to bed."

twenty-eight

DIRECTLY OPPOSITE the spired gatehouses of the Great Bridge, on the street called the Draperie that ran along the north bank of the Seine, stood the Châtelet, the prison of Paris. Most of the governance of the city went on in this old square stone tower, the keeping of the prisons and the watch, the granting of charters, the regulation of trade, all in the charge of the provost of the merchants.

To this office King John had just appointed Etienne Marcel, the draper, the richest man in Paris, who had once admired Everard for his bold speaking. Now Everard went up to the Châtelet, his hat in his hand, and his guts knotted, hoping Marcel remembered him.

It was hard enough even getting to the front door of the place. The broad street bustled with wagons, mules, and people, coming and going and just standing around talking; around the door into the prison swarms of idlers gathered, men of the watch in their blue-and-red hoods, unhired day laborers who drifted down from the Place de Grève just up the street, curious people and gossipers. Everard elbowed and shouldered his way through them to the open door and went in.

Inside, the crowd was just as dense, in the open stinking room where the lower magistrates sat hearing the watchmen's charges and ordering people into the prison in the basement or the stocks at the Place de Grève. The stairs were so packed that Everard had to slide by, step by step, with his back pressed to the wall; he went up past the second story, where two watchmen guarded the closed door with pikes, and there, some dozen steps from the top, came into the back of a crowd so thick and immovable he could go no higher.

He stood there awhile, breathing the foul air, and wondering if this would do him any good. Even if Marcel remembered him, Everard was probably of no more interest or use to him than any other of these men. Wedged between the crowd and the wall, his head beginning to ache from the bad air and the stench of many bodies, he lost heart; he thought of going home. Then, abruptly, someone came out of the room at the top of the stairs and bellowed, and half the men around him turned and began to force their way back down the stairs. After them came a redheaded man so tall he had to stoop to clear the ceiling, whose rumbling deep voice filled the stairwell and sent men scurrying away like rabbits. Everard slipped by, up, and into the top room.

The light here was better than in the stairwell, and he blinked and ducked his head against the dazzle. This room too was stuffed with people, noisy with conflicting voices. At a big table at one side, in front of the only large window, was Marcel himself, leaning over a paper spread out on the surface before him, and talking to several men clustered around him.

Three or four scribes sat at writing desks on the other side of the room; there were ledgers piled up head-high against the wall behind them. As Everard shook his head clear, one of these scribes slid down from his stool and rushed over to Marcel, waving an old stained piece of parchment.

"Please, Master Provost, I can't read this."

Marcel turned to deal with him. Everard went up toward the big table; the paper spread out on it was a drawing of some kind. He craned his neck to see over another man's shoulder, read some of the markings on it, and realized that it was a plan of the city of Paris.

"Now." Marcel wheeled away from the scribe, back to his map; he had a stick of charcoal in his hand, and he reached out to scrawl a huge X over the left half of the paper. "All this is wrong. Saint-Sulpice isn't even on this side of the river. Go out and do it right, hah, do you understand me?" He straightened, a short, square man with a red face and eyes like sparks from the fire, and immediately he saw Everard.

"Who are you?"

Everard straightened, his hands behind his back. "I am Everard le Breton, Master Provost. We met — "

"What do you want?"

"I — " Everybody was staring at him. Everard put his shoulders back. "I want work, Master Provost."

The provost grunted at him. The fierce bright eyes snapped. "I can't hear you now. Wait, if it's important."

Everard backed up a little. Marcel was sending off the men around the table to work on the map; he gave orders in a voice edged with impatience, as if they should all know already what he wanted of them. Someone else came up to him with a ledger, and they put the great bound book on the table and bent over it together.

The morning dragged on. Everard waited by the wall, watching a constant stream of men rush in, speak to Marcel, and rush out again; suddenly Marcel himself hurried out of the room, and Everard followed, determined to be there when at last Marcel was free to heed him.

Marcel was never free. He went all in a rush over to the City Island, and there in another crowded room spoke to someone in the king's parlement, and when he came striding out of that chamber and saw Everard again, waiting, he said, "Not now," and rushed away again, and Everard followed him back to the Châtelet.

There all the scribes were waiting with questions. They buried the provost in papers, and Everard went back to his place by the wall. He wondered if this was some kind of joke Marcel was playing on him. He was hungry and thirsty, and he could have been at the White Rose, composing rigorous logical assaults on Aristotle. A scribe came up to Marcel, waving an old torn stained charter.

"Please, Master Provost, I can't read this."

Marcel jerked his head up, his face red, and glared at the scribe; suddenly he swung his gaze around toward Everard.

"Can you read this?"

Everard came up and took the document; the ink had faded almost to invisibility, and the Latin was wretched. " 'In this third year of our good King Louis, ninth of the name — ' "

Marcel snatched the paper out of hands. "Good. Take this idiot's place. The work's simple, watch the others, do what they do. Take this." He gave Everard back the charter; to the other scribe, he said, "Go. You're finished with me."

"But, Master Provost — "

"Go!" Marcel roared. "Collect your penny at the treasurer's and don't come back."

Everard went quickly over to the desk the hapless former scribe had just left; he thrust away the feeling that he was stealing the other man's place. The desk was battered and the stool too high. A huge ledger lay open on it, with rows and rows of writing in a dozen different inks and hands. He settled himself, uncertain, and glanced at the scribe to his right. Within a few moments he understood what to do. He reached for one of the row of quills stuck into the inkhorn at the front of the desk and bent over the ledger to record the old charter in his hand.

It was mindless work, but around him the room buzzed and throbbed, men came briskly in and out, and Marcel's voice rose, again and again, sharp-edged, with questions, with orders. Everard's back prickled up. He felt suddenly at home here, in all this uproar. This busy practical world seemed somehow within his reach, within his power to manage — a loom on which he might weave a new justice. Again and again, during the day, he raised his head and looked around him, calculating, as if he surveyed a new battleground, ready to be won.

At the end of the day, Marcel called him over. They had shut the doors at last and the big room was almost empty of men. On top of Marcel's table lay the great plan of Paris, and the provost leaned on his arms over it, his gaze traveling over it, as if he walked the city in his mind.

When Everard came up before him, the provost raised his head.

"Your work today was acceptable. I will have you as a scribe, twopence a day. You come at dawn, you leave at dusk. On Sabbaths you stay home." He frowned, still braced on both arms over the table. "I remember you from somewhere. What is your name?"

"Everard le Breton," Everard said. "I went with you to speak to the king once."

The memory burst over Marcel's face like a sunrise; he straightened, his arms wheeling out, and confronted Everard full on, his eyes snapping with amusement. "Oh, yes! The scholar with the quick tongue and the uncomfortably close argument. Why aren't you in the Studium, hah? No — let me guess — you let your quick tongue run away with one of your close arguments, didn't you, and they threw you out for thinking too much."

Everard said, "Well, you have it right."

"Hunh." Marcel was staring at him shrewdly. "I admired you for what you said before the king, but I would not admire it if you spoke so to me. I want loyalty and hard work from you, and that is all. Do we understand each other?"

"Very well, Master Provost," Everard said.

"Good. Then I will see you tomorrow, at dawn."

When he reached his house at last, long after dark, Bonboisson was there, sitting at the table with Jeanne. Seeing him, Jeanne gave a great gusty sigh, and rose up from her place.

"Husband, you must be hungry," she said, and gave her brother a sharp look, and went off to the pantry. Everard came to the table.

"Where have you been?" Bonboisson said, in a raspy voice. "What's this about leaving the Studium?"

"I've left the Studium," Everard said. He sat down on the bench opposite his brother-in-law. A piece of paper, folded, lay under Bonboisson's elbow, and he nodded to it.

"Is that something you need to have read?"

"I did," said the vintner. "That's why I came here." He snorted, rubbing at his nose. "You left the Studium! Why, for God's sake — everybody said the inception was so brilliant!"

Everard shrugged; he had no interest in explaining it all to Bonboisson; instead he said, "I have gotten work with Marcel."

"Marcel. The provost?"

Everard nodded. Jeanne had returned with a cup of wine and a loaf and some cheese.

She said, "You did find work, then."

"As a scribe," Everard said. "For twopence a day."

Bonboisson's breath exploded from him. "A scribe! You left the Studium — a place of honor — to be a common scribe in the Châtelet?" He gave a roar of contemptuous laughter. "By God's blood, Everard, which way are you going?"

"Shall I read that for you?" Everard said, nodding to the paper under Bonboisson's elbow.

The vintner grunted. His face was still rolled up with amusement. "No — the child did it." His voice quivered, as he said it; he glanced at Jeanne, as if to confirm it.

"Did she?" Everard said, surprised.

"Oh, yes," Jeanne said. "She figured it all out, with a little guessing here and there — "

"It was just a list of grapes and wines and prices," Bonboisson said

roughly. "I could have worked it out myself, probably, with a little
. . ." He rubbed furiously at his nose with his forefinger. "So you'll
be working for Marcel," he said to Everard. "He's a taskmaster, they
say."

"I think so," Everard said.

"Well," said Bonboisson, and put out his hand across the table.
"Good luck, Everard."

Everard shook his hand. "Thank you."

A few days later Marcel called him from his desk to the big table at the
back of the room where the provost did his business. The captain of the
watch was there, the towering redheaded man in the red-and-blue
hood.

Marcel's face was the color of a new brick. He leaned on the table,
braced on his fists, and snapped at Everard, "Will you go to the rector
of the universitas for me?"

"To the rector." Everard glanced at the watch captain, Jean
Mailliard. Taller by a head than Everard, who was tall, Mailliard
tended to stoop a little, his great head tilted forward slightly, and his
pale eyes, always half closed under bulging rust-red eyebrows, looked
down with a sour contempt on everybody unlucky enough to be around
him. Now the captain set his hands on his hips, his gaze shifting
steadily from Everard to the provost and back again, his heavy-lidded
eyes brimming with suspicion.

Everard faced Marcel. "I will do what you ask. What matter have
you with the universitas?"

"Every street thief and nutshell grafter in Paris runs like a rabbit
for the Studium whenever Captain Mailliard's men give chase, and he
will not order them into the Studium after them." As he said this,
Marcel gave a strange, ferocious stab of his eyes and twist of his lips
at the watch captain, as if thereby he could throw his words like
daggers.

"They have ancient charters," Mailliard barked, "promising them
immunity — ancient royal charters — "

"I will talk to the rector," Everard said. "They have their own
watch, also, who should be doing a better job, perhaps."

"Go," said Marcel, with another sneer at the captain.

Everard talked to the rector, getting nowhere. The master of the universitas refused to admit any problem with criminals lurking in the Studium. Instead he led Everard into a discussion of Aristotle's theory of violent motion.

This theory of the Philosopher's was a major difficulty in his physics, since it required the constant application of force to keep a moving object in motion, an idea not supported well by the practical observation of such things as a thrown stone and an arrow shot from a bow. The rector had a theory of his own, that any sufficient force on a suitable object might impart a motion to it, which would carry it along until some contrary force stopped it.

"That's ingenious," Everard said. "For thinking like that I had to leave the Studium."

"You were too hasty," said the rector, raising one finger. "Too literal. The secret is to put your ideas forth as ways of calculation merely. Not facts, you see, but useful fictions. Metaphors."

Everard said, "You mean, as if they were lies."

The rector snorted at him, unperturbed. "It was for thinking like that, Master Everard, that you had to leave the Studium. Good day."

When Everard reported to Marcel, the provost gave him a grim look. "Well," he said, "it's my fault entirely, for asking more of you than your own poor powers. Go write this man his charters." He pointed him toward the first of a line of men waiting at his desk.

At the center of all things was the world, dross and decay, sin and imperfection, earth, fire, water, and air. Around it, suspended in a crystal sphere, moved the moon, at the edge of corruptible things, its face marred by proximity to degrading change. Next then was the circle of the sun, and then the other planets, each propelled by its angel soul, each rolled through heaven in its crystal sphere, each sphere more noble than the last, the whole encircled in the firmament, studded with the fixed stars, beyond which was only the quintessence, the fifth element, perfect, unchanging, inviolate.

Or so Aristotle said.

Everard took Jeanne and Sylviane up through the bedroom window to the roof and they sat together under a blanket and he pointed out the stars to them. He told them how the cosmos was ordered, as he had been taught, and Sylviane said, "It's beautiful. Like a crystal staircase up to God."

Then she turned to him and said, "Is it real?"

He looked up at the stars. To the rector, certainly, they were only useful fictions of the mind of God.

In the sky above him there were stars without number. God had made them, and therefore they were real, and the planets and the sun and moon were real, and they moved and therefore their motion was real, and if so then the crystal spheres could not be real. He said, "No, I don't think it is."

Beside him, Jeanne sat, her knees drawn up, her eyes raised toward the sky. He said, "What are you thinking, wife?"

For a moment she was silent. Finally, slowly, she said, "I am wondering why it is so hard to think about that which is just before my eyes."

He laughed. Putting his arm around her, he drew her close against him. Sylviane shot a fierce look at them, and worried her way in between them, as she usually did, but they sat there a long while, watching the stars.

Stripped of their meaning, the stars drew him like beacons, watchfires at the boundaries of a new world.

Marcel's work, on the other hand, was within his reach, and the results were immediate. The city was still starving — even those with money could not buy bread — and Marcel put himself to this problem like a knight lowering his helmet and leveling his lance.

He called in several master millers he suspected of hoarding grain, accused them, and asked for their cooperation; if they withheld it, he promised them that he would bring them to ruin. Everard was there when he said this, and he looked at the faces of the millers and saw their mouths tighten, their brows furrow.

Yet they stood together, and refused even to admit that they had stocks of wheat and barley somewhere, stocks that were increasing in value every day as the poor made soup from dandelions and burdock, and housewives like Jeanne walked for hours from bakery to bakery, searching for a few loaves for sale.

When they had gone, Marcel said, "Now what should we do, Master Clerk."

Everard said, "Send the watch to ransack their warehouses."

The provost barked with laughter. "God's blood, a brigand at heart. I thought you were a scholar, boy — where's your faith in words and numbers? I have a letter for you to write."

The letter Everard wrote was to friends of Marcel's in other places, merchants whose trade gave them friends and business allies in the countryside, even as far off as Flanders and Germany. Through them he found grain for sale at a reasonable price, although far from Paris. The provost sold off the profit to be made in the future on this grain and used that money to buy it and ship it down the river.

The successful sale of the first shipment attracted other shipments. The grain came in bargeloads, more than the millers could handle, a flood of grain. Suddenly the price of a loaf of bread began to shrink. Everard, sitting at his table, heard from Jeanne that the bakeries were full of good bread, and that the bakers were selling it ever more cheaply, and he said nothing, but spread the butter on the bread and smiled to see Sylviane eat the soft brown center of her slice and leave the crust for the chickens.

Now the hoarded stores of grain were losing value by the hour. When they saw Marcel on the street, the master millers cursed him to his face, and the provost laughed at them — all Paris laughed at them, and loved the provost — and calmly Marcel bought all the hoarded grain he could, at the cheapest price in years, and stored it away against the next famine.

"This is what power is," the provost told Everard. "To do good for the people."

He smiled, his small fiery eyes flashing, and struck Everard on the shoulder, always his parting salute. The next day he was planning to rebuild the walls of Paris, which had been crumbling for generations. Everard began to think that if any man on earth could do his whole will, that man was Etienne Marcel.

twenty-nine

JOSSERAN DID NOT RETURN to Vaumartin. Instead he went into Normandy, where like crossed swords the powers of France and England met.

These northern lands lay under the illusion of a peace. The Black Prince kept court in the south, in Gascony, where he was striving to win back the ancestral lands of the Plantagenets that generations of French kings had steadily usurped. The English kept Calais well garrisoned, but across the Channel, Edward of England was occupied fighting his ancient enemies, the Scots. Even in Brittany, where there had always been a war, the fighting season opened with no call to arms, since all the great Breton lords whose task it was to sustain the war were captive or dead.

After he left Paris, Josseran went from place to place in Normandy, from castle to castle, talking to his friends among the Norman lords, trying to stir them to help him against King John.

They listened to him, these lords; they gave him and his two men-at-arms their hospitality, but they offered him no help. Vaumartin meant nothing to them. What they took from his arguments was a sense of John's danger to themselves, and what they offered him was a place in their own armies, to defend their own lands. So he passed one whole year, and the better part of the next, traveling and talking, to no use.

At last he joined the company of his friend the Sire d'Aubrey, mostly because d'Aubrey was actually fighting. Around Calais there was always some fighting going on, mostly raids on travelers and counterattacks on other raiding parties. There was loot in it, but no real honor. Sometimes d'Aubrey attacked some holding of King John's, sometimes King Edward's, lest either grow too great; he was fond of describing this as a form of gardening.

"I keep them pruned and tied back," he said, with a laugh, and thrust out his chest, and preened himself as if he were master of Normandy.

They were sitting before the fire, deep in the night, waiting for a courier from Rouen. Josseran said, "So would I do, also, at Vaumartin."

"God's bones," said the other man. The hearth was to one side of them, and threw out an orange haze over them; the rest of the room was dark, the servants sleeping at the far side of it, gently snoring. D'Aubrey leaned back. "What does Vaumartin matter now? This is where the kings stand face to face — "

Josseran reared his head back, angry. "Yet Vaumartin — "

D'Aubrey struck the tabletop with his hand. "Your thinking's too fixed upon one place! See the thing large, my friend — more than your patrimony is at stake here." His chest expanded. He loved rhetoric, and the sound of his voice swollen great with opinion. "The king cannot turn his attention from Normandy, now that Edward has Calais. As long as they are balanced, like weights on a steelyard, we are free between them."

Josseran slid back on the bench, his hands flat before him, and stopped listening. A wave of desperation overtook him. Here he was useless to Vaumartin, begging for help, waiting for someone to come to his rescue. The door at the far side of the hearth opened, and a page came in.

"My lord, the courier is come."

D'Aubrey ignored him, staring solemnly at Josseran, dropping each word with pecular weight, as if he coined them specially. "For all our sakes, better that the war should never end, that neither king should ever win, but if one must, let it be Edward, who is farther away, and less able to meddle with us."

Josseran nodded to the page. "Acknowledge the courier, my lord."

D'Aubrey nodded. "Send him in."

A man in a dusty leather jacket strode forward, bent his knee, and said, "I have messages for you, my lord." His voice was hoarse. With both hands he set a leather pouch on the table before d'Aubrey.

The Norman lord reached for them. Josseran crooked his finger at the page. "Bring this man some wine, some meat." As the boy scampered off, Josseran nodded to the courier. "Sit. What's the news?"

The courier sank down on the bench. "Nothing much, my lord, save d'Espagne's murder."

"What?" Josseran said.

D'Aubrey jerked his eyes up from the dispatch he was reading. "What did you say?"

The courier looked from one to the other. "Have you not heard? It is all the buzz, everywhere — the king of Navarre and his brothers lured Charles d'Espagne into ambush at L'Aigle and there put as many knives in him as the old sow has piglets."

Josseran said, "Well, God bless him for that."

D'Aubrey grunted at him. He put down the dispatch and thrust it and the rest of the papers away. "He killed him. That was a mistake." His brow was rumpled; he looked suddenly older.

"A mistake," Josseran burst out. "The man was an insult to us all." Even as he spoke, he began to see that d'Aubrey was right, and he fell silent, frowning. The Norman was scowling at him.

"He should have taken him hostage. Then he would have had John also in his hand. Now he has nothing at all, save revenge."

Josseran straightened. "John will strike back, that much is foreseeable."

D'Aubrey reached for the dispatch he had set aside, his brow wrinkled. "I have no objection to letting him deal with Navarre."

Josseran leaned forward now, urgent. "If you let him take Navarre, he will overrun you as well."

D'Aubrey said, "You don't see the way of things here, Josseran. Sometimes it's a matter of waiting and watching."

"Give me command over your knights," Josseran said, "and I will lead them."

"Lead them! Where? To do what?"

"To strike wherever John has an influence, every tollhouse, every manor, every caravan of tradesmen — wherever he can be bled. We'll open a dozen wounds in him!"

"All the while the king's raising an army to lead into Normandy? You're mad, Josseran." D'Aubrey leaned back, his face half in shadow. "You'd draw him down on us — ah, but then, this isn't Vaumartin, is it? My lands are expendable to you — "

"What do you mean to do, then?" Josseran cried. "Sit and smile and bow and give him whatever tithe and tax and ransom he can lay on you?"

"I'll do what I know to be prudent and wise, in the long view."

"Which is to strike! Now, before he is ready!" Josseran half stood, his hands braced on the table. D'Aubrey was staring at him, his eyes glowing in the light from the hearth. Desperate, Josseran flung his own words back at him. "What is it, gardener? Has the weed grown greater than your hoe? Is the rose now to prune you to a stump?"

The Norman's face went rigid. "You step near the bounds of our friendship, Josseran." His voice grated, harsh.

Josseran sank down again on the bench. As if he saw a map, he saw d'Aubrey's mind: while John was languishing in Paris, the Norman lord would take every advantage, nibble at the edges of the king's power, talk loud behind the king's back, but now that John was stirring, now that John's attention was aroused, d'Aubrey would keep small, and speak in a small voice. And do nothing. Josseran rose.

"I ask you once more, my lord," he said. "Give me command, that I may fight our common enemy."

D'Aubrey said, "Perhaps it would be better if you left."

"I will," said Josseran.

"Where are we going?" Simon asked, the younger of the two men-at-arms. "Home to Vaumartin?" His voice was eager.

Josseran said, "I must have an army."

He could not slink back to Vaumartin a failure. She would flay him with her tongue, then, until he struck her down.

They were riding south from d'Aubrey's castle, down toward the great Calais road. Their way led them over a broad plain, studded with clumps of poplars. On his left hand, the dawn was breaking, a smear of salmon-colored light under the lowering blue-black sky; the wind was moist and soft, promising rain. Josseran rode with his head down, his hands on his saddlebows, his mind churning.

"Richard," he said, "up ahead, there is a crossroads tavern, am I right?"

The man on his right hand said, "Yes, my lord."

"There will be idlers at the tavern," Josseran said.

"My lord?" Richard said, puzzled.

"If I offer them loot, they will join us," Josseran said. He straightened, looking around him. He had fought up and down this country now for months; quickly he began to think over it, seeking some quick and easy target. "If we can pull off one good raid — "

Simon turned sharply toward him. "My lord, you won't find many knights at that inn."

Josseran's shoulders moved. "There will be idle men, though.

Willing to go out on a night's raiding, and if we can get them some swift reward, more will follow."

Richard said, stubbornly, "Not knights. Not true men-at-arms, either."

"A soft target," Josseran said, grimly, talking over their voices. "All we need are a few men to carry pitchforks and hoes, for God's love — at first."

They kept still. The dawn was creeping up over the horizon. Just above the level of the ground a mist was forming, filled with pearly light. The wind had died, leaving the humid air heavy as a web against his face. Ahead where this road met the Calais road, the inn waited, full of men that Josseran could take, and shape, and use.

He drew the sweet damp air into his lungs. He had been a fool to wait for someone else to come to his aid. Now was the time to take matters into his own hands. Beside him, Richard and Simon rode silent, and he felt their uneasiness with this, but they were loyal; they would stay with him, whatever he did, and eventually they would see that he was right. He gathered his horse. Ahead lay the inn, and the seeds of his army.

Beside Josseran, in the dark, Richard put up his hand to sign himself with the cross, and Josseran caught his arm and pulled it down.

"No," he said. "We don't want God to watch this."

Richard gave him a sideways look. He and Simon composed one third of the raiding party. The others, behind them, murmuring, were boys or drunks, but they had hands, they carried weapons, and they were a beginning.

Ahead lay their quarry: a village on the outskirts of one of King John's Norman manors. Josseran raised his hand and started forward, keeping his horse to a walk, and the others followed him in a ragged line.

There was a low burst of talk among the strangers, which Richard silenced with a single sharp word. Josseran kept his gaze forward.

The village lay in a fold of two low hills, planted with grapevines; the wall of brush and thorn and earth that surrounded the huts seemed to rise from the ground like one of the hills. As the little company of armed men rode forward no alarm was raised, no sentry hailed them, not even a dog barked, yet Josseran's heart knocked against his ribs as if he faced a mighty army.

He led his little ragtag band up to the wooden gate in the earthworks, and sent Simon up and over it, climbing like a monkey, to pull the bar back and let them in. Now deep inside the village a dog did bark, but it was too late now. Josseran rode into the center of the ring of hovels, onto the short grass of the common field, and with a wave of his arm sent the others around to rouse the villagers.

One hand on the cantle of his saddle, he scanned the buildings of the village, while his men went around and shouted and banged on the doors and threw them open. Most of these homes were tiny one-room huts, although there was a small church at one end of the common, and a larger house with a window near by it. The barking dog let out a single high shrill yelp and was still.

Simon lit a torch. His face was taut, the corners of his mouth sucked down. He gave Josseran a long look but said nothing. The dawn was breaking now, the light brighter in the sky than on the ground, as if the night's dark and cold still lurked in the grass. Josseran's new army was prowling the village, dragging out the peasants by twos and threes onto the common.

They wore only their shirts, their feet bare, their heads tousled. Their eyes were dazed and they looked around them as if they were in a strange place here. A woman wrapped in a dark cloak went by Josseran, sobbing, a baby in her arms and another child clutching her by the skirts and crying. Soon another woman came over and stood beside her, one arm around her.

A bearded man rushed up to Josseran, his face lifted. "What is this? This is the king's village — we are the king's people — "

"Which is why you are suffering," Josseran said.

The man's eyes widened, wild in the blaze of Simon's torch. "I demand — "

Josseran put his foot on the serf's chest and kicked him down. "Shut up." He raised his eyes from the peasant sprawled in the grass to the two other men who had come up behind him, to see how his protest was received, and said, "Keep him quiet or I'll kill him. I'll kill all of you. Now get over there and wait."

Lying on the ground, the bearded man cried, "The king will have you hanged for this, whoever you are!" The other two seized him by the arms and pulled him away, into the swelling crowd of villagers.

Josseran rode once around these people, huddled in the blaze of Simon's torch. Still lined with sleep, their faces lifted toward him, fearful, already sinking from him before he spoke. In their midst the bearded man who had challenged him was on his feet again, his arm around a woman in a long white gown. Josseran swung around, toward Richard, sitting on his horse with his hands on his saddle pommel.

"Go search the houses. Take everything valuable — gold, silver, any treasure you can find."

A moan went up from the mobbed villagers. A baby was crying, in the back of the crowd, its mother shushing it and jiggling it desperately to silence it. Josseran reached across his body and drew his sword, and from the whole whimpering herd there went up a moaning wail of despair.

The bearded man stepped forward. "We have nothing. You waste your efforts here — we are poor folk."

"Whatever you have, I'll take," Josseran said. "If you have nothing, the more pity on you, because I'll burn this whole village, and you with it."

A woman shrieked. All the children were crying now. Packed together for comfort, their arms around one another, the villagers in their huddle lifted a score of white faces toward Josseran, half in hope and half in terror. The bearded man stepped forward.

"We are the king's people. King John's people — "

"King John is my enemy," Josseran said. "His name will not defend you against me — just the opposite! If you want to live, pay me. I am your lord now, not him. You owe all you have to me, not him — by the power of my sword!"

Josseran's wolfpack army dragged a blanket toward him, loaded down with plunder, and laid it on the grass. Josseran rode over to inspect it and swore.

"This is nothing. God's blood!" On the blanket was a heap of housewares, bowls of wood, of pewter. "You idiots — " He glared at the knights. "Look harder!" He wheeled around, back toward the villagers, who shrank away from his stare. "Get that one out here!" He jabbed with his sword at the bearded man.

Richard said, quietly, "This is a poor village, my lord."

He stood by Josseran's stirrup; he spoke from the deep old friendship between them, a warning in his voice, a question. Josseran turned away from him, toward the bearded man, who stumbled forward in the grip of two of Josseran's new knights.

"You. Which house is yours?" Josseran poked at him with his sword. "Come along — drag him if he won't walk — it's that one, isn't it?" He swept his gaze around the circle of houses, found the big one he had already marked, with its two wide windows, its doorstep, its little crowd of outbuildings. "Bring him!"

Richard and Simon stayed to guard the villagers. The new knights, crowing, hauled the bearded man away after Josseran, into the dark, to the house with the doorstep.

The bearded man was saying, over and over, "I have nothing, I have nothing — " His face was moon-white above the semicircle of his beard. Josseran leaned down and spanked him with the flat of his sword.

"Take him inside." Swinging his leg up over the pommel of his saddle, he slid down from his horse.

There was a floor in this house, made of wood planks; his feet thundered on it when he walked in, the house's owner stumbling half-dragged after him. There was a hearth, where a banked fire glowed dimly under a layer of ash. There was a cupboard against the windowless wall; two stools stood before the fire. When the other men came in they crowded the place.

Josseran ran his sword back into its scabbard. "Stir up the fire." He went on into the back of this room, where there was another door, and opened it.

The smell of beasts greeted him. Cold air rushed over his face: this room was a stable, open at the far end. He turned and went back into the house, looking around again, and saw a curtain opposite the hearth.

This hanging cloth covered an open doorway into another, tiny room, filled with a wooden bedstead. The bedclothes were tossed over. He went into the back of the dim space, under the sharply sloping roof. Between the foot of the bed and the wall was only enough space for a chamberpot. Through chinks in the wall the moonlight shone in dots and oblongs on the floor. He went back into the next room.

His new army had stirred the fire up high. Before it they had the bearded man on his knees, pushing his face toward the flames.

"Tell us! You've got something here worth stealing."

Josseran strode roughly in among them, pulling them back. He wanted to get done with this; if he hurried it, he would not have to think about what he was doing. He gripped the bearded man by the shoulder, turned to the others, and said, "Go and search the rest of the houses — even the meanest ones. Get us also whatever horses they have, and something to slaughter for a feast — pigs, chickens, something we can carry. Beer or wine — whatever they have."

The firelight shone on their faces. He hardly recognized these men of his, having led them quickly out of the innyard, and kept his face forward the whole ride here. They hesitated, unsure of him too, and he reached for his sword and they backed up and turned and filed out of the house.

Josseran drew the sword. In this rude low place it seemed like a talisman that glowed and shimmered by its own light. He laid its blade down on the hearth before the bearded man and with his hands on the back of the peasant's neck forced him down on his knees before it.

Quietly he said, "You are the great man in this village. I see that by your house and by your speeches, outside. I saw the vineyards outside your fence here. You have some hoardings, surely — this is the nature of your kind. I will have them, one way or another. You can give them up, and have your life left, to hoard up some more. Or you can die, now, here, on your own hearth, and never have anything again."

The bearded man was breathing loudly, his mouth open, his eyes glazed. The fire on the hearth clothed his face with light. Josseran kept his hand on the man's back, pushing him, keeping him from resting even on his knees, and slowly the peasant's head bowed forward, and his shoulders sagged.

"Under the hearth," he said. "The stone moves."

Josseran grunted. With a shove he cast the man to one side, where the peasant lay as he fell, watching him with a grim face. Before the hearth the floor was made of flagstones, one great stone in the center, and smaller ones around the outside. Josseran felt along the edge of the big stone, found a place to grip it, and lifted.

The stone was heavy; it took all his strength to hoist it over to one side. Turning, he looked into a hole before the fireplace, in which sat two leather sacks.

When he picked them up, they clinked. He laughed, exultant.

"Damn you," said the bearded man, "and damn King John for letting you do this to me."

Josseran laughed again. He stood, taking his sword up off the hearth and sliding it back into its scabbard. "Get back out to the others," he said, and bent for the sacks.

The door burst open. One of the new knights said, "My lord, come, we've got some trouble."

Josseran straightened. "Bring this." He tossed the sacks one after the other into the other man's arms. "Come on."

The trouble was in one of the little huts on the far side of the green, where Josseran's innyard army had found someone willing to fight.

He stood in the doorway of the hut, a club in his hands, a boy only, with a wild shock of hair, and eyes wide and staring. When Josseran came up the other men stepped back; one of them slumped against another, cradling a broken arm. Josseran drew his sword again.

"Come out now," he said, "or I'll kill you."

For answer the boy lifted the club and charged him, a sudden rush of two steps. The club swished through the air at Josseran's head. He ducked under the blow and lunged with his sword, and the boy bounded back into the doorway, where the hut protected him somewhat.

Josseran yelled. Big and strong the serf was, but he knew nothing of fighting. With the sword in both hands the knight lunged at him, got him moving one way, and swung around at his unguarded side. Desperately the boy fended off this attack, but Josseran came at him from the other side again, and this time his sword licked in under the club and went clean through the boy at the middle.

The watching knights gave a gasp, a sigh, more than a cheer. The boy sagged. He struggled to live, his eyes wide and staring; the blood was erupting from his belly and chest, yet he fought for life. Josseran went by him, to see what he had defended so well.

Inside the hut there was nothing, a ring of stones for a fire, a pig in a stall, a heap of straw for a bed. On this bed a girl crouched, whimpering and terrified.

Josseran turned around. His belly heaved. Voices shouted at him in his mind, but he emptied his mind; he thought nothing, he made himself think again of the sacks of money that would buy him an army, a real army, not drunks and fools who let a boy with a club beat them, a boy with a club, who still sat there on the doorstep, as Josseran went out, his eyes wide and staring, even dead.

"Come on," Josseran said. "Let's get out of here." He sheathed his sword.

thirty

THE TWO SACKS were heavy, but most of their burden was in copper and silver. Still, with so few to share it, there was plenty, and the peasants' pigs and chickens and cider made a feast that went on for two days, and as word spread of this success more men came to join Josseran's army.

He raided another village, larger, not far from Rouen, where some of the people fought back. Josseran's army slaughtered these serfs and rampaged all through the night, attacking everything that lived, carrying off the villagers' goods and housewares and animals, burning the houses, even fighting one another over the booty. In the dawn, he led an army of exhausted men away into the forest.

On Ladymas, King John declared Josseran de Vaumartin an outlaw and his lands forfeit to the crown, which brought everything out into the open at last.

A few days after Josseran heard the news of the ban, he had visitors.

His army now numbered well over fifty men, some with attendants, each with a horse or two or three and his armor and weapons. They had settled themselves in a little hill town in the south of Normandy, taking over the houses and making the local people fetch and carry for them. They had plenty of money, so the local people minded little. Josseran kept watch on all the approaches, and so he knew well ahead of the strangers' arrival that they were coming.

Richard brought them. Josseran was sitting under the oak tree in the center of the town, having his hair cut. He slouched in a heavy chair from the priest's house, his feet up on a stool, and watched these unknown men approach him.

Their leader was tall and brawny, dressed in fine riding clothes, with spurs on his heels. After him came some squires; at the edge of the green, a groom in a hooded cloak held their horses.

This groom seemed muffled up for a sunny summer day, and

Josseran looked at him more sharply. Then the knight came up before him.

"I take it you are Josseran de Vaumartin?"

Josseran lifted his eyes. He still sprawled in the heavy chair. The woman behind him was combing his hair and trimming it evenly with a knife. He said, "Leave off, girl," to keep from getting his hair pulled when he moved, and she stepped back, and he stood slowly up from the chair.

"I am the Sire de Vaumartin," he said.

"My lord," said the knight quickly, and bowed. "I am very pleased to have found you. Your fame has spread throughout Normandy and Poitou. It's said the king himself trembles at your name."

Josseran said nothing. His gaze flicked for an instant toward the groom by the horses. Around the green his men were gathering, curious, among them the townspeople.

"I have come to bring you the regards and best wishes of my master," said the knight. "And hopes for opening a communication that will — "

"Enough of this wordplay," Josseran said. "Who sent you?" He strode off toward the groom with the horses. "Or should I not dispense with intermediaries, and come face to face with him?"

The groom wheeled around, tall and straight in the long cloak; just as Josseran reached him, he put up his hand and swept back the hood.

"Shrewd enough, my lord," said the king of Navarre. His eyes glittered.

Josseran grunted at him. "Well now, we've come to the meat course. Come indoors, Your Grace; no need to overstuff the commons with gazing on a king." He turned, gesturing to Richard to keep watch on Navarre's men, and led him away to the town church, which he had taken to live in.

"You know about the ambush in L'Aigle," said the king of Navarre.

"I heard your brothers murdered Charles d'Espagne," Josseran said. "A little hastily done, I thought."

Navarre was walking around the altar end of the little church. Made of stone and wood, its walls washed white, it was cool and dim in the summer heat. Josseran had taken down the crucifix and the altar rail. His bedding lay in a disorderly heap before the altar. Navarre, tall, slender, spare, paced along the room, looking things over.

"Such a haste as will destroy King John. Now I mean to draw the king himself into my grasp. I am here to offer you the chance to take a part in that — to have your revenge as well — because I honor you and what you have done."

Josseran's fist clenched. "To take the king himself."

Navarre wheeled toward him. The bleak shape of the church wall framed him. He said, "To wring from him all that belongs to me — to you — to all of us!"

"By God," Josseran said, "if I had him here now — " He strode away across the church, unable to keep still, his rage working in him like a fire. At the wall, he swung around. "What do you mean to do?"

"I must have your hand on this first," said Navarre. "That you will join me in it."

Josseran's ardor cooled; his head rose an inch, his belly tightening. "I cannot promise such a thing, unless I know what you intend."

"I cannot tell you such secrets without your bond of honor."

"My honor is bound. I will reveal nothing."

Navarre's face changed, like a shadow passing over it, a flicker of annoyance. He turned away, dark and ascetic in the stark frame of the church, a priest of plots. Josseran's skin tingled; every nerve was warning him, every inner eye.

He said, "If you will not reveal yourself in this, Your Grace, then we are done here. I shall keep you here no longer."

Navarre's head swiveled toward him. "You must speak no word of this to any man — before it is worked."

"I am a knight. I give you my vow."

Navarre came closer to him, his face sharp. "On Christmas Day I shall meet with the dauphin, Prince Charles — "

"The dauphin!"

"I have him utterly in my power. He worships me. I have told him how his father and grandfather have abused me and robbed me, and he sees it his sacred duty to restore to me what I have lost." Navarre's eyes shone like lamps; as he spoke of his trials his voice sweetened, his lips curved in a smile almost womanishly soft.

Josseran made a sound deep in his chest. There was a panicky flutter in his gut. "Do not trust the Valois. Any Valois."

"Bah. You know nothing of this. He is a fool, this fish-prince, but a useful one. At that I will leave it, until you join me."

Josseran turned away, putting his back to Navarre. To seize the king would end it all, quickly, in one decisive stroke. A captive King John would have to sign over Vaumartin to its rightful lord, forever, unbound, untainted. Sign over also what he owed to Navarre — which might include the throne itself.

He said, "I will not enter into an alliance with a Valois."

"You will not be doing so, I promise you. The dauphin will not be in it for any longer than necessary."

Josseran turned to face him, convinced. "No. If there is a Valois involved, I will not be a party to it."

Navarre's face stiffened, harsh. "God's blood — what is there in a knight that stiffens him below the neck but not above? You're being an idiot, Vaumartin — this is in our reach!"

He thrust out his hand, palm up, and the fingers closed suddenly into a fist; Josseran thought at once of a spider's legs closing, and he drew back, shaking his head.

"No. Get out of my town, Navarre. I am not interested in this."

"You idiot," Navarre said, between his teeth, and strode down past him, going the length of the church to the door.

Josseran stayed where he was, his head slightly turned, listening to the king's departure; when the door slammed, he raised his eyes, and gave a long sigh.

A few moments later the door opened again. He looked around and saw the woman who had cut his hair.

She said, "Richard wants to know if these men are to leave."

"Yes," Josseran said. "He should see them gone. Then bid him come here to me."

"Should I come back, my lord?"

"Yes," he said. He put his hand up to the back of his head, where the hair was half long, half short. "Yes."

thirty-one

THE WINTER KEPT THEM all quiet for a while. Snow fell all through January. Josseran heard nothing more from Navarre himself, although the rumors flew that he and the dauphin had their heads together, brewing something up like two witches over a cauldron.

Early in the spring, Josseran led his army to attack a custom-house, on a bridge over the Seine. The guards and soldiers retreated into the high stone tower that commanded the bridge, against which Josseran's men had no power, save to keep them there.

Then Josseran filled boats with straw and broken barrels and set them afire and let them drift down under the bridge. The blazing barges ignited the wooden bridge, and roasted the king's men in their tower like a stew in a pot, until they threw their weapons out of the tower into the river and lowered the treasure chests of the king's tolls to Josseran on a rope. Then he let them escape.

The king sent an army to hunt Josseran down, and he withdrew with his men into the hills of Poitou. He dared not go down to Vaumartin with them, since his own estates could not support so many men, so he seized a fortified town near the border, and from it preyed on the whole countryside. After a while, the local people paid him tribute; travelers gave their tolls to him and not the king.

In the summer he heard that Navarre and King John met under a truce flag, but nothing came of their talking but false smiles and lies. The whole of Normandy seethed with gossip and prophecy. The English kept to themselves in Calais, and while Navarre walked free King John could not attack the Plantagenets.

Josseran's army drew more and more knights; his army swelled large as any king's. There were folk, fawning, who called him the king of Normandy.

He dreamt, sometimes, of Vaumartin, and woke full of a deep and painful longing. He never dreamt of Isobel.

"Oremus." With a great shuffling of feet and rustling of skirts the congregation knelt down. Lost among them, Josseran bowed his head to pray. He crossed himself, asking God humbly to forgive him for all his sins. Kneeling on the stone floor, one of hundreds of penitents, anonymous in his brown cloak, he raised his eyes to the crucified Christ hanging above him, swaddled in purple cloth for Passion Week, and offered prayers for his wife, his dead brothers Clair and Yvain, his missing nephew Everard.

He shut his mind against the memories of hating his wife, and abandoning his brother and his nephew. He was supposed to love them; here, in the church, in the perfect cosmos of Christ, he loved them with his whole heart.

It was Palm Sunday. Lent was almost over, season of repentance. After Easter the fighting season began again. There were rumors flying everywhere — that was another reason for him to steal down from his hilltop stronghold to Caen, to pick up the news — that King John had summoned a parlement in Paris, to raise money for a general war; that Navarre in Rouen had the dauphin in the fold of his cloak; that the Black Prince in Aquitaine had sworn a vow to crush John into submission before Assumption Day. Josseran thumped himself on the chest with his fist.

"Mea culpa. Mea culpa. Mea maxima culpa."

One among hundreds, he rose, the priest's voice swelling strongly out over him, telling of forgiveness and mercy, and the press of folk around him shifted and stirred and Richard came up beside him.

"My lord."

"Wait for me outside," Josseran said, between his teeth.

"My lord, you will want to know this now."

The priest was blessing the congregation. Josseran's hand moved over his own breast. Splendid in his ornately embroidered vestments, the priest turned and approached the high altar, bowing, his hands pressed together. The altar boy lifted the ewer, to cleanse the priest's hands; they would offer the Eucharist soon, and he wanted to receive the Body of God. Yet what Richard had said nagged at him. He crossed himself again, his eyes on the altar, his mind on Richard. Finally he turned and went out of the church.

In the porch's shade, he swept his narrowed gaze quickly around him, out toward the sunlit square, saw nothing harmful, and faced the man-at-arms. "What is it?"

Richard said, "King John has taken Navarre prisoner."

Josseran let out an explosive sound, all the air punched out of him. He went three or four steps forward, toward the sunlight. Richard followed him. On the steps of the church porch, Josseran wheeled around.

"When? How did it happen?"

Richard said, "Navarre was feasting together at Rouen with the dauphin Charles. King John with a hundred of his knights surprised them. They say he slaughtered all the Navarrese but the king himself, and him he bound hand and foot, and hauled off to a dungeon in castle Arleux."

Josseran grunted again. His skin tingled. "I warned him. I told him not to trust the Valois." With the back of his hand he thumped Richard's chest. "There's a lesson in this, you see. Navarre thinks himself so clever, and yet there is always someone cleverer yet." He laughed, unamused. "Better to consider yourself too stupid than too smart, you see."

Richard said, "You think that the dauphin betrayed him."

"That's what I think." Josseran started down the steps, his henchman at his heels. "Where are the other men?" He had brought ten of his trusted men into Caen with him.

"I have them gathered in the horsemarket, by the main gate, where they will not be obvious."

Josseran's head bobbed, approving this; his legs strode out, carrying him at a fast walk across the sunny square, through the crowds of idlers.

"Navarre should have thought twice." He spat into the street, his mind buzzing with the implications of this. With Navarre out of the way, King John could march against the Plantagenets, could turn his interest to other rebels also. He gestured to Richard to come up beside him.

"Yes, my lord."

"We'll have to go back and get the rest of the men," Josseran said.

"Then where are we going?" Richard asked.

"To Vaumartin," said Josseran.

thirty-two

A WORKMAN was only as good as his tools, Marcel had often enough heard. He ground his teeth, glaring at the tool currently resisting his hand: the mason Rimbeau.

"I don't care what you've heard elsewhere, Rimbeau! There is going to be another war."

"The astrologers in the rue des Marmousets are saying that when the English come we'll avenge Crécy and drive the Plantagenets out of France forever. Why do we need — "

"God's blood!" Marcel jerked his fist up; with difficulty he kept himself from striking the mason, standing large and grimy before him, stinking of mortar. "What else do the stars say, Rimbeau, hah? Do they tell you you needn't work any more? That they'll drop bread into your lap? Damn you, do as I tell you!"

His temper forced out the last few words in a shriek, and to recover himself Marcel walked away up the wall a little.

King Philip Augustus, indefatigable builder, had raised walls around the city of Paris, but ten generations of neglect had toppled them stone from stone. Even to rebuild those walls required huge amounts of new stone, mortar, and work. Here, in the last unfinished stretch, where the Saint-Honoré road rolled through the fields and meadows into the fringes of Paris, the work had to begin anew, at the ground, and after six months of planning and labor Marcel still had not managed to get a single course of stone laid down.

What Marcel wanted was for the road to enter Paris here through a huge double gate, the Saint-Honoré gate, with its own armory, with offices for customs collectors and their staffs. The gate stood now only in Marcel's mind. The wall ended in open fields, in heaps of stone, in half-dug ditches and unmixed mortar smelling like cellars. By the road the old tower that would one day be the armory stood roofless and half ruined. The workmen who were supposed to be building wall and gate and armory sat around idle in the shade below the plane trees, whose lower leaves were whitened with stonedust, and listened to their master argue with the provost.

Marcel walked a long way beside the wall, fighting his frustrations, and tramped back to Rimbeau.

"The astrologers say what will make them rich. I remember how in the last war the English burned the gardens of Saint-Germain-des-Prés and shot arrows into the shambles on the south bank. Build me my wall, Rimbeau, or I shall find a better man to do it."

The mason's lips compressed into a flat straight line, like the seam between two building stones. "Yes, Master Provost."

"If you need more men, perhaps we can find them, but I suspect you need only get a good day's work out of the crews you have. But if you cannot do that — "

"I will," said Rimbeau, and started toward the men lingering near the wall; when his attention turned on them, they sprang up at once and started heaving stones around. Rimbeau plunged in among them, shouting and striking at them. Marcel backed off a little, his eyes narrowed, his nose pinched against the burning smell of lime, his attention caught by a little troop of horsemen coming down the road from the city.

They had reined up, a good way behind dust and uproar around the new gate, but now one of them rode forward, a boy in a silk doublet, on a splendid bay horse. Marcel stopped where he was, folding his arms over his chest. Out of the old tower came a tall figure in a long black coat: his clerk, Everard le Breton, who had been inside making lists. He too stopped to watch the pretty boy gallop up.

"Hello, you," the boy shouted, in an imperious voice. "Hold off with your work, now, and let the dust settle, so that His Grace the king might ride through here without getting his clothes dirty."

Marcel put his teeth on edge. He glanced around him and saw Rimbeau and his workmen already leaving off their chores, backing up with flourishes and awkward bows toward their sovereign. Shirkers. The provost glared at the boy in his pretty coat.

"Well, get on with it!"

The boy, who was perhaps ten years old, jerked up his head and frowned. "You can't talk to me like that! I am a Prince of the Lilies — "

"Well," Marcel said, "get on with it, sir." He backed up, into the rubble and the white dust; Everard crossed the road to him.

The boy tarried, his eyes narrowed on the provost, his lower lip thrust out, his arrogance competing with his youth. From the group of men waiting behind him on the road came a shout, and the little prince wheeled his horse and galloped back to meet them. Marcel glanced at Everard.

"What did you find in there?"

Everard shrugged. "The bottom story is sound enough, the floor is paved, and the ceiling's good. The door has a stout lock." He turned to watch the horsemen riding toward them.

King John wore a green coat stitched with silver thread. In his wide-brimmed hat there was an ostrich plume and a medal of Saint Denis. He reined in before Marcel, compelling the provost to kneel, his clerk kneeling, all his workmen kneeling, while the king looked broadly around him, one hand on his hip.

"Well, Marcel," he said at last, "you are doing some excellent work here."

Marcel said, "Your Grace is very kind."

He watched the king with a keen eye. Repairing old walls was within his power as provost; building new ones was not.

The king said, "Are you then going to make a gate here? Tell me what you are doing."

Marcel drew a deep breath, and began cautiously enough, describing how he intended to close the old rounds of the walls again, but as the king smiled on him and nodded, the provost grew bolder. Pleased with his design, proud of his enterprise, he told the king how the new gate would stand here, how the new armory would make this a stronghold in war, in peace a symbol of the might of Paris.

The king was beaming at him. Marcel said, "If you wish, Your Grace, I could take you around the entire circuit of the wall. You could inspect — "

John shook his head. "I have seen enough. Excellent work, Master Marcel, indeed, although, of course, of no urgency — we shall destroy the English long before they reach Paris. This all must be costing you quite a quantity of money."

Beside the provost, the clerk Everard suddenly stirred and cleared his throat. Marcel said, "We have raised the money from duties and charters — "

"And you must have a lot of it somewhere, then," said the king. "Which I shall require of you, Marcel, immediately, for my war against the English."

Marcel clamped his jaw shut. Around him no one spoke; he and the king stared at each other, the king smiling, the provost not. At last, in a neutral voice, the provost said, "The king commands."

"Excellent," said the king. "I shall send someone to the Châtelet this afternoon, to fetch it." He raised his hand and spurred his horse, and the little troop in their jeweled clothes galloped out through the gate that was not yet there.

Marcel said, "Damn him!" And turned and kicked violently at the dirt.

Everard said, "Well, that's unfortunate."

By the wall, the workmen were gawking after the king, and murmuring into one another's ears. The master mason came around a hod of stone toward Marcel, and as he walked he peeled off his canvas apron.

He did not stop as he passed Marcel. He said only, "Send for me, Master Provost, when the stars drop some more money on you," and flopping his apron over his shoulder, he strolled away down the road. One by one, the other workmen followed him.

Marcel spat through his teeth. He kicked the ground again. "God damn him!"

Everard said, "He has no idea how much money there is."

"He'll find out." Marcel's shoulders slumped, round under his coat, and he cast a long sad look around him at the bits and pieces of his dream. *Of no urgency,* the king had said.

"That's the weakness of a wall," Everard said mildly. "It only protects us against the enemy outside."

Marcel lifted his head, gathering himself; he refused to be stopped in his designs simply because he had no money. He said, "Is the tower empty?"

Everard shook his head. "Not at all. There's a lot of lumber in it, and some unworked iron — " He took a piece of paper from his sleeve, on which were several lines of notes. "Some pikes, barrels of arrows, even a bombard."

"Don't let the king know," said Marcel. "He'll take it all."

He started off down the road toward the center of Paris, and the clerk fell into step behind him. They passed through a cluster of little houses, where the women sat in the sun plucking chickens, and the children chased feathers; these people called out as Marcel went by, and he waved his hand absently to them.

He said, "Is everything I do to come to nothing, for the sake of the king?"

Everard said, "He thinks little of the wall."

"Yes — thank God for it. If he appreciated it, would he let me go on building it?" Marcel shook his head again.

Everard walked along beside him, his head turned, staring away into the orchards and fields that they passed. He said, "The wall alone will stop no one. Nothing. Not inside or outside."

"Yes, yes," said Marcel. They had talked of this before, of the need to put armed men on the wall, if they were attacked.

Everard was plunging on into it again. "He won't fortify Paris to fight the English. He'll ride out, with all his knights — all the defenders of the city will go with him."

Marcel said, "Good riddance."

The clerk turned and smiled at him. "Yes, yes — good riddance, especially if we can keep them out once they've left."

The provost grunted. "How could we do that? You get on this idea like a wild horse, Everard, and it runs away with you."

"Anybody can defend a wall. If they are prepared for it. Women with broomsticks, children with stones, if they know what to do."

Marcel gathered in his breath; his energies, frustrated with the gate, flowed suddenly into this new course. He imagined defying the king from the wall, of turning John back, of denying him, and his chest swelled. A peculiar excitement lifted him like a wave of the sea. "Damn him." For a moment, he indulged himself with the notion of revenge, he saw himself enormous, King John small and shivering at his feet.

Everard said nothing more. He was looking broadly around him at the houses and shops they passed. Marcel's imaginary triumph over the king faded into the gray foretaste of defeat.

He said, "What sort of army do you suppose you could make, from ordinary men?"

"One committed to defend their own homes," Everard said. His head swiveled toward Marcel. "A militia of the citizens. We could go through the guilds, have them turn out their apprentices, have them march together one or two days in the week, give them particular posts on the wall, to guard — "

Marcel gave a short, dry, humorless laugh. "You have thought it all through, have you? Have you given thought to what King John will do to us — to them — to you — for having thought of it at all?" He walked on a few strides. The dust crunched under his feet. Ahead the spires of Paris pierced the air, wands raised toward Heaven's gate.

He said, "Do it, then, Everard — but keep it always as something that can be undone. Hah? You understand me?" He lengthened his stride, his face raised toward the lofty church towers of Paris. "Now, let us get on with our work."

thirty-three

ONE DAY'S MARCH north of Vaumartin, Josseran's army stopped and refused to go any farther.

They had ridden down through the hills of Mortain, over the poor rough countryside of Maine and western Anjou; there was nothing to plunder, no villages worth raping, not even much to eat, for man or horse, and with each day's passage men had slipped away, so that the army seemed to shrink with every stride. Then when they crossed over the bridge of Saint-Croix, and saw before them the barren hill ranges of Brittany, rising rank on stony rank into the featureless distance, the whole band drew rein and would follow Josseran no more.

He cursed them, rode around them shouting into their faces — eighty unshaven, slouching, saddle-worn men in stolen armor — and they gathered around him and tried to reason with him, as if they were priests.

"On this road there's no more for us tomorrow than there was yesterday," said one, a red-faced man named Jean-Louis, who had joined up after the first raid. "I say we go east, King, to Champagne and Burgundy, where there's been no fighting. There will be plenty of plunder — we'll live easy there."

The other men gave a rumble of agreement. Josseran laid his hands on his saddlebow. The men filled the road here, overflowing onto the scrubby sunbrowned slopes on either side; the hillsides here were barren and bleak and close, the horizon looming high around him like a trap, and he felt uncomfortable stopping like this, although all he could see was a hawk sailing through the sky.

He turned to Richard. "Go on and scout ahead of us, as far as you can."

"My lord," Richard said, relief light in his voice, and reined his horse around; but Simon, next to him, lingered where he was, his gaze on Josseran.

"My lord — should we go as far as Vaumartin?"

Josseran looked into his face, and saw there the man's homesick yearning; if Richard reached Vaumartin, he would not come out again.

"Go," Josseran said. "I'll be there soon enough."

Simon looked from him to Jean-Louis and back to Josseran. "With these?" he said.

Josseran's temper mounted, a heat in his chest. Since his boyhood Simon and Richard had followed him without question. Now their questions bred questions in himself. "I am going to Vaumartin," he said, loudly. "Go there now and wait for me!"

Simon stared at him a moment longer, as if he did not quite see him there. Finally, he said, "Yes, my lord," and swung his horse's head around. Richard was already disappearing over the next rise in the road; Simon lifted his horse into a canter to follow, and did not look back. The sound of his horse's hoofs faded away into the wind.

"Devil take them," Jean-Louis said, loudly. He gave Josseran his broad gap-toothed grin. "Let's go to Champagne, King — we'll follow you there like the angels after Jesus Christ Himself!"

Josseran leaned his hands on his saddlebow. "Vaumartin is my castle. I have brought you here to defend it."

"We'll get you a new castle," someone bawled, behind Jean-Louis. "Who cares about this one, in this poor shabby place?" There was a roar from the others, men turning to nudge one another, nodding, agreeing, facing him again, an untidy mass of faces, empty of understanding.

Josseran straightened. He knew no way to compel these men, who followed him out of greed and lust, not loyalty. Their pledges to him went exactly as deep as their purses. Bitterly he began to curse them for cheat-knights, but shut his mouth. He turned his head away, his heart a canker in his chest.

The bond should have begun with him, as their lord, their liege, their sword-father. Yet he had never troubled himself with them, in any way that would connect them to him. He knew only a handful of them by name. All that had ever mattered to him was their arms, their numbers. He had paid no heed to where they had come from, or why, or even what it was they wanted, riding with him. He it was who had failed.

The wind might have blown them here. The wind might as well

carry them away. He said, "Go to Champagne, if you wish, but without me."

Jean-Louis said, "King — you lead us. You have brought us wonderful victories. You've made us rich — you can do it again."

"Who cares about him, anyway — if he won't lead us?" A lanky boy pushed forward, one of those who had followed Josseran out of the Calais tavern. He thrust his way up toward Josseran, but it was to the other men he spoke. "Who needs this king here, either? Let's elect one of us the king — any of us could do as he has done — "

He glared at Josseran, his hand on the sword in his belt. "I say we do without him!"

Josseran flung his head back. His throat tightened, full of scalding words, and he reached across himself for the sword at his side. The boy half drew his own sword, his face knotted into a growl. They glared at one another.

"I could kill you in a single blow," Josseran said, slowly. "But what glory would there be in that for me?" His mouth tasted of ashes.

"Coward!" the boy cried, in a voice that cracked.

Josseran let go his sword hilt; he planted his hands on his saddle pommel, and looked broadly around him at the other men. "You know nothing of chivalry, therefore you know nothing of cowardice, either, boy." He spat into the road. "Find another outlaw to lead you."

"Let's ride, then!" Jean-Louis shouted, and flung up his arm, and with a creak of leather and a rumble of hoofs the great band swung around and scrambled off again, back up the road, raising a cloud of dust that showered around Josseran like dirty snow. Not one of them remained behind.

His chest constricted, as if bands of iron encircled him. Without knights, he could not defend Vaumartin. Yet what made an army of knights was not mere men, but their common faith, their honor, their chivalry. The shabby riders shambling away up the road from him were not knights, for all they fought and killed. He had been a fool to think he could save Vaumartin with such men.

It came to him suddenly, in a wave of despair, that he had already lost Vaumartin. He had lost it when he yielded to Isobel and took Everard to Crécy; he had lost it again at Crécy when he abandoned his brother and his nephew, lost it since, over and over, with lies, deceits, dishonor, lost it even as he struggled with all his strength to keep it.

Into his mind sprang an old memory, long cherished, of honor and respect and pride, and an offer of friendship, artlessly extended across grim barriers of war: a dream of chivalry.

Alone in the road, he swung his horse's head around. He dared not return to Vaumartin, not without his honor, but to the south, in Aquitaine, there was a man who might redeem him. He urged his horse on down the road, to find the Black Prince.

thirty-four

AFTER THE BLOODY FEASTING in Rouen, when John seized the king of Navarre, all of Navarre's holdings in Normandy rose up against their Valois overlord. Chief of these strongholds was the great city of Breteuil. With kingly pomp and many roundly spoken vows, John proclaimed his intent to bring these rebels to their knees, and after the usual deliberation and delay, he set forth to impose his will on Breteuil.

Bonboisson and his family and Everard, Jeanne, and Sylviane went to watch the king ride out of Paris on this mission of honor. They sat in Bonboisson's wagon, a wooden island in a sea of cheering people, while the king and his chivalry paraded down the Draperie with a flutter of silks and a bright gleaming of armor, the blaring of trumpets and the shrilling of pipes.

Bonboisson's two daughters cheered and waved their kerchiefs at the first contingents of knights, until Mère Bonboisson slapped them into silence; even then, their eyes glowed, as if the passing glory raised a glory in their hearts. Sylviane sat in a corner of the wagon and wrote on her slate, her head down.

Bonboisson said, tight-lipped, "This idea of a militia, Everard, I do not hold with."

Everard shrugged. "Nor does anyone else, apparently." They had gotten little enthusiasm from Paris for the citizen militia. On either side, the crowd roared; the king's young sons were riding by, magnificent in red-and-blue doublets.

Chief among them, the dauphin looked pale as ashwood. He rode holding on to his saddle with one hand. He looked sickly, as he had been all his life, wan and limp. He seemed incapable of forceful action. His botched conspiracy with the king of Navarre appeared on its surface to be the work of a weak and submissive mind.

Yet the violence at Rouen had worked in his favor, in favor of his house, removing a deadly rival, and the rumor ran strong in Paris that the dauphin himself had plotted that — had lured Navarre to Rouen to deliver him over to King John. Everard watched him pass with an intense curiosity.

A shower of small objects pelting the front of the wagon distracted his attention. Servants walking along beside the king's son were throwing handfuls of sweetmeats into the crowd, and the surge of the mob as they fought for these prizes rocked the wagon; Everard bent forward, one hand out, to shield his wife a little.

"It is the king's right and duty to defend us," Bonboisson said, "as you will see, and all France, when he has hanged these Breteuil rebels from their own gateposts."

The constable appeared, on a capering stallion, surrounded by knights in burnished armor. Silk ribbons streamed from their helmets, their bridles, the tips of their lances. There were bells on their harness, catching the sun, the jingling lost in the thunder of the crowd. Some pipers followed after them, setting up a shrill merry music, and the two Bonboisson daughters leapt and cried out, clapping their hands together. Mère Bonboisson bent forward to swat at them again.

"Be seemly, you girls!" She cast a furious, bitter look at Jeanne. "You encourage them in this, you know — letting that child do as she pleases."

Jeanne said, mildly, "Sylviane, sit up straight."

The girl raised her head briefly, shot a fiery look at Mère Bonboisson and Jeanne, and bent over the slate again. Mère Bonboisson grunted.

"Too late, Jeanne! She's in the Devil's hands now. You should have done something long ago. It's too late now."

Bonboisson said, "It's not my duty to fight. I am a subject of the king of France, by which I am called to obey him, and you and Marcel also, Everard. When the king finds out what you are trying to do, he'll take it ill, I warn you."

"What are we trying to do?" Everard asked. Perhaps Bonboisson abhorred the militia, but he had not stopped talking about it since he heard of it.

"You and the parlement both," said Bonboisson, and pressed his lips shut.

Everard laughed. The king had called a grand parlement, to raise the tax money to pay for his war, but the parlement had refused, and then, pompously, had announced that henceforth they would raise the money, they would conduct the war. Unfortunately for their pretensions, no one listened to them save themselves. Marcel called them the School of Idiots.

Mère Bonboisson said, "She's a bad example for my girls, Jeanne. I am sorely disappointed in you."

Jeanne leaned down and touched Sylviane's shoulder. "Sit up, child, watch the procession." Without even raising her head, Sylviane thrust her rudely off.

Everard looked around him, at the great boisterous crowd that packed the sloping strip of ground that lay between the pavement of the Draperie and the river's edge behind him. On the far side the people scrambled up the high fronts of the buildings and hung out the windows and dangled their feet over the eaves of the roofs. The thunder of their voices made his hair stand on end, and now suddenly their uproar doubled and doubled again: the king was coming.

The sun flashed on brass, on steel. Three long ranks of trumpeters strutted down the center of the Draperie, blasting warlike notes through their long shining horns. On either side ran pages, their green doublets flecked with fleurs-de-lys, casting handfuls of money and candies into the crowd.

Then came the king's favorites, their horses prancing and cavorting at the screams and howls of the crowd. The plumes on their helmets swept the air; their harness swung heavy with gold and silver embroidery. Their armor was chased and polished. On their shields shone the emblems of the greatest blood in France, a menagerie of noble lions and unicorns, leopards and boars. They carried their helmets in the crooks of their arms; above their flashing steel corselets their heads looked ridiculously small.

The shouting rose to a feverish hysteria. There on his magnificent bay horse, one hand raised above his head in greeting, came John himself, enormous in his armor, looking more like some mythological beast than a man.

Beside Everard, Bonboisson suddenly sprang to his feet, rigid with respect. "The king!" he cried. "Hurrah for the king!" His voice was only one of thousands. Along the edges of the crowd, men broke ranks and rushed toward the king, and the knights around him galloped up to throw them back. John, smiling, swung from side to side, accepting the homage of his people; his face was red and sleek with sweat. Everard, sitting, watched him ride by.

"You have no sense of propriety," Bonboisson told him, reproachfully.

Sylviane turned to him. "Look, Father, what I've made."

Mère Bonboisson laughed contemptuously. "A few stupid hentracks."

It was a poem. Everard read it through twice, once out loud for the rest of them, although it was in Latin, which none of the others understood. The crowd around them was subsiding into a satisfied murmur, their lust for pageantry contented.

"It would be better if you used the right grammar, here," he said.

"But then it won't rhyme," Sylviane said, and gave him an angry look.

Everard shrugged, handing the slate back to her. Beside him Jeanne leaned past him toward the girl, to pat her cheek, and turn back one of her long curls.

"If you must wreck the language to say something, it cannot be worth the words," Everard said.

Sylviane's cheeks went red. "I like it! Very much!"

"You would probably like it better if it were better done," Everard said.

Mère Bonboisson harrumphed again, smiling. Sylviane sat bolt upright. Her cheeks burned. Abruptly she flung the slate down and scrambled over the side of the wagon and ran off into the crowd.

"Sylvie!" Jeanne cried, and started up; Everard caught her arm.

Mère Bonboisson's face wore a limpid smile. "There. You see?"

Bonboisson stared at Everard. "You are too harsh with her."

Jeanne wheeled on him. "Why did you do that?"

Everard drew his wife down firmly on the wagon seat. "Go home with these folk here," he said, and smiled into her furious frightened eyes. Getting up he climbed out of the wagon and went away into the crowd, after his daughter.

Even in the dense surging crowd, he caught up with her almost at once. They walked along awhile without speaking, going away from the Draperie, down toward the riverbank, side by side.

At last, Sylviane said, "You took their side against me."

"You know that is not so," he said.

"You said yourself that words don't matter."

"Did I? What a fool I was. The poem itself is only words. If the poem is to matter, then, must it not yield to the rules of the words?"

She sighed; she cast a long look at him. He took hold of her hand, and she let him hold it, as if she were a little girl, or his sweetheart. In her pale flaxen hair the sun struck a glint of a rainbow. They left the crowd behind. On the shelving riverbank, where the gravel crunched under their feet, she looked up at him, her eyes narrow.

"Who am I — really? What was my father's name?"

"Italo del Borgo," he said. "Your mother was Elisabetta del Borgo."

"Sylviane del Borgo," she said, drawing the name out in long rolling tones. "Sylviane del Borgo! It's a pretty name, isn't it?"

He said uneasily, "Yes, it is."

She whirled toward him, her face bright and wild. "But you are still my father." She flung her arms around him and hugged him, her whole body pressed against him, and then she spun around again, and ran away from him, down the riverbank toward the quays and stone bridges, and Everard walked slowly along in her wake.

thirty-five

BYPASSING Vaumartin, Josseran rode south, toward the city of Bordeaux, where Prince Edward kept his court. The way was desolate, the road empty. The only other travelers he saw went in packs, bristling with arms, and cast wary looks at him as he passed by.

He guessed how he looked to them — a dusty rider on a road-weary horse, his pack horse as worn and dirty as a peddler's. He was glad of their aversion. He was deep sunk in his aloneness; his mind was dark and grim. He felt himself to be traveling through a featureless spaceless void, to be nowhere, and no one, until he reached the prince.

At a toll bridge over the Dordogne, in the hot sun, he waited for a chance to cross, the only mounted man in a crowd of wagons and people on foot. A steady stream of people was hurrying across the span of the bridge to the far side, and it took him nearly an hour, in the hot sun, to reach the gate.

As he waited, against his will he overheard scraps of the gossip of these others, and in their voices, arose the name of Edward of Aquitaine again and again.

When he came to pay his toll, he asked, "What is this of the Black Prince?"

The customs man took his penny, laid it flat on his table, and began to cut it in half. "God have mercy on us. They say he rides again." He lifted his hand from his knife long enough to cross himself. The blade had bitten a bright gouge into the copper.

Josseran took back his half of the penny. "Where does he ride?"

"North, they say — burning and raiding — the south is safe. That's where all you folk are going, anyway, and so it must be safe."

Josseran reined his horse around. "Not I."

"What?" The customs man looked owlishly at him. "Well, then, the toll — "

Josseran laughed, contemptuous, at the deformed coin the man held up to him, and swung his horse around and rode away.

Now he spoke to anyone he saw, riding after them on the road, stopping them in their tracks, badgering them for all they could tell him of the Black Prince. In an inn on the bank of the Dordogne, he heard of the siege of Breteuil, where the people held out valiantly against King John; farther up the road, he met the first of the rumors that an army of English knights under Henry of Lancaster had landed at Calais to go to the support of the beleaguered city. When he asked about the Black Prince, folk only crossed themselves and shook their heads.

Three days later, as he quartered his way eastward, he saw a fountain of black smoke rising into the sky ahead of him.

It took him almost until sundown to reach the blackened ruin of a manor house, burned to the stone floors, the only sound the buzzing of a great cloud of flies that scattered up from a dead cow that lay bloating in the court. A quick circle of the place found him the broad trail of a great mass of men, leading off through trampled fields into the northeast.

For many days thereafter, he did not stop to eat or sleep until sheer exhaustion forced it on him. Steadily he pushed his weary horses on. The trail was easy to follow, in daylight and at night under the waning moon. Ruins marked it, fields and vineyards and the wretched villages of the peasants who worked them, burned and trodden down. There were no living folk here, no beasts. When, reluctantly, he paused to let his tired horses feed, he had to search awhile to find them grass. He himself ate such game as he came on. Now and then, in a ruin, he found a handful of grain the pillagers had overlooked, or a few apples.

One day, at twilight, he smelled wood smoke.

The army's trail had taken him down a broad road, west of the great river Loire, through rolling meadows and stands of oak; being wary, now, of every man, he had not ridden down the middle of it, but off to one side, where no one could come on him without warning. At day's end the road wound down into a narrow valley, where sudden outcrops of rock burst up through the green on either side, beetling over the path. Josseran swerved his horses around and worked his way along the rough crest of the hill.

The sun went down through low red clouds like gouts of blood. Josseran drew rein, his muscles quivering with fatigue; his horse's head drooped.

There ahead of him, indistinct in the gathering darkness, a tower rose from the sheer side of the valley, like another upthrust of the rock. The wind shifted suddenly, and he tasted the flavorful tang of smoke on it. His horse flung up its head, and its nostrils fluttered; between his calves its great barrel swelled, and it let out a blast of a neigh like a trumpet call.

Josseran leaned down, his hackles rising, to put his hand on its nose. From the valley below him a horse answered, first one bugling whinny, and then a chorus.

He straightened. An eager gladness took him, a boyish excitement. Rummaging quickly through his pack, he found a rag, still white enough to be a sign of peace, and tied it to a stick. His horses needed little urging, although they were weary; they smelled the other beasts below, in the valley now filled with the night like a black pit, and they scrambled down through leaf and branch, slipping and sliding, banging loose showers of rock, down toward the night camp of the Black Prince.

The prince said, "And this is Jean de Grailly, Captal de Buch, as they style him — as fair a knight as ever a lady swooned over."

The heavyset unsmiling man before him muttered a greeting and held out his hand, and Josseran shook it.

"My lord, we have not met before, yet I have heard such tales of your prowess I think I know you well enough."

The prince clapped him on the back. "Fair words enough, my lord. With you among us, we make the greatest company in Christendom, I think."

"God grant us victory, then," said Josseran.

They stood in the prince's tent, in the meadow below the tower Romorantin; he had now met all the prince's captains, who stood around him in a circle, their faces grim, dusty, drawn with weariness and war. The round bald head of Sir John Chandos, the English knight, glistened in the light of the only lamp.

"I hope, my lord, your sudden appearance here marks some end to the bad luck we are having with this tower, which refuses to yield to us."

The prince's eyes flashed. He was as Josseran remembered him, tall and lean, with russet hair; although it had been years since they had met before Calais, he was so much younger than Josseran that he seemed a boy still. Now he spoke with a boy's impatient ardor.

"I cannot see how any man with a fighting heart could ride beneath it and not want to take it on."

"Yet if we linger here too long," said Chandos, "the fighting season will have come and gone, and all our power will be wasted."

The Captal de Buch said, "Now that we've begun, we cannot turn our backs on it — to do so would be to lose honor, and without honor we have no power at all."

"Well spoken," Josseran said, sharply.

The Black Prince smiled at him. "I see you are still a prince of chivalry, Vaumartin. Good enough. Now, let us all to bed, and tomorrow we shall put ourselves to Romorantin, and see what mettle they might have."

The other men raised their voices in a growl of agreement. Clearly most of them were very eager to get away from here. Josseran could understand that; there must be little forage left for the army, and in fact, as he had come in through the camp, he had marked that most of the Prince's men were elsewhere, probably out scouring the countryside for something to eat.

As he went toward the flap of the tent, the prince caught his arm and held him back. The other men filed out and left them there alone.

"Now," said the English prince, "sit down here, and drink a cup with me."

Josseran sank down on a stool, and the prince sat down beside him. They passed a leather flagon of wine back and forth. Josseran said nothing, out of weariness, and a sense that the prince had his mind full of his own thoughts.

"Chandos wants me to leave off here," the prince said, after a moment. "I think most of the others agree with him."

"Not de Grailly," said Josseran. The wine was making his head light.

"He is a Gascon," the prince said, with a quick short gesture of his hand. "He cares not whom he fights, so long as he strikes blows."

He stretched his legs out before him. Josseran handed him the flask. The little lamp that burned on the stool behind them cast their shadows long and wavering against the dirty canvas of the tent wall. The prince turned toward him suddenly.

"Take this well, Josseran — yet I wonder you have come here to me, since I know your own country is in peril, and King John has declared you forfeit of Vaumartin."

"He reaches for Vaumartin with his hand," said Josseran, steadily. "With you, I may strike him in the heart, and so stay his hand."

"Well put. And shrewdly thought of." The prince smiled at him. "But where is your wife — is she in danger?"

Josseran turned his head away. "I have not seen my wife in some years now."

The prince reached out and gripped his arm. "I am sorry to hear that."

Josseran bowed his head. Almost against his will, he spoke, his true heart's words ripping through the bonds of his dignity and pride, tumbling from him in a wild rush. "The last thing she said to me was full of hatred. I have lost everything, my lord. My love, my wife's joy, my only child — I have lived by the code of chivalry, done all as I was taught to do, and therefore I have nothing left."

His own words shocked him. He dared not look at the prince, for fear of how he might receive this unmanly outburst. Then the other man's arm pressed down around his shoulders.

"God is harshest with those He loves. That is our chivalry, is it not? We must not seek after softness and ease and pleasure but only to offer up our lives in His name." The prince embraced him. "We are brothers, you and I, Josseran, in our hearts. I have always known it. Now you have come home to me. You are but weary. Tomorrow your heart will be whole again — when you have slept, when you see valiant deeds to be done. Offer up your soul to God, and sleep. Tomorrow will be different."

Josseran raised his head and looked him in the face, seeing the bright faith shining in the prince's eyes. He said, "You humble me, my lord."

"Keep heart," the prince said, and smiled at him.

Josseran nodded. His soul lifted a little. He had come here for healing, and the prince would heal him. If he but believed again, then all would return to him, as it had been. If he only believed, then all would go well. He rose and let the Englishman take him to a corner of the tent, and there on a low cot he slept.

thirty-six

THE PRINCE SAID, "Leave off, Chandos! I will not yield here — my teeth are in it."

The balding knight strode away, his arms jerking up and down, as if he fought invisible foes. Around the prince, the other men stood scowling down at their feet. On the rock slope behind them, straight as a sunbeam, Romorantin stood against the sky.

The prince nodded to the messenger. "Go rest — you made a long ride, you must be weary."

Josseran put his hands on his hips. The sun blazed down from a cloudless sky; no breeze stirred the oppressive humid heat. A trickle of sweat ran along his ribs under his shirt. The disorderly camp around him seemed stunned and drowsy in the oven of the day. Down by the stream, a squire was leading a string of horses to water, past the drooping dusty willows; later they would take the horses off somewhere to feed, because all the graze here was gone, even the little trees that dotted the meadow eaten to the bare twigs.

He thought, We have to get out of here. He dared not say so, and his soul quailed anyway, just to think it: to fail here was to fail in some other way, forever.

Chandos tramped back toward them, his eyes like chips of quartz in his sun-darkened cheeks. "Read the letter again, my prince. Read what it says."

"I have read it."

"Have you understood it? Breteuil has fallen! King John has taken Breteuil — "

"I have read it," the prince roared, and Chandos clamped his mouth shut. The prince glared at him, his brows low, his cheeks sucked hollow.

"I will not yield here! I will have Romorantin!" The prince stalked away, stiff, his voice cracked with frustration.

Josseran said, "In that case, we must take it as quickly as possible."

The other men murmured, shifting their weight; de Grailly folded his arms over his chest, and another knight scuffed his foot along the ground. Chandos said, "You have some plan, then, Vaumartin?"

Josseran cast a look up at the tower above him. He was thinking of another tower, on a toll bridge in Normandy.

"Dangerous," he said. "Costly, perhaps, in men."

The prince came striding back, his head up. "Speak it."

"We could burn it out," Josseran said.

Someone grunted. Another man said, "We've tried that."

"Not from below," Josseran said. "From above."

"Above. You think to call down angels — "

"Build another tower, beside it," Josseran went on, stubbornly, his voice riding over the other, objecting voices, his gaze steady on the prince. "Rain fire down on them from another tower."

Chandos glanced at the men around him and nodded. "Risky, yes."

"We have to get out of here," said one of the Gascons. "If King John has taken Breteuil, then he is no longer bound there, he will be riding, and his army you know, outnumbers ours by very many."

The prince's face was fierce. "Yes. We'll do it. Now." He gripped Josseran's arm, a short hard clasp. "Let's go, Josseran. Show them what to do."

"Yes, my lord," said Josseran.

On the tower Romorantin, someone screamed derisively and whistled; a shower of arrows pelted down around Josseran, pinging off the shield he had rigged awkwardly on his back. Dirty rivulets of sweat dripped down his sides, and his legs shook with weariness and haste. Ten feet above the ground, he clung with his hands and feet to the corner of the makeshift tower, holding the sides together while three other men, sheltered inside the frame, lashed the corners fast. An arrow stuck in the green wood near his face.

"There, we're finished, Josseran."

He let go; he jumped down to the ground again, dropping the shield, and landed on his hands and knees. In the savage heat he was working all but naked. His fingers and his knees bled. Around him stood other half-naked, scraped, filthy men, and they stood a moment, looking up at their craftsmanship, teetering against the sky, ugly as a witch's work beside the clean upward sweep of Romorantin.

They had assembled the walls in pieces, down in the meadow, lashing together willow twigs and long, stronger boughs from up on the hillside, where oaks grew. Over this framework they had bound green hides. These flat panels they had now rigged together into a three-sided structure that stood merely one third the height of Romorantin, and from the tower above them came shrill taunts, and more arrows.

"Now what?" said the Captal de Buch, standing with his hands on his hips. "If we climb up onto this thing now, to build it higher, they'll just pick us off like limed birds."

Josseran shook his head. "Build it up from the bottom." He cast a look over his shoulder at Romorantin, and turned to look down at the camp.

The prince had summoned the rest of his army in from their foraging, and bands of men were coming steadily into the camp. As soon as they arrived the prince set them to work, cutting more wood, building more ramshackle panels in the meadow. Josseran could see him there among the other men, shirtless, stooping and hauling like any serf. Chandos, once he saw what was to be done, had flung himself into it; now he and thirty other knights were dragging the next stage of the assault tower up the brown rutted slope between them. Josseran stooped and hooked his shield up on his shoulder again.

"We'll need water," he said, briefly. "Lots of it."

"Water," said the Captal, disbelieving. "What — "

"And more rope," Josseran said. He saved his strength for the task ahead; he did not want to argue with the Gascon, whose mind worked best on simple and immediate matters, like fighting. Chandos, puffing and red-faced, hauled up the next of the great wooden frames.

He cast one quick look over the ridiculous structure before him, and nodded. "Good enough. Let's go."

The Captal still stood there, glowering. "I don't see — "

"Water," Josseran said to him. "Buckets of it. And more rope."

"But — "

"Do it," said Chandos, and spat. His hands were raw. Bawling an order to the men around him, he stooped to lift the next section of the wall, and Josseran bent and gripped the slick round edge of the frame. All together, they heaved the piece upright. The Captal de Buch stamped away down the slope, grumbling.

Near the foot of tower Romorantin grew some young pine trees. Josseran with his sword trimmed away the lower branches of these trees, and used their trunks and higher branches to support the assault tower as he raised it, section by section, in the shadow of Romorantin. By midafternoon Romorantin's defenders had stopped shouting insults and jibes. From the top of the besieged tower a thick black coil of smoke was rising.

Chandos said, "They see what is happening here." He rubbed his broad callused palms together, slimed with blood and sweat. His bulbous pocked nose had a long scratch across it.

Josseran wiped his forehead. His eyes stung. Before him the rude structure of hides and trees hung like a gross parody of the graceful stone shaft of Romorantin. "Let's get the last piece up."

The English knight smiled at him. "You should rest. You must be worn to the bone, Josseran."

"We cannot stop," said Josseran.

He was tired, but the hard work absorbed his mind, his moving hands gave him purpose. He dreaded what thoughts might come to him if he stopped.

They had run out of hides now and were covering the last section of the assault tower's wall with their tents, with saddlecloths and pack covers. Josseran himself soaked each in water first, until the water ran out over his hand when he squeezed, but the heat was drying everything out like tinder; by the time they raised the last course of the tower into place, the walls were steaming. While they lashed the base of the tower fast to the pine trees, the men in Romorantin began to shoot burning arrows into the walls.

The sun was going down. The prince ran back and forth around the tower, organizing groups of knights together to bring water to douse the flames. The tower swayed and wobbled; even the trees that held it up seemed to totter. A fire began to spread through the middle section above Josseran's head, and he left off what he was doing to climb up inside the structure and beat it out with a wet blanket.

Inside, twenty feet above the others, he hung there a moment, too tired to move. The tower around him was like a great basket. At Vaumartin the peasants had a custom on midwinter's day of putting birds in baskets and setting them afire; they said it gave the sun strength. Suddenly he imagined himself one of those birds, beating his wings against a blazing world that creaked and tilted around him. He slipped quickly down along the pine tree to the ground.

The sun set. On Romorantin the defenders got long poles and reached out and thrust and pushed at the ungainly basket rising up beside them. Again and again they tried to set it on fire; again and again the attackers climbed up to put the fires out. In the dark, the defenders could not see well enough to shoot at them, but the work of building was more dangerous; several men fell to their deaths. Near midnight, Josseran at last felt sleep overcome him, and he lay down at the foot of the pine tree and gave himself up to oblivion.

Just before dawn he wakened to the sound of argument.

Chandos was saying, "You cannot go. If you fall, our whole enterprise is lost."

The prince stood with his hands on his hips. Stripped down to the waist, he looked no more royal than a skinned squirrel, his bare back blistered with sunburn, the spine knobbed. Josseran got up and stood beside him. The prince gave him half a glance.

"How can I ask any of them to go where I am loath to go? It is my honor, Chandos — "

Josseran said, "I will go." He turned to look up at the tower he had made. Beside Romorantin, soaring up into the starry sky, the ramshackle tower tilted crazily, ragged and ugly.

Chandos said, "Yes, he should go." He nodded to the prince. "This was his idea — give him the honor." His gaze stabbed at Josseran, who caught the edge of ambivalence in his words, and smiled.

"We should start now, before the sun rises."

The prince was still staring hard at Chandos, his fists on his hips. Josseran laid his hand on the other man's back. "I'll go."

"My heart goes with you," the prince said, turning toward him. "I shall be right behind."

Chandos came a step toward Josseran and gripped his arm, urgent. "When you reach the top, cast down a rope. I have some torches made."

He led Josseran a few steps to the foot of the tower and showed him the torches: great switches of straw, bound together with chunks of resinous pinewood. Josseran nodded. "Good."

"You won't have long to do it," Chandos said. "Do it fast, Josseran." His gaze pressed on Josseran, as if he could send his own spirit aloft in Josseran's body, do the work while keeping safe below. Abruptly his hand rose, and he made the sign of the cross in the air between them. "God keep you, boy."

Josseran went down the slope, to where a small fire burned; most of the army lay asleep in the meadow, rows of bodies, like a night graveyard. At the fire he sank down on his haunches. There was a flask of wine on a blanket by the pile of wood, and a piece of cold roasted meat, which he ate.

His belly clamped down over the food, unwilling to accept it. The thought flitted through his mind that it was a waste to eat, since he would be dead soon. Part of him startled at that, and at the sense of relief that attended it.

Emptying the wine flask, he tore open the top and made a firepot of it; this he hung around his neck on a cord. He took no weapons, only a coil of rope, hooked over his elbow. The prince was going along the rows of the sleeping army, rousing them quietly.

An army of dead men. They would all die someday; they bore their deaths within them already. Josseran shook himself, fighting off this humor, and went back up to the crazy tower.

The pine tree that steadied it grew up only about half the tower's height, but it was sturdier than the man-made thing, and Josseran climbed the tree instead of his own creature. Below him, in the dark, men were quietly gathering. He heard no sound from Romorantin, saw no movement on its notched rampart. The pitch from the tree clung to his hands, and he had to pull them free of the knobby trunk as he climbed. The rich smell was sweet to him. The firepot pressed against his chest and grew warm, and he slung it over his shoulder, to hang down his back.

He was not afraid. As he climbed, he made his prayers, he consigned his soul to Jesus Christ, Who forgave all sins. He asked God to care for Isobel and for Everard, whom he had wronged; he thought of his brothers, whom he would soon see again.

But in his death, he would free the prince of Romorantin; he would send the prince on to his destiny. That was worth a life, especially a life as botched as his.

He reached the top of the pine tree. Now there was no way to climb save the rickety tower of woven willow, which swayed in the slightest breeze.

Putting out his hand, he grasped the nearest thick branch and stepped into the tower. At once it began to wobble and creak under him. Below, voices murmured; the other men crowded around the base to hold the thing still. In the middle of it Josseran climbed up, his feet slipping on the peeled willow; a branch broke under his weight, and he fell sideways and the whole tower leaned over. The firebox banged his back, painfully hot now, burning him. He took a deep breath, looked up, and scrambled as fast as he could up through the collapsing web of branches.

The sun had not yet risen, but the sky was brightening, pale pink streamers of cloud floating by like the banners of the day to come.

Perched on the top of the crazy basket, swinging back and forth like a bell, he flung down the rope and dragged up a great bundle of straw and resinous pine.

On the tower Romorantin someone yelled.

"Josseran!" the prince cried, far below him. "Watch — "

Josseran dropped a coal from the firebox into the straw. All along the top of Romorantin, men were running, coming toward him, and their voices rose in a growing chorus. He ignored that. They could not kill him fast enough to keep him from destroying Romorantin.

In the straw the flame shot up, its bright glow blinding. The assault tower was swaying back and forth; he swung his own weight with it, leaning far backward, and then jerking himself forward, so that the tower tilted wildly in toward Romorantin, and at the end of its arc, he flung the straw over the rampart.

The defenders shrieked; they closed on the blazing straw, but Josseran had another ready for them, and hurled it over, a ball of flame that whooshed through the gap and hit the roof and rolled down, scattering sparks and chunks of sputtering pine resin. Before it came to rest, Josseran flung another after it.

Whatever that torch hit, on Romorantin's rampart, burst into a roar of flame that shot upward into the sky, crackling and erupting black smoke. They must have had a cauldron of oil waiting, to throw down on the attackers. Within moments the whole roof of Romorantin was blazing. Through the leaping flames the thin screams of the men trapped on the rampart filtered like trapped birds, cries of despair, prayers and curses.

Josseran screamed, triumphant. Then, below him, he saw the flames creeping up through the willow branches, and he smelled the stinking of burning hides.

He had no way down, save through that blaze. The fire burned stronger and brighter, and the tower seemed to sink down gently on one side, giving way as part of it burned through. He gasped, and breathed in enough smoke to make him choke. His eyes stung. The tower heaved and bucked and rocked.

God, he thought, I burn in Hell already. He shut his eyes, afraid, his feet hot, his calves singed. He tried to pray, words streamed through his mind, names and words, but he could not string them into order; like birds they burned to nothing in the flame, left him naked to the blind disorder of the flame.

"Josseran — "

This was death, this coming apart.

"Josseran! Can you reach me?"

He turned blindly toward the voice, feeling the tower go down under him, and something wrapped itself tight around his waist. His skin hurt. He gulped. Someone held him. The tower slipped away from him and he dangled in cool darkness. He sagged, unconscious.

When he woke, Romorantin was a blackened ruin on the hillside. The fire had scarred the land around it, burned the little pine tree to a stump, turned the fragrant brush to smoking twigs. The tower he had made lay wrecked beside it.

The prince said, "You alone brought down Romorantin, Josseran."

He turned his head away.

thirty-seven

AFTER THAT, things began to go wrong very fast.

Prince Edward's army marched west, hoping to find some town or farmlands to pillage for supplies, but the country had been fought over for so many years it was a wasteland. The prince's advisers argued with him every day to give up and turn south, but the prince was determined to continue on to Normandy, to join forces with his Uncle Lancaster, free the king of Navarre, and destroy King John in open battle.

But day after day they starved, eating mice, roots, wildflowers, the horses gnawing the bark off trees, until when they reached the westward-flowing Loire, even the prince lost heart, seeing nothing around them but desolate wild country.

So they turned south, to retreat back to Gascony.

Then, in the shimmering summer heat of an August afternoon, not far from the ancient town of Poitiers, the prince's vanguard ran up on the heels of a swarm of French knights. King John was ahead of them. They had no retreat.

The prince did what he could. On Chandos's advice, he gathered his army up on a winding ridge, its crest within sight of the spires of Poitiers. On the gentler slope to the south the prince put all his pack animals and baggage wagons; he faced the oncoming French across a steeper slope, rutted by the rains, studded with low-growing bushes.

At the foot of this slope was a strip of marsh, with a broad meadow beyond, nearly flat and covered with windblown grass. Before the prince had gotten his own banners raised on the summit of the ridge, the first knights of the French army were moving into this meadow.

Josseran took his horses down onto the flank of the ridge, looking for something they could eat. The smaller packhorse was faring well enough, but the war-horse's ribs showed, his belly tucked up. He tore up mouthfuls of the green grass, but the grass was too young to nourish him; he needed oats and hay.

Still the great horse moved with a quick, nervous grace, swinging its head up at every sound, snorting, its huge hoofs lifted lightly as a lady's slipper. Josseran took it from one little patch of grass to another, keeping the packhorse off to the side, to nibble on leaves.

He struggled against the dull weight of his thoughts. He had lost his faith, he saw that. It was not that things were so different, now, but that he saw them differently. Ten years before this he had made a mistake, he had chosen to do something that seemed small at the time, not very blameworthy, more listening to his wife than anything else, but from that day the crack in his honor had widened and deepened into an abyss that was swallowing him whole. He had been betrayed, or had betrayed himself, worse than ever he had betrayed Everard.

In the battle to come, he would die; God would not sustain him, who had no faith. He longed for that death, for the end of pain, even as he feared the judgment to come.

His wanderings with the horse had taken him to the eastern end of the ridge, where the road from Poitiers swung across it, narrow and rutted, fenced by high thorn hedges on either side. Along it, now, a party of French were riding, with a truce flag fluttering on a lance in their midst.

Josseran stiffened; he recognized many of these men, and as they saw him, they knew him also. One called, "Vaumartin!" in surprise, and another drew rein and stared hard at him.

"Tell King John I am here," Josseran shouted. "Tell him today no tricks will save him." The bellow scoured his throat raw.

One of them shouted an answering challenge; an arm thrust up into the air, defiant. Under their truce flag they galloped away up the hill. Josseran turned to his horses. His skin crawled. All their hot words seemed like foolery to him now. They spoke of chivalry and gallantry, but that was a disguise: what they did was brutal, the savagery of beasts, prettied up with words.

Yet what else did he have? He could not turn from it; already in his belly the dark rage was swelling, his heart thundered, longing for the battle, for that moment when he faced death, when he knew, truly, that he lived. What else was there? His fears subsided into a contemptuous disdain. His life mattered nothing, anyway — a thrashing of the heart, a passing lust and then gone, and some other would take his place, make a cage of words to live in, love and fight and die in the endless meaningless fire. Boosting himself up onto the packhorse's back, he kicked and whistled the two animals back up the hill, toward the camp, where things would begin.

thirty-eight

IN HIS FAMOUS BLACK ARMOR, the prince
paced up and down, staring across the slope and marsh between
them at King John's banner. "The longer they put off fighting, the
worse for us."

Josseran growled in agreement. He was hungry, had eaten nothing
today, and very little the day before. By the tent, Chandos was talking
to the commander of his archers. The prince left all such details to the
old soldier, who knew everything; he had already bidden most of the
English knights to fight on foot, with axes and swords.

They were ranged now on the steep broken slope before the prince,
squatting or sitting in the sun, most of them thirsty, all of them
hungry to the bone. They faced the broad meadow where the French
knights were only beginning to form ranks. In the center of the
meadow the French banner, the Oriflamme, hung limp from its staff in
the windless heat.

In the wagons under the trees at the top of the meadow would be food,
wine, fodder for the horses. Josseran swallowed the sudden tide of water
in his mouth. Swinging around toward the prince, he said, "Let me go
out and challenge them. The sooner we bring this on, the better."

De Grailly said, "They have more men moving in, see? They must
have great bands of knights still out on the road."

The prince nodded to Josseran. "Do it."

Josseran put his helmet on. The world shrank to a little patch of
ground directly before him, visible through the visor. De Grailly
himself held his horse.

"God go with you."

"If you see King John," said the prince, "tweak his nose for me,
Josseran."

Josseran took his lance in his right hand; he slid his left arm through
the straps of his shield. "I'll cut his ears off."

He made the horse do a little quick footwork, showing off, and the knights raised a cheer for him. All around them, in the camp, on the slope, the other men turned to see. With all eyes on him, Josseran wheeled his horse and rode down between the thorn hedges toward the French camp.

He held his horse to an easy canter, conserving its strength; it wanted to gallop, it fought for the bit, its ears pinned back, but he knew better than to use it all at once. At the foot of the road, he swung around and loped along the foot of the slope, with the marsh between him and the French, and began to shout taunts at the French.

"De Clermont! Still serving this false, lying king, are you?"

On the meadow there was a concerted rush forward, men on foot and men on horseback, to the far side of the strip of marsh.

"Vaumartin! What a traitor! Riding with the English — "

"I still have my honor, at least," Josseran called. "You've all lost it to King John, who's cuckolded you with all your wives — as he was cuckolded with his — "

Ahead, the ridge curved around, cutting him off, and he swung his horse around. His rein shaved the lather from the horse's sweat-soaked neck. Back there, the Englishmen were all whooping and jeering at Josseran's last jab at the king, and the French knights were lining up along the marsh to intercept Josseran, a shifting gaudy row of riders, their lances stabbing the sky.

"Get back, you fools," Josseran roared; his horse stumbled, exhausted already, and he let it regain its footing and reach stride again, his legs tight around its barrel. "It's John I want — let him come to my challenge. Is he really a king, or just a stuffed doll?"

"By Saint-Denis!" Forty feet ahead of him, a knight he did not know screamed out, lowered his lance, and charged across the mire.

Josseran gathered himself and his horse. The first knight never reached him; his horse staggered into the marsh, stuck its leg into a hole, and collapsed, throwing the knight headlong. After him came a wild charge of men, smarter or luckier, who found ways through the muck.

The first of these came straight at Josseran, who set his lance, put his spurs to his horse, charged fifteen feet forward, got his lance on the other man's shield, and knocked him cleanly off. Another man shot by him, his horse veering off at the last moment, his blow missing Josseran's head by an inch.

"Saint George! Saint George!"

The English battle cry shrilled in his ears. Around him now were English knights, fighting on foot, catching the Frenchmen in the marsh, or on the broken slope where they could not charge. Josseran wheeled his exhausted horse around and vaulted out of the saddle.

On the ground, he saw things very differently. The English had run down the slope together, in good order, their ranks tighter than the French ranks, which, attacking across the swamp, quickly got separated from one another. The English stayed together, also, and fought together, two or three of them taking on a single Frenchman. Quickly many French saddles emptied.

A loose horse bolted past Josseran, almost knocking him down, and galloped on, straight in among the French. Josseran plunged in after the riderless horse, using it like a plow to break up the field before him. One French knight jerked his own horse back out of the course of the runaway, but his head turned to follow its passage, and Josseran got in under his guard, struck up between the other knight's elbow and side, and flung him to the ground.

"Quarter — quarter — "

With the knight helpless before him Josseran had to struggle to keep from striking him dead. With a jerk of his head he tore his attention off to the next enemy. Across the swamp a horn blew. Around him men grunted and thrashed and flung themselves on one another like wild beasts. His own sword dripped blood. Someone was screaming in his ears. His mind floated above this like a bird, looking down, oddly detached. His arm thrust and pumped, his legs stalked across the slimy earth.

He knew he would die here today. God would grace one of these knights around him with the honor of killing Josseran, who had fallen from grace. Yet that seemed like a respite to him, or like an atonement.

A face heaved up before him, framed by its helmet, the red mouth round in a tangle of beard. Was this the man? Josseran raised up his sword and strode forward, ready to die, wanting only to do it well, with courage, and with honor.

All through that bloody day, in the relentless sun, he fought on the slope below the banners of the Black Prince, and he did not die.

He killed; he struck down men as they swung their swords at his head, as they came at him from the side, as they charged on horseback toward him, as they leapt up from the ground behind him. He knew he himself was hurt — his left thigh ached whenever he could stop and think about it, and his head hurt inside the helmet. His throat was raw with thirst.

Along the slope he ranged like a wild animal, striking down Frenchmen, one of a horde of similar madmen, striking and striking, until on the slope the bodies lay like sheaves of harvested wheat. He did not die.

Later, in the twilight, when the English knights were overrunning the fields, surrounding the few bands of Frenchmen left, and making feasts in among the French baggage wagons, he went up to the top of the ridge. There Chandos sat, as he probably had throughout the day, on an empty barrel, where he could see everything, direct men here and there, compose this battle like an entertainment.

Certainly everything he saw delighted him. He beamed at Josseran as the Breton knight came up.

"Someone bring this man a cup — he has earned as full a cup as any man in Prince Edward's army, by my vow." He nodded to Josseran. "We have wine now, Vaumartin, as well as victory."

Josseran stood beside him, his legs trembling with fatigue, and let a boy unlace his greaves. To his amazement, someone did give him a cup of red wine, certainly looted from King John's stores, in the wagons on the far side of the meadow.

He said, "God have mercy on King John, whose wine is better than his chivalry." He drank deep, and his head reeled.

From here he could see the whole battlefield. For the first time he realized why the fighting on the slope and in the marsh had gone so well. The whole road between the thorn hedges was buried in bodies stuck full of arrows, dead horses and men, which the English archers were now picking over in the dusk.

He said, "John tried to charge along the road?"

Chandos said, "As you say, he knows his wines better than his battle tactics."

Josseran murmured under his breath. The man who had brought him the first cup of wine had brought him another; the boy who had stripped off the weight of armor on his legs was working now on his corselet.

The twilight deepened. His mood sank to a cold and stony darkness.

He should have died, who had lost his faith; some more noble knight should have struck him down. Instead he made himself a hero to these other men — although Chandos it was who had won the battle, sitting here on his little keg, and John who had lost it.

Although his armor was off now, he felt the burden of his despair like a weight of iron.

This was his punishment: not to die. God would make a mockery of him, would let him be the hero he had always longed to be, a perfect knight. But Josseran would have no sweetness from it, no pride, no honor, no soul's nourishment. He was hollow as his armor. This was his punishment, to have what he wanted.

Chandos was staring down into the dusk. He said, "What's going on out there?"

Roused from his gloom, Josseran peered down the slope. Down at the foot of it, just beyond the marsh, a great knot of men, mostly on foot, screamed and fought like boys on a field, fighting over their ball. He straightened. In their midst was a mounted man, who was shouting.

"The king," he said.

Chandos erupted up off the keg. "Send for the prince! Get me my horse!"

Josseran took several long strides down the slope, toward the men below. They were fighting, but not with the knight in their midst; they were fighting one another for possession of him, and in their midst, he was shouting, over and over, "Let me surrender — give quarter — I am the king! I am the king — "

Chandos on his horse galloped down past Josseran, down to the milling crowd below. From another part of the field, the prince was riding up; like Josseran he had fought all day on the bloody slope of Poitiers. Josseran watched them ride into the noisy group around King John.

He laughed. Here was another mockery. Outnumbered and exhausted and starved, they had destroyed the flower of the French, and captured King John himself, now soberly giving up his sword to the Black Prince. Josseran turned and walked away; he began to think there was no God.

thirty-nine

IN THE DEEP of the night, Jeanne woke; there was a pounding somewhere, and the rhythmic thudding brought her slowly out of a profound sleep, so that she was sitting up in her bed before she realized someone was knocking on the door of the house.

Beside her Everard lay snoring. He had gone late to the White Rose the night before, and had come home drunken. She got him by the shoulder and shook him hard.

"Everard — Everard!"

Still the thundering went on at the door below. Everard stirred, groaning, and she got out of her bed and went to the window, pushed the shutter open, and leaned out.

The waning moon still hung above the gable of Bonboisson's house. Her own front door was out of her sight, around the corner of the house from the window, but she could see several horses waiting there, a dark restless mass in the moonlight. She turned.

"Everard!"

"I'm coming," he said, swinging his feet out of the bed. He put one hand up over his face. "What is it?"

"Nothing good," she said, pulling on her heavy outdoor cloak over her nightdress; Sylviane was downstairs, near this uproar, and she went hastily toward the door. "At this hour, nothing good." She went down the stairs in the dark, one hand on the wall.

As she reached the hall she heard the door opening. She went quickly down past the table, toward where her daughter stood, holding the door open, her white nightdress luminous in the moonlight.

"Sylviane — "

The child turned, and beyond her Jeanne saw a bulky man with a broad face, several other men behind him, who said, "Mistress, I am here to see your husband. Will you let me in?"

"Come in." Jeanne went up behind Sylviane, her hands on the girl's shoulders. "Go light a candle," she said, and pushed the child gently toward the back of the hall; she glanced toward the stair, where Everard had not yet come. She faced this heavyset man again, pushing irresistibly into her house, and said, "I am Jeanne Bonboisson, Everard's wife. Are you not Etienne Marcel?"

"I am," said the bulky man, and smiled at her. He was not much taller than she. Yet of all the men now shoving into her hall he was the one she did not take her eyes from. He went straight to the hearth, and she followed; as if this were his own house he threw a log across the firedogs and jabbed with the poker into the banked coals below.

Now Sylviane brought the candle, and on the stair Everard appeared, in his shirt.

"Master Provost." He came swiftly down the stairs. The other men ranged themselves by the fire; the provost was still stabbing the poker into the shooting flames.

He turned, the poker in his hand, facing Everard, and said, "Well, now, Everard, God is making His will more evident, I think," and smiled.

Everard said, "What's happened?" He glanced at Jeanne and nodded toward the pantry, and she went off, reluctant, to fetch some bread and wine.

Behind her, Marcel said, "There's been a battle, and King John lost it. Not only battle and army, but himself as well: he is the prisoner of the Black Prince."

Jeanne, hearing this, caught her breath. From Sylviane, at the pantry door, came a little gasp, and Jeanne put out her arms and the child came toward her.

"Help me," Jeanne said, and led her into the pantry.

Sylviane said, "But — the king, Mother — what will happen to us now?"

"Help me," Jeanne said only, and got the cups and a tray, got wine, a loaf of bread, a knife, and carried them back out to the hall.

Everard was saying, "Where was this battle?"

Marcel pulled the end of the bench around. "At Poitiers."

He sat himself down on the bench, put his hands on his thighs, and smiled at Everard. "Now I have come here to give you the chance to leave my service, Master Everard."

Everard's gaze flicked toward Jeanne; he said mildly, "Why should I do that, Master Provost?"

"Because what I am about to do will put us all at some risk," said

Marcel. "I mean to hold Paris, against the English, against our own king, if need be, to keep her safe, and no man knows really what the end of it will be."

Jeanne set the tray down on the table; her hands trembled, and she gripped the heavy knife and sawed through the bread, her eyes on the blade. She knew well enough what her husband would say, and he said it calmly; she had heard more passion in his voice over a rainbow. He had been expecting this.

He said, "I am your man, Master Provost."

Etienne Marcel thrust out his hand, and Everard shook it. "Well done," said Marcel. "Well done. Now, come with me, I have a horse for you — we must seal up the city, and make our plans."

Everard said, "I'll get my shoes on," and went up the stairs two at a time.

The other men with Marcel had drawn near the fire, and as Jeanne poured out the wine they each came for a cup. Marcel himself turned to her, reaching for a cup, his small deep-set eyes like points of flame. He said nothing to her. Everard pounded down the stairs, pulling on his black coat, and Marcel wheeled toward him.

"We are ready!"

They strode out the door, their feet loud on the floor, their voices high and full with importance. The door slammed behind them.

Jeanne put the cups on the tray. Her hands still trembled. She was unsure if she was angry or frightened. Sylviane came toward her, her eyes wide.

"What will happen to us? What will we do now?"

"Now," Jeanne said, "we will go wash cups." She looked down at the child's pale anxious face and put her arm around her shoulders. The world might be crumbling, yet there was work to be done, which remade the world. "Come now, I need your help."

At dawn, in every church in the city, the priests shouted forth the news of the king's defeat and capture at Poitiers. The news poured through the streets like a river of gossip, rumor, and wild conjecture; when Everard walked back up the Draperie from the rue Saint-Honoré, the streets were full of people, standing in little groups, urgent with talk.

No one was working. There was a mob in the Place de Grève, but none of them was looking for work. They milled around in the broad square as if it were a holiday, and at the smallest sign — a flight of birds, a random shout — they surged together in a panic, screaming that the English were at the gates. As Everard worked his way through them, more people appeared, rushing in from every side street, coming to the comfort of the mob.

Along the waterfront, the barges were hauled up unloaded by the quays. Between the Tour Roland and the Tour d'Acre, which guarded the river's edge, was the scaffolding where murderers and traitors were hung, a rough platform of wood. In the loops of chain that dangled from the crossbar hung the remains of some long-dead criminal; the crossbar was lined with black crows, which fluttered off when Everard climbed up beneath them, onto the platform.

He looked out over the crowd, shaken; these were too many people, too huge and inchoate a power; he and Marcel would never appease them, never bring them to obedience.

His gaze caught on a bright pennant, off to one side. To right and left, the Place de Grève was lined with tall old houses, whose stepped rooflines, blackened with age, were now festooned also with more people, scrambling for a better view. There at the east side of the Place, in front of the vast old house where the duke of Normandy sometimes lived, was a little band of armed and mounted knights, one of them carrying a red banner.

Those were the king's men. If Marcel faltered, they would ride into the gap.

He faced the great surging clamorous throng. Their numbers and their restless tumultuous energy awed him. There had to be some way to call them to their own defense. He went to the front of the platform and raised his arms.

"People of Paris!"

At first, no one heeded him. From each throat rose a separate voice, contending, feeble compared to the mass, and yet the mass itself was only a collection of feeble contending voices.

"People of Paris, hear me! Paris — oh, Paris!"

Slowly those nearest were turning toward him, and unable to hear him they hushed those around them, and a waiting stillness spread over the crowd. They turned toward the platform; those at the back of the mob pressed forward to hear, jamming those in front up against the platform, which suddenly quaked under Everard's feet; he caught hold of the scaffolding's upright to keep his balance.

"People of Paris, hear me! King John is taken prisoner by the enemy — we are without a king!"

The crowd roared at that. Everard's scalp tingled. In spite of what he had said, their panic and disorder were fading. Pushed together, all facing one way, they were forming into a single monster creature of incalculable power. He shot a glance at the knights on the duke of Normandy's porch.

"People of Paris!" he shouted, his throat already skinned raw. "We need no king!"

From them all went up such a roar that Heaven itself seemed to quake. A runnel of sweat coursed down Everard's side under his heavy coat. He had seen, at last, on the opposite side of the mob from the king's knights, Etienne Marcel coming into the Place de Grève.

Everard lifted his arms. "Together, we can defend ourselves, our families, our homes, and our city against all enemies — those outside our walls — and those within!"

As he shouted that, he thrust out his arm, pointing above the heads of the mob toward the knights loitering before the porch. The mob swung around to see, and a growl burst from them; some of them surged toward the knights, but Everard's voice held them back.

"Now — heed me, Paris, heed me — we must have a leader, and who better to lead us than he who has led us already through famine and hardship — "

The crowd's imagination leapt ahead of his words. Already their voice was building, confident, expectant, a swelling murmur of a cheer.

"Marcel — Marcel — "

Everard shouted, "The king cares nothing for us! The provost cares for us like a father, has fed us, sheltered us like a father, and now here he comes! He will lead us through this trial — him we can trust! He will keep Paris — "

On the far side of the Place, by Normandy's porch, the band of knights started forward, plowing through the mob toward the platform. Opposite, at the edge of the Draperie, a little wedge of men was pushing through the crowd; their red-and-blue hoods bobbed. The murmurous voice of the mob swelled to a yell of welcome.

"Marcel! Marcel!"

The name boomed off the fronts of the buildings. Flung in the faces of the king's knights, it blocked their way, it pushed them back, out of the crowd, while Marcel himself, in the little wedge of watchmen, reached the platform and climbed up onto it, walked forward, raised his arms, and stood there, wrapped in the acclaim of the people.

"Marcel! Marcel! Marcel!"

Everard stepped back. The captain of the watch, Jean Mailliard, climbed up beside him, tall and stooped and grim.

"People of Paris," Marcel cried. "What you have heard is true! The king has been defeated in a terrible battle. If we are to survive, we must defend ourselves — "

From the duke of Normandy's porch a knight rode forward a little way into the crowd. "The king is taken, but he is still our king! We must keep faith with the king — "

Marcel waved his arms over his head. "There is no reason to fear! The walls of Paris are strong, the people of Paris are resolute — "

The knight shouted, again, "Do you keep faith with your king, Marcel?"

Again Marcel ignored him. "We shall have an army of the citizens of Paris! Each of the quarters will have its own troop, its own captain — "

"Marcel," the knight shouted, "are you loyal to King John or not?"

Marcel wheeled. His face was dark red. He bellowed, "I am loyal to Paris, and to the good of Paris! King John betrayed us! King John it is who has not kept faith!"

At that the crowd howled, moving again, its restless undirected power rippling through it, and before Normandy's porch, the knights gathered themselves and thrust forward into the crowd again, headed for Marcel.

They came hard, spurring their horses, trampling down whatever lay before them. The crowd there yielded, like a crack opening; the column of knights gathered speed and rushed toward the platform.

Marcel did not waver. He flung out his arm, pointing at the knights swooping down on him.

"These are the men who have fattened on our labor — who have starved our children for the sake of their fat bellies — who have lived easy on our groans and toils, and then told us that it was God's will — "

At the front of the band of knights, their leader reached for his sword and drew it free. The crowd immediately before him wavered, shrinking back, their voices thinned to cries and whimpers. Everard took a step forward toward his master, but Mailliard reached out and held him back.

"Marcel doesn't need any help," said the watch captain, and grinned.

The band of knights was cutting through the mob, coming straight at the provost. On the edge of the platform, visible from one end of the Place to the other, Marcel thrust out his chest and with both hands pulled open his coat.

"Yes, slay me — for I speak the truth. I love the people — I fight for the good of the people — so slay me! Keep faith with your king and slay — "

The crowd screamed. Those directly in line with the knights had pulled back from their threat, but now the mob surrounded the king's men. At the trumpet of Marcel's voice they lunged forward again, closing tight around the column of armed and mounted men, closing like a fist on a handful of grapes.

Their commander's horse reared. The rider swung his sword down, and perhaps it struck some body below, but nothing stopped the mob. The horse reared again, lashing out with its hoofs, and the crowd shrieked and a hundred arms waved, reaching for bridle and reins, for the knight now stabbing and slashing frantically from the saddle, and abruptly the knights at the back wheeled around and fled.

Everard shouted, some wordless triumph. The crowd's scream of victory pierced his ears, and he put his hands up to the sides of his head. The leading knight spun his horse and spurred for safety. Objects rained down on him, stones, mud, turds, people's caps and shoes. Someone clung to his horse's tail. He lost his sword; as he reached the edge of the ground, his horse went down.

The knight landed running. The other nobles were waiting, their horses' hoofs in a mad dance, in the mouth of the next street, and just ahead of the screaming crowd their commander reached them.

He vaulted up behind another man's saddle, and with a clatter of hoofs the knights galloped away.

The crowd screeched. Long after the knights had gone the people flung insults and mud after them. Waving their arms and cheering, they rushed toward Marcel, for whom they had won this victory. He reached down from the platform, and they got him by the hands, by the legs, lifted him up, and carried him off, a leaf on a vast tide, toward the Châtelet, and as they went, they cheered his name to Heaven.

Marcel, climbing the stairs toward his chambers, was peeling off his coat; his face, red as a robin's breast, streamed with sweat. When Everard caught up with him the provost gave him a crisp nod.

"We still have much to do today. We must find some way to recruit more men and officers for our militia — "

They tramped up the stairs, talking about the militia, leaving below and behind the crowds that had followed Marcel; but as they came toward the top of the stair, another crowd met them.

Not the poor. Not the crowds of the Place de Grève. Men in rich coats, these, with gold chains around their necks. Men with pages, with underlings, with papers in their hands, and false self-serving smiles on their faces, and bows as smooth as oil, bows they made toward Etienne Marcel as he passed.

"My lord Provost — if I may have only a few words with you — "

"My lord Provost, I must speak with you — "

The provost led Everard on into the chamber. "Who are these people?"

"Men who know where the power is," Everard said. "The fat churchman is the bishop of Laon — he's an agent of the king of Navarre's. You can guess what he's after."

Marcel said, "I cannot spend myself on frivolous matters." But he was smiling. He puffed out his chest, smiling, his eyes small in his broad red face. "Tell them they shall have to wait. Where's Mailliard?"

They bent over the chart of Paris, talking about the militia, how it was to be raised, and how armed and led. Pages came in and out, begging admittance for their masters, and Marcel sent them all away.

"They shall have to wait." Whenever he said it, Everard could see his satisfaction in it, that he kept these great men dangling. "Tell them to wait."

Everard pointed on the map to the Saint-Honoré gate. "This is the weakness. I was out there this morning, as you suggested, and we can erect a temporary gate easily enough. That will close the wall."

"We'll double the workmen. The stone is available." Marcel reached for paper. "We must have the walls secure, in case the English come, or brigands, or — "

Another page rushed in. "My lord Provost — my lord — "

"Tell him to wait!" Marcel boomed.

"My lord — the dauphin has come."

"The dauphin," Everard said, startled, and straightened up. "I thought he was taken prisoner with the king."

Marcel was glaring at the page. "It's a lie."

"No, my lord — " The child bounced on his toes. "It's truth — the dauphin is in Paris!"

Everard ran his tongue over his lips. Marcel met his gaze. Loudly, the provost said, "He does not matter, not now."

He said it liked a challenge. Everard said nothing. Marcel said, again, "He matters nothing." His voice was too loud. He turned with a sudden anger to the page. "Tell them to wait!" Bending over the map, he reached for his pen, and Everard stooped over the map beside him.

orty

"WHY HAVE YOU COME?" Marcel shouted, furious.

The dauphin pulled nervously on the cuffs of his coat. He was a thin, pale youth of not quite twenty, with the long Valois nose and pointed chin.

He said, "I thought to find Paris in a desperate condition, with the king captive — instead I see great well-guarded gates, ordered streets, the watch in their usual patrol, people going about their usual business. I am told I have you to thank for this, Master Provost."

Facing him across the palace council chamber, Etienne Marcel with a sharp gesture thrust that mollifying remark angrily to one side. "Why are you here, then?"

One of the two knights behind the prince stepped forward. "You shall address the dauphin as 'Your Grace.' "

The dauphin waved him back. "I am here to protect my kingdom. To defend my people — "

"You are here to hide."

"No! I — "

"You fled the battlefield, didn't you — you left your father behind to be taken, and you fled."

Again the knight stepped forward, and again the dauphin waved at him to be still.

Everard, standing behind the provost, cast his glance around the room. He had been here before. On the wall was an arras of the Nine Worthies, which he remembered, and he remembered also the humiliation of that meeting with the king, and he glared across the room at the dauphin, who had the idea that all he needed to do was appear in Paris to be accepted.

The dauphin puzzled Everard. Sick and weak, scarcely out of boyhood, he seemed too feeble to make his way among men like his father and Navarre, and yet he had bested Navarre, somehow, at Rouen, he had escaped from Poitiers, where his father had fallen prisoner, and here he was moving quickly, with decision.

Within hours of arriving in the city, he had called every important man in Paris to this council — the chancellor and the provost and the bishop, the abbots of Saint-Denis and Sainte-Geneviève, the rector of the universitas, the presidents of the parlements, the great merchants of Paris, and the knights who had come with him from the battlefield; the little room was stuffed with men, who now, in the wake of the provost's accusation, were staring at the young man before them, even the knights waiting for some explanation from him.

The boy stood straight and calm. "Yes. You have it right, Master Provost — I fled the field. But the field was lost. Had I stayed I would only have been taken, with my father and my brothers — "

"We are better off without you," Marcel said, and now, from the far side of the room, where, with his canon beside him, the old bishop sat slumped in a chair, came a snort of displeasure.

Everard had given the canon one sharp look when he came in: it was Claude de Brises, his enemy from the universitas.

"Let him finish, Provost! He is the only prince we have, now."

"I say we need no prince," Marcel said hotly.

His own men murmured over that, and the dauphin stepped forward, pleading now with them all, although he addressed his words to Marcel.

"Provost, you can rule Paris, and have done so admirably, and I have no desire to prevent you from continuing to do so, but there is more than Paris in this, there is the kingdom of France. Do you propose to rule it too?"

Everard grunted. This at least was true. Against his will he was coming to the prince's point of view; that in itself impressed him. He glanced at Marcel and saw a similar understanding settle on the provost's face.

The dauphin went on, his voice quiet, so that they all had to be quiet to hear him. "I fled the field, but I have not fled the kingdom. I have not got the grace of courage, but France cannot long survive the exercise of such courage as I saw at Poitiers. I have come here to defend and protect my kingdom, of which Paris is only a part. You men here represent the widest interests of the realm. I have called you here to form a regency council, and to name me regent. I promise to heed your wisdom in all things, to be guided by you in all things, to work together with you all to lead our country through this peril."

His words reached them. All around the long narrow room, the watching faces eased and opened to him. The bishop leaned to one side, to whisper to his canon. Everard glanced at Mailliard, standing beside him, and saw the watch captain frowning, his great head lowered, his red brows hooding his eyes.

Marcel said, "You Valois have gotten yourselves into this. Why should we trust you any more, after all we have put up with — the taxes drawn like drops of blood from our veins, and then squandered on tournaments and wars and feastings — "

The dauphin lifted his hands, pleading with them. "I know you have been shabbily cared for. I promise to listen to you — to be guided by your real needs. I will be king one day, and I want to rule well."

"Where are the English?" asked one of the merchants, a miller named Gilles. Everard shifted, wary. This was one of the men whom Marcel had outwitted over the grain shortages, a year before. A large man, bald, he was standing on the far side of the room from Marcel. "If you ran from one battle, I can't see how we can expect you to defend us against the Black Prince."

"The Black Prince is marching to Calais. He exhausted himself defeating my father." The dauphin licked his lips. He looked tired. The mere effort of talking was almost two much for him, this sick, weak boy — how could he defend them?

Yet he was talking, and his words were compelling.

"I have noticed — the English have won some great victories over us in the field, now and in the past, and yet ever they have failed to follow their advantage. They cannot turn victories on the battlefield into the conquest of the kingdom. If we do not fight them — "

"If we do not fight, we are already beaten," said one of the knights, and around the room the other men all growled in assent.

"The English are not the only difficulty, anyway," Everard said. "The countryside is overrun with brigands, mostly hired soldiers the English bring here to fight battles and then turn off their payrolls after the battle's over. We have our militia here to defend the city, but to drive out the brigands you will need an army. Can you lead an army?"

Marcel grunted. "Answer that with a mere look at him. No. We must have an army, and a captain to lead it. Not a weakling boy."

The bishop of Paris said, "Yet this weakling boy is by every precedent clearly the regent of the kingdom of France."

"There's no money to pay a captain," said the bald merchant.

Marcel wheeled and glared at him. "Perhaps we should tithe you, Gilles."

"You have already drained me white as an Easter candle," the bald man snarled.

Everard gave a shake of his head, alarmed, and stared at the back of Marcel's head as if he could force his thoughts in through his skull; this was no place to unearth old feuds.

"There is one," said Marcel, "who would be our captain willingly, for the sake of his freedom and our support."

Everard twitched at this. The dauphin's head shot up. Behind him one of the knights swore; the bald merchant folded his arms across his chest.

"And what shining knight is that?"

"The king of Navarre," said the provost, his gaze narrowly on the dauphin.

The prince said, "Navarre is imprisoned by the order of the king. He is a dangerous and treacherous man, and I will not endure to have him set free."

In the provost's broad red face his eyes were squinted almost closed; a half smile touched his lips. "I thought you were agreed to abiding by the will of the whole council."

"Do you agree, then, that I am regent?" the dauphin said, swiftly.

Everard pressed his lips together. This boy was feeble in body, but his mind was strong enough; he had nailed the provost, and Marcel knew it. His smile melted off his face. Behind him, the bald miller said, "Yes, yes, he agrees. You are the regent, we are the regency council. Aren't we, Master Provost?"

Marcel's jaw set hard; he stood square, as if he were driven into the ground, and would not move. He said, "I want my money. The king stole my city treasury from me, just before he left. I want it back."

"You shall have it," said the dauphin.

On his left, one of the king's men said, "Your Grace, be not so hasty."

Out of the side of his mouth, his gaze oblique, Gilles said, "Not so great a man now, is he, our provost? Just one among us all."

The king's man said, "We will need money."

"I trust my council," the dauphin said. He smiled at Marcel.

JEANNE SAID, "I need your help."

Sylviane had her slate in her hands. "I am writing a poem."

They stared at each other across the table, like crossing swords. Jeanne said, quietly, "Then I will make a bargain with you. If you help me for the rest of the morning, when the nones bells ring, you shall be free to do as you please."

"But — I'm — I have the ideas now, Mother."

"And if you want," said Jeanne placidly, "you can teach me."

That brightened Sylviane's face, like the sun coming from behind a cloud. "All afternoon?"

"All afternoon," said Jeanne.

"You must do whatever I bid you."

"Anything."

The girl went to the table and put down her slate. "I will help you, then."

They went out to the garden and began to pull onions. At every sound from the street, Jeanne's ears strained, and her nerves jumped.

Her neighbors gossiped, down the street; a tinker came by, his pots jangling on his back, calling out his trade. Everything seemed so usual, so ordinary, and yet she could not steady her mind: as little as she knew of what was happening in Paris, she knew it was not usual.

With Sylviane, she sat on the back steps and braided the onions into strings. Before nones, Everard came home.

She got him a piece of a savory to eat, and a cup of wine. He sat on the step and watched them braid the onions.

She said, "Have you met with the dauphin, then?"

Everard said, "Oh, yes." He leaned back on his elbow, his coat open, his white shirt open down the front; she resisted the urge to put her hand on his bare chest. Deep lines marked his face. He smiled at her.

"What is he like?" she asked.

He gave a shake of his head. "He is a Valois. He understands the underside of power as if he received the knowledge with his baptism. But — "

He looked away. In the street some boys were playing ball. The ordinary sounds grated on Jeanne's ears like a clash of arms. She laid another string of onions in the basket. Beside her, bent, Sylviane worked over the coarse dry stalks; the stepmother leaned forward suddenly, and touched the child's hair.

"You are doing well, Sylvie — a good job."

The girl looked up, a tendril of her fair hair floating over her cheek. "It's only braiding onions," she said scornfully, with a glance at her father.

Everard said, "He's . . . interesting, the dauphin. He's full of ideas, good ideas, he talks well — " He rubbed his unshaven jaw. "We need him, I think."

Jeanne took the last string of onions from her stepdaughter. "I thought you and Marcel were going to rule Paris by yourselves."

He laughed at that, some edge in his laughter, some anger, or some fear. "Well, anyway, perhaps we could, but someone must rule the kingdom, too, and that we cannot do."

"You think the dauphin can? I heard he is too weak to mount a horse."

"He's ill," Everard said. "Nonetheless . . ."

He stroked his jaw again, his young beard rasping under his fingers. He said, "Among other things, if we work with him, we are not rebels."

Jeanne looked sharply at him. "Hunh. I'm glad you're considering the consequences."

"We need a king," Everard said. "Without a king, there is no France — only a collection of cities and manors, each with its own allegiance. But the king needs us — and the dauphin seems aware of it." His smile returned. "We can make something here, Jeanne — Marcel, the dauphin, the rest of us. We can make a new way of things, more just and right than before."

Sylviane got up; Jeanne held up the basket to her. When the child took it their hands touched. Out across the city, abruptly, the first of the church bells began the toll that marked the hour of nones.

She said, "Everard, will you help me up?" although she could have risen by herself.

He stood, reaching down to her, and lifted her onto her feet. With her hands on his arms, she looked into his face, and said, "Are you pleased, then?"

"I'm afraid," he said. "So much can go right here. So much can go wrong."

He bent down and kissed her full on the mouth, greedy, fierce. She put her arms around his neck. On the step, Sylviane said, "Mother — come inside, now."

He stepped back, smiling at her, that same smile, tense as a bowstring. "I have to go back to the Châtelet."

"We will be here," she said.

That seemed simple enough, but it touched him; he bent again and brushed his mouth over hers, and hugged her again. Sylviane called once more from the hall, impatient; she was a tyrannical teacher, very harsh. Everard went off down the street, back to his high matter. Jeanne went into the hall, into her child's tutelage.

The dauphin did not sit idle; he made himself open to all men of any importance in Paris; before a great crowd at the Place de Grève he sat with all his knights and counselors and heard the grievances of the people; he agreed that members of the Estates should sit on his regency council; he agreed to consult with them on all matters of the kingdom, especially taxes and the spending of money; he agreed, in fact, to everything anybody asked of him, save that the king of Navarre should be released.

This annoyed Etienne Marcel. He saw how the prince's reasonableness and openness made him friends around the city. He especially saw how anyone who disliked Etienne Marcel found a charitable ear and a kindly look within the dauphin's chambers. When the regency council met again, to talk about giving the dauphin money to raise an army, Marcel was all but alone in denying it.

However, although the whole council disagreed with him, yet they had to yield to him, because the only money available was in the six great chests from the city treasury, which the dauphin had already promised to turn over to Marcel. In the end, the dauphin got no money at all.

The dauphin, however, had not yet actually returned the six chests. Marcel, working all day long at the unfinished Saint-Honoré gate, took heed of this, and waited.

"They think they can snap their fingers in our faces again," he said to Everard. "Mark me, there is something going on deep, here, that stinks."

Everard had brought him papers to read and sign. While Marcel supervised the work on the temporary gate, Everard was carrying on the usual business of the provost's office, which meant walking in and out of the city several times a day.

He said, "You should allow the prince some money."

Marcel grunted at him. These days the high color was rarely gone from his face. A sheen of sweat covered his forehead. "Giving money to a Valois is like dropping it into the Seine."

Everard held out another sheaf of papers. "It seems to me that you have a very strong position in this, strong enough to be able to yield a little. He has already given you Paris. If you took the long view of this — "

The provost lifted his head, his eyes narrow. "Are you his man, or mine?"

The clerk said, "I am your man, as I have shown you, over and over, since I began with you."

"Then keep faith, and keep silence. I have no need of your opinions in this matter. Conform to me, or find another master, do you hear me?"

Everard took the signed charters from him. "I have no difficulty with my ears, Master Provost."

"I am aware of that," said Marcel. "Do not concern yourself with the dauphin. When I have Navarre to throw against him, he will disappear like a dewdrop in the sun. Now, go, do as I bid you."

He turned, his hands behind his back, supervising the work on the gate. Everard went away down the road to the Châtelet.

forty-two

ON THE DAY that the temporary gate at Saint-Honoré finally closed the gap in the wall, the dauphin delivered the city treasury to Marcel.

The money was still packed in the six chests with the city's locks and the city's seals on them. Marcel caused them to be opened, so that he could count the money; he expected to find the chests half filled with sand, or some such thing. Instead, when Everard opened the first of the leather sacks and spilled the money out onto the floor, every single coin was clipped.

Marcel exploded with a roar of rage. Everard went back to the chest for another bag.

Every coin he brought out had been cut, the scar still bright and new, and very deep. The money could still be spent, but no one would accept it at face value any more. The stolen silver had probably been melted down by now to hide its dishonorable origin. Marcel slammed his hands down on the table.

"You cannot trust the Valois. They are all thieves." There was a big pile of money in front of him, and he pushed it with both hands toward Everard. "Take this." He got to his feet so fast his thighs struck the table, and half the money slid off.

"What are you going to do?" Everard said. He knelt down and began to scoop the violated money into its leather sack.

"I am going to show this thief who is master of Paris," Marcel said.

He strode out onto the stair. Everard came after him, leaving half the money on the floor, but the provost did not send him back; he would need every man he had in this, and as he went through the Châtelet out to the street, he recruited them: guardsmen just getting off duty, and the dozen idlers loitering around the steps of the prison.

"Parisians!" he called, as he walked out across the Draperie. "I need your help now — if I have ever been your friend, now be the friend of

Etienne Marcel!" With twenty people hurrying at his heels, he strode up through the gate onto the Great Bridge, more men following after with each step.

"The dauphin has broken his word!" Marcel shouted, as he walked. On the busy bridge, packed along each rail with shops and stalls, people turned to listen, and stopped what they were doing and rushed to join him. "He's stolen our money — like all those other times, whatever we have, they take!"

"Marcel," someone called, and there was a cheer. The people coming across the bridge toward him slowed and turned and joined the mob streaming around him. He walked from the bridge onto the City Island, the crowd around him now chanting his name.

"Mar-cel! Mar-cel!"

Everard strode up beside him. "Master Provost, what do you mean to do?" His face was taut and his black eyes burned.

Marcel said, "Ask no questions of me, Everard."

"We must have his good will," Everard said, relentlessly. "We cannot rule Paris without the kingdom."

Marcel turned to his right, saw a guardsman, his face red with excitement, striding along beside him, and gripped him by the sleeve. "Take Everard! Hold him back — " Without slowing in his march, he thrust the guardsman toward Everard; the clerk's eyes opened wide, and he turned and ran.

The provost plunged forward. He forgot about Everard. Ahead, the street before the palace was aswarm with people, all heads now turning toward the provost and his following; he saw Gilles the miller up there, standing in a circle of his hangers-on, and veered through the wide, rough-paved street toward him.

"Gilles! Here to whisper in the prince's ear?"

He swept into the palace past the other merchant, who wheeled ponderously to glare at him. Marcel shouted to him, "You think you can work behind me, do you?" Then he was past Gilles, too far away to talk any more, Marcel himself now caught up and carried along in the excited stream of people.

The doors to the palace stood open. The crowd poured in through them. Marcel lengthened his stride. For the first time he looked around him at the men on either side. On his left and behind him were three guardsmen in their red-and-blue hoods; on his right, some of the idlers from the prison, and some other rough-looking men, caught up in the rush over the bridge, common men, day laborers, who owed their bread to Etienne Marcel.

These were men to do his will. He flung his fist in the air, and they burst into the council chamber.

It was empty. Marcel led his little army in a charge across the room, to the door beyond, where a stairway began that took them up to the dauphin's chambers.

The stairwell was narrow; it throttled the onrush of the crowd. Marcel went two at a time up the stairs, the guardsmen and the laborers clamoring excitedly around him. He reached the door at the top of the stairs and tried the latch.

"Locked," he said, and the men around him looked at him, grinned, and lunged.

Their weight drove the door inward off its hinges and crashed it down flat before them. They charged in over it, across a room of light, beautiful furniture, carpeted in wool flowers, paneled in wood. At the far end, by a shuttered window, the dauphin turned in the midst of a little group of his counselors.

Marcel strode up to him. "I want my money," he said, and struck the dauphin in the chest.

The youth coughed. From behind him one of his knights sprang on Marcel like a lion.

"You'll treat my lord the regent with the respect and honor due him!"

Marcel staggered back, his arm up between him and the knight. Before he could speak, one of the guardsmen behind him lunged past him, his pike set in his hands. The blade jutted in past the provost's side and through the space between him and the knight and buried itself to the crossguards in the knight's body.

A plume of blood shot up from the knight's chest, and the man crumpled. The dauphin's face dropped open, as if his mouth were a wound. His eyes widened with horror. Stiff, slow, he reached down toward the body at his feet. From either side of him his other knights launched themselves forward, and the guardsmen around Marcel attacked them. Through the door behind them streamed more of the mob, howling.

Marcel staggered back, his hand raised. Around him they were battling one another, in such close quarters that their elbows struck him, their grunts exploded in his ears. Stumbling across the room, banging into people, he put his back to the wall; he had no weapons, but he snatched up a stool beside him and held it like a shield. The room was full of battling men.

"Cease — hold — I beg of you!" the dauphin cried. He still stood in the center of the room, frozen in his tracks, the body at his feet, blood all over his hands and arms. Another of the knights fell, and another. Marcel gathered himself and stepped forward.

"Halt! Stop — stop — "

The dauphin wheeled toward him. "Please — I'll do anything — " His long white fingers clutched at Marcel's sleeve.

The provost thrust him back, toward the wall. The noise was subsiding a little. The mob still filled the room, some few still fighting one another, but most of them were looting the place. A steady stream of people was rushing out the door, each carrying some piece of plunder. Wide-eyed, he saw two men picking at the gilt trim on the walls.

Marcel strode forward, braver now, with the room emptying, the three knights dead. "Stop — in the provost's name — "

The few men remaining in the room stood still. They turned slowly toward him, three guardsmen in their red-and-blue hoods, and a few rough-looking men off the street, the dauphin, and the provost.

"Hold," Marcel cried, in the sudden silence, and went forward into their midst. Through the crowd outside in the stairwell, Everard pushed and shoved his way to his master's side.

"What are you doing?" he shouted into Marcel's face. "What have you done here?" One hand still on the provost's arm, he turned and swept his gaze around the room.

On the floor the bodies of the dauphin's men lay in lakes of blood. The dauphin whispered, "Holy Mother — Holy Mary Mother — " and crossed himself. His eyes were huge in his white face. His clothes were smeared with blood.

Marcel shook Everard's hand off his arm. The sight of the blood sent a new excitement galloping through his veins, an unsteady lightness like drunkenness. What had been done was done; now he had to make the best of it. He went up to the dauphin and seized him by the shoulder and shook him.

"This is what happens to thieves, whether noble or base! You stole what was ours, you are no king, but a thief! A thief!"

Everard reached out and gripped his arm. "Leave off. You'll ruin everything."

Marcel was panting; his nerves rippled, and his stomach heaved. He cast a quick glance around the room, at the swarm of men who packed it, and faced the dauphin again.

"I want my money back!"

"I'll give it to you — anything — "

"You will release the king of Navarre!"

"I will," said the dauphin. "I will."

"And you will take this — " Marcel grabbed the red-and-blue hood off the head of the nearest guardsman. "Wear this, and make yourself one of the people of Paris. When you have seen how we must live, then perhaps you will be ready to be a king — when each of us is a king also."

The dauphin took the cloth in his limp white hand. An unintelligible murmur escaped his lips. Marcel swept another look around him, found Everard staring at him, his face unreadable, and said, "Clean up this mess." He straightened, throwing out his chest, triumphant again, master of Paris again. He looked once more at his beaten and cowering enemy and forced his way back through the crowd, out of the room.

The dauphin sank down on one knee. Robert de Clermont, his friend since boyhood, lay at his feet, his body ripped in a dozen places, his head flattened. Blood ran from his eyes, his nose, his mouth. The smell was nauseating. Feet crunched and scraped by him, and he put out his hands to protect the body.

"Come along," someone was saying. "Get out. Everybody get out. Move!" Slowly the room was emptying. The dauphin drew in his breath, feeling as if for long moments he had not breathed; fresh tears dribbled down his face. The door shut.

"My lord — " A hand on his arm urged him gently up onto his feet; he wobbled a moment, dazed, and slumped, and the same hands caught him and set him down on the floor with his back to the wall. "Get some wine. Damn you, yes, I mean you, can you do nothing save gawk? Do as I say!"

The dauphin wiped his face on his sleeve. He leaned against the wall. The room was empty now save for the dead bodies and the man in the black coat, Marcel's Breton clerk, who had cleared out the mob, and who now turned from the doorway, a cup in his hand, and knelt down by the prince.

"Here, drink this."

The young man sipped once, took the cup and drank all. Leaning his head back against the wall, he shut his eyes.

Feet tramped heavily through the door, and he jerked his head up again. The Breton clerk led in two heavyset pages. When they saw the room, both stopped and gasped.

"What happened in here? What happened to everything?"

"Wait," said the Breton, and he went into the next room, where the bed was, and yanked down the bedcurtain. Bringing it back out to this chamber, he spread out the fabric on the floor. "Help me," he said to the pages. Bending over the nearest of the three bodies, he began to lift it.

The pages hung back. The clerk shouted, "Help me!" and they sprang forward and together lifted the broken bones and jellied flesh of Robert de Clermont onto the bedcurtain and wrapped it tight around him. In such wise they gathered up the remains of the others, and the pages lugged them out the door.

The dauphin turned his head to look around him. His father had used this room most, King John, reclining now in captive splendor among the English. King John would not recognize the room. The mob had destroyed it. Everything small was taken, books and cups and the painted miniatures that had stood on the sideboard, the pots and the stools, the bedclothes. The furniture too heavy to carry was smashed, and even the gilt trim was peeled off the paneled walls.

The clerk shut the door on the last of the bodies. He turned and surveyed the room with a glance, and the dauphin held up the empty winecup.

"More." He put one foot under him and slowly stood up.

The clerk went out a moment and came back with a ewer. The dauphin leaned against the broken sideboard. By his hand the shining wood surface was gouged to a clump of splinters. He passed his hand over his face; the tall Breton poured wine into the cup and set it next to him.

"Everard," the dauphin said, remembering his name.

"My lord," said the other man.

"They were like beasts," the dauphin said. He leaned against the broken sideboard and drank more of the wine. "They tore my friends to pieces — are these the people I am supposed to care for as a father cares for his children?"

"Did you know that the money was clipped?" Everard asked.

The dauphin said, "I needed money! He was refusing to give me anything — we must have some money!" He folded his arms up on the sideboard and put his head down on them. "I have . . . I have much to learn."

Suddenly he gave way to tears again, remembering, and the words flew from him like tears. "Is this power? Is this governance? Savage blows and threats of death and brutality? Are these my people?"

The clerk made no answer. Mastering himself again, the dauphin raised his head, and found Everard's gaze on him, his face fretted with deep lines.

"You must help me escape," the dauphin said.

"Escape? Escape to what?" Everard said.

"I have to get out of Paris." The dauphin went toward the window, his hands moving. Every footstep outside his door brought the hackles up on end along his spine and nape. He had to find someplace safe, somewhere he could lock the mob out. "Help me."

Everard said, "My lord, do not flee now. You've given Navarre his freedom. Marcel will surely bring him here to use against you. If you leave, you are giving him Paris."

The dauphin laughed; he breathed with a suck and rasp in his chest, and he yielded to a spasm of coughing. "Navarre deserves Paris." He strode off across the room again, trapped here. "Help me!"

"If you run away now you will never come back," Everard said.

"I'll bring an army back," the dauphin said. "I'll hammer down the walls — I'll lay the mob low with arrows — "

Again he began to weep. He put his hands over his face, hands that had never been strong enough to bend a bow. Everard stood silent before him a moment, while the prince fought to control himself.

At last, pensive, the Breton said, "You can sail — I have seen you often, in your boat on the Seine."

"Yes," said the boy, lowering his hands, grateful. "Yes."

"I will meet you tonight, then, at the foot of the king's garden," Everard said. "On the shore there."

The dauphin nodded. Everard was staring at him, his dark eyes bitter, his mouth twisted, his shoulders slumped. The dauphin turned away from the condemnation in his face and reached again for the wine ewer.

The sun was setting. Gleaming with the last pewter light between its shadowed banks, the river wound away toward the gilded horizon. Already the little boat had drifted a good way off the Island, past the low sandy shoals where the two streams of the river merged again in a washboard of black ripples.

Now Everard stood on the shore and watched the lone sailor haul his canvas up into the evening's breeze. Pink with the sun's failing light, the sail filled with wind and turned, and the boat rose lively under it, lying over.

What is the power of reason? Everard thought. The power of reason is to destroy faith.

Marcel was his master; there was no man he cared to serve but him. Yet what Marcel had done against the dauphin filled him with terror and foreboding. Marcel needed friends; everything he did now made him enemies. He was like a fly caught in honey; every move he made enmired him. Now he was bringing into this turmoil the king of Navarre, to be his captain, a man whose only feats of arms were murders. This was the world that reason made.

Everard thought: Is this God's trick, then, Italo? The human soul thirsts for justice, longs for order, but the world thrives on injustice and disorder and decay. Is that the answer, Italo?

Out there the little boat had all but disappeared in the gray twilight. The sun had gone down. The sky was fading. Everard turned, put one foot before the other, and thereby made his way home again, in the darkening, the corrupted city.

forty-three

"THE DAUPHIN has been proclaimed regent,"
said the Black Prince. "Paris is his, and the place is apparently
well fortified."

"The dauphin's a boy," said Chandos. "Isn't he? What do you
know of the dauphin?" He turned toward Josseran de Vaumartin.

The Breton murmured something; he would not let them use him
for a spy against France. Still reading the letter, the prince walked
away, up the little room, with its fine fittings, its carpet, its brass-
studded oaken table.

"But there's unrest in the city, and the people are calling for the
release of Navarre!" He wheeled. "That's interesting. If Navarre were
free, there might be some work to be done here yet."

He folded the paper quickly in his hands and thrust it at
Chandos. "Put this in my chest. Let's go. Our royal guest awaits us."

Josseran went after him down the stairs, toward the great hall, where
every night the prince gave a lavish entertainment for his captive, the
king of France. Halfway down the stairs, they could already hear the
feverish gaiety, and the prince turned to him.

"He is making the best of his circumstances, is King John." He
laughed.

Josseran jerked his mouth into the shape of a smile. The prince
looked sharply at him.

"You are a dull companion lately, Josseran. What's the matter?"
He reached out to slap his shoulder. "Come, come — you look
too sober, you need a little of what has King John aroar right now."
He went on a few steps ahead, eager, and Josseran went after him,
trying to shrug off his low humor.

King John leaned back and laughed, his mouth wide and red, his winecup in his hand. With a broad swat of his right arm, he struck his companion on the shoulder.

"A good jest! Let's have a few more good jests — let's have a drink to all good jests!" He lifted his cup high, so that the lamplight gleamed on it, saluting the whole table. "Who has another, now? Who can make the king laugh?"

The hall blazed candlelight, swarmed with servants. Around the several long tables sat a hundred knights, and at the king's challenge, fifty of these leapt up, trying to outshout each other. Opposite them, on the far side of the room, Josseran leaned his elbows on the littered table and stared away.

One of the knights cried, "There was a lady once, who wished to deceive her lord — "

"No, no, we've all heard that one!" John reached out and struck him, knocking him back into his seat on the bench. "Another jest — a new one! Who has a new one?"

Midway between him and Josseran, at the front table, Prince Edward said, "My lord, you are merry tonight."

The king lounged expansively along the bench, his arms stretched out. His mustaches were damp. "Such a generous and noble hospitality as you have given me here, my dear lord prince, would make a merry man of Saint Anthony!"

Josseran swung around, his temper like a razor. "Yes, by Holy Heaven, he should have gotten himself taken sooner, had he known how jolly it would be."

The prince murmured, "Josseran, Josseran." Across the room, King John straightened, his smile gone.

"What is it, Vaumartin? Is it not enough that you have defeated me?"

Josseran lowered his head; it was not his place to speak out here, and in fact he knew not what it was that galled him so, in the king's rejoicing. He was himself half drunken. He turned his attention to his winecup and did not answer King John, his enemy, over whom he should have been gloating now.

Several of the other knights had jokes to tell, for the entertainment of the captive king of France, and soon the whole table was aroar with laughter again. Josseran sat there alone, his shoulders hunched, as if he were defending his gloom against their lightheartedness.

They had marched north to Calais from Poitiers, with the king, with all the booty of the battle, and not a Frenchman had stirred to make their way troublesome. Now, since they had come into the city, Prince Edward spent the idle days and nights in feasts and entertainments for his royal captives. He had poured wine into John's cup with his own hand, delivered fine speeches to him of nobility and pride, until Josseran's teeth gritted and his belly was afire, and John had smiled and drunk and feasted like a base clown.

Now the whole hall rocked with laughter at some joke of the king's youngest son, ten years old, who had stayed faithfully by his father throughout Poitiers. A shock-haired boy in a bright red coat, he stood up and told his tired little jest, and more at him than at his joke, the knights shouted and clapped and bellowed with mirth, until the candles in the sconces on the walls shook and the cups bounced at the table. Someone laid a hand on Josseran's shoulder.

He turned; the prince was sitting down beside him on the bench, the men around him with murmurs and bobbing bows making space hastily for him there.

The prince said, "Josseran, it grieves me to see you so low."

"Yes," Josseran said, furious, his gaze going across the room again, to the king guffawing in the middle of his servants and attendants, "I should be merry, should I not, merry as a king — merry as he who left his kingdom desperate and undefended — " His voice rose to a shout. " — Left France to groan and weep while he rejoices in captivity!"

The room clashed into silence. Everyone was staring at him. Across the wide room, King John stared at him, his face rigid.

"How dare he speak so to my father the king!" The boy prince sprang across the intervening space like a mosquito, his hand raised. Prince Edward nodded, and coming from one side somebody caught the child's hand, and drew him firmly back toward his place on the bench.

King John said, "I demand . . ." His voice was thick with wine. His head swayed, not quite balanced on his thick bull's neck. "I demand an apology."

The prince's hand still lay firmly on Josseran's arm. "Of all the knights who have offered up their lives in our cause, none has my love more securely than Josseran de Vaumartin."

Josseran said, "Your Grace, you do me honor — too much honor. I will remove myself, lest I stain your honor." He rose, staring across the room at the king, and walked down behind the table to the door. No one spoke; all eyes followed him. When he went out to the next chamber, the room broke into a buzz, a roar of talk.

He went down the stairs. In this castle of Calais there was hardly room enough for the prince and his attendants and his royal captive, and Josseran had been staying in a house in the city. He was glad for the dark and quiet and cool air of the staircase.

In the castle courtyard, where the guards were changing their watch, he stood in the cool darkness listening to their little ritual, passing on the watchwords and the weapons, giving the news of the night.

"All's quiet in Calais. All's quiet in God's good night."

The courtyard's flagstones gleamed silver in the moonlight. Overhead, the full moon ghosted through the sky; later, the fog would veil it, and turn the night dark as hellgate. He could smell the sea, its tang flavoring the eastbound wind. Someone hailed him, and he answered. A guard let him out the postern gate, into the street.

His heart seethed, his mind an uproar; he could not slick down the turmoil of his feelings with any film of words. There was a heat in him, a tingle in every nerve, a soreness in his mind that would not ease. Miserable, he went down the street toward his house, wishing he had come on John on the field of Poitiers, and slain him there.

The prince had placed some servants and retainers with him. One of these opened the door for him, a candle in his hand.

"My lord, there is someone here."

Josseran said, "I want to see no one." He wanted more wine, to get very drunk, to drown his rage. The servant with the candle led him into the house.

"My lord, she has been waiting many hours."

"She? Who is it?"

"This way, my lord."

He went after the man through the wide dark hall, into another chamber, much smaller. A candle burned on the table against the wall. Beyond it, half in shadow, a woman turned to face him.

"Isobel," he said.

Cool, wrapped in her headdress and cloak so that only her face showed, she came a few uncertain steps toward him. Her voice was wary. "Josseran — my lord — "

He put out his hands to her. "Isobel. What are you doing here?"

Slowly she reached out and took hold of his hands. "I was not sure how you would receive me, my lord — and grateful I am for your welcoming. But my news — will put you against me, I fear."

"Tell me."

She gathered herself visibly to speak. "I have lost Vaumartin."

"Lost." The news was like a blow in his belly.

"The Comte de Nesle came with a company of men, to lay siege to it — I had no men, no stores. I had to surrender."

His jaw clenched. He lifted his head, thinking of Vaumartin, and in his grip her hands moved, drawing back. He turned his gaze on her again. To see her again, without the hatred like a mask over her beauty, wakened every sweet memory in him. The sight of her overwhelmed him; even Vaumartin seemed unimportant to him, with her standing there before him.

She was pulling her hands free of his. He tightened his grip. He drew her closer to him, looking down into her face. He said, "Yet you came back to me." His voice shook. He searched her face for the hatred and rage that had driven him away.

She raised her eyes to him. Her lips were soft, her eyes gentle. She said, "Since you left, I have known no restful hour, Josseran. I have come to beg your forgiveness — to beg you to take me back — "

He pulled her into his arms. "I should never have left you." Tight against him, her body was as warm and vibrant and eager as his own. The thought shot through his mind that now they were free of Vaumartin. That startled him, but only for a moment; after that, all his heart and mind were lost in Isobel.

At noon, the next day, at dinner, Josseran fell sick with a camp fever. Knowing what it was, the servants and Isobel got him at once into his bed, and she sat by him, and the servants sent for a priest.

Josseran tossed, restless, on the bed. "Isobel," he cried.

"I am here, my love."

"Isobel, you must find Everard. He is in Paris, if he lives, at the Studium, perhaps. Find him. Everard le Breton, he calls himself. Make amends to him."

"Josseran," she said, "don't use up your strength."

"Find him! I will suffer like this in Hell, if you do not get his forgiveness for me — "

The prince said, "Has he had the Sacrament? Who is this Everard?"

Josseran said, "My prince — keep faith." His voice creaked. The prince leaned toward him again, and he was dead.

Isobel sat back, her hands shaking. She crossed herself. The prince turned toward her, his face twisting.

"Ah, God — God — that such a one as this could die so low!" He put his hands to his face and broke into weeping.

Isobel drew back from him. Her husband's eyes were shut, peacefully shut. She covered him with the sheet and snuffed the candles out. Her own calm surprised her. She had come too late, she thought, over and over.

What he had said to her was welcome, giving her purpose over the next few days. She went out into the front of the house, to find a servant who would help her get to Paris.

forty-four

MARCEL SAID, "I will hear nothing more of
this, Everard. The dauphin is gone now, fled like the coward he
is, and nothing will stand in my way. If I am to save Paris, I must have
absolute loyalty — complete obedience. I mean to make Navarre my
captain, and nothing you can say will stop me."

Everard turned to Mailliard, standing by the door. "What do you
think of this?"

Mailliard lifted his great shaggy red head. "I don't think — I do as
I'm told." His voice rumbled, with amusement, with annoyance.

Marcel grunted at him. "A point well made." He glared at Everard,
his broad face set, his eyes flinty. "I think you will understand, Master
Everard, why I am giving you this work to do, here, while I go to greet
the king of Navarre, and do my business with him. There is much
work here, as you know."

Everard said, "As you will, Master Provost."

Marcel went out, the watch captain with him. Everard sat down at
his desk and began to write charters.

He heard the roar of the crowd when the king of Navarre came
down the Draperie, and later he could hear thunderous cheers from
the Place de Grève, where Marcel and the king spoke before the city.
Later a messenger bringing him some documents said that the king
spoke very well, eloquently and at length, about the evils done him
by the Valois, who had stolen everything from him, and how he was
rightfully king of France and with their help would become so in all
men's eyes.

"Has he an army?" Everard asked.

"Some few hundreds of men-at-arms. His brothers, and some other
knights. Not a big army. And he looks not much like a king," said the
messenger. "All in black, he was, on a black horse, not even a fancy
medal in his cap — not much like a king, I'd say."

Everard bent over the charter on his desk. "The name deceives. Watch his hands." He dipped his pen into the ink. The messenger left.

One of Jeanne's hens set a clutch of eggs outside, under a bush at the back of the garden. The wife was afraid that the neighborhood dogs would get her, and so when the hen had begun to brood, Jeanne cast a cloth over the bird, nest and all, and lifted it all up gently with the hen in it and carried it into the house and put it down by the chimney corner.

Sylviane had put a heap of straw down there, and the corner was warm. Jeanne left the cloth over the hen, until she could grow used to her new place.

"Now leave her alone," she said to Sylviane, who was squatting down to peer closely at the nest. "She must be quiet awhile. Now leave her." The door opened, and she looked across the hall to see who was coming in.

It was her brother, Bonboisson. He had a pail of cream with him, which he gave to her, to make butter, but he did not leave when she had taken it; he sat down at the table and stared at her.

"What is it, brother?" She dipped her finger into the thick fresh yellow cream and tasted a dollop of it, rich as angel's milk.

"Where is Everard?" Bonboisson asked.

"He has some work at the Studium." She called to Sylviane, who came out of her room, and took the cream away to the pantry to put into the churn. Presently the sound of the churning came from the pantry. Jeanne said, "Would you like a cup of wine?"

"You know I told them I would do nothing in this militia," said Bonboisson. "Well, I have changed my mind."

"Have you," she said, straightening. In the chimney corner the hen twittered under the cloth.

"I thought — before — you know what I thought, that it usurped the king's place, for men like me to fight, but now — " He flung his hands up. "All has changed. The Death juggled everything, Jeanne." His face was deeply graven. "The king taken, now the dauphin fled also, and this Navarre now claiming that he is the king — " He put his hand over his face. "I am a fool, to be talking about such things with a mere woman."

She said nothing to that. He leaned his arms on the table, staring into the fire.

"Everything was so easy, for my father. He knew who the king was, what his duties were — what his taxes would be, what his prices would be! God's love, Jeanne, how can I plan, when I know nothing of what may come? How can I know what to do?"

She said, "Everard will probably be home for supper. Come talk to him then."

"Everard. He knows no more than I — he but rides it better." He laid his hands down flat on the tabletop, as if to prop himself up, and stared at her. "Tell Everard I shall join his militia."

"Then you've made up your mind certainly?" she said.

"Yes." He nodded. "I'll be one of their captains, if they wish — some of the other vintners will assign their apprentices to my company. We've talked about it before."

She said, "You are very brave, brother."

He looked sharply at her, as if she mocked him. His face was still stiff with uncertainty. He said, "What do you think of it, Jeanne?"

She glanced toward the fireplace and faced him again. "God, Who keeps the hen, will not forsake His people of Paris."

He let out a snort, half laughter, half scorn. "Such things as a woman says." He turned his face toward the fire again; she rose to go down and help Sylviane with the churning.

The provost devoted himself to his dealings with Navarre, leaving the small work of the city to his clerks. Some of this business took Everard into the Studium, to talk to the rector. When he was done, he went to the White Rose for his dinner.

As he was sitting there drinking the last of his wine, the tavern around him filling up with scholars coming out of the afternoon lectures, someone came to his bench and sat down next to him. He looked up, and saw Claude de Brises.

The bishop's nephew wore a fine black cassock trimmed with gold braid. His cross was begemmed gold. Everard said, "Well, I see the world's won out again." He put down his empty cup and got to his feet.

De Brises put out his hand to stop him. "Wait, Everard. I want to talk to you."

"To me?" Everard swung around toward him, his hand on his hip. "Aren't you afraid you'll learn something?" He ran his eyes over de Brises's clothes, marking the beautiful boots of soft black leather and the rings on his fingers. "You should thank me, Claude, for God's love — you could not look so splendid on a master's fees."

De Brises's face reddened. "Will you leave off firing at me so that I can speak to you? It's all over Paris that you and Marcel are on the outs — "

"Untrue," Everard said, briskly.

"That he needs you, and you are loyal, and so you can stay on together — "

"That is not so," Everard said. "I am going — "

De Brises said, "Are you afraid to listen to me?"

Everard stood where he was a moment, and then at last he went back to the bench and sat down again. "Stop shouting at me. What do you want?"

The canon sat back, smiling, his eyes narrow. In the haunted towers of the Studium, he had wandered like an orphan, but clearly the exercise of power was hearth and home to him. He said, "Leave Marcel. There are many men in Paris who hate him — "

"That's folly," Everard said, shortly. "Marcel's the only man who can master the city. If he goes down, Navarre will step in and take it all."

De Brises leaned toward him, his face intent. "There are many men in the city working in support of the dauphin. You yourself — "

His voice broke off, his gaze diverted across the room. Everard turned. Through the tavern door, into the crowd of black gowns, tramped a dozen men in gaudy jackets and boots, popinjays among crows. Some of them had feathers in their hats. They all carried swords. The little tavernkeeper sped toward them with his head bobbing in bows of greeting, and with many scrapes and flatteries he marshaled them and their fat purses toward the big table. The rest of his custom sat like the furniture and stared.

"Navarre's men," Everard said.

Swiveling his head, de Brises brought the full force of his glare back to Everard.

"Who but the dauphin can rule the kingdom now? Marcel has betrayed us all, Everard."

Everard grunted at him. "Therefore I should betray him? I have taken his penny, I am his man, and will be until I — "

A roar from the front of the room drowned his words. Everard twisted around to see; all the scholars nearby swiveled their heads toward the big table, where the soldiers were gathered. One of them, black-bearded, red-faced, had pulled the serving wench into his arms.

"Here's my conquest! I've been waiting for you, my doll, since Poitiers — "

Everard found himself suddenly on his toes, stiff as a bolt, his blood racing. All around him the benches scraped and the tables groaned; everybody else was standing also. The serving wench put her elbow into the blackbeard's throat and swung her arm roundhouse to smash him across the face. He let her go with a yell.

"'Sballs, she's stronger than any of those knights we fought at Poitiers! The French should send their wenches into battle!"

De Brises said, in a voice choked with fury, "These men fought for the English at Poitiers."

He lunged forward. Everard caught at his arm.

"Wait. Stand — "

De Brises flung off his hand. "Will you not fight for anything?"

All around the tavern the scholars were up on their feet; being of the Picard nation, most of them were French. The soldier was howling like a lovestruck hound after the serving wench.

"Come, my little French dumpling! I'll — "

From all sides the scholars leapt on him. De Brises let out a roar of encouragement. Everard stepped back. The whole place was brawling, every black coat in a mad tangle, fists pumping, while the soldiers neatly fitted themselves in a corner and fought off the attacks. De Brises climbed up onto the bench and began to shout, "That way! Over there, you fools — get them from the side — someone go out by the window!" Everard left.

The watch was changing, and the Châtelet was jammed with men coming in off duty and other men going out. Jean Mailliard was in the ground-floor room shouting orders and reading from a long list in one hand. When Everard came in and strode purposefully toward the steps, the tall watch captain called, "Marcel's not here, if you're looking for him."

Everard went over to him. Mailliard's voice filled the room, resounding off the stone walls like a thunderclap, and his watchmen scurried around like rats doing his bidding. There seemed many more of them than usual. Everard looked around him, surprised.

"What's been going on?"

"We had a little trouble in the Place de Grève," said the captain. He folded his piece of paper and stuck it inside his shirt. "Marcel is out at the Hôtel de Plaisance."

The outlandish name brought a startled snort of derision from Everard. "The what?"

"Navarre's house, outside the city," Mailliard said. He rubbed his great beak of a nose, his eyes agleam. "The Hôtel de Plaisance."

Everard said, "What sort of trouble did you have at the Place de Grève?"

"A pack of Navarre's soldiers came in and started beating up people."

"Hunh." Everard cast a look around him at the watch, now rapidly leaving to go on duty, their staffs and lanterns in their hands, and their long red-and-blue hoods flying. "There was a brawl at the White Rose, when I was there, that Navarre's men intended to start."

The watch captain scratched his nose again. "I don't plumb this. You think they did it on purpose?"

Everard nodded. "Where is this Hôtel de Plaisance?"

"Out the Saint-Germain gate." Mailliard caught him by the sleeve. "Where are you going? Don't be a fool! Who's to do the work if you go too?"

"You can, Mailliard," he said, and laughed at the look on the tall man's face. With a sort of salute, he went out of the Châtelet.

forty-five

THE HÔTEL DE PLAISANCE lay just back
from the Saint-Germain road, in a grove of plane trees and old
oaks. Everard had no trouble finding it, since half of Paris seemed
already to be there. He made his way through a crush of wagons trying
to get in through the main gate; the porters, red-faced and throat-sore
from screaming, ignored him.

In the courtyard there were more wagons, and people unloading
them, tuns of wine and sacks of cheeses, whole sides of beef and strings
of sausages, parades of servants to carry it all away into the kitchens and
pantries. Everard picked a way through this turmoil and got into the
house itself.

Wanting to look around, he did not ask at once for Marcel, but went
through the great hall, a vast room in the new style, with a whole wall
full of glazed windows that let in the light of the late summer afternoon
in sheets and veils. Several men were rolling out a carpet over the slate
floor, and before it was even laid flat, other servants were setting up a
table and some chairs, real Italian chairs, with backs and arms. He
went on through a series of smaller rooms, just as crowded and busy,
looked out along a tiled walkway into the garden, and circled around
behind the house, admiring the richness and luxury of the appoint-
ments.

When he reached the hall again, the carpet was down, the chairs and
table in place, and most of the servants gone, save for two or three
laying a fire in the great hearth. Everard went toward the windows. On
a table there stood some pots and bowls, and a huge heap of flowers,
perhaps to be set about the room, also a new Italian fashion.

He stood looking out the window into the garden, wondering at all
this sudden bustle here, at the intentions of Navarre, who had sent his
men into Paris to make trouble. To raise the animosity of the people.
It seemed a strange way to aspire to power.

Through the corner of his eye, he saw a rainbow.

He turned. The table was covered with a white cloth. Among the bowls and pots collected on it was a sphere of Venetian glass, half full of water. The sunlight passed through it; around the bottom edge on the white cloth was a smear of purple edged with yellow.

He picked it up in both hands. When he took it from the sunlight, the color vanished. When he held the bowl in the sunlight again, and put his face close to it, all along the round edge he saw the rainbow again, the purple color darkest and most evident, but every other color tucked in alongside it.

Abruptly, as if scales had fallen from his eyes, he understood. Grosseteste's theory of refraction and reflection suddenly fell into place in his mind. A raindrop, like this glass bowl, had two surfaces, the front and the back; the light entering through the front bounced off the back and bent again through the front surface, splitting the beam of light into its fan of colors.

He trembled as he stood there, the cosmos in his hands. For an instant it seemed to him that the whole order of the world had been revealed to him, woven on a loom of light.

"Who are you?"

He wheeled, the glass bowl still in his hands, and faced a tall man of about his own age, with close-cropped hair and dressed all in black. Something rang in his memory, sword on sword. He knew he faced the king of Navarre.

He said, "I beg Your Grace's pardon. I am seeking Etienne Marcel."

"Marcel," said the king. "You know me? How?" He drew closer, one hand on the tabletop, his eyes keen. "Go on as you were — with the glass."

Everard laughed, uncertain, and put the bowl down. "I was idle, Your Grace."

"No, no, I have an interest in the occult arts, and I know that certain adepts can read much in a sphere of crystal." The king gave him a piercing look. "And you knew me at once. Why do you seek Marcel?"

"I am — I have business with him."

"Convey it to me. I shall see him momently."

"Your Grace, I — "

Some small movement in the doorway caught his eyes, and he looked around, relieved, to see Marcel himself coming into the room. In these bright, airy surroundings the provost in his heavy dark coat looked solid and squat as a tree stump. He said, "Everard. What brings you here?"

Everard said, "Master Provost, I must talk to you privately."

"Speak," said the provost, with a flick of his gaze at Navarre.

They were watching him expectantly now, and he saw no reason to dissemble. He said, "Did you know that His Grace the king's army is made up of men who fought at Poitiers — for the English?"

Marcel let out a grunt of surprise. Navarre's face was impassive; he said nothing.

Everard went on, "Today, some of them came into the White Rose while I was there and made a great point of announcing they were Englishmen, and started a brawl. In the Place de Grève there was a similar brawl." He turned his gaze on Navarre. "What purpose there is in inciting the people of Paris to hate these men, and those who command them, I leave you to guess at."

Marcel's head swung toward Navarre. "Is this true?"

Navarre said mildly, "When I was released from prison, for which I will forever be in your debt, Master Provost, I had need of an army. I recruited one from men available to me. If they are a problem, I shall remove them from the city."

"Do so," Marcel said.

"I shall." The king inclined his head slightly. "I am your captain, sir, I will do whatever suits you."

"Well said." Marcel faced Everard again. "You see, things are well in hand here. You may return to Paris, and await my further orders."

Navarre said, "Perhaps your lieutenant here would care to remain awhile, and join us for some supper. He and I were engaged in a conversation pleasing to me when you came in."

"I must go back to the city," Everard said.

Marcel said, "Go then," in an irritated voice, and gave Navarre another sharp look. Everard strode swiftly out of the room.

forty-six

NAVARRE'S MEN WITHDREW from Paris; for a while the city was calm. De Brises preached against Marcel from the high pulpit of Notre Dame, and on every street corner monks berated the passing crowds on the evils of ambition and power.

Two days after the feast day of the Martyrs, when Bonboisson went down to the river to buy wine coming up from the east, no boats came into Paris, and for some days after that there were no boats. The price of bread began to rise; groups of people collected in the Place de Grève and around the Châtelet, spreading rumors and panic. Somehow the story got around that in the countryside the serfs were rising against their masters, and killing all that they could lay hands on. People were moving into the city nearly every day now, to escape from the brigands who haunted all the roads, and they carried with them a plague of fear.

Then on Saint Denis's Day a single boat came down the Seine, but it was burned to the waterline, and the only men on it were charred corpses. Marcel sent for Navarre, and they agreed to take some action together to remedy this evil, although no one knew precisely what the evil was.

Marcel went to the Hôtel de Plaisance to hold counsel with Navarre about the brigands, and he took Everard with him. Marcel said, "I expect some civility and humility from you here, Everard. This is a king who entertains us."

Everard said nothing. He dropped back a step, to go into the room behind Marcel. Ahead lay the same long sunny hall where he had found the rainbow. The tables had been joined together to form an L-shape; already most of the places on the benches were filled with people.

On the short leg of the L, Navarre sat, in a fancy chair. When Marcel was announced, he rose, smiling, and so the whole room got to its feet, and Marcel entered the room as if he were its master.

Everard saw how this pleased the provost, and he set his teeth together. He went after Marcel across the soft carpet with its pattern of flowers. Navarre came forth, both hands out, to greet Marcel as if they were brothers. Everard swept his gaze around the table.

Half the great men of Paris sat there. Gilles the miller was among them, his eyes sharp, and some other merchants, their drab clothes like bark and stem among the richly colored coats of Navarre's courtiers, and there, where the table bent, sat Claude de Brises.

The king himself led Marcel to his place beside him, at the head of the table. To Everard, he said, "I am delighted, master, that you have honored us with your presence." A serpent's smile slithered along his face. With one hand he gestured toward de Brises. "I understand you two know each other? Here, my lord priest, make room for Master Everard."

De Brises shifted on the bench, and Everard circled the table and sat down in the space he had made; each kept as far from the other as he could. Navarre, on De Brises's far side, smiled broadly at them.

"No welcoming words? I thought you were schoolfellows."

De Brises murmured, "I see you are still part of this cabal."

"What are *you* doing here?" Everard asked him.

"He commanded me," said the bishop's nephew, and his face reddened. "As if he ruled all Paris!"

"He does," Everard said. "For the moment." He glanced up at Marcel and Navarre, on his right side.

They were talking together, their heads leaning toward each other like lovers. The provost laughed. He reached for the tall goblet of glass before him on the table, and when he lowered it again, a page ran up to pour more wine into it. Something Navarre said made the provost nod profoundly, as if they shared some fundamental truth.

The king now turned toward Everard. "My captain's scouts have located the source of our trouble — a band of brigands, on the river, raiding all the traffic. Tomorrow we shall go out and drive them off."

"We," Everard said, startled.

Navarre leaned forward to see him past Marcel's bulk. "My lord provost says he has an army of his own."

"The militia," Everard said. His gaze shifted from the king to Marcel. "They are for the defense of the walls. You can't mean to lead them outside the city."

"They are stout enough fellows," said Marcel.

"Master Provost, they are townsmen, apprentices, laborers — "

"You told me yourself they could fight."

"They can defend a wall! They can't be expected to go into the open field — "

"My knights and I will support them," said Navarre, smoothly.

Marcel was staring at Everard, his eyes like cold fires. "I will hear no more of this. Understand?"

Everard shut his mouth. In his belly a writhing sense of alarm uncoiled and spread and climbed along his nerves; he glanced down the table, the other way, and saw all these men sitting calmly at this table, listening, untouched.

Navarre was watching him steadily. "My dear Everard. Recently I had occasion to glance over some writings of yours — brilliant, quite brilliant, if I may say so."

"Writings of mine?" Everard said, startled. De Brises glared at him.

"Yes — some lecture of yours at the Studium. What I saw was merely a student's notes — you should correct them, and put out a proper copy. I understand they're very widely circulated."

De Brises hitched himself up, his shoulders high, and his big hands before him on the table. "That heretical lecture of yours," he said.

"Heresy! Indeed," said Navarre, his mouth smiling, his eyes unsmiling. "You'll end up at the stake, my dear, with de Brises here piling on the faggots, mark me. But it's wonderful stuff, nonetheless."

Everard shifted on the bench; he could feel de Brises's stare on him like a hot coal, or the twist of a thumbscrew, or the tightening of a noose. Navarre was still watching him with his intent, unblinking gaze, and Everard lifted his head and met his eyes.

"Thank you, Your Grace. Perhaps I shall take your suggestion to heart."

The king smiled wide at him. "Do so."

Everard lowered his gaze. He had come here like a fool, walked into this of his own will; he deserved this. Around him, the servants were moving, bringing food to the table, and the soft click of knives and cups and the sounds of eating enveloped him. He did not eat; he stared at the pewter plate before him and did not lift his hand even to take his wine.

After a few moments, Navarre said, "Let's have my magician come forward."

The magician clearly had been waiting somewhere for this command. He was tall and thin, and wore a long robe embroidered with magic emblems. Standing before the table, he waved his wand, producing from the empty air a scarf, a flower, a shower of coins. The dinner guests gasped and applauded.

Navarre said, "This fellow came to me from Spain, he says, where he learned deep secrets from a Jew."

"Blasphemy," said Claude de Brises, through a mouth like an iron trap.

"You think so," said Navarre. "I myself believe — as Adam believed — that such false names are hung on knowledge to keep it out of common reach."

"Adam," said de Brises, startled.

The magician brought out a little table, padded and cushioned with purple silk, and stood it at some little distance before the king and his guests; on it was a silk scarf, which he whisked away to reveal a box made of glass and gold. The purple table showed through the clear sides of the box, and the magician lifted it up off the table, waved his hand all around it, turned it over, to show that it was empty.

Everard shifted his weight a little; he glanced at Navarre, remembering Italo, his demons, his tricks, his passion for stories that defied reason. Navarre was watching the show with a rapt attention. The magician held up both arms, his hands empty, made some elaborate gestures, and suddenly produced the wand again, as if from the air.

There was a gasp now from the few women, and all around the room the servants paused in their business to watch. The magician made more gestures, a dance of the arms, around and around the box of glass, and abruptly he struck a dramatic pose, one arm cocked high over his head, the other with the wand poised above the box.

De Brises himself was caught on this, hanging forward intently. Everard put his hand over his mouth. The magician's arm swept down, and the wand tapped the top of the box with a sharp ring, and suddenly from the empty box, a white dove flew into the air.

A yell of amazement went up. The dove wheeled around in the confined space of the room. The magician raised his hand and the white bird fluttered toward him and landed on his finger. All around the table, Navarre's guests exploded in applause.

The magician paraded the dove back and forth awhile, bowing and nodding to the acclaim. Navarre turned to Marcel.

"What do you think of that, Master Provost?"

Marcel grunted at him, his jaws chewing, massively unimpressed. "Get him to do it with a few hackbuts instead of a bird."

Navarre swung around to this left now, to the priest. "And you, Master Claude. What do you make of this?"

"Evil and frivolous," said de Brises, in a harsh voice. "By such things do demons beguile the weak and silly souls of men. This magician is a demon in disguise, or his Jew gave him one, who does these wonders."

The king made a face. "What a leaden spirit, to take no joy in tricks. Master Everard, did you enjoy the magic?"

Everard glanced at the priest and turned his gaze on the king of Navarre. "It was no magic, Your Grace, as Your Grace well knows — only a trick. The dove always was in the box. The box is made of mirrors, not of glass."

Around the table there were a hush, then some breathy sighs of disappointment, and a low murmur of comment struck up. The magician hustled forward, teeming with objections. Navarre waved him away.

"Go — find some gypsy, to teach you newer tricks. If a magpie out of the Studium can see through you, I will not keep you another moment."

The magician started toward the far door, his steps quickening as he neared it. Navarre lifted his voice. "Let's have some music." He leaned forward, reaching for his winecup, sipped, and held the cup out to one of the people on his right.

On his left, de Brises said, stiffly, "I know nothing of false magic."

Navarre leaned his elbows on the table. His face was bland, but his fingers twined together, plucking and pulling at each other.

"Very clever, Master Everard."

Everard straightened. Everyone else was eating, even the canon beside him. "Perhaps so. I am sorry to have destroyed the effect of Your Grace's entertainment."

Navarre leaned on his elbows. His hands like predatory birds pecked and tugged at each other. "Certainly you disappointed poor Claude here, who wanted to find devils in it, not mirrors."

Everard said, "My lord de Brises sees what he expects to see, like all of us." He glanced at the canon. De Brises turned the back of his head to him.

Navarre said, "Tell me how you knew the magician's trick. Had you seen it done before?" A page brought him wine in a glass cup.

Everard said, "No, I had not seen the trick, but I knew it could not be done. Therefore the dove was in the box, therefore the box was not of glass."

"You knew it could not be done. You mean, you knew only a true adept could perform such a feat, and you realized poor Master Eichorn is not an adept?"

"No," Everard said. "I knew it could not be done at all. If the substance of nature were so easily tampered with, we should all be in graver danger than from mere plagues and famines."

Across Navarre's smooth face passed a ripple of feeling. His hands locked together into one fist. "Do not delude yourself. The true adepts can move worlds."

Everard shrugged, his hands behind him. Navarre leaned toward him, urgent, his voice sharp.

"I swear to you, you are mistaken. I myself have seen such things done, when it could not be otherwise."

"Then," Everard said, "you were duped."

"I am not duped!" Navarre shot up onto his feet. He lunged toward Everard, his jaw leading, his voice rising to a shrill shriek. "I have never been duped! I know the deepest secrets of the cosmos, as you, my foolish fellow, will never know them — I have seen such things — "

On his right, Marcel reached out and gripped his sleeve. "Your Grace, calm yourself."

Navarre flung off his hand. "How dare you — how dare he — " Unsteady on his feet, he stood swaying before them all, every eye on him, and the recognition that he was watched came over him like a veil. With a visible struggle he mastered himself. He sat down suddenly, as if pulled down. Marcel glared past him at Everard.

"Get out, Everard."

Everard rose. "Is this the king you want, Marcel — this trickster, this gamester — this king of illusions?"

Marcel still had Navarre by the sleeve and was holding him in his place. "You are impudent and insolent. Everard — "

"And I am right, Marcel." Everard flung his arm out toward the box of mirrors. "That is what he offers you, you fool — not true support, but a gull, a ploy — he means to destroy you! Take the militia out with him tomorrow, and he will turn on you and slaughter you, and Paris with you — "

"Get out!" Marcel roared, his face red.

Everard stared at him, seeing in him still the man he had loved, confident and practical and strong-willed and free, and his hand fell to his side. He said, "God help you, Master Provost. God help Paris." He turned, and walked out of the room.

Forty-seven

W HEN EVERARD reached his house the night had fallen over Paris. On the long walk back from the Hôtel de Plaisance he had half made up his mind to take Jeanne and Sylviane and flee, although he knew nowhere to go. He went in through the door, and by the fire, his wife straightened, turning, slight as a willow twig in her long gray dress, and at the table, her brother, Bonboisson, looked up.

"Well — what news have you got for us from the great ones?"

Jeanne came past him. "Are you well? What's wrong?"

He went to the table and sat, looking Bonboisson long in the face, but it was to his wife that he spoke.

"Where is Sylviane?"

"Asleep," she said, startled. "Where else would she be, at such an hour? What's wrong, Everard?"

"Will you fetch me some bread and wine? I'm very hungry."

She went off at once toward the pantry. Bonboisson said, "I thought you dined with the king, Everard."

Everard said to him, "You are a captain in the militia. Tomorrow Marcel will order you to follow him out of the city, to fight the brigands on the river, but you must not go."

"Not go," Bonboisson repeated. "Why?"

"Because it is a trap. Navarre is behind everything — I am sure of it. He means to lure Marcel outside the city and destroy him, and then he will have Paris."

Bonboisson's face settled. All the light came from the fire, to one side, and so Everard saw only half his brother-in-law, one eye, one cheek, part of a mouth. The vintner raised his hands.

"And you. What are you going to do?"

"I don't know," Everard said. "Take my family and go — "

"Run away," Bonboisson said.

"God's blood," Everard said. His wife was coming toward him with the wine and the bread. "Everything I have ever tried to do, Bonboisson, has come to nothing. Yet — I swear to you, before God, I have meant only good by it. Now — "

Jeanne sank down on the bench beside him, her warmth beside him. He turned toward her. "You and Sylviane alone have prospered in my house, and that has been your doing, not mine, wife — "

"Everard." She leaned on him, her head against him.

Bonboisson said, "I disagree. What you and Marcel did after Poitiers — what you did before, standing against the king — that was right and good, Everard. I thought not so, at first, but now — "

"You must not go outside the walls tomorrow," Everard said.

"Yet I will," said Bonboisson. "I will go out and defend my city."

"Oh, God."

"If I do not, who will? You should come, too."

"I have left Marcel — he has dismissed me."

"He need not see you," said Bonboisson. Massive, dark, he leaned across the table, and the firelight streamed over his brow. "If you are right, then we shall have a leader among us, to help us. We will need you all the more, if you are right."

Everard gripped the knife; he had begun to cut the loaf, but he could not eat. He said, "Navarre's men are trained knights. In the open field, they will hack you to pieces."

"If we do not go," Bonboisson said, "they will take Paris anyway, won't they?"

Jeanne reached out and got the knife from him and cut the bread. Everard jerked his head toward her. "What do you say, wife?"

She said, in a low voice, "I am only a woman, Everard."

Bonboisson said, "Come with us. I have my horse to ride, and a pike. I can find you a horse, if you can ride."

Everard suddenly saw himself bareback on a plowhorse, a hoe in his hand, tilting against an armored knight. He gave an unsteady, unhappy laugh. In his vision the shield of the knight was Vaumartin's green-and-gold cross. He put his hands to his face.

"I am a coward," he said.

Jeanne murmured something. He lowered his hands again, facing Bonboisson.

"I will go," he said. "Tomorrow."

"Good," said Bonboisson.

forty-eight

BONBOISSON'S HORSE was his wagon horse, fat and placid as a cow. There was no horse for Everard, which was something of a relief; he walked along beside the vinter's stirrup, keeping the bulk of the horse between him and Marcel, all the while they were at the Saint-Honoré gate, waiting for the rest of the militia to assemble.

Their numbers were impressive, even to Everard, who had worked to recruit men from the beginning. Most of them were young men, apprentices, laborers; they carried clubs and axes, long knives in their belts, here and there a pike like Bonboisson's, six feet long from the butt of its staff to its nasty three-barbed tip. Noisy, in no order, they waited for Marcel in the yard before the gate, a great milling throng, while on the walls their women and children and friends gathered to see them off, as if this were a festival.

Everard stayed close by his brother-in-law. In his belt was the longest knife from Jeanne's kitchen; in his hand was the axe he used to chop wood.

The sun rose, high and hot. Marcel appeared at last, in a corselet that shone in the sunlight like a mirror. When he first appeared, on the gate, the whole militia cheered him until their throats were raw.

"People of Paris — "

He harangued them awhile, on the need to defend the city and keep the river open, on their own righteousness and glory. Bonboisson had brought a flask of wine, which he and Everard shared, until someone passing by got it, and then they never saw it again. At last, with a blast of trumpets, the gate opened, and Marcel led them forth into the world.

They walked along the road, still in a great disorderly mass, some singing, some already straggling off, a few even turning to steal back into the comfort of the city. They passed through fields and pastures, over flat land, the road veering down at last to parallel the river. Bonboisson on his horse shaded his eyes and looked down the road.

"I don't see anything," he said.

"Where's Marcel?" said Everard, walking beside him, one hand on the stirrup.

"Ahead of us. He has a sword, by God." The vintner's voice sharpened. "Here comes someone."

"Who?" Everard strained to see ahead, but all he could make out was the backs and heads of the men around him. Off to his left, a line of trees rose like plumes.

"I think it must be Navarre and his knights. Ah, they look like real soldiers — Marcel's going forth to meet them."

The militia stopped suddenly, the men bumping into one another; behind Everard two of them began to fight. He pulled on Bonboisson's stirrup. "What is happening?"

"Marcel and Navarre are talking." Bonboisson looked down at him. "You see, perhaps you were wrong, after all."

"Perhaps," Everard said. He thought, I have been wrong about everything else, why not this?

A horn blew. They moved forward again, shuffling along in the dust and the heat. The axe was heavy on Everard's shoulder. He could see nothing, save the heads and backs around him, the horse trudging along beside him.

"Navarre has ridden off," said Bonboisson. "We're coming into a wood."

Everard lifted his head. "Where did Navarre go?"

"I don't know. Ah, the shade will be good — it's hot out here. I wish you had not lost the wine."

"I did not lose it," Everard said. "You gave it away."

Bonboisson turned, his face darkening, to argue, but before he spoke there was some other sound, faint at first, whistling, like a flight of birds. Bonboisson straightened, looking around. Everard dropped his axe; reaching up with both hands, he grasped Bonboisson's coat and hauled him down out of the saddle.

The vintner shouted, angry, half off his horse, and then the first arrows struck.

All around them men screamed. The arrows came in whistling and thudded into flesh. Everard shouted, "Get down, get to the river!" He could see nothing; he knew more arrows were coming, and he let go of Bonboisson, who understood now, and snatched up his axe.

All around him, men were crumpling to the ground, or lay there already, stuck full of arrows. Bonboisson's horse reared up with a harsh frightened neigh and collapsed, an arrow through its neck, another in its barrel behind the girth. The vintner staggered back away from it. Everard got him by the shoulder and thrust him down, into the shelter of the horse's bulk. Around them men were screaming.

Now Everard could see around him. In that first attack, half of Marcel's army had fallen dead or wounded on the road, and many of the others were running aimlessly away. The wood lay off to his left. Behind him was the river. Before him, a broad fallow field, golden in the late-summer sun, sloped away in a long gentle swing to the south, and down this slight rise a stream of knights was galloping, spread out, their arms raised, their swords flashing.

Everard straightened. There would be no more arrows; they meant to finish off Marcel's men one by one, with swords. He looked quickly down the road for the provost but saw nothing except the mad tangle of the militia, some dead or thrashing, some fleeing, some gathering in tight knots to try to fight. Around Everard were several other men, a boy with a hoe, a man in a leather jacket with a wooden club, some others, looking dazed, their arms at their sides, and he roared at them.

"Come here — get down behind the horse — take some shelter and get ready!" The charge was hurtling down on them. Bonboisson gripped his pike as if it were a sword, and Everard snatched it away from him and thrust it back into his hands in the proper way, with the butt against the ground, and the pronged head pointed toward the horses thundering down on them.

He stooped for his axe again, and the knights galloped down on them. He heard the crunch of bone breaking, the gurgle of a man dying, the thunder of the hoofs overwhelming in his ears, the stink of sweat and blood like an incense. Memories rushed on him. He thought of Yvain, his uncle. He laid around him with the axe, fending off the wild rush of horses. Something banged him on the side. He went to one knee, flung the axe up over his head, and turned off a sword blade aimed at his skull. Bonboisson was just before him, kneeling behind the dead horse, the pike held stiffly out in front of him. Then the charge was by them, the knights veering off to avoid the river, wheeling back, circling around into the fallow field, forming up for another charge. A horn blew.

Everard flung a look around him. Of the dozen men around him, half were dead. The boy with the hoe had a gash across his cheek; the man with the leather jacket stood with one arm dangling useless, his face gray with pain and shock. Bonboisson stood sound, his eyes huge as washtubs, his mouth wide open.

Everard shouted at them, "Come on — stand together — you there, with the hoe, hold it like Bonboisson's pike — see — " Out there on the golden summer grass the knights swung their horses toward the road and charged.

"Stay together! Stay together — "

The rank of horses hurtled down on them. The ground shook under their hoofs. The knights looked like giants. Their swords darkened the sky when they raised them. Before them the militiamen cowered down in the road, but when the knights reached them, and leaned from their saddles to strike, the townsmen struck back.

Everard leapt forward, ducking under the swing of a sword, and got his axe around, level, as if he chopped trees. The blade sank deep, deep into flesh, and a horse crashed down past him, hitting the hard road headfirst. The knight reeled in the saddle, and the boy with the hoe sprang on him. His feet widespread, he hacked down with the hoe, and the blade skidded with a screech along the knight's armor and hit the joint between corselet and armplate and sank deep.

The knight screamed, helpless; his horse pinned his leg, and his sword was gone. The boy jerked the hoe free and raised it again and chopped down again and this time struck the knight in the neck, not killing him, too inept to kill, but the blood fountained up, and the knight was still trapped under his horse's weight. He screamed, "Quarter! Quarter — " but the boy was giving no quarter; his face was clenched into a demonic fury, and he raised the hoe again, and struck again, and again, and again, each time carving another wound, throwing up more blood, hacking the knight to pieces.

Beyond him, the other knights were wheeling their horses around, light as butterflies in the burning sunlight. Their charge had carried them by Everard and his little band and they were circling back toward the field, where the downward slope gave their charge more weight. Bonboisson straightened, panting, his face wild. Before his horse now lay another horse, a knight's great caparisoned war-horse, down and thrashing. Bonboisson's pike was bloody its whole length, and there was blood all over him.

Everard cast a look around him again. Of the six men who had stood here moments before, only four remained, but they were in a full fury now. A short blond man scrambled over the fallen horse and lifted the dead knight's sword in both hands. He bounded back among the others, and they stood together, sobbing under their breath, their eyes glazed, a wild rage of battle on them.

All up and down the road, it was the same. Marcel's militia lay in clumps of bodies, only a few of them still standing, but among them sprawled men in armor. Everard's chest swelled. A maniacal exaltation filled him.

"Come on — let's take them, this time — stay together!"

In the field, the knights gathered again to charge, and with a yell they rushed forward, coming from both sides. Around Everard the green boys and the vintner were learning fast. They swung around, their backs together, their weapons raised up. He went quickly along their rank, pushing them shoulder to shoulder, getting their weapons aimed up.

"Fight together! Make them come to all of us at once — "

Their faces were taut and wild. As the knights rushed down on them, they crouched, their hoes and rakes and clubs bristling around them, and at the last moment the knights wavered. Faced with the solid clump of men and weapons, they faltered and veered off, without a blow struck.

Bonboisson gave a hoarse cry of triumph. Among the knights, one shouted, cursing the others into order. Everard went again along the rank of the militia.

"Keep together! Aim for the horses, when they come again."

The knights were lining up again, to charge again, the horses tight-reined, their hoofs tearing up clods of earth. There were ten or twelve of them. The rest were busy down the road, where others of the militia still fought among the heaps of dead.

Everard knelt down at one end of his little rank, the axe in his hand. Had Navarre's men sent for archers, they could have slaughtered these townsmen at their leisure, but their arrogance would not let them do that; they would come again, to redeem their honor in their enemies' blood and their own.

The horn blew. The knights bounded forward, coming straight down toward the clustered rakes and hoes, the single pike like a lily stalk among them. The militiamen tensed, crouching; Everard heard a frightened voice reciting prayers.

The knights formed a loose line that swept down the long grassy slope. In the middle three or four of them pushed ahead of the others; just before they struck, the two ends curved around to take the little knot of the militia from the sides. Everard wheeled around, his back to Bonboisson's shoulder.

Behind him was a crash and a thunder of hoofs and a scream. A great horse wheeled toward him, coming at a slant, the man in the saddle leaning down to slash with his sword at Everard's head. The townsman ducked down under the blow; with all the strength of his shoulders he swung his axe out, and the blade bit deep into the horse's knee and sent it somersaulting to the ground.

Everard bounded out of the way. The knight was rolling out of the saddle, landing lightly on his feet, and Everard lunged at him and he dodged. Everard rushed at him again, his breath hot in his throat. The knight danced away from him and whirled, and suddenly he was alone, separated from the other militiamen, and this knight and another had him between them.

He shrieked. He laid about him with the axe, and they gave way, the broad head of the axe whistling in the air. He feinted, trying to draw them one way, so that he could get back among his friends, but they lunged together toward him, the man on foot before him, the mounted man behind, and something struck him in the leg, and he went down, and the world spun away from him, and he fell into a bottomless oblivion, an empty black pit that was dying.

On the wall, someone shouted, "Here come more of them!"

Sylviane cried, "Maybe that's Father — " She rushed forward toward the gate. Jeanne snatched at her, trying to hold her back. The crowds here frightened her, their panicky excitement frightened her, they filled the whole wide yard before the Saint-Honoré gate, and at every cry, every sight, they surged and screamed and seized one another, half wild.

Sylviane got away from her, running quick as a boy through the crowd. Jeanne went after her.

For the last hour now men had been straggling back into the city, dazed and exhausted, too breathless and frightened to say much but that there was fighting on the road, and many were dead. Two steps behind Sylviane, Jeanne climbed up a ladder to the top of the wall. Her belly was cramped with fear and her hands shook. She was terrified for Everard, and she was afraid of what she might see, but she could not have stayed behind, in her house, and let this go on without being there.

Sylviane's shoes were gone. Her dress was filthy and the hem was coming down. Her hair streamed around her in a wild dusty glory. She scrambled up onto the wall and leaned over.

"It's the provost!" She leaned over the wall and shouted, "Provost! Where is my father?"

Jeanne caught her, panting, and held her. "Sylvie, be still!"

The wall was crowded with men and women, packed shoulder to shoulder. The girl pulled out of her mother's hands and wormed her way through them again.

"Look! They're all bloody — "

The gate was creaking open. Jeanne gripped Sylviane's skirt in one hand, so that she would not lose her, and turned to look down over the edge of the rampart.

In through the gate came a stream of men. First among them was the provost on his horse, hunched over, his face gray. He drew rein, and from the foot of the tower by the gate, the tall redheaded watch captain strode forward to meet him.

"What happened?" someone shouted, near Jeanne. The whole crowd was screaming, every voice separate. Someone behind her bumped into her so hard she stumbled. She clutched her daughter's skirt and craned her neck to see. Everard was not with the provost. She turned toward the rampart again, looking down the long dusty road, and in her heart something pulled and pulled, aching after him.

"What happened?"

In the roar of the mob Marcel rode in silence, his face grim; he bent from his saddle and spoke to Jean Mailliard, while through the gate came a steady trickle of men, covered with dust and blood.

"We were betrayed," someone called, as he staggered across the yard, and slumped down at the foot of the tower.

From the far side of the street a man in a priest's gown strode forward, his face dark. "Betrayed! Then Everard was right. Provost, those who trusted you, you led them to disaster — "

Still in his saddle, Marcel looked up and thrust out his arm to point at his accuser. "Get you gone, de Brises, before I strike you down, you dirty dog."

The crowd was shifting away from the gate. Their attention focused now on Marcel, before the tower. The provost straightened, looking around him, and someone shouted, "What happened? Who betrayed us?"

From the crowd other voices rose.

"Tell us what happened!"

"Where's my husband?"

"Where are the rest?"

"He took them out and gave them to the brigands — Marcel betrayed us to the brigands — "

At that the crowd gave up a many-throated roar. Something ugly in their collective voice raised the hackles on Jeanne's neck, and stirred a horrible rage in her gut. Her free hand clenched into a fist. She cast another glance down the empty road, and faced the provost, her teeth together.

Marcel waved his arm at them, striking at the crowd. "Get home — you do no good here."

Mailliard still stood beside him, his hand on Marcel's bridle. The provost turned to him and said something Jeanne could not hear; he started his horse forward, but Mailliard held him back.

"You'd better stay, Master Provost — you have accounting to make."

Marcel stiffened. His broad face was the color of a brick. "I need account to no one! Paris is mine — "

The crowd roared at him. "Don't let him go!" Near the front of the mob a woman with straggling gray hair shook her fist at him. "You'll give answer, Master Provost!" Surrounding him, the great shifting surging pack pressed close around him, and a shrill chorus of their voices rose again, shrieks and whistles and cries, more like animal voices than human.

"Did you sell us to Navarre, Marcel?" That was the priest de Brises again, hurling his preacher's voice through the tumult.

"Damn you!" Marcel jerked at his reins, trying to get his bridle out of Mailliard's hands. "You deserve no better — you are clay, the pack of you — "

"Mother!" Sylviane screamed. "It's Uncle Bonboisson!"

Jeanne whirled. Everyone on the rampart had turned their backs to the road, to join the great mob swelling around Marcel; she fought her way through them to the wall, where Sylviane stood balanced precariously on the top ledge.

Sylviane cried, "Uncle Bonboisson!"

"Oh, sweet Mother of God." Jeanne crossed herself. There on the road, a man was staggering along, something draped across his shoulders. She recognized her brother. What he carried was another man, loose and flopping, whose long black scholar's coat was as familiar to her as her own hands. She ran for the ladder.

In the yard, Marcel roared, "Damn you all! Mailliard, give me the keys to the armory — get the weapons away from these madmen."

Mailliard lifted his great red head. "Not until you account to us — "

Marcel reared back. "Account! To you? To swine and dogs? This is my city! I do as I will here — you, Mailliard, you are dismissed — you are no more the watch captain — "

"You'd kill us all if you could, wouldn't you, Marcel?" de Brises bawled.

"Yes!" The provost in his fury flung his gaze around him at the mob. "You worthless, shiftless — "

They attacked him. In one wild rush they came at him from all sides. Mailliard scrambled out of their way. The provost's horse blared a neigh and went down like an ox before the poleaxe. Marcel disappeared under the mob. Jeanne whined between her teeth. She turned her head away, and struggled through the swirling crowd to the gate, standing slightly open. Behind her the mob screamed in a triumphant lust.

Bonboisson shuffled toward her. His face was gray. Everard on his shoulders was limp as a sack of corn. There was blood all over them. She cried out; she ran to help him, to lift the weight from him, and they went together into Paris.

forty-nine

BONBOISSON SAID, "He saved us, I think — he knew what to do, as if he had done this all before."

Jeanne touched her husband's forehead. There was no wound on him, save a tremendous swollen bruise on his head, but he had not wakened or stirred. He was pale as candle wax, even the bruise livid. She had seen men lie so who never woke, until they wasted away and died.

Bonboisson had told them all about the battle on the road, in great and bloody detail. He said again, "Everard saved us. And we saved Paris, I think. You mark they have not attacked the city. Though they slaughtered us on the road, we took many of them, and they may think the price too high, now that they have tested our mettle, to take on the rest of us."

She sat with her hands in her lap, watching Everard's face.

"You brought him home again," she said. "God reward you for that, brother."

The vintner's face reddened a little. In a low voice, he said, "I did not fail. I was afraid — I misdoubted — but when the burden was on me, I bore it." He turned toward her, some new strength bright in his face. "Care for him, sister. Pray for him." He put out his hand to Sylviane, behind her. "Come to my house, child, while your father sleeps."

"I'll help my mother," Sylvie said. She was sitting very stiff and straight, as if she wanted to look older.

The vintner nodded and went heavy-footed out of the room and down the stairs. A moment later they heard the door shut.

Sylviane rose to her feet, resolute. "Mother, shall I fetch more water?"

"There is water aplenty," said Jeanne, absently, her gaze on her husband.

"Then I shall sweep and clean," said Sylviane, stoutly, and went down the stairs to the hall.

The city was quiet. All the gates were barred; Mailliard's watchmen patrolled the walls, with such of the militia as were left, and dozens more, who swore they had been there also, in that battle on the road. No one knew who ruled Paris now; the priests in their pulpits, the monks on street corners preached calm, patience, waiting. There was very little to eat.

Everard woke at last, weak and trembling. He lay in the bed and Jeanne fed him soup with a spoon.

He said, in a voice scarcely louder than a whisper, "How did I get here?"

"My brother carried you," she said.

"Bonboisson. He is alive, then. What of Navarre?"

"He has never come back," she said. "My brother thinks you frightened him away."

His chest heaved in an exhausted laugh. His eyes moved toward her. "And Marcel?"

"Dead. The mob killed him."

His eyes shifted. "He deserved better than that." His hand pulled feebly at the bedcover. "What a hell this life is."

"Rest," she said. "Rest, Everard. Hoard your strength."

His lips moved. She fed him more soup. In a moment he said, "I know the rainbow now."

"What?" she said, startled.

His voice was tremulous. "At Navarre's house. There was a thing of glass. I saw — I know what makes the rainbow." His eyes shut; she thought he would sleep, and she put down the bowl, but he spoke again. "Every certainty I try to stand on crumbles away beneath me. Yet God has given me the rainbow." His eyes opened; he looked toward her. "What does that mean?"

She shook her head at him. "You should rest. Get your strength again." Putting her hand on his forehead, she stroked his hair. His eyes closed; perhaps he slept again; perhaps he thought about the rainbow.

She went to the church and lit a candle for him. The church was crowded with folk praying. She said her prayers to the wooden crucifix and to the faceless dream behind it, like dropping stones into an infinite well.

Going home, in the gray autumn drizzle, she went up the street past the old priest's house, where the cherry tree stood naked as a corpse, and when she came to her own step, she found some people waiting.

Three were servants; the fourth was a woman of middle years, very beautiful, who wore the dusky black of mourning. One of the servants held a cloak over her to keep the rain from her. When Jeanne came up to them, they all turned to face her, and she looked into this woman's magnificent eyes, and some old memory stirred, something Everard had said once to her, words she could not quite remember.

"My lady." Puzzled, she glanced around her, wondering where Sylviane was. "May I serve you?"

The woman lifted her jeweled white hands to the hood of her cloak. "I am Isobel, the Dame de Vaumartin. I am seeking Everard de Vaumartin."

"Everard," Jeanne said, unsteady. "Everard le Breton is my husband."

"He goes by that style now," said this woman, with her skin like silk, her voice like music. "Properly he is Everard de Vaumartin — properly he is the Sire de Vaumartin."

Vartin. Jeanne steadied herself. Such a freight of feeling came over her that she could not move or speak. The silence grew awkward, this strange woman staring at her, waiting, and at last the wife said, "Will you come in, my lady?"

"Thank you," said the Dame de Vaumartin. Jeanne went up the steps and opened the door, and let her into the hall. The servants stayed outside in the rain.

Sylviane stood on the foot of the stair. She said, "Mother? What is it?"

Jeanne said, "This is — " She cast a look at the splendid woman, who walked calmly into the center of the hall, looking around her.

She said, "I am Isobel de Vaumartin, my child." She sat down on the bench, shrugging off her cloak, which fell unheeded to the floor. "Are you Everard's daughter? No — you are too old, I think, and too fair, for such a raven as he was."

Sylviane went toward her as though drawn to her. "I am Sylviane del Borgo," she said.

Jeanne had not known she even knew the name. It was as if the child separated herself from her, saying that name. Jeanne's heart thrashed with a wild alarm. She looked once more at Isobel de Vaumartin, beautiful as an angel.

Everard had said once that this woman would make nothing of her, and now she was come to do it. Jeanne went up the stairs to the bedroom.

He lay in the bed as she had left him. His eyes turned toward her, and he smiled.

"Jeanne. Where were you?"

She laid her hand on his forehead. Bending, she put her mouth against his. Then all at once she was weeping.

"Jeanne," he said. "What is this? Jeanne?"

She straightened. "Everard — there is a woman downstairs — she says her name is Isobel."

He pushed himself up on his arms. "Isobel." His voice was low and thready. He hung his head, struggling to rise.

She put her arm around his shoulders; he leaned on her, getting his feet to the floor, and turned his face toward hers. "Is she alone?"

"She has some servants with her."

"But no man — no knight?"

"No."

He stared at her, his face drawn, and put his hands out. "Help me up."

"Everard, who is she?"

He said only, "Help me."

She gripped his arms and helped him stand, and held him while he got his balance. "Get me a fresh shirt," he said.

"Everard, stay in bed. I'll bring her here."

"Get me the shirt."

She brought him a clean shirt, and he sat down on the bed and put it on. His hands shook. The fluttering in her heart would not subside. He raised his head and looked at her.

She said, "Who is this woman, Everard?"

He shook his head, as if to tell her would devour all his strength; he got to his feet again, wobbling, and slowly went toward the door. She went ahead of him, down the stairs, down to the hall.

There at the table Isobel de Vaumartin sat, with Sylviane beside her, the slate in her hand. As Jeanne came down the stairs, they turned toward her, and she saw they had been laughing.

"What a lovely child," said the Dame de Vaumartin. She reached out to grip the girl's hand. "And so clever! What a pretty poem this is!"

Sylviane glowed. She cast a look of admiration and awe at the lady Isobel. Jeanne swallowed. Between these two, somehow, there had grown up in a few moments what in years and years she herself had struggled for and never won. She felt her life being ripped from her in shreds. She went down the hall to the pantry, for some wine.

When she returned, Everard was coming down the stairs.

He wore no coat, but only his shirt, unlaced; he looked rough and wild. Across the room his gaze found Isobel, and she rose, laying aside the slate, forgetting Sylviane.

Everard said, "What are you doing here?"

Isobel said, "Josseran is dead, Everard."

He came down the last three steps, his hand on the wall, his face taut. "Then what are you doing here?"

"To . . . make amends," she said. "You are the Sire de Vaumartin, Everard."

"I have always been the Sire de Vaumartin," he said, harsh.

"Everard — " She raised her hands, palms up, toward him, begging. "Josseran told me — I am to — on his deathbed, he bade me find you and . . ."

Tears coursed down her cheeks. Her voice wavered and trailed off.

Sylviane gave a low cry and would have gone to her, but Jeanne reached her and held her back. Isobel raised her face, all bright with tears, toward Everard, who stood frowning before her.

"We wronged you, Everard — we sinned against you — and yet, oh, Heaven give me witness, of it we have had no pleasure, no good at all, these years." She pressed her hands together. "I pray you, forgive us. What we did to you has been our punishment itself."

Jeanne clutched Sylviane against her; she watched Everard's face, frozen in its dark scowl, and held her breath. Before him Isobel bowed her head.

"He died, my Josseran — not gloriously in battle — he died of a fever, in exile, alone, burning with the fever — my Josseran — "

Everard said nothing. His face was set like stone.

She said, "We lost our love, we were estranged for years, because of what we did to you. And in the end, we lost Vaumartin as well."

"Isobel," he said.

"When I came here, I thought it would be hard to find you, but everyone in Paris knows you. They speak of you with pride and love, they say even the dauphin is in your debt. You can recover Vaumartin. You can make whole what we tore in pieces — "

Sylviane jerked free of Jeanne's grip; she rushed across the hall to Everard. "Father," she said. "Vartin — we can go now to Vartin!"

He stood without speaking, ignoring her, his gaze on Isobel. Sylviane caught his hand. "Father!"

Looking over her head, he spoke to Isobel de Vaumartin. "I have a life here of my own, Isobel. I have my Jeanne, my daughter."

Sylviane cried out; she wheeled, her face pale and wild, and took two steps toward Isobel. Beyond her, Everard said, "I am no knight, nor would have been one. Had you not driven me out, what would I ever have had that was real? I need not Vaumartin."

Isobel said steadily, "Then it's gone. It's all gone."

Her body sagged, and she put out her hand and felt feebly beside her for the bench, and sank down on it, miserable as any beggar woman. Sylviane stared at her. Everard brushed by the girl and sat down beside Isobel, and she turned to him, blindly, her hands raised. He opened his embrace to her, and she wept against his shoulder.

Jeanne sighed. The panic flutter in her breast died away; she blinked, as if she wakened from some dream.

Everard said, "Here, Isobel, drink." His voice was gentle, pitying, tender. He glanced at Jeanne, who brought the cup of wine to Isobel, and she took it with a grateful look.

"Tell me about Josseran," Everard said. "Wife, fetch us something to eat, if you please."

Isobel said, "On the great street, I saw some shops — let me send my grooms for a feast."

Everard shook his head. "We have bread and cheese and wine enough, Isobel. We need nothing you can give us."

"And want nothing, I see." She lifted her gaze to him, her hands in her lap. "Everard, I thought to find you full of hate."

"I hated you," he said. "The last ten years, I have hated you and Josseran. Until now." He lifted his head, looking at Jeanne. "Bring us dinner, wife. Sylvie, help your mother."

Jeanne said, "Come, Sylvie," and went into the pantry.

They ate, and talked, and even came to laugh at things, somehow, late into the evening. At last, Everard said, "What will you do now, Isobel, if you cannot go back to Vaumartin?"

The Dame said, "Prince Edward of England has offered me a place in his wife's court. I shall go there."

She sat with Sylviane beside her; the girl had shown her all her poems, and Isobel had given her a ring from her little finger. Now Isobel put one arm around the child's shoulders.

"Let me take Sylviane with me."

Everard lifted his head. "What!"

"Oh, Everard — you see what she is. Here, what will become of her? Let me take her with me to the English court, where her gifts will thrive." Her eyes were wide and melting.

Sylviane said, "Father!" in an urgent voice.

Everard looked from her to Isobel, and then to Jeanne, sitting quietly on the bench. He put out his hand and took Jeanne's in his grasp. "What do you say, wife?" Across the table, Sylviane looked keenly at their joined hands.

Jeanne's face was white. She had hardly spoken, all through the evening, but had watched only. Now, in a murmur, she said, "Let her do what she wills."

Everard turned to Sylviane, and said, "What do you wish, Sylvie?"

Isobel said, "Come, Sylvie. It will be wonderful. Gardens, and beautiful clothes, and people who will care about your poems. You'll be made much of, there."

The child raised her head. She cast a look at Isobel. "It sounds wonderful — like the stories my father used to tell me — he used to promise me that someday we would go to such a place."

Everard glanced again at Jeanne, sitting still as an icon on the bench.

Sylviane got up; she went around the table to stand by Jeanne's side, and reaching down, she took her free hand. "But I cannot leave my mother and my father."

The Dame de Vaumartin stiffened. She smiled, but it was a false smile. Shocked pride marked her face; her eyes were dark, and her voice was stiff. "I shall not ask you twice."

The girl said, steadily, "I cannot leave them, who love me."

Isobel said, "Then my business here is done, and I shall go."

Everard rose, his hand out to her. "Where will you stay this night?"

"I have — friends," she said. "You know that."

She was noble; every other noble was her friend. He took her to the door, and they said some few words in farewell. The rain had stopped. He stood there, on the threshold, watching as she went down the steps. Her groom helped her into her saddle, and they rode away, down the dark street. Everard shut the door and went back into the hall, to his wife and daughter.

LIN THE EARLY SPRING the dauphin rode into Paris, with the canon de Brises at his right hand, and a great army at his back, and the city yielded quietly to him, its rightful master.

The dauphin took his place in the palace, and thereafter, in a steady stream, the great men of Paris came to him, bowing and kneeling and saying honeyed words to him, each to swear that he had always put his faith in no other than the regent, and never, no, never, in Etienne Marcel.

The dauphin heard everyone; he received them all with mild words and welcomes. He took no vengeance for the way he had been run out of Paris. Mailliard kept his post; no man suffered at all for the return of the regent.

Then, after many days, he sent for Everard le Breton.

The dauphin had learned his lessons. Forced at first to use the palace, on the City Island, for his business and his residence, he swiftly took over a country house of the old duke of Burgundy's in the Marais, the swampy scrub just beyond the city wall in the north, and there began to make himself a home secure from the rages of the mob. It was there, in this half-ruined, half-begun place, that Everard came face to face with him again.

"Well," the dauphin said, "you see I have come back."

Everard stared at him a moment, until the prince thought that the tall Breton had forgotten their last meeting, but then Everard said, "You see I never left."

The regent jerked his head up, affronted. "Are you chastising me?"

"Had you remained, much of what happened here might not have taken place," Everard said. "But it did take place. Now you think to come back in and rule us, as if everything were the same as before."

The dauphin bit off the angry words that climbed into his throat. In his exile, he had imagined his return, over and over, and always he had thought that he would return to Everard's welcome.

In spite of his anger he saw the truth in Everard's words, and he spoke to that truth.

"I have not forgotten," he said. "You suffered much, you and all the people here, and some say that suffering ennobles men. I shall try to give you honest rule, and truthful, as you deserve." He put out his hand to Everard. "But I want you to come to my court — to serve me and my kingdom."

Everard lifted his head. "I have seen too much of governance."

"Yet — you saved me, once. And you saved Paris. I have heard that from many a man — how you alone dared speak against Navarre."

"I need no reward for that, Your Grace."

"But I would reward you. Is there nothing — no post, no money, no privilege I can give you to show my favor?"

"None, Your Grace, truly."

The dauphin shook his head, angry at this arrogance masquerading as humility. "Nothing. But I've read your book, you know — "

"My book?" Everard said, startled.

"On light and grace. My uncle the emperor had a copy — he is fond of heretics. That in itself puts you in some danger, Everard. You need friends — powerful friends — to protect you from those to whom ideas are anathema."

"Well, perhaps." Everard smiled at him. "Actually, you know, there is a thing you could give to me."

"Name it," said the dauphin, pleased.

"I want a bowl of clear glass." The Breton shaped a sphere in the air with his hands. "Perfectly round, like a raindrop."

"A bowl," the dauphin said, puzzled.

"Yes."

"You shall have it."

"Thank you, Your Grace."

"And nothing else."

"No, nothing else," said Everard, and bowed. "I shall go home, if it please you."

"Go, then," said the dauphin, brusquely, and they parted.

Later, walking home, Everard considered what he had done, and knew he was a fool. The dauphin would have made him rich, made him powerful, would have protected him against such as Claude de Brises, who was already acting bishop of Paris and who would soon receive his shepherd's crook and hat from Rome. Now he had nothing, no money, no work, no future at all.

Yet as he walked he rejoiced. The spring air was warm and sweet; with a clear glass bowl, he could study the rainbow at will. He could rewrite the lecture notes that were circulating as his book, correct the inevitable errors, and add what he had learned. If his life was uncertain and full of risk, that meant that he was living it well.

He had reached his own street now. Before him, at the bend, was the old cherry tree, a white cloud of blossoms covering every ancient limb. His step quickened. Ahead of him was all he loved. He turned the corner to his house, and there was Jeanne.

Rue Saint ... Ger ... main

Four l'Evesque

Abeurouer

Abeurouer Jehan Popin

Le Grand Pont

R. devant la Court le Roy Barrillerie.

LES SAZ

JARDINS DU ROY

Le Palais

La Court le Roy

S.te Chapelle

S. Michel

S. BARTELE...

Lu Vie...

Abb. S.te

B

l'O...

Abeurouer

La Rue de l'Abbé de S.t Denis

Rue Pavée

La boucherie Hyrondelle

La Rue de Hyrondale

La Grande Boucherie

La petite Boucherie

S. ANDRI

Grant Rue Saint Germain et

Hostel de Nazare

R. de Guiguet.

R. derriere S.t Andri

Cimetière S.t Andri

R. Guiartaux Poitevins

Rue Percée

Rue Poupée

Pilori

Porte

... de la

Serpent